Praise f[...]

'One of the best new fantasy [...]
Steven Erikson's *Gardens of the Moon* . . . I want more'
ALIEN ONLINE

'Vigorous, violent fantasy adventure' **INTERZONE**

'There is a gritty desolate tone in depicting the grime
and horror of conflict; Cobley's skill lies in establishing a
sense of reality unusual in fantasy'
TIME OUT

'Darkly different . . . writing to rival David Gemmell'
GUARDIAN

'Fantasy doesn't come much better than this'
ALIEN ONLINE

'Resonates with dark magic and violent deeds.
Cobley takes fantasy to new places'
INFINITY PLUS

Michael Cobley was born in Leicester in 1959. While studying engineering at Strathclyde University, he DJ'd at the students' union by night, and later wrote an acerbic column of comment for the campus paper. Since 1986 he has had short stories and articles published in several magazines and anthologies, and was responsible for the rambunctious Shark Tactics pamphlet.

Shadowmasque is his third novel, continuing the stories and themes begun in *Shadowkings* and *Shadowgod*.

SHADOWMASQUE

Book Three of
The Shadowkings Trilogy

MICHAEL COBLEY

**POCKET
BOOKS**

LONDON • NEW YORK • SYDNEY • TORONTO

First published in Great Britain by Simon & Schuster UK Ltd, 2005
This edition published by Pocket Books, 2006
An imprint of Simon & Schuster UK Ltd
A CBS Company

Copyright © Michael Cobley, 2005

This book is copyright under the Berne Convention.
No reproduction without permission.
® and © 1997 Simon & Schuster Inc. All rights reserved.
Pocket Books & Design is a registered trademark of Simon & Schuster Inc.

The right of Michael Cobley to be identified as author of this work
has been asserted by him in accordance with sections 77 and 78 of the
Copyright, Designs and Patents Act, 1988.

1 3 5 7 9 10 8 6 4 2

Simon & Schuster UK Ltd
Africa House
64–78 Kingsway
London WC2B 6AH

www.simonsays.co.uk

Simon & Schuster Australia
Sydney

A CIP catalogue record for this book is available
from the British Library

This book is a work of fiction. Names, characters, places
and incidents are either a product of the author's imagination or are used
fictitiously. Any resemblance to actual people living or dead, events or
locales is entirely coincidental.

ISBN 0-7434-1601-5
EAN 9780743416016

Typeset in Bembo by Palimpsest Book Production Limited,
Polmont, Stirlingshire
Printed and bound in Great Britain by
Cox & Wyman Ltd, Reading, Berkshire

Acknowledgements

Here, at the end of this long road of a story, I realize that there have been many people who played a part in the general ongoing gallimaufry of my life, and thus influenced the Shadowkings books in one way or another. So many that inevitably I will find that I've missed someone out, which is why I'm apologizing in advance in case I stupidly forget one or another of you. No slight intended, on my oath!

But the roll-call of thanks (as best as I can assemble it) goes out to Ben Ball and Melissa and the S&S team, who have exhibited great patience in awaiting the final volume. To my agent, John Parker of MBA (and to Susan and Dana and the inestimable Tim Webb), to the mighty duo, John Jarold and Darren Nash for insight and detail, and to Steve Stone for his wonderful art.

To Stewart Robinson, buddy and loft-owner, to Dave Wingrove (for being the diamond geezer's diamond geezer!), to Derek Cameron, Lorna, and to Dave McGilvray for letting me rant at him about all things Blairish (still got that party card, then, eh?), to Graeme Fleming for some of the greatest prog gigs of all time, to Debbie Miller for being an ace writer-buddy, to Ariel for keeping the website ticking along, to Neil, Al, Phil, Gary, Craig, Paul, Barry, Duncan, Lawrence, Jim S and Jim C, Elsie and Veronica and all members of the GSFFW Circle, past and present.

To Ian McDonald (for the craic), to Bill King (for introducing me to KE Wagner), to Eric Brown (for being a top bloke/writer/father but not necessarily in that order), to Keith Brooke for dedication and being infinitely plus.

To Mark Roberts and Jeff Vandermeer, without whom the Thackery Lambshead assemblage of imaginary afflictions would never have pustuled their way into our lives, to Storm Constantine and Gabriel Strange at Immanion Press, to Cuddles whose enthusiasm and encouragement never waver, to Andrew J. Wilson, and to Alistair Travis and his guitar-totin' Hippykillers.

To Raymond, John, Marion, Pam, Jean, Helen, Andy, Billy, Jim, Mags, Leslie, Susan, Liz, Sophie, Angela, James A, Joe, Carol, Martin, Aneeta, Lorna, and all the other dozens of great people that I became friends with while working at Atrium Court, floor 5, between '98 and '04, not forgetting the steadfast and welcoming Jeff, Yvonne and Kenny!

The soundtrack for the writing of this book was provided by a grand pantheon of the subtle and the brain-crunchingly heavy. Mention must be made of the wonderful electronic soundscapes of Ashok Prema and Bjorn Lynne; the epic symphonic metal of Rhapsody, Luca Turilli and Ayreon; the heavy blues of Spiritual Beggars, the Quill and Grand Magus, not to mention the finest musical export to come out of America this decade, Monster Magnet. Also, the latest CD by Yello, and a wonderful late release from Bill Hicks, 'Shock and Awe', one of the standup gigs he did in Oxford.

For my brother, Peter

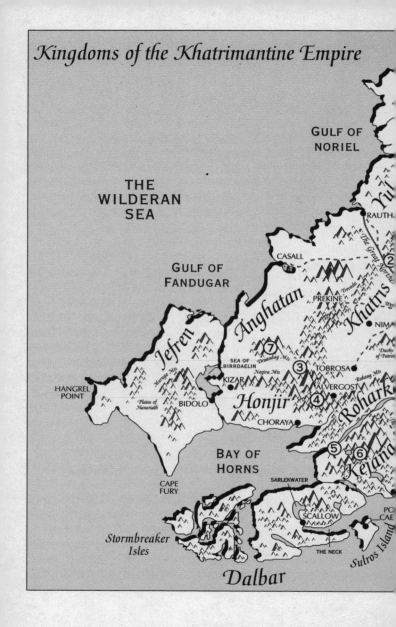

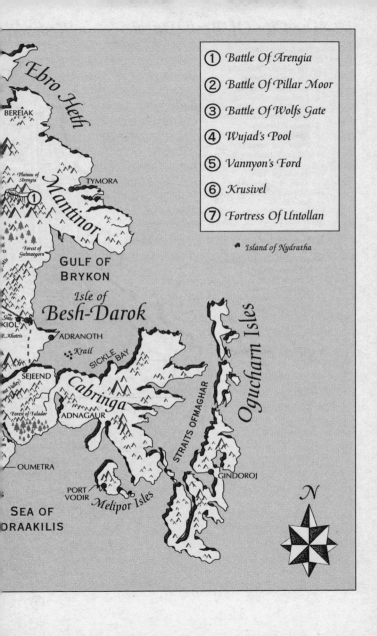

The City Of Besh-Darok

1) The Gallaro Gate
2) The Shield Gate
3) The Gauntlet Gate (sealed)
4) The Imperial Palace
5) Lord's Glade (despoiled)
6) Earthmother Temple Of The Glade (pillaged)
7) The Glade Grove Of Burial (desecrated)
8) Mage Halls (razed to ground)
9) Ironhall Barracks
10) Riverside Barracks
11) Chapel Fort Barracks
12) College Of Hendred's Hall
13) Earthmother Temple at Wybank
14) Five Kings' Dock
15) Kulberisti Longmarket
16) Four Guilds Merchant College
17) Guildhouse
18) Garrison Of The Order Of The Fathertree (razed)
19) Shrine Of The Rock, Fathertree Temple (demolished)
20) The Long Quays
21) Fishers Quarter

Bridges Of The Olodar (heading upriver):
a) Knights Bridge
b) Queens Bridge
c) Bridge of Hawks
d) Bridge of Spears
e) Veterans Bridge

Keshada

Gorla

Prologue

The seed of darkness is buried in the ground,
Nurtured by years of rain and pain,
And stroked by the tresses of blinded Night.

Ushald Drusarik, *The Twilight Emperor,* Act I, Sc. ii

The square, high-walled courtyard of the Sejeend Imperial Academy's eastern cloister was smothered in late spring blossom from the four spiraleaf trees which dominated the lawn. A flock of greenwings trilled and swooped on the breeze which blew down into the cloister, stirring up swirls of blue and yellow blossom. In the east wall of the main building, under the sheltered cloister walkway, was a door. It opened and a slender man emerged. His dun leather skullcap and ankle-length black cloak marked him as one of the Academy's clerks. Pale brown hair was tucked under the cap's edge. Cold, grey eyes in a narrow, pinched face regarded the swooping greenwings with disdain. Locking the door behind him, the clerk turned and stalked across the blossom-strewn lawn, his thin-lipped mouth taking on a bleak smile as he saw the crownhawk that was relentlessly harrying the greenwings.

The eastern portal was a pair of tall, iron gates guarded by four masked sentries armed with bucklers and maces. Their iron shields and bronze masks bore the crest of the Imperial Academy, a book and a crown, as did the seal the clerk wore prominently on a chain about his neck, though the sentries still squinted at it for long moments before grudgingly allowing him to pass. Seething inwardly, the clerk said nothing as he hurried out to the stone steps that curved down one side of the thickly wooded hill on which the academy had been built.

At the foot of the steps was a high stone wall and a heavy wooden door. Being daylight, it was unlocked and its ancient hinges squeaked as he tugged it open and stepped out into a tree-lined, cobbled street. A steady traffic of carriages, pedestrians and the occasional sedan was passing to and fro along it. The clerk's face was impassive as he made his way determinedly over to the other side where a busy bridge spanned a deep, leafy gully. There, a gravelled path diverged from the road and sloped down into the gully, following it north towards the centre of Sejeend. The clerk paused to glance over his shoulder, a hard suspicious look, then hastened down the path.

The steady rushing sound of the river Kala filled the tree-shaded air, mingling with birdsong and the chatter of voices. People sat at the tables of small alehouses that had been built into the steep sides of the gully. Children dashed after pets or each other while kulesti players went from table to table. The clerk did his best to avoid them all as he continued northward.

Formed by the Kala across many centuries, the mouth of the gully was a steep-sided notch in the face of the hundred-and-fifty-foot cliffs that towered over the city of Sejeend. Once it had been blocked by an ancient, fortified wall from before the Khatrimantine imperium – the clerk could see the ruined remains all the way up on either side, massive blocks half-buried by vegetation. A large, moss-burdened piece of masonry with a curved underside jutted over the path, carved with bear-like shapes. The clerk glanced up at it without pause as he left the path to cross the river by a low, wooden footbridge. Shafts of sunlight cut through the leafy canopy of huge agathons, turning the Kala's running waters to flowing, sparkling crystal, making insects into glowing motes. The clerk entered one of the slanting sunbeams and was dazzled for a second before rejoining the shadows on the other side.

His pace was quicker now, bootheels knocking on the wooden riverside walkway as he followed it out into the city. Four- and five-storey buildings began where the river disappeared beneath a horse-ornamented stone bridge, the last sight of it before it re-emerged somewhere near the harbour. The clerk's course took him westward along a narrow street, between a row of opulent townhouses, abodes of the rich, and the high wall of a burial grove and through the grove's arched entrance.

Sheltered by its enclosing wall, the grove was thrown into deep shadow by the torwood trees, each burdened with loops and coils of sweet-scented litrilu blooms. Devotional chimes tinkled amid the lower branches while a few solitary figures in mourning robes tended some of the heavily ornamented gravestones. All of these were built into or near the foot of the cliff and it was towards one of them that the clerk now made his way.

It was the sepulchre of a military man, his resting place a great piece of granite carved in the likeness of an archaic, palisaded barracks, with stern-looking, sword-grasping guards at each corner. The clerk squeezed past a tall bush which concealed the gap between the tomb and the cliff, then crouched down and felt around a stone in the tomb's base. A moment later he lifted out a small but weighty leather pouch. Replacing the brick, he straightened and turned to face the cliff, a rock face patched with lichen and sprouting tiny plants and grassy tufts. He studied it for a moment, then smiled and spoke a word.

The rock rippled like water and a rust-streaked iron door suddenly appeared. The clerk produced a spiked key from within his robes, opened the door and stepped inside.

When the door closed behind him the darkness within was broken only by a thin thread of radiance around the door's edge. He took a small lamp from a waist-high niche in the wall that he found by touch, lit it with another word of power then started along a rough, narrow gap in the rock. Protrusions in the crudely hewn walls caught at his robes but he went on, following the passage as it curved and sloped down into the roots of the cliffs ancient, solid stone.

And further down until it levelled and widened out into an oval chamber. The oil lamp's flame cast his shadow across uneven walls daubed with symbols and adorned with rotting charms made using wood, cloth and blood. His attention, however, was fixed on the face which rose out of the sandy floor. Sculpted from grey clay, it was some six feet or more from crown to chin. Wide, sightless eye-hollows stared up at the chamber's darkened ceiling and the lips were parted as if ready to speak.

The clerk stared at it for a moment, then brought out the pouch and opened it. He bent down and poured a little of the contents, a fine ashen powder, into the eyes and the mouth and a shallow channel which defined the face's outline. Straightening, he tucked the pouch away, took a step back and uttered a string of harsh, guttural syllables.

Suddenly light flared up from the face, forcing him to avert his eyes. When he glanced back after a moment or two, curling coils of vapour veiled the hot green glow which shone from the eyes and the mouth, and the enclosing channel. As he edged closer, the bright emerald orbs in their clay sockets turned to look at him. The mouth smiled a blazing, unpleasant smile.

'. . . *late, Jumil . . . once more you are late . . . perhaps you should be punished . . .*'

Stark fear leaped into Jumil's features.

'No, please, Great Shadow, please! I came as quickly as I could – one of the senior masters delayed me . . . stupid Frolek and his inane questions!'

A glowing tendril unfurled from the bright mouth's corner then struck like a snake at Jumil, wrapping itself around his neck. The clerk let out a cry and fell to his knees.

'Great One, I beg . . . spare me, oh please! – I have done everything you asked of me . . .'

'*Everything?*'

'. . . yes, I swear it – there are now five flocks of NightKin, all founded according to your instructions, Great Shadow . . .' The clerk Jumil was breathing heavily in his fear, sweat beading his face. 'Apart from the leaders, each is . . . unaware of the others and believes itself to be the only flock . . . I will soon begin preparing them for their . . . journeys . . .'

The clay face, aglow with green power, seemed to scowl at him for a moment, then the entwining tendril released his neck and withdrew into the mouth. The clerk slumped on all fours, visibly trembling with relief, gasping for breath.

'*And our enemy, the Watchers – how have you dealt with them?*'

A smile twitched across Jumil's features. 'Ah, not yet, but soon. I have thought deeply on this and I have devised a way to send fragments of the Broken against them.' His smile grew calmer, bolder with satisfaction. 'Another day or two and we will be ready.'

'*And Emperor Magramon's death two nights ago,*' said the face on the chamber floor. '*Was it your doing?*'

Jumil shook his head. 'No, my master, I would never have done such a thing without your express command. According to trust-worthy accounts, it seems that the exalted Magramon simply choked to death on a gezel stone at the high table, in full view of the Lord High Minister and several others. Crown-Prince Ilgarion is due to return tomorrow, and will most surely be offered the throne.' He rubbed his neck. 'How will this affect our plans, master? The Carver pilgrimage tactic is well advanced, although I know little of our progress in Honjir . . .'

'*Do not concern yourself with events in Jefren or Honjir — I have other overseers besides you. You may be assured, however, that my plans will remain as they are, although some details may change depending on the character of this Ilgarion.*'

'A bitter man, that one,' Jumil said. 'He was raised to the Apparency on his eighteenth birthday and has had to wait nearly thirty years to ascend to the throne. As Emperor he would be just as traditionalist as his father, especially with regard to any external threat. It should make his first session with the Conclave of Speakers interesting . . .'

'*A man who understands the value of power,*' said the face. '*Yet lacks experience in its use. Good — the pilgrimage tactic will sting his pride, though you may need to intensify his urge, twist the knife. On the subject of the Watchers, are you any closer to discovering their identities?*'

'Sadly, no, Great Master. All my spies have learned is that there are eight or nine of them, that they venture forth in hoods and masks and that they are well versed in the cantos of the Lesser Power.' The clerk frowned. 'Well versed and highly skilled.'

'*This does not please me, Jumil. I want them hunted down and slain!*'

The fear came back to the clerk's features. 'Great Shadow — I am doing all that I can. My plan for the Broken will finish them . . .'

'*To be certain of this, I am sending someone to assist you, one of my trusted servants.*'

Jumil's eyes widened in eager anticipation.

'One of your servants, from your glorious Nightrealm? How will he cross into our world, master, and how soon?'

'*A great temple, correctly purified by incantation and well provided with sacrifices would have made an acceptable gateway. But the intrinsic aspects here do not allow for such luxuries, thus I must employ simpler methods. A sacrifice, one already prepared over several weeks, one who will become the bloodgate by which my servant shall enter your world.*'

'*And he will be arriving soon, Jumil, very soon.*'

Lurid green fire was shining through webs of cracks in the malleable clay face. '*I'm sure that you understand that by now.*'

The clerk did not answer. Squatting on his knees, leaning forward on clenched fists, he seemed unable to move or utter a sound. A shivering ague had him in its grip and as sweat ran down his neck and arms, the eyes in his frozen, open-mouthed face were full of ghastly horror. They stared imploringly at the great face on the chamber floor which only laughed quietly as it watched him.

A few moments later the eyes ceased their terrified darting, slowed to lifeless stillness. The body itself seemed strangely rest-less in small ways, as if muscles were shifting and flexing, limbs tensing and relaxing, bones turning in their sockets back and forth. Although dead, the body of Jumil straightened and the head moved with sluggish jerks, its face looking slightly misshapen, the skin sickly and taut.

Something cracked, and the clerk's body slumped forward. There was a sharp ripping noise and blood spattered the chamber floor. There were more cracks, wet tearing sounds, a moist intake of breath and a throaty hiss. A dark, slender form writhed amid the gore, tore apart what remained of Jumil's head and then crouched there, breathing heavily.

'*Welcome, Xabo,*' said the Great Shadow's face. '*Welcome to the Realm Between.*'

'Master, I . . .' A hoarse voice paused for a savage bout of coughing, then went on. 'My head is rent by a fever of strange imaginings . . . my thoughts scarcely seem my own . . .'

'*You have come into this realm through a bloodgate, formerly one Jumil Felok, and it is his essence and memories which are clouding your mind. Let them find a place there, Xabo, and savour them — you will have great need of them in the days ahead.*'

Harsh emerald radiance from the great face gleamed on wet, black limbs and cast glittering highlights across a hairless, gaunt face from which dark red eyes stared.

'Yes, I can see pieces of his past, master, and read their meaning . . . there are many connections . . . although I still feel that the Duskgeneral would have been a better choice than I.'

'*No — there are other duties for which he has unique abilities. Focus on your form for soon it will change, limbs, skin and face — Jumil's memories are not the only aspect that you will take on.*'

The smooth, black head nodded. 'I am to become Jumil Felok, master, prepare the NightKin flocks for the great task, and crush these Watchers before they become a danger.'

'*Exactly so, except that the danger is already real, Xabo. I know this to be so because I have very recently discovered the identity of their leader . . . truly, when I discovered this knowledge, the past came alive to me. You know him, Xabo, as the one who turned and tried to betray me at the crux of the great struggle . . .*'

The creature called Xabo stiffened.

'Him? I thought that one had died.' Hate glared from his eyes. 'How I would exult to see him exhibited in your dream-courts, highest!'

'*Yet still he lives and seeks to frustrate my will once more. He goes by the name of Calabos now . . .*'

'That name,' said Xabo. 'It is . . . familiar. A poet, a dramatist . . .'

'*In time, all of Jumil's memories will become clear to you, much of it vital to the demanding work that lies ahead. So for now, my faithful one, rest, build your strengths and prepare for your new role. Become acquainted with all that Jumil has accomplished with the NightKin — he mentioned using what remains of the Broken against the "poet" and his underlings. This would be a most satisfying way of grasping a long-awaited retribution . . .*'

Silently nodding, Xabo crawled away from the bloody wreck of Jumil's body and sat against the chamber wall, brooding, watching, waiting.

Part One

Chapter One

When Death's baleful hand,
Lies heavy on heart and soul,
Summon all of thy strength,
And dream the dream of life.

Abbess Halimer, *Cautions & Aphorisms*

The light of the day was fading through shades of rose and grey as Corlek Ondene made his way up Baraskel Hill by way of the old Treemonks' path. The fresh smell of new leaves and burgeoning flowers hung in the cool air, and early blossom lay in small drifts against low bushes or scattered across the simple wooden benches that he passed every twenty paces. This was a place of communion and devotion, yet as Corlek walked through the scented stillness his thoughts kept straying to the letter which he carried in one of his robe's inner pockets. A four-year-old letter, which had reached him three years ago as he lay shivering with fever in an ocean-lashed tower out on the westernmost edge of the Stormbreaker Isles.

In the letter his elder brother, Rhanye, had written of their father's tragic death in a boating accident at the mouth of Sejeend's harbour. After that had come a short account of how the Emperor's ministers then found a way to rescind the family's right to their manor and estate (which was later bestowed on an unnamed court favourite). However, the Emperor insisted that his mother and brother be allowed to reside in the old summer house and receive an adequate annual stipend 'as a measure of the crown's unfailing generosity . . .'

Corlek smiled bleakly as he trudged on, easily able to imagine

Rhanye speaking those words with unrestrained sarcasm. The letter went on to reassure Corlek that despite their reduced circumstances all was well, and ended with the words – 'In the six long years since your unjust and undeserved exile, not a week has passed without our giving prayers and offerings at the Earthmother shrine in Drum Park. You are always in our thoughts, brother. May the Light be with you . . .'

Every word was graven into his memory by the hundred or more times he had read it these last three years. During the latter days of his mercenary wanderings every sentence had become a small treasure, a fragment of the life he had abandoned a decade ago. Yet nowhere in the letter had Rhanye mentioned the reason for Corlek's mad flight from Sejeend and the lands of the Empire because, Corlek knew, his mother would have read it before its despatch.

It would have been improper to mention that a young knight newly raised up to the Iron Guard, the Imperial bodyguard, had dishonoured the Emperor's own daughter, would it not, Mother? he thought. *Especially when that young knight was and is your own son . . .*

The ground levelled out as Corlek emerged at the cleared, open crest of the hill, a flat, grassy area lit softly by a pair of glass-chaliced oil lamps. Dominating the clearing was a fountain shrine dedicated to the spirit of the divine Emperor Tauric I, the liberator of Sejeend who gave his life in the final struggle to vanquish the Lord of Twilight. Standing over a shell-like bowl was a pale marble statue of the boy-emperor, hands holding aloft a banner while his feet bore down on the back of a five-headed, reptilian beast from whose fanged jaws water poured. But there was a finger-length crack in the fountain's bowl, an old one by the long stripe of green mould on the underside and the channel worn into the ground by the leaking water. In the lamplight, the rivulet looked almost black as it trickled away down the other, steeper side of Baraskel Hill, beside the curving rack of worn, wooden steps.

Corlek's mind was full of memories of Lyndil, the Emperor's daughter whose beauty and grace had stolen his heart and his mind and shackled all his senses. The Emperor's fury on discovering their dalliance had been such that Corlek was advised by one of his father's friends to flee the capital or face charges of treason followed by certain death.

But now Magramon was dead, and his body was interred in the royal vaults on the Isle of Remembrance. Looking southwards across the outer estates of the city, he could make out the lanterns of the burial grove by Drum Park. It was a man-made hill amid the city, but was called the Isle of Remembrance by the Earthmother priestesses nevertheless. With night now encroaching, a carpet of lights was beginning to spread through the streets and districts as porch lamps and street cressets were lit. Suddenly he laughed, full of the belief that he was on the verge of new beginnings, new hope and a new life. All that remained was to seek out his mother and brother and see what might be salvaged from the old.

He followed the wooden stairs downward, alongside the leaking water which veered away near the foot, disappearing into a bushy copse. With the hill behind him, Corlek hurried along a log-surfaced road with small, hedge-bordered fields to either side as he headed towards a slow-winding river called the Deinlok. Beyond it lay the northern districts of Sejeend and the former estate of the Ondene family. As he neared the bridge, he had to pause as a caravan of ten or more horse-drawn wagons coming from the north rumbled across. He guessed that they must be carrying the first harvest from the rich fields of eastern Khatris. The impact of horses' hooves and iron-rimmed wheels passing over heavy planking combined to create a mighty din and as the last rolled onto the bridge Corlek tugged the wide brim of his hat a little lower, shouldered his travelling sack and followed close behind.

'Back to civilization,' he whispered to himself as he reached the other bank of the Deinlok.

Rather than follow the wagons uphill into the northern suburbs, he ducked right along a grassy riverside track. In darkness he hurried, led by childhood memories which told him that before long he would come to a great, tilted kingsgold tree in whose bark he and Rhanye had carved their initials far back in their youth. At a bend in the river he paused to light a small, shuttered lamp then looked about him – sure enough, there in the undergrowth was a leaning tree. The initials were still there, if a little higher.

Hanging the lamp at his waist, he tugged on his gauntlets and began tearing away a screen of dogthorn and winding grass, searching for the flat stones and split logs they had laid down over the boggy ground which blocked the way to the eastern boundary of the Ondene estate. Bushes and saplings had taken root but the stones were still there, providing a path for him to follow. But when he emerged a little while later from the trees, muddy and scratched, he was confronted by a tall, heavy palisade rather than the flowering fences which had once served as an enclosure for the servants' huts. Following it round to the right, he saw where it joined the old west wall which was a combination of wood, turf and slate – eleven paces along from there he crouched down behind a clump of bushes and found his secret entrance, a small section of the wooden surface which fell inwards after several moments of determined pushing. As he crawled into the short, root-fringed tunnel on hands and knees, he laughed quietly as he imagined the surprise on his mother and brother's faces when they opened the door to him.

The lamplight showed the square wooden framework of the hatch that opened on the slanted earthwork beyond the wall. It took a while to push it open against all the grass roots which had woven together down the years but he was soon through. He put the log section back in place before backing out and fitting the grass-covered hatch into its square hole.

Lights were burning in some of the servant cottages and he could hear voices talking as he crept northwards to the old coppice beyond which the summer house lay. Skirting the trees he used the bushy undergrowth for cover yet when he pushed his way out of the foliage on the other side he thought for a moment that he had lost his way. Instead of a two-storey house with a small greenhouse, there was only dark, empty ground leading via a slight rise to the bush-bordered gardens that stretched away to the lamplit walls and bright windows of the high manor. But he knew that from the balcony over the manor's main entrance you could look straight down at the seated arbour at the rear of the summer house, so this was where it had to be . . .

A ghastly fear rose up in him and heedless of any observer he opened the shutters of his lamp and stumbled across the bare, hard ground, searching . . .

'Stand where you are, ser – and put out your light!' came a man's voice from the dark behind him.

He whirled on the spot, one hand reaching for his sword . . . then he froze when he saw the spear waiting poised about two feet away, aimed at his throat.

'The lamp,' growled the spearman. 'Put it out.'

As he did as he was told, he saw that the other man carried a hooded lamp on a chain about his chest. Faint glimmers highlighted the spear's wooden shaft and the dark iron of its tapering point.

'Who are you?' the man said. 'Why are you trespassing?'

But Corlek was full of panicky foreboding.

'Ser,' he said. 'I beg you, please tell me what happened to the summer house . . . it used to stand on this very spot . . .'

'How . . .' the man began, then set his spear aside as he raised up his lamp to shine in Corlek's face. There was a gasp.

'Master Corlek!'

The man turned the lamp towards himself and Corlek immediately recognized him as Rugal, the Ondenes' stablemaster. But his ten-year-old memories were confounded by what he saw – once a tall, vigorous man, Rugal was now gaunt and stooped, black hair gone grey and long while his eyes looked watery and full of pain and fear.

'Rugal – what happened?'

The older man suddenly gave him a grim, piercing stare.

'Can't you smell it, young master?' he said. 'Breathe in deep.'

Almost against his will he did so and found that he could smell something, a faint charred odour, like old ashes . . .

'The summer house . . . burned down?'

'Caught fire like a book in a furnace,' Rugal said. 'When the alarm was raised, I rushed through the coppice with everyone else, thinking to help your brother and the Lady Ondene, but the flames . . . they were everywhere, great sheets of them roaring up the outside of every wall . . .'

'By the Void,' Corlek groaned. 'No . . .'

Rugal turned and wandered off a few steps, as if seeing and reliving it all again.

'My clothes were smoking, the heat was so terrible – it drove us back. There was no water nearby, except for the well up behind the great house.' A few steps and he was back at Corlek's side. 'But there was nobody coming running from it to help. No, they were all out on their balcony, watching.'

Corlek felt hollow and bereft, his legs trembling and weak. 'Was anything recovered . . . anything . . . ?'

'Nothing left but burned ashes and cracked stones,' Rugal said in a hoarse voice, leaning on his spear. 'Them up at the house wouldn't have a memorial stone on the grounds, and they offered nothing towards the cost of one. But I was having none of that . . .' He suddenly began walking towards the coppice. 'Come this way, young master. You'll be wanting to see it.'

Stunned by the terrible news, Corlek stumbled after him in the darkness, following the gleams of his hooded lamp through the night and back into the dense foliage of the coppice. Rugal led him into its heart where the oldest trees grew, safe from cutting, and behind a screen of vines and dog-ivy he opened the lamp's shutter a good way and held it higher for Corlek to see.

In some past year lightning had struck one of the elder trees, leaving it a stump from which smaller limbs had sprouted. The trunk itself had later been shaped by a wood carver, whittled into a finely detailed sculpture of leaves and berries and entwining vines, in the midst of which were the faces of Corlek's mother and brother, eyes closed but smiling as if in peace. Below their images three small, tiered shelves had been carved into the wood, each one bearing a number of thimble-sized votive candles. Rainwater had gathered in each one's tiny flame-melted cavity.

As he reached out to touch the beautifully rendered faces, the tears came at last, silently in the silence.

No family, no bodies, no bones, and no graves, he thought emptily. *No home, no hope . . .*

'Nothing left but my name,' he murmured, pausing as a faint pattering and the quivering of leaves announced a passing shower.

Taking off his hat he raised his face to the cold raindrops for a moment or two before letting Rugal lead him out of the coppice. The old servant closed his lamp's aperture down to a gleam, just enough to show the way back to the secret exit in the palisade earthwork. When Corlek understood where they were going, a certain realization roused him from grief.

'You knew,' he said. 'You knew about our hidden door.'

Rugal chuckled in the darkness. 'Of course, and it was me who planted those bushes on either side of the wall. Thought an escape hole might come in handy . . .'

Nearing the wall they both fell silent and moved in a stealthy crouch. At the concealed hatch, as Rugal knelt to tug it loose he whispered to Corlek an address and a name.

'They are old friends of my family,' he said. 'Tell them you were sent by Father Wolf, young master, and they will keep you safe and fed for a time. Then we'll find somewhere safe outside Sejeend for you to go, though when Ilgarion is crowned peace will become a rare commodity and nowhere will be safe.'

'What do you mean?' Corlek said.

'You may not have heard but in the last week those fanatical Carver-worshipping Mogaun routed Mantinor's largest army. And what with that Carver prophet uniting the Jefren templarchies . . .'

Corlek shook his head, having only heard vague rumours about the threat which the Carver worship-dominated land of Anghatan posed to eastern Honjir, which had been an Imperial protectorate for nearly fifty years. But he had found that difficult to take seriously since the Nagira mountains lay between the two countries.

Next to him, the grassy hatch came away in Rugal's hands and Corlek crouched down to crawl through, pausing to look back at the old servant.

'Thank you, Rugal – thank you for your kindness and for the shrine. It was . . . more than fitting . . .'

'I would have done more, had it been possible, master Corlek. Now, I wish you good health and a long life, both of which you are more likely to find someplace other than in this city. That is my advice, which I am sure you'll not be taking.'

Corlek gave a bleak smile, then said: 'Perhaps I will, Rugal, but for the moment tell me the name of the people who own the estate now, the people who watched my mother and brother burn.'

Rugal hesitated and Corlek waited. Then the old man leaned in close.

'They are the dor-Galyn, a powerful family and close favourites of Crown Prince Ilgarion. Their eldest son was recently sent up to the Iron Guard as a captain.' He placed the grass plug down by the gap in the earthwork. 'Have a care, young master. May the Light reveal your path.'

As Corlek crouched and entered the low tunnel, the hatch fell back into place with a muffled impact, plunging him into utter blackness. On the other side he leaned back against the wall for a moment or two, staring at the smothering, leafy darkness, hearing his heart thud in his chest, turning that name over and over in his mind.

Dor-Galyn, dor-Galyn — I need to know more about them.

Then he sighed and pushed through the undergrowth, out towards a road that led into Sejeend's commercial districts. He paused at the roadside, thinking again of the carven shrine that Rugal had shown him. Eyes closed, he whispered a prayer for his mother and his brother, then set off.

Chapter Two

He gathered all the world onto a stage,
Rivers, forests, cities, all,
And let the savage capers of heroes,
Tell a timely tale of truth

Epitaph on a poet's tomb in Adnagaur

The smoke of a hundred pipes and the main hearth's leaky flue hung in a grey veil across the high, crossbeamed common room of the Four Winds Inn. The place was warm and busy with evening custom and many drinkers were standing near the tap counter or in clusters by the massive fire, or along the balcony that hung off the streetside wall, right above the main entrance. Scores of conversations merged into one continuous din of voices punctuated by laughter and coughing while in one corner a couple of musicians were playing requests on fiddle and whistle.

The Four Winds lay at the one of the main crossroads in north Sejeend, between Blueyard Market and the Earl of Westerbow dramahouse. Thus many trades had their representatives among its customers, farmers and merchants from the plains of eastern Khatris, drovers from further along Gronanvel, fur-trappers back from the shadowy gorges of the Rukang mountains, fishermen and oyster-catchers, weavers and carpenters, soldiers and scholars. All were watched over by the senior tapsmen and a brace of brawny, hard-eyed men carrying weighted bludgeons.

Another observed the noisy crowd from a small table beneath the balcony, glancing up occasionally when those above stamped or otherwise caused the woodwork to creak audibly. Attired in a long, dull green coat over well-worn travelling clothes, Tashil Akri drank sparingly from her jack of small beer, lending an ear to some of the chatter going on nearby while keeping an eye on the main door. She had a mask, little more than a plain eyemask in red cotton, but it was pushed up to sit on her tangled brown hair just as several people within sight had done. In fact, almost no one in the tavern was actually wearing their masks, apart from a tall gaunt man she had glimpsed across the crowded room.

As people came and went, the big door swung open and banged shut repeatedly, admitting frequent gusts of cool evening air, but Tashil stayed where she was to be sure of catching Calabos as soon as he arrived. She had been at the safe house at Vannyon's Ford, having just returned from the Honjir Wall, when she received mindspeech contact from Dardan who was passing on an urgent message recalling the senior Watchers to Sejeend. Since Magramon had died only a few days ago, Tashil guessed that the two events were not unrelated.

With her wicker-seated stool making cricking sounds, she took a generous mouthful of beer and leaned back against the wall, feeling the aches in her limbs. Without really trying she focussed her underhearing on the Treemonks kneeling by the fire, hearing their murmured rumours of the persecutions in north Anghatan and the torture of other monks in Casall . . . then she shifted her attention to the head tapsman as he told one of the serving girls to point out a trouble-making customer . . . then managed to over-hear the short luck prayers that the dice-throwers were muttering under their breath before making a play . . .

Tashil relaxed, knowing that further temptation might lead to using the Lesser Power itself, and that would be foolhardy.

'You never know who might be listening,' her old mentor Tregaylis once told her. 'Being a Watcher means resisting the urge to use the Godriver in unwise situations. It also means being able to recognize such situations . . .'

It also means learning how to wait, she thought wryly. Passing time while waiting for others invariably led to eavesdropping as a way of relieving the boredom, just as she was doing with the argu-ment taking place in the corner behind her. Three maskless scholars from a northbank college were exchanging drolleries and retorts with a group of well-dressed students from the Imperial Academy. As a veil for her Watcher activities in Sejeend, she managed a small shop selling books, parchment, inks and stones, and recognized the three scholars from past custom, while the Academy students she knew not at all. The argument had opened with general insults concering each other's institutions and style of attire, then moved on to more erudite matters. The Academy students, it transpired, were dramaturgic seminarists and cast members of the Imperial Academy's annual production.

'I see,' said one of the scholars, a handsome, golden-haired youth she remembered as Brondareg. 'Then I imagine that you would have everything hired for you: theatre, stagehands, costumes – and audience!'

There was a chorus of guffaws at this barb and Tashil edged round to gain a better view.

'You betray your ignorance with such low wit, ser,' came back one of the Academy students, whose mask was a silvery affair decorated with eagle motifs. 'Anyone of consequence would know that Academy plays are always well-attended. Why, last year's production of *The Great House Of Hallebron* drew a full house every night.'

Entirely true, Tashil thought. *But since it was also sponsored directly by the crown, it would have been practically treasonous for any of Magramon's court nobles to not go and see it.*

Brondareg nodded judiciously. 'Hmm – *Great House* is a good enough play . . .'

'Whereas its sequel is by far superior,' added one of his two companions, a short stocky young man in a threadbare brown doublet, whose name escaped her. 'But *The Fall Of The House Of Hallebron* is far too provocative for these times . . .'

Another of the Academy students, his bronze and jet mask decorated with wolves, shook his head. 'From your shabby demeanour and sneering tone I would place you as apprentice scoffers, or would-be pedantic tutors!'

Brondareg turned to his friend. 'Why Ghensh – this fine fellow seems to have heard of us!'

Then the two scholars gave exaggerated, hand-fluttering bows to their accuser, provoking more laughter from the onlookers. Meanwhile, their third companion said nothing, just lay slumped forward on their long narrow table, head resting on a couple of leather-bound books around which his arms were wrapped.

'Guilty as charged, good ser,' said Brondareg. 'Perhaps you could enlighten our meagre souls by telling us which work is the object of your Academy's ambitions this year?'

'*The Twilight Emperor*,' was the lofty reply.

At which the third scholar sat bolt upright, a dark-haired young woman who glared across at the haughty Academy boys as they lounged against their own table.

'That overheated, bombastic muddle by Drusarik?' she said. 'Surely not . . .'

Tashil grinned – the girl was Viorne and she was half-Mogaun, just like Tashil.

'You should keep a civil tongue in your head,' snapped the eagle-masked student. 'Our stagemaster is a direct descendant of Drusarik himself!'

'But *The Twilight Emperor* has a ridiculous ending,' Ghensh said. 'Tauric and the Lord of Twilight duelling in the depths of the Void while hurling florid invective at each other . . . there is nothing in the historical record to even imply that that is what happened!'

'Whereas others prefer to plod along behind the antiquarians,' said Wolf Mask, who then suddenly lunged forward and snatched away Viorne's books. 'As I thought – *The Great Shadowking War* by Beltran Calabos . . . why, you're all disciples of the Noble Relic!'

Tashil had to force herself to say nothing in Calabos' defence. Amid the laughter, Viorne and Ghensh rose angry-faced from their seats but Brondareg gestured them to remain as he calmly got up, took a couple of steps towards the Academy students' table and, smiling, held out one hand. Tashil watched him lock gazes with Wolf Mask, who held for a moment then shrugged and gave up the books. Brondareg in turn handed them back to Viorne, who quickly stowed them away. Then he sat back down and took up his beaker.

'Not disciples, good sirs,' he said. 'Merely seekers after the truth, which Calabos pays more regard to than Drusarik, it must be said . . .'

Tashil was finding the students' bantering quite amusing but as the next retort was uttered, she was distracted by a sustained draught of cold air. Turning, she was in time to see a large, black-robed and hooded figure sit down at her table. She was about to object when the burly newcomer laid a familiar copper-inlaid, ironwood walking stick on the table before him then pushed back his cowl. Pale eyes that were both piercing and kind regarded her from beneath bushy eyebrows while a strong hand bearing a plain ring stroked a neat beard as grey and tightly curled as the hair on his head. Hanging below his chin was a half-mask made of plain, stitched red satin with no motif other than a third eye staring openly from the brow.

'Dardan informed me of your imminent arrival,' he said. 'So I decided to meet you myself. Besides, I haven't been here for many years . . .'

Tashil smiled, and indicated the still-squabbling students behind her. 'You just missed a clash over one of your works – *The Great Shadowking War*, to be precise.'

Beltran Calabos frowned, then shrugged. 'Were there any deaths or maiming as a result? No? Hmm, maybe I should revise it, after all . . .' He caught the eye of a serving girl, ordered a pot, then leaned forward. 'We'll leave shortly, once I've reminded myself what Hethu ale tastes like.'

Once the tankard was brought, he sipped it a couple of times then drank off a great quaff of the dark brown beer. Wiping his moustache, he smiled and nodded.

'So how was your journey from Vannyon's Ford?' he said, so quietly that she could hear him only with her undersenses.

'Exhausting, master,' she replied in the same way. 'Two changes of mount, and only this padded stool is allowing me to stay seated. Are you expecting anything . . . untoward?'

'Ilgarion returns in a day or two,' said Calabos. 'To claim his crown and issue more warnings about the "Carver menace", no doubt. Meanwhile, all word and trace of the NightKin has dried up – we know that we did not kill them all that night on Redstone

Beach a month ago, so they must be planning something . . .'

'Assassination?' Tashil said grimly.

'Or kidnapping, or blackmail or . . .' He stared into his half-empty tankard.

Tashil was about to question him, when a loud but steady voice cut through the babble surrounding them.

'I think that you've made a mistake, friend – now why don't you return that pouch to the young master?'

All went quiet in the corner as Calabos glanced up and Tashil looked round. Most eyes were fixed on a seated man who was holding out a bare, long dagger with the point pressing against the side of another man frozen in the act of walking past Ghensh, one of the three scholars. They, too, had turned to watch.

'You mystify me, ser,' replied the accused, a scrawny man in shabby town attire. 'I know not what you speak of.'

The man with the dagger sighed and leaned forward. Tashil saw that he was a grim-faced, unshaven man in a long, shapeless coat and leather leggings. His black hair, tied back in a short tail, was streaked with grey while his features were those of a man in his prime. But his expression was one of steady, almost calm contempt for the other who stood before him. 'Let me refresh your memory,' said the man with the dagger. 'As you made to leave you brushed against the young man there –' He nodded towards Ghensh, '– during which you relieved him of his money pouch.'

'Mother's name!' Ghensh cried, fumbling at his waist. 'It's gone!'

The thief smiled weakly. 'Ah, you mean the pouch I found on the floor . . . I was about to give it to the head tapsman, but fortune allows me to return it to its rightful owner in person . . .'

Dropping the pouch into the outraged Ghensh's outstretched hand, he bowed then disappeared into the crowd. As an excited din of conversation erupted, Ghensh offered thanks to the stranger who only nodded and went back to his ale. Tashil grinned and turned to see that Calabos had suddenly pulled his hood up to partly conceal his face while peering past her shoulder.

'Is something the matter?' she asked.

'You might say that,' he muttered. 'I seldom feel calm when a face from the past suddenly appears in the middle of a crowded tavern.'

'Ah, Ser Dagger, you mean.'

He nodded. 'Corlek Ondene, as I live and breathe.'

Tashil shrugged. 'Who?'

'Ten years ago, he was the youngest soldier ever to rise to a captaincy in the Iron Guard, the Emperor's personal bodyguard. But while he was an outstanding warrior, he was callow and careless in other matters — he became entranced by the Emperor's daughter and bedded her—'

'With her agreement, I assume,' she said archly.

'No doubt. When Magramon found out he swore he would cut off Ondene's head himself, after doing the same to his manhood.'

Tashil was both appalled and amused. 'How did he escape?'

'Someone in the palace warned him and helped him climb down from one of the guard towers, and someone else spirited him out of Sejeend. That was the last that anyone saw of him, but the repercussions went on for months, years. Ever heard of a play by Momas Gobryn called *The Trial Of Aetheon*?'

'I know the title but I've never seen a copy, nor seen it enacted.'

Calabos' smile was brittle. 'Nor would you while Magramon was alive — Gobryn wrote it as an allegory of Ondene's folly . . .'

Suddenly Calabos paused, bowed his head and let the cowl fall forward across his face. Before Tashil could say anything, Corlek Ondene brushed past their table on his way to the door. He was now wearing a battered, wide-brimmed hat and while he did not look directly at either of them, Tashil saw a look of bleak despair in his features as he passed by. And there was something else, a minatory feeling that chilled her as if a beast made of ice had breathed on her. Glancing up, she saw that Calabos too had felt it, his bearded face seeming almost haunted while a fierceness shone in his eyes.

'What was *that*?' she said low and quiet as Ondene reached the door and stepped outside.

For long moments Calabos said nothing, then drew a deep breath.

'A forebodeance,' he said. 'Ondene is going to his doom. Come!'

Standing quickly, he snatched up his walking stick and made for the door. Tashil hastily downed the last of her ale and hurried after him.

Outside, cold dense fog from the river drifted through the narrow streets, strengthening the dread within her. It was rare for her to experience a forebodeance so strong that it forced its way into conscious thought. As she followed Calabos along from the Four Winds she started to wonder why he was so concerned about Ondene. Then her attention was diverted by voices as she crossed before the alleyway that ran up the side of the tavern – a wedge of brightness spilled into the darkness halfway along as two figures stumbled out and began trudging off to the other end, followed by a third who closed the door on the light and the chattering din. Listening a moment, she recognized the voices of the three scholars from earlier, then hastened to keep with Calabos, who halted suddenly at the next corner to survey their surroundings. The light from a few porch lamps and street lanterns was smothered to a weak, isolated glow by the fog. The grey roads ahead and to the left ran level while a rightward turn led up a hill. Of Ondene there was neither sight nor sound yet Calabos pointed to the right and said, 'This way.'

Matching her companion's gait, Tashil strove to focus on her undersenses and after a moment thought she could see signs on the cobbled road, faint outlines of footprints left on the fog-dampened stones, the spoor by which Calabos tracked their quarry. Once more, her curiosity came to the fore.

'So, how did you come to know Captain Ondene, master?' she said, recalling how Calabos had covered his face back at the tavern.

There was a dry chuckle. 'I knew his father, Arnos, Baron Ondene, thus I knew the family – 'twas I who helped the boy escape the city back then, but I could not save Arnos or his wife and older son.' The humour in his voice had turned to bitterness.

Then his whole demeanour became more alert as he regarded the cobbles with unwavering intensity, pointing with his walking stick. Tashil could just see where other footprints had converged on the single set of tracks and formed a smeared muddle from which lines of scuffed marks led diagonally across the road towards a small, wooded park. Shadowy trees were were bordered by a low stone wall broken by an arched entrance through which the tracks progressed.

'They've taken him, and it was only moments ago!' Calabos said, breaking into a run. Dashing after him, Tashil could make out at the edge of her undersenses faint sounds of struggle, twigs breaking underfoot, foliage brushing against clothing . . .

As they hurried into the park and up a wide path amid the tangled gloom, Calabos gave his stick a twist with his hands, separating it into two pieces which he stowed away in his robe.

'I'll use Engulf to smother their lanterns,' he muttered. 'Then you'll move in and retrieve the unfortunate Captain. Agreed?'

'Yes, master,' Tashil said as she sifted through her memory for an appropriate spell.

The wooded park was a shapeless, dark mass in the night, except for the fitful lamplight that glimmered through the trees and bushes from a point off the main path along which they now crept. Cruel laughter and grunts of pain reached Tashil's ears as she called up the thought-canto Leech and set it spinning in her thoughts, a loop of whispers, reverie-shapes and dream-tastes. Calabos was now standing a few feet away with both hands held before him, gripping each other. With her attuned eyes she could see the intense purpose in his features as he stared at his clenched hands.

'Ready?' he murmured without shifting his gaze.

Tashil breathed out her unlocking word, and the thought-canto flowed down into her hands which now flickered with an icy-blue web of power.

'I am now,' she said.

Calabos nodded once, eyes fixed on the flickering lamp glows. Then his hands sprang apart as the Engulf spell burgeoned forth and an utter, pit-deep darkness rushed in, swallowing every detail and every gleam of radiance. Tashil was already slipping swiftly through the trees when blackness fell, but her sight was now firmly aligned to her undersenses, allowing her to see the surroundings as ghostly, webby forms and spidery outlines.

Moments later she reached a clearing where four wraith-like

figures of men were either sprawled on ground, or struggling
blindly against entangling roots and thorny vines, while giving out
angry, baffled shouts and curses. But with her glowing hands she
silenced them one by one, sending them into insensibility with a
light and precise touch. All succumbed instantly except for one
who was wearing a crescent-shaped amulet that hung down from
his indistinct, dishevelled garments. The amulet resisted her
thought-canto, brightening for a second or two before lapsing into
dullness while its owner slumped into immobility.

Tashil did not realize how tense she was until she felt the relief
that followed. She quickly turned to the figure of Corlek Ondene
who, bound to a tree, had already suffered a beating. Untying him,
she realized that he was scarcely able to stand so she was forced
to half-carry him with one of his arms braced across her shoulders. She was struggling with him through the bushes when she
felt Calabos' strong hands relieving her of the burden. By the time
they stumbled out of the blackness and down towards the road,
Ondene was completely unconscious and Calabos had to carry
him over one shoulder.

'How long before those roughs start to awake?' he asked,
breathing heavily.

'Not quite half an hour,' Tashil said.

'Good.'

At the park's arched entrance he halted and lowered the unre-
sponsive Ondene down to a seated position against the stonework.

'I have my horse and carriage lodged at a hostelry just a street
away,' he said. 'If you watch over our friend, I shall return very
shortly.'

So saying, he departed at a run, leaving an apprehensive Tashil to
shiver in the cold and stand over her charge while eyeing the dark
wood behind her. Yet all seemed tranquil, the deserted park and street
ruled by a chill, deadening silence. Then something disturbed the edges
of her undersenses, a tenuous, uneasy feeling that she was being
watched from shadows along the downward street they had climbed
from the tavern. She turned her head enough to glance that way and
began attuning her sight, reaching through the intervening distance
with perceptions that made the grey veil of shadow and fog melt . . .

Then the clatter of hooves and wheels broke her concentration
and a moment later a two-seater drew up, and Calabos clambered
out. The moment of unease passed and Tashil bent to the task of
helping to lift Ondene into the carriage, then climbed up and
squeezed in beside him. Back in the driving seat, Calabos took
up the reins and flicked the horse into motion. Great clouds of
vapour fumed from the animal's mouth and nostrils as it hauled
on the traces.

'Where are we taking him?' Tashil said. 'The Watch-house?'

Calabos shook his head. 'I think it would be better if we made
for the townlodge – we should be safe there.'

Tashil knew that was certainly the case – Calabos' lodge was
built like a fortress. So she sat back in the hard seat as Calabos
steered the carriage round to head down the other side of the
park, towards the eastern districts of Sejeend.

*From a shadowed doorway, a tall, gaunt figure stared at the horse-drawn
vehicle as it rattled away from him. The timely intervention of the two
mages had saved him the trouble of having to retrieve Ondene from his
predicament, yet they struck him as suspicious, especially that powerful
older man who at all times had a secretive air about him. The young
woman may have been weaker in power but she was still able to perceive
his presence, even this far back along the street.*

*He sniffed the cold fogginess of the air and was so reminded of sea
mist that he smiled. He longed for a return to the* Stormclaw's *deck,
but he and his companions had been entrusted with the guardianship of
Ondene's mystery by the exalted Prince Agasklin himself, who hinted at
mysterious lines from the Book of the Vortex. Thus duty commanded that
he follow Ondene's rescuers and discover their destination, which would
not be difficult given their nature.*

*Stretching, he rocked his head around to loosen the stiffness in his neck,
then set off in trudging pursuit.*

Chapter Three

From the first crystal morn,
To the final luckless night,
He trod a hundred islands,
And slept in a hundred caves,
With Time at his back,
Like a vast, lost country.

Ralgar Morth, *The Last Shieldring*

Crossing and recrossing the threshold of awareness, Corlek Ondene was harried and hedged in by pain. It seemed that he was being taken from place to place in a cart of some kind, then later physically carried. Snatches of conversation slipped through the fitful fog in his mind to disrupt those other recollections that were stubbornly marching to and fro. How his attackers rushed him from all sides before dragging him into the wooded park, how they tied him to a tree and began beating him, and how one said 'You should never have come back . . .'

Then he was aware of lying on something soft and warm amid the dimness of a room bathed in the amber of fire and lamplight. There were another two people there sitting either side of the bed . . .

And then there was only one, her cool and gentle hand stroking his brow, brushing back his hair. In the buttery yellow firelight her features took on the semblance of his mother, her aristocratic sternness softened by a careworn sadness. '*My son,*' he seemed to hear, '*My poor, ill-treated son . . .*' Then the firelight wavered and her features became that of Lyndil, the emperor's daughter, who just smiled at him for a long, sweet moment before the flame-shadows

danced across her face, changing it to that of a young woman he
did not know . . .

But the ebb and flow of wakefulness took her away and after
another spell of oblivion he became aware of another presence,
taller, darker, who stood by the bed, and whose irresistible scrutiny
he felt as a great pressure upon every fibre of his being. Only
when that strange burden eased did he realize that the knots of
pain were gone.

The dark figure's face was hidden in the dimness of a capacious
cowl while, in contrast, firelight glinted brightly on the brass-
ornamented sheath of a straight longsword hanging on the wall
behind him. Some old aphorism about becoming the sword's edge
whispered through his mind like a vagrant memory before sleep
surged over him, its heavy waves rolling in from a deep ocean of
weariness.

Healing Corlek's wounds in tandem with Tashil had been a satisfying task but by the end of it she was fighting to stay awake.
Calabos, while feeling the strain of the work, had deeper reserves
of strength to draw on and eventually had to insist that since they
had done all that they could she should retire and rest. Yawning,
she had finally agreed, bid him goodnight and trudged away to
the nearby chamber he had set aside for her.

Leaving Calabos to contemplate Corlek Ondene, last scion of
a disgraced and anulled house. As he stood there in the darkness
by the bed, a brief but perfect recollection came to him, that of
a sunny day at the Ondene estate in the company of the Baron
and his hawks. A day when a far younger Corlek had come running
from the manor, bursting with exultation and eager to show to
his father the parchment with seals and ribbons, confirming his
new cadetship in the Imperial cavalry.

'Do you ever recall what I said to you that day?' Calabos
murmured to the insensible Corlek. '"Train hard and you'll become
the edge of the emperor's sword; survive and learn and you will
become the edge of your own sword." What have ten years of
exile taught you, I wonder?'

Then, unexpectedly, the man's eyes fluttered open and looked straight up at him. Yet they held little focus and alertness as their gaze drifted here and there, half-closing, showing the whites as the eyelids trembled for a moment or two before opening again. This time Corlek's eyes wandered for only a moment before fixing on the longsword hanging on the wall behind Calabos, who frowned, alert to any change in it. But there was nothing, no disturbance in the weapon's tranquillity. Corlek muttered something unintelligible, turned onto his side and fell asleep.

Sensing that this was a healing slumber, Calabos left the darkened room and climbed the main stairs to the second floor and entered his own chambers. Before long he had disrobed and was pulling heavy, woollen blankets over his head. Clearing his mind, he slowed his breathing then embraced sleep like a swimmer striking out from the shore.

But his hold on the recesses of his mind was less than perfect this night and cryptic intrusions came in fleeting encounters amid a gloomy, thready fog. Shades of black, silver and grey predominated. Moans of despair, sighs, muted shouts and cries of pain came from all around. Part of Calabos wanted to wake from this unfamiliar dreamstate but curiosity kept him there, observing a succession of grotesque visions – a man with a cat's head; a number of opaque, wraith-like children floating in midair, swapping their heads and limbs as they danced in a figure-of-eight; a golden-haired woman carrying a torch and pursued by a one-eyed barbarian who caught and killed her, then stripped away her flesh to reveal not bones but knives, swords, arrows, axes, all clotted with gore; a great black bull, its eyes and mouth filled with golden fire which left trails of burning letters in the air as it galloped. The letters were ancient Othazi script, and they spelled out a variety of curses and imprecations.

Then the slow-swirling tendrils of ashen fog convulsed as if something huge had passed nearby and gaps opened up, revealing faces amid the leaden veil, men and women who stared at Calabos as if in recognition, although he knew none of them. There were expressions of anger and cold contempt and as they all glared at him they began silently mouthing one word, a name, over and over and over . . .

Quickly, Calabos broke free of the dream and woke to a cold room made grey by the faint traces of dawn slipping past the edges of the window drapes. He sat up and swung his legs out to rest bare feet on the polished wooden floor, while his thoughts remained filled with the images from his dream.

Not a good sign, he thought. *Not good at all.*

It had been a long, long time since he had experienced a dream so freighted with such disturbing imagery. Clearly he had to discover the meaning of those symbols and there was only one man he could trust with such truths but to visit him would entail a two-hour journey on horseback north to a town amid the Rukang foothills. Shrugging, he rose and dressed in dark, heavy garments suited to travel then left his room and descended to the lodge's lamplit main hall where two night guards were on duty. He beckoned one over, a Kejaner called Gillat, and told him to wake Osig the stable boy and have him saddle the mare for a morning ride. As Gillat hurried off, Calabos donned boots and a riding cloak. Fastening the latter to one side, he paused before a large oval mirror near one of the lamps and studied his reflection for signs of the truth.

Before him stood a tall, grey-haired man noticeably past his middle years, yet retaining a certain vigour. While the dark-brown doublet and trews were sombre and formal, the calf-length cloak gave him an imposing, dramatic air. But he could not escape the sight of those disembodied heads soundlessly chanting in unison one word, a name that he knew so very well.

Calabos felt an old dread in the pit of his stomach. In the past, only a few images had slipped by the disciplined barriers he laid across the deep wells of memory, glimpses of snow-covered battle-fields, the massed ranks of dark armies, and horrifying carnage. Paradoxically, however, such disturbing dreams could be the first shreds of proof that the influence of the Lord of Twilight had returned to haunt Sejeend.

Three hundred years of living, he thought. *Nearly a dozen lives lived, five score of friends and lovers gathered and discarded, ships sailed along every coast and every city seen and delved, and still I can feel your mark upon my very spirit, a scar so permanent and profound that it can instantly recognize in others the least remnant of you . . .*

Again, the faces from his dream filled his mind's eye, pitilessly
staring, all mouthing that name again and again . . .

Byrnak, Byrnak, Byrnak, Byrnak . . .

Calabos closed his eyes as if in pain, gritting his teeth.

*No, that name belonged to another, one who was part puppet and part
mask, one who did not survive the death of his god . . .*

He opened his eyes and stared into their reflection in the mirror
and saw a stark and grim resolve.

Who can tell from where I received the touch of undying? he thought.
*Perhaps it was the consequence of being a god's garb or my immersion in
the Wellsource, or both. But I've had three hundred years of living, and
worn a dozen faces and a dozen names, and any one of them gave me
more self-knowledge and inner strength than that other . . . no, Byrnak
is dead — Calabos lives!*

A side entrance in the lobby opened, letting in morning light,
cold air and Osig the stableboy. 'Master, your horse awaits you.'

Calabos nodded, gave Gillat a short message to pass on to Tashil,
then followed Osig out to the stable courtyard. The air was cold
and a fitful gust shook blossom from the old apple tree in the
corner of the yard as Calabos swung up into the saddle of his
horse, uttering a grunt of exertion for Osig's benefit as the stableboy
opened the heavy yard gate.

Moments later, with the gate closed and bolted behind him, he
spurred his mount into a trot along a narrow street that led between
townhouses and loomshops, heading east before curving north. A
while later he came to a pair of immense iron gates bolted into
equally imposing sections of city wall, a crossing point that marked
the city of Sejeend's notional boundary. There were several other
gateways around the city, some guarded, others — like this — unattended and lying open.

Beyond, the road continued with houses and buildings still
spreading outwards. As he rode through, Calabos smiled, recalling
a time when these gates really had been a barrier to the outside.
Sejeend had been so much smaller back then, when Tauric III
abandoned the melancholic, half-deserted isle of Besh-Darok and
moved the Khatrisian capital here. He frowned, trying to recall
the name he had been using at that time . . . Malban, that was it,

who had been a cultivated and laconic swordmaster, tutor to the sons of the nobility and rich merchants alike.

He remembered the sight of Tauric III's court flotilla sailing into Sejeend's wide outer harbour. It had been late in the afternoon on a clear summer's day, with heat coming off the stones of the city and the setting sun filling half the sky with a spreading display of roseate clouds shot through with fiery orange. Flying hundreds of flags and driven by banks of oars, the massive Imperial barge had led the stately procession of noble ships and wallowing cargo galleys overladen with all the treasure and chattels of the palace at Besh-Darok. He had observed it all from the protruding balcony of a cliff-edge tavern called the Brinksman which had once afforded a magnificent view of the estuary and the surrounding lands. From that vantage, the court flotilla with its warship escorts on either flank had resembled a huge jewelled regalia converging on Sejeend.

Calabos laughed quietly as he rode – the Brinksman had not lasted long after that, demolished to make way for the gardens and walkways of the grounds of the new palace, which was only half-complete at that time.

I almost wish I'd bought the place, he thought. _Then dismantled it and put it back together further along the cliff. Perhaps I will rebuild it, when the years have wound well past this year . . ._

The town was called Hekanseh and it nestled among the verdant, wooded foothills south of the Rukang mountains. Like many other towns north of Sejeend or west along the banks of Gronanvel, Hekanseh was a former village which had expanded in the prosperous stability of the last 100 years or so. Unlike them, however, it was host to a House of Seclusion, one of several scattered around the empire. The houses had been founded and administered by the Healer subchapter of the Earthmother order as refuges for the care and study of the sick in mind. It was Hekanseh's own House of Seclusion which was his destination, and one of its residents his intended advisor.

Calabos avoided the town's main road and square, choosing instead a narrow track which skirted the western edge of Hekanseh.

He came to a gravelled road which sloped up a hillside, and turned along a bushy gully between tall trees. Before long the road levelled off as he emerged from the trees to see a small, weatherbeaten mansion from whose squat belltower the Healer's banner hung. Wallthorn and dog-ivy had grown wild across the frontage, partially obscuring some of the tall, decorative windows and providing a fringe of foliage for the wide archway through which he steered his mount.

He dismounted in the small enclosed courtyard, just as a young Healer novitiate in the green livery of the chapter came forward to take charge of his horse. Behind him approached one of the senior brothers who carried a long plain walking staff, swinging forward in time with his gait.

'Welcome, ser Calabos,' the Healer monk said impassively. 'We were not expecting you for another week or more.'

Calabos maintained an amiable demeanour despite the man's coldness. This was Niloc, the most important monk at the House, after Bishop Daguval, a haughty, humourless man whom Calabos enjoyed irritating by posing as a dim aristocrat.

'Well, good brother Niloc,' he said airily. 'Having gone for a ride beyond my usual daily round in a wander which brought me close to splendid Hekanseh, I thought to derive some virtue from the day by visiting my poor cousin. How is he, pray tell?'

For all Niloc's skill at concealing his disdain, it was clearly visible to Calabos' eyes. It was a guilty pleasure this, prodding the man's prejudice by playing the city-bred fool, yet it was also a necessary one.

'He has apparently displayed considerable lucidity these past few days,' Niloc said. 'But you will have to ask the bishop—'

'Could it be the diet you're feeding him?' Calabos said. 'Or perhaps it's the water, eh?'

Calabos could almost sense the acid remark rising to brother Niloc's lips but it was forestalled by the appearance of the bishop at an open door in the corner of the small courtyard. Bishop Daguval was a short, balding man with a large presence, and a strength of character that showed in his features. The slight dishevelment of his green robes seemed to emphasize his personality.

'Ah, good Calabos!' he cried. 'An unexpected pleasure is it to welcome you to the House this day . . . thank you, Brother Niloc, for greeting our friend. I think that I should take charge of this fellow now.'

Niloc gave a small bow of the head. 'As you wish, your worship.' Then with a cool nod to Calabos he stepped through the door and was gone.

The bishop shook his head and with a forefinger tapped Calabos lightly on the chest. 'One of these days you'll overplay that buffoonery and Niloc will become less than courteous . . .'

Calabos gave a wry laugh as they entered the building. 'I doubt that he gives me any serious consideration,' he said. 'But I take your meaning.'

Inside, a long, tall corridor led to left and right, dimly lit by small, round windows set high on the walls. Calabos paused to look directly at the bishop.

'How is he?'

A sombreness came over Daguval like a garment he was well used to wearing. Calabos had a high regard for the man's intellect and compassion and knew that there would be no evasions and no soothing nonsense.

'For the last week and a half he has been surprisingly lucid,' the bishop said. 'Possibly his longest period of unbroken sanity since you brought him to us . . . until last night.'

Calabos' heart sank and recollections of his dream flickered in his mind's eye for a moment. 'He took leave of his sense once more?'

Bishop Daguval nodded sadly and led Calabos to a nearby archway beyond which rough stone steps wound upwards.

'But there is an odd libration to his inconstancy of mind, as if his sanity is a pendulum that swings to and fro between the light and the dark but according to unknown principles,' the bishop said as he ascended the stairs ahead of Calabos. 'I'm afraid he's gone back to carving.'

'I see,' Calabos said as he climbed with heavy footsteps. 'Have any of his . . . talents manifested themselves?'

'Hmm – not as yet.'

Daguval was fit for his age and showing no strain when he reached the head of the spiral stairs. Calabos, as a matter of habit, deepened his breathing and leaned slightly on the wall as he mounted the last step. They had arrived at a narrow landing with two doors.

'You know,' Daguval said, 'last week he and I had the most fascinating discussion about Cabringan poetry from the reign of Droshan the First. Was he ever an archivist, I wonder . . . if such a query is permissible?'

'I would not be violating my trust to say that certain archives were in his charge . . . prior to his tragic misfortune.'

Bishop Daguval nodded gravely, then turned to one of the two doors and gingerly pressed his ear against the dark-grained wood.

'All seems to be calm,' he said. 'You may enter, as you wish. I shall await you in the vigil cell.' He indicated the other exit.

Calabos faced the door, thoughts aswirl with apprehension. Then he steeled himself, opened the door and stepped inside.

The room was low-ceilinged and oblong, with a bed recess in the same wall as the entrance. The grey, rough-mortared walls were bare except for a framed piece of embroidery depicting trees and indistinct lines of verse. Embers were slowly dying in a small hearth in one corner where there was also a half-empty basket of kindling, a solid wooden chair and a low, three-legged stool. A burnished brass oil lamp hung from a shoulder-high iron bracket, adding amber radiance to the weak light that filtered through the single, curtained window. In the middle of the room was a square, heavily built wooden table littered with carpenter's offcuts, odd lengths of branch stripped of bark, and a few pieces of planking. Some of them bore evidence of woodcarving, rough semi-reliefs of horses' heads, ships and fish. The corner of the table closest to the door had also been engraved, a fantastic tangle of leaves, berries and vines with the snouts of tiny foxes peering out here and there.

An offshoot of tendrils and foliage wound along the table edge to where the figure of a man clad in a grubby yellow smock sat bent over a flat section of golden torwood. As he worked on the piece with a small implement held tightly in his hand, his hunched posture managed to convey a kind of furious intensity. Calabos smiled to himself as he regarded his old companion, his self-chosen charge.

'He is here!' said the man as he put down the implement and turned.

Three hundred years or more had not blunted the piercing severity that shone from Coireg Mazaret's eyes during these periods of derangement.

Calabos met the unbalanced gaze as understanding settled into his thoughts. *The Lord of Twilight is here . . .*

'You're certain? How can you know?'

Mazaret uttered a dry, contemptuous laugh and rummaged through the heap of wood pieces before him. 'How else would I know? By my sensing of the Wellsource, naturally. It still lives in the deepest deeps of the Void yet I can feel every quiver and ripple in its constricted flux. Some of it, however, is bleeding across the realms and now His hungering spirit is abroad once more.'

He paused as he found what he sought among the now-scattered sections of branch and beam, a dark piece which he clutched to his chest as he went on. Calabos attended closely while a sense of inner dread crept over him.

'His hungering spirit,' Mazaret repeated, a feverish light in his eyes. 'He never died at the crux of that final battle, you know, not wholly, not truly — I've read your dramatized account and you were wise to not to fabricate some improbable scene with the boy-Emperor overmastering the Prince of Dusk . . .'

'So where is He?' Calabos said.

'He reigns in blackness,' said Coireg, a slow, malign smile coming to his lips. 'In glittering, soaring, magnificent blackness . . .' He half turned in his seat while considering Calabos with a sly, sidelong glance. 'Tell me — do you ever think of the dead, poet; your dead?'

Calabos gritted his teeth. *For three centuries,* he thought, *the same cursed question . . .*

'Not my dead,' he said.

'The great plains of Khatris laid to waste, its towns and villages ransacked, their inhabitants slain or enslaved—'

'Not my dead,' he repeated sharply.

Coireg stood to face him. 'Was it not your hand that plundered the lands of Yularia and Anghatan of their menfolk? Many tens of thousands they were and every one was emptied out by your Acolyte servants then made into fit vessels for more ancient, loyal spirits . . .'

'Not by my hand,' Calabos said grimly.

'. . . then there's the dead Mogaun, the dead of Besh-Darok, and those of your masked slave army who died twice.' Mazaret had moved towards him and was almost an arm's length way. 'A vast, smothering host of the dead, an abyss of agony, an ocean of blood.' His grin was savage. 'Your dead. Your hand.'

Gaze met gaze, will locked with will. Calabos had to consciously resist the pressure of this unhinged, malefic presence before him while keeping in mind that it was only a fragment of Coireg Mazaret, twisted and deformed by the inhuman tortures of the spirit that he had undergone three centuries ago.

'The I that I am,' Calabos said in a low voice, 'scarcely existed when Byrnak was stumbling along the path laid down for him by another. When He . . . was freed by the melded sword, Byrnak ceased to exist, leaving behind a walking shell and a few instincts and habits, enough to rattle around inside and create the semblance of being . . .'

Before him, Mazaret laughed darkly. 'But you remember, don't you?'

It was true. His mind, even after all these years, remained the voluminous storehouse of another's memories but it went beyond that. His hands were the hands which had held the axe which had lopped off Kiso's hands and feet on the fateful night of Tauric's capture; his powers had subdued Ystregul, the Black Priest, and imprisoned him in that spell-laden casket after the first abortive assault on Besh-Darok; his chest which had been pierced by the melded sword in the hands of Nerek . . .

Calabos breathed in deeply and slowly exhaled, feeling the tension ebb.

He feared yet required the recurring encounters with Coireg Mazaret's madness, likewise a consquence of an immersion in horror and the full force of the Wellsource.

'My memories are my own,' he said. 'To embrace or reject or treat as I see fit.' He leaned forward a little and met Mazaret's unfriendly gaze. 'That aside, it would be of great use to us if you were to tell me where He is . . .'

Mazaret's smile grew sly. 'In the Nightrealm, the domain of the Eternal.'

'Which is where?'

But Mazaret was not listening, his febrile stare wandering around the room. 'Do you remember what I said to you atop the great keep of Rauthaz?'

Calabos' recollection of that moment was effortless and all that had been said paraded through his mind even as Mazaret gave his own recitation.

'Ghosts in the sky and sea and the black chasm of the night . . . armies and nations of ghosts . . .'

Mazaret held out his hand, at last offering the piece of black iron-wood to Calabos who warily accepted it as the words continued.

'. . . a world full of ghosts, full to overspilling, hungry enough to eat the flesh of the sky and bones of the land, leaving nothing, only shadows . . .' Then he stepped back, his face gone pale with fear and his eyes seemingly fixed on something unseen. 'The world is a ghost, a flimsy parchment skin stretched across a blackened skull . . . !'

Then the eyes rolled up, showing the whites, and he keeled over, knocking a chair aside as he fell to the floor. Calabos leaped forward to catch him. A moment later, as he laid him out on the plain grey pallet, there were signs of returning awareness, a groan then a weak coughing as the eyes fluttered open. Calabos poured a beaker of water from a jug on the floor and offered it. Gratefully, Coireg nodded and drank.

'You are a good friend,' he said at last. 'I wish that I were less of a burden to you and more of a help.'

'You've been more help than you know,' Calabos said. 'From the very outset of our journeying.'

'If only I could be now . . .' Coireg Mazaret shook his head gingerly. 'Everything my shadow half rants about these days is over-laid with an esoteric symbolism that I cannot penetrate.'

'He was quite unambiguous about our old adversary,' Calabos pointed out. '*He is here . . .*'

'And he mentioned a place . . .' Mazaret paused to yawn widely, 'somewhere called "the Nightrealm, domain of the Eternal". It seems familiar.'

Calabos frowned. 'I've heard it too, but it must have been since the war — I cannot recall where or when . . .' Certainty evaded him, but as he thought on it some possibilities suggested themselves. 'It sounds like part of a ritual prayer, or perhaps an invocation . . .'

He stopped, realizing that Coireg Mazaret was fast asleep.

Truly, Calabos thought, you are a sailor upon your own restless seas, trawling strange catches from the deep.

Carefully, he placed the jug and beaker on the floor but within easy reach of the boxbed, then rose and quietly left the room. Out in the narrow hall, he took the ironwood carving from his pocket and examined it. The detail was very fine, which made the subject matter all the more disturbing — it depicted a flat surface from which the forms of people protruded, faces, head and shoulders, hands and arms. All seemed to be struggling, as if drowning . . .

Then the other door opened and the elderly Bishop Daguval emerged, and Calabos unhurriedly slipped the carving away out of sight.

'Did you find him in a tractable mood?' said the bishop.

'Intractable,' Calabos said with a wry smile. 'Yet oddly informative.'

'And now?'

'Sleeping soundly,' Calabos said. 'The madness lifted from him but left him exhausted . . .'

Daguval nodded sagely. 'Yes, my friend, that is a familiar consequence, but I shall prepare some broth in case he wakes later.'

'Thank you for all you have done,' Calabos said, moving towards the stairs. 'Unfortunately, I must return to Sejeend. When he next regains his senses, tell him that I shall return in a few days.'

'I shall,' the bishop said. 'May you have a safe journey.'

Calabos smiled then descended the stairs, thinking about Mazaret's words and the carving and, for once, quite forgetting to walk like an old man.

Chapter Four

Tiny bells can ring clear and wide,
In the sacred silence of great temples.
Small stones can disturb the still mirrors,
Of calm and windless lakes.
Thus, the purer the light,
The darker the shadow.

Keldon Ghant, *Prayers At Midnight*

Vorik dor-Galyn finally found the cluster of shabby workshops, but they seemed much further back along the steep-sided dale of the Kala than the clerk Jumil had suggested. A steady trickle of city-folk passed along the walkways still, yet Vorik had doffed his mask, relying for concealment on his cloak and cowl and the foliage-muted light of mid-afternoon.

The workshops were part of a long, low rough-tooled building divided into small, open sections where the likes of farriers, fletchers and weavers plied their trade. He approached the dank, shaded end of it and leaned against the corner post. Before long the visible path in either direction became deserted so he swiftly made for the rear of the vacant workshop where he used a crude key to open a rickety door. Beyond it was a dark narrow room reeking of mould. From an inner pocket he took a velvet pouch and tipped out a bright, glowing gem hung on a long chain. Wrapping it around one wrist, Vorik could see that a layer of broken detritus covered the floor so he picked his way to the end of the room where a tall cupboard stood against the outer wall. A second key, smaller and finer than the first, opened its heavy door to reveal an empty interior with only a few wooden hooks still fixed to the back at head height. He reached in and twisted the hook furthest to the right, whereupon the back of the cupboard split down the middle and swung inwards, opening on a dim passage.

A wave of stone-cold air brushed Vorik's face as he clambered through, then closed first the cupboard door followed by the secret doors. Turning, he held up the light-gem to illuminate his surroundings – the passage had been hewn through the solid rock in a manner which made all the surfaces uneven yet oddly free of roughness or sharp protrusions. Then he noticed something embedded in the rock, irregularities that looked like teeth. But even as he fingered them in the light of the gem, a voice came from further along the passage:

'Don't loiter, Vorik! You know how I hate to be kept waiting!'

He jerked upright in surprise, uttering an oath under his breath. It was Jumil, sounding close enough to be just past the first curve of the passageway before him. But when he hurried round it there was no one to be seen, just more tunnel sloping gently down-wards into darkness.

He must have dashed on ahead of me, Vorik thought. *What fool's game is this?*

Vorik felt his anger rise as he hastened along the tunnel. Ever since those cursed Watchers snatched Ondene away last night his temper had been on a short leash, and up until recently he would have been unconcerned about expressing his anger before Jumil, or even berating him on occasion. But almost a week ago, after not hearing from the clerk for two days, Vorik received a message ordering him to find four willing men among the city's dregs and bring them that night to a safe house by the West Wharfs. This he duly did, arriving with the new recruits in a cart. The house was a primitive dwelling, little more than a single room with a scullery and pantry in an alcove and a couple of smoky lamps hanging from the two supporting posts. Jumil was waiting within, and he locked the front and only door when they were all inside. Vorik had been in the mood to deliver a stinging rebuke to him but held his tongue when he saw the sheathed broadsword hanging on the man's hip.

Jumil had directed the men to sit in four chairs already arranged in a square in the centre of the room. What happened next seared itself into Vorik's memory.

Jumil had regarded them one by one, then announced that he had need of only three of them, pointing them out. The fourth he approached, laid a hand on his shoulder and asked him to say something about his family. A strange light entered the seated man's eyes as he began to gibber on about parents and cousins, yet Vorik had thought nothing of it. For the next moment or two.

The clerk had listened to this prattle, nodding at this point or that, then calmly drew forth his sword and hacked off the man's leg. Vorik had cursed in shock, as did the other three men, yet their companion still gabbled on and on as if nothing had happened. There was blood, yet only a steady trickle, and the words kept coming even as Jumil lopped off the other leg and both arms until he was standing in a welter of gore with the still-living torso sat on a red-drenched chair, talking insanely. Silence came with the final blow, after which Jumil promised the other three, pale and quivering with fear as they were, that there would be great rewards for obedience and loyalty.

Then he told them to await his orders and dismissed them. All three were near rigid with terror as they quickly left: Vorik, on the other hand, had a stronger disposition towards carnage, having served with the Imperial army in Eastern Honjir, teaching bloody lessons to Carver trespassers. But the sight of this made him realize that something fundamental in Jumil had changed, for the bloody performance had been as much for his benefit as for the three new hirelings. And Vorik had more knowledge than they of the great powers Jumil had at his disposal, powers that Vorik often dreamed of possessing.

It was this ambition that had drawn Jumil to him some months previously, leading firstly to the Revelation Initiation, a sorcerous ritual which made manifest the powers of Shadow, drawn from the Lord of Twilight himself. Although much diminished, he was apparently still at one with the Wellsource which enabled him to conduct his stratagems from a refuge hidden beyond the many veils of the Void. Secondly came Vorik's ordination as Master of the Flock which brought with it the responsibility for recruiting NightKin and the promise of power.

All of this trailed through Vorik's thoughts as he hurried and stumbled along the strange tunnel which wound this way and that, steadily descending into the cold bedrock beneath Sejeend. After a time the tunnel turned and opened out to a low chamber lit by torches jutting from sockets in the walls.

'At last. Your sense of urgency leaves a great deal to be desired.'

Jumil was over at the far wall, garbed in his customary long black robes. Next to him, standing with his face to the wall, was a naked man, his arms and leg trembling, his head covered with a hood.

'I came with all speed, honoured one,' Vorik said carefully, as if his anger were an obstruction he had to speak around. 'But I did not realize how long the passage was . . .'

Jumil waved aside his excuses. 'No matter – you are here, thus we can begin. From my own discernings, these Watcher fools are holding council at this very moment . . .' He smiled. 'Which is the best moment to serve our notice.'

'How can I serve you in this?' Vorik said.

'This tactic requires me to carry out two strenuous incantations,' Jumil said, studying the wall nearby. 'And even though we have a sacrifical source, the effort shall still render me near helpless at the conclusion. At that point, I need you to carry me from this place along that passage –' He indicated a second dark entrance which had escaped Vorik's attention, '– to the ancient chamber of wards where you will place me on the floor by the face of the Great Shadow.' He glanced at Vorik. 'Is that clear? Have you any doubts about your task?'

Vorik felt the heat of his anger at this patronizing prod. 'No doubts, master,' he with forced calmness. 'I understand – completely.'

Jumil regarded him with amusement for a moment then turned to the wall and the other man. 'Good, then let us proceed.'

The naked, hooded man had made neither sound nor motion during all of this and remained so as Jumil laid one hand on the dark grey rock and began to recite some kind of spell. Vorik felt a chill go through him as the sorcerer crooned strings of syllables in some ancient tongue from before the fall of Jagreag. Then bright threads began to appear on Jumil's bare upper arm, weaving along towards the wrist like burning veins. Across the back of his hand they writhed, growing brighter as they entwined about his fingers, and from where his fingertips were pressed against the rock the threads continued to spread.

'The call shall be uttered,' Jumil muttered, 'and the call shall be heard. Calabos and his vermin will hear, but only he will know what it means.'

'What does it mean . . . ah, master?'

Jumil glanced at him for one tense moment, then gave a wintry smile. 'You know the fiction that the self-deluders of this empire tell themselves about the downfall of the Prince of Dusk . . .'

'Yes,' Vorik said, unsure of where this was leading. 'The final battle in the depths of the Void, Tauric the First vanquishing our Lord . . .'

'Just so, but it was a banishing, not a vanquishing. The history tellers weave an elaborate web of fancy, but they know nothing of the Broken, the servants of the Great Shadow. Well, soon the lies will snap and shatter like the three-hundred-year-old mask that they are . . . ah, at last the rock is ready.'

The burning threads had crept across the wall, criss-crossing in a patternless way until a section of the stone surface resembled a strange, random mosaic. Jumil let his hand fall limply to his side, then raised the other to pull away the naked man's hood. Vorik narrowed his eyes, recognizing one of the original four men that he had recruited several days ago.

'Behold, my conduit, my channel to the bones, the very viscera of this land!' With one hand, Jumil pushed the middle of the man's back. 'Go forth now, enter that splintered embrace.'

Arms at his side, the man stepped forward and into the rock wall of the chamber. Vorik stared, transfixed. Bright-edged fragments of the surface shifted, eased aside as if they rested upon some thick, malleable substance. Soon Jumil's servant − or sacrifice − was halfway into the wall, one leg and both arms sunken to the elbows. The other leg was swallowed, then the buttock and lower back, followed by one shoulder and the next . . . then Jumil muttered something in a low voice and the man's progress ceased.

Vorik watched, fear warring with his hunger for power such as this. Jumil spared him a brief glance, exertion plain in his face as a roseate radiance began to leak from his eyes and mouth.

'Remember,' he said. 'Carry me to the chamber of the wards and place me by Great Shadow's face.'

'It shall be done, master,' Vorik said.

Jumil nodded sharply then turned to face the wall with the naked man's still visible shoulder blades, neck and back of his skull. He began a low, droning chant that grew in urgency as the strange glow in his eyes and mouth became brighter. Soon they were hot, luminous nodes of golden fire and Jumil's swaying stance and clenched fists betrayed the great strain he was under.

The chanting rose in pitch, culminating in an unintelligible, two-syllable word. In that instant the glow of the chamber's torches dwindled to nothing as the fires in Jumil's face leaped forth to lance into the back of the trapped man's head. The floor of the chamber shook and a grating, roaring sound came from all around, slowly resolving into a deep booming voice which made the dust on the floor crawl and the air in Vorik's chest resonate horribly.

Terror gripped Vorik as that awful voice spoke on and on without cease in raw bass tones that reverberated around the chamber.

Here, it seemed to say, *Here is the place. Come to us!*

There were eight people in the common room of the Watchers' lodge. Six coats and cloaks lay draped over chairs brought closer to the hearth's fire, while their owners reclined on divans near the heat, or otherwise sat or stood.

The other two present were Tashil and the fugitive Corlek Ondene. On rising that morning Tashil had received a message from one of the guards explaining that Calabos had left earlier on urgent business and would return in the evening. The poet had also requested that she keep Ondene as mollified as possible since the guard were under orders to prevent him from leaving the lodge in case he was still being hunted.

This did not prove an easy task, resulting in three angry outbursts and one struggle with the guards down in the main hall. Tashil tried to explain that this confinement was for his protection –

which was confirmed later by one of the lodge messengers who said that posters bearing Ondene's face and a fifty-regal reward had been put up in the markets and squares 'by order of the Iron Guard'.

Ondene's response was to become cold and withdrawn, and he was now sitting alone in the window seat across the common room, alternately reading a book on Roharkan history and staring morosely out at the pouring rain. Tashil had decided that it was tolerable enough for her to leave him be and devote herself to her fellow Watchers who had arrived following a mindspeak message from Calabos.

The senior Watchers were a disparate group, their manner of attire as varied as their origins. Like Sounek, for example, a tall, well-kempt man who affected the air of a Khatrisian aristocrat when in truth he came from a humble Tymoran family. At the other extreme was Dardan, a wiry, craggy-featured man in his middle years whom Tashil knew to be the estranged scion of an old Cabringan noble house, although his garments sometimes resembled those of a gamekeeper or a travelling artisan.

As Tashil's gaze came to rest on Dardan she was surprised to find him watching her in turn. He gave a wry grin and came over to where she stood at the end of the mantelpiece, out of the fire's hot glow. Tashil felt a sting of embarassment, wondering if he was going to remonstrate with her. Dardan was highly respected within the Order of Watchers and was effectively Calabos' second-in-command.

'So – which of us do you find the most intriguing?' Dardan said in a quiet, amused voice.

'I couldn't possibly single out any one person from this honourable gathering, ser,' Tashil replied. 'Think of the consequences . . .'

'Quite right,' said a stalwart, red-faced mage called Chellour who sat before the fire with a heap of parchments in his lap. 'I would find it most upsetting were I to be ranked lower than, say, Dybel . . .'

Dybel, a tall, lantern-jawed man sitting on a stool on the other side of the fire from Tashil, smiled and shook his head. 'Be careful what you wish for, my friend . . .'

Hearing this, Dardan shrugged. 'Then perhaps we need another focus for our curiosity, like yonder brooding student of the rain,' he said, tilting his head in Ondene's direction.

Tashil had prepared for this. 'Oh, that's Stom – he's just a guest of Calabos who's been restoring some old statuettes.'

Dardan's smile was accompanied by a dry chuckle.

'No need to play parlour games, lass. I recognized the notorious Captain Ondene the moment I entered the room.'

'Is that really him?' said Inryk, an edgy, untidy-looking man who turned in his armchair to peer across the room. 'He doesn't seem very dangerous—'

There was a muffled thud as Ondene suddenly closed his book and glared round at him.

'I have been considered sufficiently dangerous to have been hired by a number of southern lordlings and castle princes in recent years, ser,' he said darkly. 'If it's any of your business.'

Oblivious, Inryk shook his head. 'But I don't see how that's relevant to why the city knotmen have been putting up posters about him . . .'

'You should pay more attention to the gossip about the nobility, Inryk,' said the sixth mage, Countess Ayoni, an elegant, mature, dark-haired woman. 'You see, the former Ondene estates were gifted to House dor-Galyn, and they have a son with a captaincy in the Iron Guard.' She regarded Corlek dispassionately. 'Who knows that Baron Ondene's last surviving son is in Sejeend, thus . . .'

Corlek Ondene's only response was a brief nod, as if to confirm her summary, but Inryk was not satisfied.

'That's all very well, but how does he come to be here?'

Eyes turned towards Tashil but before she could even begin to frame an account of the previous night's events, there was the sound of a door opening and closing in the antechamber beyond the arched entryway, and footsteps crossing the wooden floor.

'Ah, Calabos at last,' said Sounek. 'Now we'll have some answers.'

It was not Calabos but another taller man who stepped through the arch, stooping slightly as he did so. Clad in a long, powder blue coat of austere cut and a plain grey skullcap, his very presence silenced the entire room. His hair was short and as silver-grey as were his well-trimmed moustache and beard which, in his weathered and bony face, gave a strong impression of authority and intellect. His eyes were a pale blue, somewhere between ice and ash, and held no pity.

'Good,' he said in a level, slightly harsh voice. 'Everyone is here, everyone except the poet.'

Startled at this intrusion by a complete stranger, Tashil wondered why the other mages looked tense and guarded, saying nothing as they watched the newcomer who returned their collective gaze with a disdainful smile. But before she could ask his name, Sounek spoke from his chair.

'This is a private meeting, ser,' he said. 'It appears that you have entered the wrong house.'

'No, Sounek, I am in the right place,' the man answered.

'I fear that you've mistaken me, ser – I am Ven Hortis, a master of antiquities from Scarbarig—'

'Sounek of Tymora,' the man went on. 'Born to a family of barrelmakers, ran away at age eleven, studied at the Green Hall in Tobrosa, admitted to the Order of Mages thirty-one years ago by my predecessor, renounced the Order eight years ago to become a Watcher . . .'

'You've worn out your welcome, Tangaroth,' Chellour said angrily.

Tangaroth? Tashil thought in amazement. *The Archmage? Here?*

'Aah, Nyls Chellour, youngest son of an Adnagauri pickpocket, made a ward of the House of Guilds, trained as a scribe and illustrator until a mage brother at the Earthmother temple saw his potential and helped him become an initiate. Admitted to the Order of Mages twenty-five years ago but left fourteen years later . . .'

He surveyed them. 'I know each and every one of you, what you were and what you think you are, even your rash young guest over there . . .'

'No, you don't, Tangaroth,' said a familiar voice from beyond the arched entrance. 'You may know details of their lives, but you do not *know* them as I do . . .'

Tashil felt a rush of relief as Calabos, looking spry and alert, entered the room, shrugged off his damp cloak and slung it over an empty highbacked chair before turning to confront the unwelcome visitor. The two men faced each other for a drawn-out moment before Calabos addressed the Archmage.

'So why are you here, Tangaroth?' he said. 'To merely dispense threats and the crown's unique menace, or is there some other reason?'

'You and your Watchers are only just tolerated, Calabos,' the Archmage said. 'Keep that in mind. Renegades, outcasts, and the offspring of enemies—' He shot a glance at Tashil with that. 'Only your marginal usefulness has saved you from the dungeons thus far.'

Tashil felt a strange hollowness, a mingling of panic and anger at the Archmage's cruel jibe. Some of the others got to their feet and Dardan clenched his fists as he took a step towards the Archmage. But Calabos halted him with a raised hand and a tight smile.

'That was a mean blow, Tangaroth,' he said. 'And not worthy of your office. You must know that all of us here have vowed to protect the interests of the empire and its people – that is why the Watchers exists.'

Tangaroth sneered. 'You seem to have forgotten why the Mage Order exists, then . . . but in any case, when Ilgarion and his court take up the reins of power he will learn of you and wonder why all of you are not under my direct control and guidance.' He shrugged. 'I doubt that any record of past achievements will stand between you and incarceration at his majesty's pleasure.'

'Unless?' Calabos said.

'Unless the Watchers perform a service vital to the sanctity of the realm.'

Everyone's eyes were on Calabos. Tashil stared at the old man's face, wishing and hoping that he would turn down this blatant coercion but to her dismay he frowned and gave a small nod.

'Go on,' he said.

The Archmage looked satisfied. 'It has come to the notice of the High Minister of Night as well as myself that the Great

Carver Pilgrimage to the Isle of Besh-Darok will be used as a veil for the assembly of an army of northern Carver zealots which will then attack Sejeend. At the same time, other Carver wreckers will attempt to sow confusion in the city with burnings, assassinations and the like. It will be the Watchers' task to spy on the few prominent Carver priestholds and their sympathizers in Sejeend, find out who is party to the plot and ascertain its details.'

Calabos regarded him pensively. 'And may I ask what the Order of Mages will be doing in the meantime?'

'Working closely with the High Lord Marshal and his commanders to counter the threat from the north,' Tangaroth said. 'Pre-emptively, if necessary.'

Tashil felt so full of outrage at this that she teetered on the brink of shouting in his face. 'Norther Carver zealots' could only mean her own people, the Mogaun tribes, but she knew that the true zealots among the tribes were the fanatical Oathtakers and they accounted for merely a small minority with numbers that scarcely constituted an army. In any case, it would be sheer madness to mount an attack on a city like Sejeend . . .

Then Sounek caught her eye and raised a cautionary finger, to which she gave a slight nod and held back, listening.

'A most singular strategy, Archmage,' Calabos was saying. 'Very well, then – you can be assured that we will carry out this investigation for you on the understanding that our integrity and independence will remain as it was under Magramon.'

'So it shall be,' Tangaroth said. 'But before you begin, it might be wise to escort your hotheaded guest out of the city – who knows what harm might befall him were he to stray out into the streets.'

'Yes . . . quite . . .'

Calabos suddenly paused, swayed on the spot then reached out to the padded back of a divan to steady himself. 'Can you hear . . . a voice . . . calling . . .'

Tashil could hear something but only in her mind, a low, rumbling voice speaking a continuous string of syllables. And even as she became aware of the sound, it grew louder and louder in her head. In the next moment, Calabos let out a strangled cry and keeled over to sprawl on the floor.

But the terrible roaring went on, even as the others stumbled forward to Calabos' aid, all of them similarly affected by the monstrous torrent of noise. It was now so loud that it seemed to fill her head to bursting and sent her senses reeling. She could hear nothing else and the mere act of trying to walk over to Calabos' motionless form was like crossing a tightrope above an abyss.

Finally it abated, faded to a murmur and whispered away to nothing with surprising swiftness. Relief was stark on every face around her, and Tangaroth was crouching by an unconscious Calabos with fingers pressed against the side of his neck.

'Unharmed,' the Archmage said, getting shakily to his feet. 'When he wakes, impress upon him the gravity of this new . . . incident.' He looked at them all. 'I'm sure that he will have recognized that as a spell of dark provenance.'

'It was an invocation,' Dardan said sourly.

'Yes, but of a kind known as a calling,' Tangaroth said. 'It is supposed to draw powerful spirits and other things to the vicinity of the caller. If this was perpetrated by Carver zealots then your task may just have become a little more arduous than I originally anticipated.'

The Archmage had regained his composure and once more carried an air of haughty disdain.

'When Calabos sufficiently revives, have him contact me with mindspeech,' he said. 'But before that comes about, you yourselves might consider sending forth a search party, for I fear that your caged bird has flown!'

With a quiet, malicious laugh, he turned and left by the archway, while Tashil whirled round and cursed at what she saw. One of the windows stood open and a book lay on the chair nearby, but Captain Corlek Ondene was utterly gone.

Chapter Five

The old tyrant was long since slain,
But his accursed bane lived secretly on,
A blight that rotted out the land,
And poisoned us all.

Ralgar Morth, *The Empire Of Night*, Canto iii

*From the deepening shadows of a muddy alley, he gazed at the Watchers'
lodge which sat across the road behind a low hedge, its dark mass broken
by the curtain-muffled radiance of a few of its windows. He knew there
were others also spying on it, the driver of a wagon, a gardener, and
someone behind a curtained window in the adjacent house, all of whom
had come to his attention after the arrival at the lodge of one who could
only be the Emperor's Archmage, such was the strength of his aura. Using
the long voice he had reported all of this to Prince Agasklin, his clade
chief back aboard the* Stormclaw, *and the response had been one of
concern, to say the least.*

*The elderly mage from the previous day arrived not long after the
Archmage. Knowing from past rumour that there was some antipathy
between the two, he had expected some hint of magery but he felt no
disturbance in the Lesser Power. Only the silence and tranquillity of neat,
well-tended gardens and streets bereft of people in the night.*

*When it began it sounded like a faint susurration in the air while a
tenuous but noticeable coldness flowed over him. Then he thought he could
hear a steady murmur emanating from the ground underfoot, a sound that
grew steadily, becoming an interleaved drone of voices, one of which intoned
an unending string of words in an ancient, primitive Othazi dialect.
Distorted amid the burgeoning roar it was barely comprehensible but here
and there he picked out exhortations to awake, to follow, to fulfil . . .*

And for some moments he imagined that this din was audible to anyone until he saw two locals stumble past in the weak glow of porch lamps, chatting away, seemingly oblivious.

Only those attuned to the Void or its powers would be able to feel such a primal outpouring, he realized. Yet this was not a direct, focussed act of sorcery, rather an inveigling incantation that was meant to flood the thoughts while an insistent compulsion worked away at the undersenses. No focus, no direction, just this pervasive torrent, gushing in all directions from some source across the river, somewhere near the cliffs.

Then, as it reached its peak, his night-piercing eyes spotted a figure clambering over a wall separating the lodge from the grounds of the house next door. Momentarily a face was framed in a shaft of light from within the lodge before slipping out of sight. Without hesitation he moved out into the feebly lit street, affecting a sot's stagger along with a limp and a slurred, wavering sea shanty. For a second, the other lookouts had noticed neither Ondene's escape nor his own weaving drunkard's walk across the road towards a lane that ran along the other side of the Watcher's lodge.

With only a few paces to go he just caught a high-pitched whistle over the sound of his own voice and quickened his stride. Once within the thick shadows of the lane he broke into a run whose swiftness and silence would have stunned any chance observer. He could not know where the hunt would lead him, but he knew that he had to get to Ondene before the other pursuers. His brothers and sisters aboard the Stormclaw would expect no less. Of course, once he had the man in his custody, his problem would then be what to do next.

He grinned a ragged grin as he ran, certain that the solution would involve some kind of radical tactic.

The sorcerous calling raced outwards from the chamber beneath the cliffs of south Sejeend. A widening ripple of compulsion that ghosted through stick, stone, brick and iron as if they were empty air. Those few who possessed a touch of the Lesser Power — fortune-tellers, weather-wives, shipboard stormsmen, horse-tamers and the like — felt it as dizziness and a hollow rushing in the ears. Those with a greater degree of talent suffered a correspondingly greater level of mental turmoil.

Then there were its intended prey for whom it was akin to barbed hooks snatching at the mind.

In a rundown district on the north bank, a pack of dogs milled in panic as the leader was attacked by one of its senior followers, an ugly brown mastiff whose powerful jaws allowed it to tear out the leader's throat in one savage wrench. With gore dripping from its muzzle it turned and lunged at the nearest of the others, breaking its neck, while the rest scattered, yelping in fear . . .

In the dungeons below the imperial palace, a wrongly imprisoned potter waited until the warder had opened the cell door before ramming a hastily sharpened wooden spoon into the man's neck and slashing it with fearsome strength. Pausing only to snatch a dagger from the still-twitching corpse he slipped out and along the torch-lit passage, heading unerringly towards a storeroom which he somehow knew had a boarded-up hatch in one wall that led to the guard's kitchen . . . but he had barely reached the storeroom door when a crossbow quarrel smashed into his temple, killing him instantly . . .

A kidnapper murdered his partner then their captive, before leisurely decorating the floor and walls with their blood, writing over and over the words – 'Here – Follow – Now – Come!'

Amid the laughing, chattering din of a dockfront inn, the fortune-teller in her corner was laying out the cards to pass the time when the wave of sorcery passed. A moment later she caught her breath when the faces and images on the cards began to move and writhe – the Mother of Eyes began flicking through the heavy book she held while glancing impatiently up from the table; the Merchant of Daggers licked his lips suggestively and winked; the Five of Gates showed three people chasing each other from gate to gate and changing their shapes as they passed through them . . .

She closed her eyes but when she opened them the cards were as animated as before. Suddenly she felt unconcerned, knowing that she had to leave the tavern and cross the river to the south bank . . . but she also owed the barkeep for her thimble-sized glass, money that she lacked, and she could see him directing a glance her way from time to time. Then a solution to her predicament came to her, almost as if some part of her had known how all along. Effortlessly she conjured a perfect illusion of herself sitting beside her at the table, out of smoky air and candlelight it seemed. At the same time she cloaked herself in the appearance of a short, shabby old pitch-stained bargee then rose and sidled her way through the busy crowd, reaching at last the low-lintled door.

Out on the dockside, only a few torches and porchlamps interrupted the night shadows and between one pool of radiance and the next she shed her disguise with the ease of a thought and began the long walk to the nearest bridge across the Valewater.

Further out the sorcerous calling travelled, an inexorably widening circle that disturbed a few and spoke deeply to even fewer. While madness claimed a miller's son in central Cabringa, a woodcutter on the east shore of Lake Ornim, and a prostitute in Oumetra, a cold and violent purpose filled a wineseller in Adranoth, an ex-mercenary imprisoned in the Port Vodir lockup, and a vacant-eyed wagoneer heading north on the Red Road.

And on the coast of north Cabringa some thirty miles east of Sejeend, a figure lay writhing on the pebbly shore of a small cove, his convulsions plain to see in the light of the torch he had dropped. There was a cry of alarm from the lookout on his perch high in the branches of an ancient torwood tree and soon a dozen or more came running from the dark shape of the blockhouse just inside the entrance to the inlet.

By the time they reached him, the spasms had passed and he was forcing himself to sit up. As they gathered round, one said, 'Are you well, Captain?'

Saying nothing, Captain Bureng — at times known as the Black Dagger of the Seas — raised one arm to the questioner who obediently hauled him to his feet. For several moments he just stood there, surveying his lieutenants who all sported beards and the occasional scar. Then his gaze rose over and past their heads and he breathed in deeply as if savouring the air, tasting the night. He smiled, his eyes widened, and he laughed, and most of his lieutenants laughed too, although with a nervous undertone in their voices.

'Bones, my bloody rogues,' Bureng said to them at last. 'I can smell the bones of the rich!'

A sudden greed lit up their faces. Mouths grinned in avaricious anticipation.

'Who, Captain?'

His glee was wolfish. 'The rich of Sejeend!'

Grins faltered and eyes glanced from side to side, trying to gauge each other's state of mind. Then one named Cursed Rikken spoke up.

'That there's the, eh, imperial capital, Cap'n.'

He nodded. 'That it is, Rikken – well done. And?'

'Perilous well-guarded it is, Cap'n. Boats and ships and guards and knights and fortress walls and—'

'All this I know, Rikken, but do you think that I'd lead you into such a drakken's lair without a plan?' Bureng smiled at them all, nodding. 'Yes, I have a plan which will bring the rich worms of Sejeend into our hands. By the next full moon I swear that we'll be enjoying their wives, wearing their gold and drinking wine from their skulls!'

Captain Bureng gave Rikken a comradely slap on the shoulder. 'When we're through, they'll be calling you the Blessed Rikken!'

Savage laughter rang across the cove but was swallowed by the night and the roar of the sea.

Tashil and Dardan were a couple of streets south of the Watchers' lodge when the latter slowed and announced that Ondene was heading in another direction.

'Which way?' Tashil said, breathing heavily as she came to a halt.

'West across the north of the city,' Dardan said, shaking his head. 'Straight towards the old Ondene estate.'

Dardan's skill at the hunting scry was incomparable so she only nodded before setting off with him again at a steady run, heading for the next corner and turning west.

They had not waited for Calabos to regain consciousness, even though that had been Dardan's initial wish. Tangaroth's jibes had stung Tashil deeply so when she said that she would go after Corlek Ondene alone if necessary, Dardan had thrown up his hands and agreed to accompany her. Then hurrying across a small square, around a weather-stained statue of Lord Regent Yasgur on horse-back, then along a narrow road of brewers and barrelmakers which filled their nostrils with the aroma of hops and malt. The road was interrupted by a small, overgrown public arbor and as they drew near to it Tashil felt a faint coldness. She was about to mention this even as they passed a mass of vine and weed-tangled bush, when there was a sound of snapping foliage and leaves flew as a snarling shadow burst out of the bushes and leaped at Dardan, bearing him to the ground.

Instinctively, Tashil called up the thought-canto Barb, focussing the Lesser Power into her right hand as she dived forward and slapped the creature's flank. There was a bright flash as the puissance struck deep and the beast, which she now saw was a heavily built hound, let out an agonized howl. Suddenly ignoring Dardan, it whipped round, trying the bite the spot struck by Tashil who had backed off smartly, expecting it to swiftly collapse to the ground.

Instead, it seemed to overcome the force and effects of the Barb canto and turn its growling attention to the two mages.

'That wasn't too effective,' Dardan muttered as he carefully stepped backwards.

'There was enough power in my hand to fell a horse,' Tashil replied, keeping her voice even and her movements slow since the hound seemed to have fixed its gaze upon her. 'What now?'

'I've readied Firedagger,' Dardan said. 'Once I get its attention, jump out of the way, and sharply, hear? Right . . .'

And with that he stepped forward and lashed out at the dog's rear with his foot. There was a deep and savage snarl as the dog turned quickly and lunged at him. Tashil had already begun her sideways dash but saw the firedagger spell lance out from Dardan's hands like a blazing red blade with feathered edges. For an instant, the road, the mages, the dog and the nearby masses of vegetation were drenched in a crimson glow. The dog let out a wrenching, grating howl as the firedagger smashed through one side of its head and seared a terrible gash down its flanks. It fell to the ground, convulsed for long seconds, its paws scrabbling pathetically, then was still, its jaws half open, its one remaining eye fixed on Dardan.

Tashil and Dardan, both breathing hard, looked at one another. Dardan shook his head, wiped his hands on his grubby ranger's coat, then laughed and Tashil was about to remark that the Watchers could do with some of their own guard dogs . . . but was stopped by a low rasping sound that made the hairs on her neck rise. Looking round, she saw that the dog was getting back on its legs again, despite the ghastly mess of its head and the gory, dripping gash in its side in which the whiteness of ribs could be seen. Bloody drool trailed from the beast's seared jaws as its growling grew in volume.

'Stand further back behind me,' Dardan said as he drew his blade, a glimmer of steel in the gloom.

Tashil was happy to oblige, but prepared another burst of the Barb canto in case.

Then the hound gathered its unnatural strength and made a great leap, its gaping jaws rushing straight at Dardan's throat. But Dardan spun on one leg and brought his sword round and down, perfectly timed to strike the back of the dog's neck. A second later the hound's carcass lay sprawled in a spreading pool of ichor while the head came to rest a few feet away. Dardan paused only to wipe his blade clean on the corpse's hide before resheathing it, then looked Tashil.

'Let's be on our way,' he said. 'Time is fleeting.'

As they ran, Tashil went over the nightmarish encounter in her head and came to a worrying conclusion.

'It was possessed, Dardan, wasn't it?' she said. 'What kind of spirit would ride an animal?'

'What and who?' Dardan said. 'We'll speak on this later – right now, our quarry has gained a good lead and may reach the Ondene estate too soon . . .'

He glanced to either side of the road along which they were hurrying. This was an older part of the city and the streets were narrow, the alleyways narrower. The buildings were more than a century old and many had gantries running along their first and second floors, or even above the eaves with rope-and-plank catwalks spanning the streets overhead.

'Our way lies across the rooftops,' he said with a roguish smile.

A nearby building, massively constructed from great blocks of grey sandstone, had a stairway hewn into its side, a rack of somewhat narrow and rainworn steps which zig-zagged up the outside wall. Up on the second floor a ladder led up to the rooftop walkway. Loose, weathered planks rattled underfoot and the wooden railings of the first catwalk they came to seemed too rickety to rely on, swaying in the open air as they crossed. But soon they reached the building on the far side of the street, clambering up over its tiled peak and down the other slope. Tashil focussed the Lesser Power through her undersight and was able to maintain her footing as she strove to keep up with Dardan's relentless pace.

During their fleet-footed traverse of the housetops, Tashil heard from the rooms below arguments, barking dogs, off-key singing, the crash of broken glass, drunken chatter, and once the sweet refrain of a fiddle played with skill and sadness. As they ducked and darted amongst the jumbled roofs, gables and cupolas, they had to be wary of being spotted by dwellers or the occasional hired guard. But at last Dardan brought them to a low balcony on a building near the foot of a sloping street of small traders and inns whose owners tended to live over the shop. Tashil was perspiring profusely but she felt exhilarated as they crouched on the shadowy balcony and caught their breath.

'Good – we've beaten him to it,' Dardan murmured, pointing downhill. 'The old Ondene estate lies at the end of this road, along which our determined captain will shortly be passing. When he does, I shall drop down, render him insensible then carry him back up here and thence to the roof from where we shall observe the confusion of those who hunt him.'

'How many of them are there?' she said.

'Four, perhaps five . . . hssst, the captain arrives . . .'

Down the dark street a lone figure came hurrying, passing through infrequent patches of torch- or lamplight. Ondene was still clad in the shirt and breeches given to him by Calabos. Watching him, Tashil felt a certain admiration for this relentless if foolish approach to vengeance while knowing that only someone without hope could act this way.

Ondene was only yards from their balcony when his gait slowed and he paused, staring down the road.

'Shade's teeth!' Dardan muttered. 'He's seen one of the hunters!'

Tashil glanced over her shoulder and saw someone duck into a doorway. Looking back she was in time to see Ondene take a few more paces down the road before turning a corner out of sight. Dardan cursed again.

'Fool – he's gone into the Wolf and Dagger coach inn. It's been closed up for a month and there's no way through to the alley at the rear. Now he's trapped . . .'

Without warning he dived round the corner of the house. Tashil dashed after him, along the side wall, up onto the railing to leap a few feet onto the sloped roof of a lower adjacent building. Dardan was already there, climbing the column of iron rungs normally used by tilers and slaters, and she was quick to follow. On the other side, two men with torches had entered the lightless enclosure of the coach inn's main yard. With magesight, however, Tashil and Dardan could see much more detail, an abandoned wheelless cart, a couple of smashed and empty crates, a toppled stack of pails . . . and there behind a pillar in the utter darkness of the far corner, crouched the wary figure of a man.

'We follow the roof round,' Dardan whispered. 'Maybe get a chance to snatch him.'

Moving low and stealthy, they crept along the slanted, peakless roof of the inn but they had gone only half a dozen yards when another three men with torches and lamps entered the yard. Dardan cursed under his breath.

'Tash, we'll have to stop this. I'll use Engulf if you . . .'

'Wait,' she said. 'There's someone down there with him!'

In the shifting glimmer of shapes revealed by her magesight, Tashil could make out a tall figure in the pitch blackness behind Ondene who seemed oblivious to this intruder.

'Void's name!' Dardan muttered. 'Who—'

He was cut short as a cry went up from one of the torch bearers. Tashil saw Ondene stagger backwards then turn to come face to face with the tall stranger, who grabbed his shirt front with one hand and made a scribing pass in the air with the other. Nearly all the torches were immediately snuffed out, plunging the yard into a darkness which, to Tashil's surprise, extended to her own magesight.

The strange, impenetrable gloom cleared after a moment or two but when all the hunters converged with relit torches on that corner of the yard, Ondene and the stranger had gone. From the angry exchanges below she knew that all the doors were still locked and barred from within. That left only one explanation – powerful sorcery.

'Wonder what Calabos'll say about this,' murmured Dardan with a crooked smile. 'Something cryptic, no doubt.'

How swiftly he had gone from captive to fugitive in those moments of confusion back at the Watchers' lodge. Then the single-minded exhilaration of becoming an avenger, an instrument of retribution on two legs, moving inexorably towards those who had let his family die.

But others had intervened, cutting off his approach to what he still thought of as his family estate. A rising panic caused him to hurriedly turn off the road and now he found himself cornered like a rat in the yard of a locked, barred and shuttered coaching inn. As he cowered behind one of the veranda pillars, he almost regretted his impetuous flight from the Watchers' protection. Were these pursuers, he wondered, anything to do with the soldiers who had ambushed him the previous night? By the light of their brands they seemed like the kind of black-hearted toughs who frequented the more ill-omened wards of the city, louts he could easily dispose of unarmed – if they came at him one by one.

Then more of them arrived with bright lanterns and he knew that the end was near. The flickering glows came closer and one of the torch-bearers shouted on seeing him, and hands brought out long knives and cudgels. Ondene stepped back into the shrinking shadows, thinking in desperation that he might find a pole or some piece of wooden debris to defend himself with . . .

And turned to find himself face to face with a tall, gaunt man with long, dishevelled hair and eyes that burned. Ondene gasped and would have recoiled but the man grabbed a fistful of his shirt and held him close.

'Prepare thyself,' the man said in a deep, resonant voice. 'And close thine eyes.'

'Damn you, let me be . . . !'

Before he could say any more, his captor whispered something and with his outstretched hand quickly sketched in the empty midair a small, silvery glyph that hung there even as his hand moved away. The strokes of the glyph were like cuts or gashes which started to widen as he stared. Everything else seemed to be slowing down, the approaching toughs moving in an unhurried manner, while the flickering flames of their torches became languid, undulant tongues of orange and yellow shot through with floating bursts of sparks, then the grey line of the glyph quickly spread apart, drowning everything in ashen silver.

His stomach lurched and he closed his eyes, believing that this was death, that he would soon awake in the Earthmother's realm, in the Vale of Unburdening . . .

Suddenly he was falling forward to land on hands and knees on something soft, cushioning, cold. Dizzy nausea made his body quiver and his head swim. An involuntary spasm kicked in his vitals and he emptied his stomach onto the ground.

'I told you to close thine eyes,' said a voice nearby.

Coughing and shuddering, Ondene turned away from the spew, then realized that he was sitting on snow and that the tall man was standing a few feet away, watching him.

Then the thought came to him – *Snow? In summer?*

Fear began to grow in him, the conviction that he had been kidnapped, rendered unconscious, and spirited off to the mountains. Breathing white clouds, he got unsteadily to his feet.

'Who are you and why have you brought me here?'

His captor gave an amused snort. 'Two questions that require more answers than I have time or inclination to provide. Indeed, the second of them may not yet have an adequate answer . . .'

'I will not listen to such games . . .'

'In that case you may call me Qothan for now, but it would be more important for you to take more notice of your surroundings, Captain Ondene,' the gaunt man said, pointing over Ondene's shoulder.

'What do you mean by my "surroundings"?' he said, turning to look.

Before him were snow-covered fields and a few steadings spaced along the banks of a wide river which narrowed towards a large bay. On the other side was a good-sized town from whose chimneys a thousand smoky trails threaded up into the icy grey air.

'Behold – mighty Sejeend!' Qothan said.

'Don't be absurd—'

Then he stopped, recognizing amid the clutter of buildings opposite the unmistakable outline of the White Keep from whose battlements fluttered a large, pale blue banner. Beyond it reared a line of cliffs topped by dense forest.

Dizziness struck again, along with a nameless fear.

'How . . . where is this . . . ?'

'Not "where", good captain, but "when".'

So saying, he walked past Ondene, downhill towards the river. In a whirl of panic, Ondene stumbled after him.

'Wait! – What must I do, what *can* I do here?'

'This sojourn will not last, ser,' the tall man said over his shoulder. 'If we reach the strand of the bay within the hour then all will be well. And if you keep up, you'll knock some of that cold out of you.'

Surrounded by strangeness and dark implications, Ondene knew that he had no other choices so he did as he was bid. And hurried to keep up.

Chapter Six

Beneath dark and restless waves,
Below deep waters and the deeper abyss,
The shout of drowned nations yet rings,
And their dreamless citizenry stirs.

Eshen Caredu, *Storm Voyage*, Ch. 9

Corlek Ondene followed the mysterious Qothan across snow-covered fields to a wood of skeletal, ice-encrusted trees. He was chilled to the bone and by the time they found a wagon-track snow was falling, a steady scatter of flakes in the white silence as the first shadows of evening began to encroach. But when Qothan continued along the track without so much as breaking step, Ondene protested through chattering teeth, swearing not to move until he had rested. Then he sat down on a boulder by the side of the track, arms wrapped across his chest.

Qothan came over to him and laid a hand on his shoulder. Ondene opened his mouth to utter a cutting remark but hesitated as a peculiar warmth burgeoned within his chest and began to spread across his body. At first he imagined the worst, that this was the onset of some terrible seizure, but as a new vitality swept through him his feelings turned to relief, tinged with frustration.

'What are those powers that you have?' he said. 'And what do you want with me?'

Qothan only shook his head. 'I am not the one to answer such questions—'

'Then who will?'

The tall man gave him a stony look. 'My own chieftain could give you answers but only if we hasten now to the bay.' Then he turned and began walking again. 'Time is not our ally, captain.'

Ondene cursed under his breath, rose to his feet and set off after him along the frozen, rutted track.

More flurries of snow came and went as they trudged down towards the north bank of the Valewater, yet Ondene felt shielded, as if he wore an invisible cloak which let in no coldness while keeping him comfortably warm.

His thoughts, however, were far from composed; thoughts that whirled around the fearful understanding of where and *when* he now was. *Time is not our ally*, Qothan had said, yet it was starkly apparent that this grim intruder upon his personal drama had employed some dark magery and hurled them both back down the long aisle of Time, to an age when Sejeend had been no bigger than a town.

But the more he dwelt upon this nightmarish predicament, the more his fears began to sharpen and close around him, so he thrust the thoughts aside and instead concentrated on matching Qothan's gait, stretching his own pace to keep from falling behind. The countryside was half wild, half cultivated, with only a few birds disturbing the muffled stillness. Before long, the wagon track widened and was joined by another coming from the north, along which a scattering of folk were travelling, mostly on foot with a couple of horse-drawn carts heaped with boxes, bundles and other possessions wrapped in rugs. A few of those who walked carried sputtering torches to light the way as the day waned, and the carts each had a lantern swinging from a bracket near the driver.

Ondene saw the weary misery in their faces and immediately knew that they were refugees, fleeing some unknown calamity to the north. This was a sight he knew well from his years as a sellsword, fighting for the princelings and holdsmen of the Dalbari coasts, and it never failed to make him feel sick at heart. As he walked alongside them he noticed that hardly anyone was talking. Everyone seemed locked within themselves by tiredness and suffering, except for a knot of children chattering to each other in one of the carts. He could make out the odd word here and there, and realized that they were speaking an old form of Mantinoran, probably in a dialect.

If I open my mouth, he thought, *they won't be able to understand me and might get unfriendly . . .*

So he trudged on in Qothan's wake, saying nothing.

The road passed through a thick copse of black, leafless trees, emerged at the bank of the Valewater and led onto a heavy stone bridge. On the other side, the road sloped up towards the gates of Sejeend but Qothan stepped off it, heading north along the shore. With a sad backward look at the refugees, Ondene hurried after him across snowy, uneven ground broken by hollows and icy pools that were almost invisible in the descending gloom. Qothan had quickened his pace and was striding through the snow. Ondene hastened to reach the man and snatched at his arm, thinking to slow him, but instead found himself seized by his own arm and dragged along.

'Wait! . . . Damn you – hold! Why this . . . mad flight . . . ?'

'I told you, captain – time is against us in this,' Qothan said, releasing him and slowing a little. 'Soon we shall be swept back to the year and the day and the hour whence we departed, thus we must be in a safe place.'

'And you know of such a place,' Ondene said.

'I do, and we must reach it very soon.' He glanced at Ondene. 'If your strength is waning I can carry you over my shoulder – it would not delay me.'

'I think I can manage.'

'Very well,' and so saying the tall man leaped forward into a long-legged run. Ondene stared in astonishment for the merest moment before dashing after him with all the speed he could muster.

Several wooden piers marched on wooden posts from the shore out to deeper water, and Qothan led the way under them, feet crunching on frost webbed shingle. Ondene's memory told him that this part of the bay was – would be – a continuous stretch of massively built wharfs and quays, so Qothan's urgency seemed inexplicable. Then they emerged from the weedy shadows beneath another jetty and Qothan grunted.

'There!' he said. 'We will only just be in time . . .'

He increased his gait and sprang ahead. Ondene, gasping for

breath, could see only a huge stony outcrop, some ancient spur of bedrock, jutting out beyond the waterline, partly exposed by the low tide. But there was no one else to ask and no one else to trust so he snarled and put on a further burst of speed.

'Do not forget to close your eyes this time, captain,' Qothan cried over his shoulder. 'The sweep is about to take hold . . .'

Sure enough, Ondene could feel nausea uncoiling in his stomach then a ripple of dizziness. His sense of balance went awry, he stumbled and tripped, arms outstretched as he fell. Sand and pebbles flew as he came down on an elbow, rolled then struggled to regain his feet. But his chest felt hollow and echoing while his hearing came and went in waves and pale webs were invading his sight . . .

He said to close my eyes, came the desperate thought. Close my eyes . . .

As he did so, the nausea and imbalance lessened, then he felt someone lift him bodily and carry him along the beach.

'Prepare yourself,' said Qothan's voice from beyond a veil of whispers and watery purling . . .

He kept his eyes tightly thut through it all but that did not prevent strangeness from intruding. Abstract visions played across the insides of his eyelids, rainbow threads and diamond flickers which coalesced into curious eye-like shapes then drifted apart, momentarily seeming to depict a great array of weapons, arrows, shields, spears, daggers, and amongst them a vaguely familiar man's face . . . then a crack split the vision in two, bisecting the face and widening into a fissure down which he fell—

He was shocked into awareness by a sudden cold which enveloped him from the chest down, cold and a heavy dragging sensation in his legs as he tried to move. In the next instant sight and sound rushed in upon him with a suddenness that made him gasp and almost lose his footing. But another's supporting arm kept him from pitching face-first into the waters.

'Calm yourself, captain. We have returned from the pit of Time.'

They seemed hemmed in by darkness and the surging slosh of waves. Feeling sand and shingle slip beneath his feet, Ondene looked up and could just make out a horizontal edge to the blackness, illumined by yellow torchlight. He laughed hoarsely, realizing that they were wading about near the foot of one of the lesser quays on the south coast of the bay.

'How did . . . you know where to go?' he said, following Qothan through the choppy waters towards the sheer side of the quay.

'Observation,' the big man said. 'Of unchanging landmarks.'

Ondene frowned. Surely this entire section of coastline was utterly changed from those earlier times, the banks having been completely reshaped and the coastal seabed dredged to allow the berthing of larger vessels. But he said nothing, for the raw chill of the sea was seeping into his body and a shivering was taking hold. They were now deep in shadows so perfect he could barely discern Qothan's shape. Then his hands were grabbed and he was led forward a few yards to touch something cold, wet and metallic.

'Climb, captain. We are not far from deliverance.'

It was an iron ladder, corroded and flaking. He could feel the crumbling rust and the slippery tendrils of seaweed as he climbed the rungs. The exertion was warming his body yet also putting a strain on his dwindling stamina so that the last few rungs demanded the greatest effort. At the top he slumped forward and crawled a few feet onto the rough, wide planks of the wharf, then just lay there, gasping. A moment later Qothan was at his side, hauling him to his feet.

'Just a little further, captain, to one of the deepwater berths.'

'A . . . ship?' Ondene said groggily.

'Yes, the *Stormclaw*,' Qothan said, supporting him with one arm. 'Aboard is my chieftain, who may have answers for you.'

They made an odd sight, two bedraggled men of mismatched heights, both soaked through and streaked with rust. Qothan explained to passers-by that his companion was drunk as a lord and Ondene felt no inclination to contradict him. His thoughts were returning to the matter of the usurping dor-Galyn family and his yearning for retribution, and in retrospect he conceded that he could have chosen a stealthier, more certain means of exacting revenge. If he had been carrying out such an assassination for someone else he would have been a shadow within the shadows, the cold, unseen blade of death. But now, becalmed in weariness, he could see that his careless pursuit was really just an urge to self-destruction which had shut out all caution and guile.

My mother and brother are dead, he thought. I must grieve for them, I must find a way to say last words to them, offer up prayers for them and bid them farewell. After that, vengeance.

Out of the smells of brine-soaked wood and rope, and the flickering glow of pole-torches, Ondene grew aware that they were passing before the jutting prows of berthed ships. Even at such a late hour there were longshoremen at work, off-loading a huge cargo barge, their backs curved beneath sacks, canisters, bolts of cloth and a hundred other items of trade. Elsewhere he saw sentries up on the vessels themselves, and port watchmen patrolling in pairs, stavelamps slanted over their shoulders.

'Ah – at last,' said Qothan.

By now Ondene was just capable of standing on his feet unaided and so followed the tall man up a gantry to a lit opening in the flank of a massive, dark shape. Climbing the gantry, however, sapped the last dregs of his vitality and when he stumbled at the top only the helping hand of a waiting crewman kept him upright. A rough woollen blanket was wrapped about his shoulder as Qothan stepped into the entry passage.

'Prince Agasklin awaits you in the auracle, Outrider,' said the crewman, another tall, gaunt man.

Qothan only nodded, then turned to Ondene.

'I can see that you are weary, captain, but my chieftain wishes to speak to you now, if you are able.'

Ondene almost laughed out loud but intead rubbed his chin thoughtfully and breathed in deeply, trying to banish some of the fatigue from his mind.

'Well, I believe I am equal to a spell of conversation,' he said. 'But not much more.'

A wintry smile cracked the big man's stony features.

'Very good, captain. This way.'

From the entryway, Qothan led him through a low archway to a wider, lamplit corridor running athwart the ship, and thence to another heading forward. They passed other members of the *Stormclaw*'s crew and every one had the same lanky height, overtopping Ondene by at least a head, as well as a similar dour air. Whenever his gaze chanced to meet one of theirs, however, he saw no contempt or dislike, but a kind of obstinate sternness.

As they proceeded along the passageway he noticed that there was a large amount of decoration on the dark brown bulkheads, most often on the arched frames of doors but also on panels of paler wood set into the darker grain. Mostly the images were of creatures in flight: birds, insects, or beasts out of legend. They looked worn and polished, much like the wooden deck-planks which felt smooth and rounded underfoot. Everything suggested that the *Stormclaw* was an old ship.

Before long Qothan came to a wide door of some rich red wood, its surface inlaid with silver and mother-of-pearl in an odd device that resembled a circlet of eyes.

'This is the auracle,' Qothan said. 'It is used for meditation and immanation, among other things.'

He pushed the door open and they entered. The auracle was a circular chamber with twelve single-seat alcoves spaced around its walls. Wooden columns rose between the alcoves to become plain spars sweeping inwards to meet at the centre of a low, curved ceiling. Its twelve sections were each painted with a crowded tableau of figures enacting some mysterious drama. The floor was tiled and likewise divided and at its centre was a raised dais where an impassive, bearded man in long grey and black robes sat in one of four ornate chairs, watching the newcomers as the door closed silently behind them.

This must be Agasklin, Ondene thought.

'Greetings, Qothanalorimundas,' the man said, rising as they approached. 'I see that your outriding has borne fruit.'

'Just so, my prince. May I introduce Corlek Ondene, former captain of the Iron Guard and sometime military advisor.'

'An honour to meet you, captain,' said Agasklin with a brittle smile that Ondene guessed was seldom seen on those lips. 'I am Prince Agasklin of the Ushralanti, clade chieftain of this ship, the *Stormclaw*. I have heard good accounts of your talents, most especially from the Armigerlord of Shieldness almost two years ago.'

Ondene was surprised, then wary. The fortress at Shieldness in the southern Ogucharns had been the subject of friction then open conflict between its master, Bazak, the brutal Armigerlord, and his neighbour, the no-less brutal Verogin, Duke of Bones. Ondene had been hired by the former to assassinate the latter and had toyed with the idea of doing away with both repulsive tyrants, but in the end kept to his contract. A poison in the middle of the night was all that was needed.

'I was glad to be some service to the Armigerlord,' he said. 'Unfortunately, with his main rival gone he lost his sense of caution and was deposed six months later by his boatmaster, I believe.'

'Not a fate likely to befall his majesty, Ilgarion, would you say?'

Ondene stared at Agasklin, wariness now shading off into uneasiness.

'You're surely not suggesting . . .'

'In the Sleeper's name, captain, not at all . . . ah, you look unwell, ser – please, take a seat here . . .'

With legs gone weak and a stomach threatening rebellion Ondene sank gratefully into one of the ornate, almost ceremonial chairs. It was, he discovered, very comfortably padded.

'No, captain,' Agasklin continued. 'Our concern is with the stability of the empire, and safeguarding the crown, and Ilgarion poses no immediate threat to either. However, there is one person in this city whose plots and evil sorcery could bring it all crashing down.'

He leaned closer and Ondene had to force himself to meet the man's dark and insistent gaze.

'Ilgarion has returned to Sejeend this night and called a mandatory audience for all nobles and city fathers. Among them will be the dark agent – his name is Jumil and he will be attending as one of several officials from the Imperial Academy. It may mean little to say that he is of slender build and has fine features – we have a likeness for you to see.'

'In situations like this,' Ondene said carefully, 'it is usual to offer a contract, and before that to state the nature of the undertaking. Do you want this Jumil killed?'

Agasklin nodded. 'Very much so, captain, but you would not be capable of inflicting harm upon such a man; by now, almost no plain weapon could draw his blood. No, your task will be to attend Ilgarion's audience at the palace – we will provide the appropriate noble garments, mask and accoutrements – and observe the man, watch who he speaks with, perhaps even contrive to overhear any exchange.'

'There are risks to undertaking such a venture within the palace grounds,' Ondene pointed out. 'What would be my recompense?'

'Five hundred regals,' Agasklin said. 'A generous amount by any standards. Yet there is another aspect which may provoke your interest, namely that this sorcerer Jumil's right-hand man is a captain of the Iron Guard by the name of Vorik dor-Galyn. It was one of his senior servants who recognized you when you entered the city, and his hirelings who tracked you through the streets. If we can expose the sorcerer, Vorik dor-Galyn and his House will face utter disgrace.'

Ondene was silent for a moment or two as he absorbed this new twist. But he remained wary, realizing that he was hearing all this from mysterious, powerful men aboard a strange ship.

'I am favourably inclined to accept your terms, ser,' he said at last. 'However, I would like to know more about your people, the Ushralanti, and their singular talents.'

Agasklin raised an eyebrow and shared a look with Qothan.

'I understand your curiosity, captain,' he said, 'and I can offer you a brief account of our history, but it will be incomplete as there are things we do not share with outboarders.'

'That will suffice,' Ondene said and settled back in his chair to listen.

'. . . and listen well, dog! You and the rest *will* go back to that inn and the surrounding streets and you *will* search high and low, and keep searching till I say "hold"!'

The news of Ondene's escape had driven Vorik into a fury.

'And I don't care what you *thought* you saw – he must still be in the city somewhere so get out there and look with both eyes. And stay away from the alehouses or it will not go well for you. Now, begone!'

Looking miserably chastened, Vorik's hireling hurried off amid the dark shadows of the burial grove, pasing through the amber glow of the gatelamp before vanishing into the night. Standing in the light of a lantern that sat on the ground by the old soldier's tomb, Vorik stared after his servant, his anger slowly abating.

Ondene had just disappeared, was the story, backed into the dark corner of a coaching inn courtyard then melted away to nothing. Impossible, of course, unless . . . unless it had been the work of someone with powers approaching those Jumil possessed, rather than the feeble trick of a Lesser Power mage.

Vorik shrugged, deciding that it could wait until Jumil had fully recovered. He turned and bent to pick up the lantern, hand reaching for its wooden handle . . . then paused and straightened once more. Frowning, he peered at the dense shadows among the tombstones to his left where the pathway lamps could not shed their light.

'Whoever is there,' he said loudly. 'Come forth and show yourself.'

After a long, silent moment a figure emerged from the darkness and approached. Behind him another three likewise came into view.

Vorik smiled unpleasantly.

'So the little hawks come fluttering round,' he sneered. 'Sadly, our master is unable to see anyone so you'll have to go back to your Flocks and await his command.'

'We're not complete fools, dor-Galyn,' said one, a slender, aristocrat called Lymbor cul-Mayr. 'We sensed that great wave of sorcery and immediately felt concern for the master. We *must* see him.'

'We must be sure that he is unharmed,' said another, a burly former pit-fighter named Amaj.

'I'm afraid that is not possible,' Vorik said. 'After his exertions, Jumil is recuperating.'

'How do we know that you've not slain him?' said Skotan, a nervous, haggard woman who had once controlled the child slave trade in Sejeend. 'He . . . he might be lying in a pool of his own blood at this very instant!'

'Ludicrous,' said the fourth, a round-faced man known as Rugilo, garbed in dun-coloured, monkish robes. 'Literally incredible to suggest that our puissant master could succumb to one such as yourself, Vorik. No – unlike my Kin fellows, I only wish to seek final guidance from our master before he orders us to lead our NightKin Flocks out across the wilds to our mysterious destination . . .'

'The answer is still "no",' Vorik said, crossing his arms.

Skotan pointed a skinny, long-nailed finger at him. 'I see only deceit and betrayal in your face – if the master is not dead, I'll wager that you're plotting his downfall!'

'Or he's plotting against us,' muttered Amaj, clenching big, calloused fists.

'You see, Vorik?' said Lymbor cul-Mayr. 'Not one of us is convinced by your intricate explanations. Why, we should just walk right past you and descend to our master's chamber—'

The ringing hiss of Vorik's sword being swiftly drawn forth brought him to an abrupt halt.

'Yes, you could try that,' Vorik said, holding his blade out with the point hovering before cul-Mayr's chest. 'Or you could turn around now and flap away back to your perches. My master – who is very much alive – will send for you in due course.' He directed a black stare at all four Flock leaders. 'Time you were leaving, and quickly!'

They glared at him for a moment or two, as if gauging their chances, then cul-Mayr brought up one gloved hand and with his finger pushed the swordpoint aside. Uttering a contemptuous snort he turned and strolled away towards the gates. The others followed suit, with only Amaj pausing to direct a silent snarl at Vorik before he too left.

He waited for the last of them to leave the burial grove before returning his sword to its scabbard and stretching down to pick up the lantern.

Weak fools, he thought. *All of them. If it had been up to me, I'd have chosen more capable leaders for the NightKin. At least my own Flock knows who's in charge.*

Lantern in hand, he turned to face the concealed door behind the tomb – and almost cried out in startlement at the figure of a peasant woman who was standing directly behind him. As he lurched backwards he snatched out his sword and, seized by sudden rage, lashed out at the woman.

Who vanished as his blade struck her neck.

In the next moment an identical woman stepped out from the

other side of the tomb, a short, dumpy woman, he noticed, attired in a patched dress and a knitted shawl. She said nothing, just stood and watched him. Feeling more certain of himself, Vorik raised his sword and casually poked at the woman's shoulder. And again she disappeared.

'I don't know who you are,' he said. 'But it's time you showed yourself.'

'If you've finished wavin' yer pig-sticker around,' said a woman's voice.

Gritting his teeth, he slid his blade back into its sheath.

'Satisfied?'

The shadows a few feet to his left shivered and brightened, resolving into the same shawl-draped woman who came over to him, pausing a few feet away.

'Someone called to me,' she said, staring intensely at him. 'And it were like a door opening in my head and a voice as big as a mountain telling me to wake up – "This way, here, follow," it said . . .' Her gaze grew hard. 'Do you know where it came from, or who spoke to me? Do you?'

Vorik considered the woman. He had heard tales of the illusions and phantoms conjured up by the mages of old but had never thought to see one as rich as this. Clearly the arrival of this woman was an intended consequence of Jumil's underground ritual.

'It was my master who called out to you,' he said, moving to the concealed door and pushing it open. 'He is in seclusion for now and unable to receive visitors, but you may enter within and await his will if you wish.'

The woman gave a sharp nod. 'Aye, that'll do.'

She kept her gaze on Vorik all the time and as she stepped past him into the gloomy passage he noticed that the irises of her eyes were edged with glittering emerald.

On the wings of a stiff, early morning breeze, three sailing ships rounded the jagged mass of a jutting promontory and turned their prows towards Krail, the notorious brigand port. Krail was a collection of shabby buildings huddled in a great natural hollow at the foot of sheer cliffs, its narrow-shingled cove and small jetty offering practically the only safe berth in this reef-strewn cluster of islets.

The largest of the three vessels was the *Mocker*, a two-masted brig that had seen better days. Aboard, Captain Bureng, the Black Dagger of the Seas, was reclining on a wicker settle, smiling as his ship heeled gently to starboard.

'Rikken!' he sang out. 'What do you see?'

'The lights of Krail, my captain,' said Cursed Rikken from his lookout near the prow.

'What else?'

'The sternlamps of four — no, five ships tied up at the jetty.'

'Are any of them familiar?'

Rikken narrowed his eyes, trying to see through the dawn gloom. 'Not yet, cap'n . . . wait — one of them has a forked prow . . .'

'Ah, Flane's *Bitter Biter*.'

Bureng's voice was suddenly very close, and with a sideways glance Rikken saw that he was now standing just feet away.

'And the *Iron Fist*, I see . . . the *Vandal Lord*, too . . .'

Rikken shivered as his master named the other pirate vessels one by one, even though their outlines were scarcely visible at this distance. Something had changed in Captain Bureng yesterday evening, something which made him look at everything and everyone with a strange and hungry malice. Yet from the moment the captain ordered his crews aboard the *Hound*, the *Snake* and the *Mocker*, Rikken felt a thrill of excitement and a certainty that Destiny was filling their sails.

With the sky lightening from louring darkness to ashen grey, the three vessels found berths at Krail's crowded pier, weighed anchors and had their hawsers lashed to mooring stanchions. Gantries banged down onto the age-blackened boards of the pier and Bureng led forth a small band of his followers, Gont and Peshik, the masters of the *Hound* and the *Snake*, and a handful of toughs, including Cursed Rikken. Minutes later they were climbing the few steps to the double doors of a decrepit, two-storey tavern called the Lucky Captive. Inside, a few tallow lamps broke the dimness with the brightest hanging over a square table in the middle of the floor. Those sitting there looked up at the newcomers and Rikken saw faces he knew and others he did not, yet all held some kind of hate or deceit.

Without hesitation, Bureng strode across the table with his men at his heels.

'The Black Braggart comes a-visiting,' said one of the seated men.

'My ears is stingin' a'ready,' said another.

Rikken saw Bureng smile widely, as if he were contemplating a feast.

'I hear some squeaking, Flane,' he said to one man garbed in a long black coat that had seen better days. 'You going to clear out the vermin or shall I?'

The two men who had offered up the snide greetings turned surly but before they could speak, Flane looked coldly at them and said, 'Shift.'

Muttering, the pair vacated their seats and Bureng sat down with Gont on his left and Peshik standing to the right. The others gathered at their backs.

'The *Bitter Biter* looks a bit worn, Flane,' Bureng said. 'When did she last have a refit?'

Flane regarded him with unconcealed distaste. The captain of the *Bitter Biter* was a tall, severe man with one eye — the other eye socket held a polished red gem.

'Too long,' was the sour reply.

'What about you, Logrum?' said Bureng, brightly, gleefully, to the hulking, bearded man next to Flane. 'Is the *Vandal Lord* ready for battle?'

'Hull's sprung in a dozen places,' Logrum said with a yellow-toothed snarl. 'But she could still gut the *Mocker*!'

Bureng laughed at that and looked at the other two captains. 'And the *Iron Fist*? . . . and the *Ravager*?'

'I need a new mains'l and rudder for the *Fist*,' said a plain-looking, unshaven man known as Raleth. 'Anyone could tell that just by looking.'

The captain of the *Ravager*, Zanuur by name, was a wiry, dusky-skinned man with a black moustache. He crossed his arms, leaned back and swung one booted foot up to rest on the table's edge.

'My problems are my own,' he said with a Jefren accent. 'I'm more interested in why you want to know.'

'Quite so,' said Flane, leaning forward to fix Bureng with his one-eyed stare. 'Not planning any surprises for us, were you?'

Smiling, Bureng shook his head as if oblivious to the distrust and ill-will that was flowing in his direction.

'Gentlemen,' he said. 'I only meant to discover your fitness and seaworthiness for a little expedition I have in my mind.'

'Mayhap we should learn what you propose before we make any judgement,' said Zanuur.

'What's it to be, then?' sneered Logrum. 'Laying ambush to cupclaw catchers off the Mantinor coast? Or robbing the dangerous kelprakers of Maghar? You can surely manage that with the ships you got.'

Bureng joined in the laughter but a hard look came into his eyes. 'For what I'm planning, I need more than three ships, in fact more than seven, much more.'

Flane snorted. 'Why so many? What prize would need such force for the taking . . . ?' Then he paused, his single eye widening. 'Surely it's not . . . ?'

'Sejeend,' Bureng said. 'The jewel of the empire.'

Logrum erupted in guffaws of laughter. 'Aah, so you've finally gone mad, eh? Attack the capital? We'd be as well to try and sail across the fields of Khatris to lay siege to Trevada, or scuttle our ships for a raid on the Godkings of the seabed, and neither o' them makes sense an' all!'

'Nevertheless,' Bureng said. 'Sejeend is the prize I mean to have.'

'How?' Zanuur said, eyes narrowing. 'Where will you find the ships and men for such an undertaking?'

'Not far from here,' said Bureng. 'Sickle Bay.'

'I lost a fine carrack in a storm there a few years ago,' muttered Flane. 'Reefs tore out her hull.'

'It's an ill place,' said Raleth. 'It's been a graveyard for ships since olden times.'

Logrum grunted. 'Hanavok's Last Battle.'

'Just so,' Bureng said. 'Tell me, have any of you heard the name Crevalcor?'

Brows furrowed and heads shook.

'He was a powerful sorcerer who lived in the Age of Legends.' Bureng's voice grew thoughtful. 'During the great war of the Shadowkings, his essence was resurrected and put to work on their behalf. During his brief second life, before the defeat of his masters, he assembled a codex of rites, rubrics and comments . . . and I have that book!'

Listening to this, Rikken swallowed hard as an uneasy silence settled across the taproom.

'What's in the book?' Zanuur said warily.

Bureng laid his hands flat on the table. 'Sorcery,' he said. 'The black sorcery of the dead – with it, I shall raise an armada from the bottom of Sickle Bay and hurl it against the defences of Sejeend. After that, uncountable riches will be mine – and yours if you join me.'

'When are you setting out for Sickle Bay?' Logrum said.

'This very moment,' was the reply. 'Do not ponder – decide now.'

'Very well,' the big man said. 'Count me in.'

When the others stared in surprise, he shrugged. 'At least, if this turns out a fool's fancy, I'll have the pleasure of dealing with him personally.'

There was laughter at this and Zanuur slapped his hand on the table. 'Aye, then I'm in too.'

'And me,' said Raleth.

Eyes looked at Flane who was studying Bureng with dispassion. 'You don't strike me as one burdened with fancy, captain. I'll take you up on your invitation.'

'Then it's settled,' Bureng said. 'And the time for leavetaking is upon us.'

As the company rose and moved towards the door, Raleth said, 'What about Buskal, master of the *Skewer*? He's upstairs, sleeping off a skinful, but if you need another ship I can always—'

Bureng cut him off with a gesture. 'We don't need him – the five of us will do. Five is perfect.'

Cursed Rikken nodded happily at this, not understanding yet filled with purpose and wild daring as his captain led them all outside and down to the ships.

Chapter Seven

With the hooks of Fear and Desire,
The gods do fish for men.

Gundal, *The Doom of Gleoras*, Ch. 1, iv

'Are you sure that you're well enough, master?' Tashil said. 'Such burdens would tax even a younger man.'

'You mistake a moment's unpreparedness for signs of infirmity,' Calabos said with a little smile. 'I'll not be ready for my dotage for at least another fifteen years.'

Countess Ayoni glanced at Dardan. 'Have you tried talking sense into him?'

'Tried to,' Dardan said. 'Once, about ten years ago.'

Calabos smiled inwardly, remembering the very predicament and the very day . . . yet still the two women regarded him with anxiety, and he sighed.

I doubt that either of you would be receptive to the notion that my true age is more than three centuries rather than three score, he thought. *Or that I'm far more physically strong than my appearance would suggest. No, I have to be plausible in this.*

The four of them were gathered at a table next to the wide bay windows of the lodge's summer room. Outside, a brief but heavy shower was just slacking off and bright shafts of sunshine made the rain-drenched garden below glitter.

Calabos spread his hands.

'My friends, your concern for my well-being truly touches my heart,' he said, looking at each in turn. 'But you must realize that we are living through testing times that will inevitably tax our strength and our purpose, my own as much as any of the Watchers. That said, be assured that I shall not needlessly exert myself or take any pointless risks.'

Dardan looked sceptical but said nothing.

'You are our linch-pin, Beltran,' Countess Ayoni said. 'Without your leadership, the Watchers would lose purpose.'

'There will be little point in the Watchers at all if darkness triumphs.' Calabos straightened in his chair and gave a roguish smile. 'Besides, I'm not exactly defenceless, you know.'

Ayoni and Tashil gave nods of acknowledgement while Dardan just shrugged.

'Anyway, to other matters,' he said. 'Earlier this morning I spoke with Sounek and Inryk, instructing them to find out more about the Carverists in Sejeend; Sounek is going to attempt to join one of the more zealous Carver congregations while Inryk will employ his enviable stealth to investigate the background of certain senior Carver priests.'

'You mean he'll be crawling across the roofs and picking locked doors,' Dardan said.

'And searching for any evidence of conspiracy, plots, bribery and the like,' Calabos said.

'So are you taking Tangaroth's suspicions seriously?' said the Countess.

'Not entirely,' he said. 'I don't really believe that the Carverists in Sejeend pose any real threat, yet Tangaroth and others close to Ilgarion have convinced themselves that they do. But there is room for doubt on our part, stemming from not knowing enough about the various Carver congregations, which is why I despatched Sounek and Inryk.'

'I haven't seen Chellour and Dybel this morning, master,' said Tashil. 'Are they likewise engaged?'

Calabos nodded. 'The sources of darkness are what they seek.'

Yet it is not last night's sorcerous calling that they pursue, he thought. *As with the Carvers, I know little about Ilgarion's inner circle and its motives, thus the palace is their goal, a secret goal.*

'But worry not,' he went on. 'I have vital tasks for you both. Countess — I assume that you will be attending Ilgarion's audience with your husband? – good, then make it your aim to watch who Ilgarion and Tangaroth speak with, and it might be valuable to see if you can overhear any conversations. It will be a state occasion so the masquering will be formal, which may be an aid.'

Calabos turned to Tashil. 'For your part, I want you to find time to stop by various inns and stalls and listen for tales of odd happenings last night. The Archmage may believe that some Carverist was behind that sorcerous calling but I'm certain that someone or something else is at work in the city's shadows. See what you can discover.' He paused to regard them both with a fond smile. 'Do I need to encourage you to exercise caution and restraint?'

The two women exchanged a look, then laughed in unison.

'Why, of course not, Beltran,' Countess Ayoni said with mock innocence. 'I will be the very soul of prudence.'

'As shall I, master,' said Tashil brightly.

Then together they turned and left the summer room. If Calabos he was right about what they faced, then the perils that awaited the Watchers would be beyond anything they had previously encountered.

'You still set on our little expedition later?' said Dardan.

Calabos nodded. 'While the rest pursue other quarry, we are the ones who will hunt the darkness to its source.'

'In that case –' Dardan stood and pulled on his battered, dark green leather cloak, '– there are some matters for me to attend to.'

Reaching the door, he paused. 'And worry not – I shall exercise all due caution. Those laundresses can be a mite nasty this time o' day!'

Sniggering, he opened the door and was gone.

Calabos grinned, shook his head. But his humour faded as solitude forced his thoughts in on themselves. He rose easily from the table, thinking to go downstairs to speak with his guards, but instead paused to look out at the lodge's walled garden. A rack of heavy cloud was moving in from the east, obscuring the sun and sending an overcast greyness rushing across the sea towards Sejeend. Calabos turned back to the room, now growing gloomy. He crossed to a long carved stand whose various niches and shelves held a variety of books and odd ornaments. He found an oil lamp, lit it with a flint-wheel, then set it atop the stand – and found that he was standing before a wall-hanging of the siege of Besh-Darok.

In fading colours, it depicted the moment when the witch-horses, led by the boy-emperor Tauric, fell upon the great army of the Shadowkings. Calabos had seen it during a visit to Adnagaur and, in a moment of wry consideration, bought it, thinking to hang it in his villa. Later reflection caused him to change his mind and donate it to the lodge where he was less likely to set eyes on it too often. As it loomed over him now, it seemed to offer a silent, mordant commentary on last night's disturbing events.

That maddening, insistent emanation had been carefully constructed from the most ancient of tongues and was, he was sure, directed at whatever survived of the Lord of Twilight's fragmented essence, a call ringing out across the nightbound land . . . and something in him had responded.

No, that wasn't right. He *knew* that nothing of that dread presence remained since it had been excised utterly by Nerek with the melded sword of powers. Could it be that there was an emptiness in him that still held the shape of what had once been there? Such that when the sorcerous wave battered through him, what anwered was merely an echo of an echo, a memory of a memory?

He shuddered. When he had awoken it was after hours of deep, unbroken sleep, a period of blankness from which he emerged without so much as a fleeting shred of nightmare or dream-vision. By his bedside had been a pale and anxious Tashil and a scowling Dardan, a reassuring sight to his dazed senses. As he recovered he heard of Corlek Ondene's escape through the common room window while all had been distracted, and Tashil and Dardan's subsequent chase through the night. Their account of his apparent disappearance while trapped in the coach inn courtyard gave Calabos pause – neither of them reported any sense of a focussed use of the Lesser Power and neither saw Ondene emerge from the shadows, either free or captive.

Which left only two explanations, either that the errant captain had found a way out of the trap undetected or that some unknown power had intervened. Then there was the question of the hirelings

sent to stalk him through the streets – were they working for
Tangaroth or were they connected to the soldiers who had set
upon him the previous night?

He studied the fleeing rout of black-masked troops on the wall
tapestry. *Unknown power*, he thought dismissively. *I know that power's
name – I can taste the taint of his corruption spreading throughout this
city. Even destroyed and scattered to the seven coasts, enough of him yet
remains to draw forth worshippers of the twisted and the profane.*

And once these dark priests began to gather more converts and
deepen their power, their purposes would gain potency and a
momentum which would become increasingly difficult to defeat
with the passage of time. It was a pattern he had witnessed repeatedly over the last three centuries.

No, not this time, he thought as he turned the lamp down low.
*We shall search out their lair and crack it open, then hunt them down
like the vermin that they are. The Lord of Twilight must never return –
never!*

The sun had reemerged from the clouds and brightness flooded
the summer room once more. As he turned away from the tapestry
Calabos could feel his hands trembling. From anger, he told himself,
only anger.

Not fear.

Outside the lodge, Tashil waved farewell to Countess Ayoni as she
climbed into her large and sombre carriage. Once it was clattering
away in the direction of the count's coastal estates, she turned and
made her way downhill through the district towards the riverside,
occasionally ducking into doorways when brief but wild showers
whipped along the street.

Near the riverbank, behind the warehouses and godowns, was
Oldyard Walk, a long, narrow street comprising little else but squalid
lodgements, a few ramshackle inns and several mean little alehouses.
Some of these she knew by reputation to be risky for a lone
woman so she stopped at some of the others along the way, keeping
to small beer and swapping tall tales and ragtalk with the regu-
lars. With her narrow features, short hair and fluency in riverway
argot, she felt safe from being recognized as Mogaun; it was a

guise she had worked hard at since her arrival in Sejeend and it had proved helpful in sidestepping the complications of bigotry.

In the Black Bottle she related her and Dardan's encounter with the unnatural hound, but told as if she had been a witness (and adding a few embellishments like the dog having yellow eyes and breathing fire). The soused ropemaker who was her chance companion responded with the meandering tale of a headless horse trotting through the streets after midnight. Further talk provided tales of the misty ghosts of Mogaun shamans prowling around the foot of the White Keep, corpses rising from the bay and wading ashore to the shingle where they were set upon by a swarm of rats and a murder of crows. But when he tried to pick her up she made her excuses and left.

Further along, in a narrow tavern called the Bag O'Nails, she plied her story again but heard little in return apart from a long-haired minstrel swearing that he woke in the middle of last night − in a small park nearby − to see a pair of dainty, ladies' boots dancing with a red velvet glove upon the grass, and next door, in the Ragged Staff, she heard of flying crockery and a kulesti that played itself. In the Iron Daemon, it was a yarn about talking mice, and in the Ship and Star, it was a group of alley cats who had given voice.

Out on Oldyard Walk, Tashil reflected on what she had once heard from an Earthmother sister about working in the temple's hall of healing, namely that after some time it seemed to her that the entire city was ailing since all she saw were sick people. Tashil smiled − right now, she found it easy to imagine that all of Sejeend was deep in its cups . . .

In the Monk's Head, however, she heard a despatch rider speak of a chilling experience he had at a coaching inn some forty miles south of Sejeend on the Red Road. After a wearying ride from Vannyon's Ford, he had stopped at the inn for the night and was unsaddling his horse when he heard a noise from a covered cart which had been parked in the stabling barn. When he went to investigate he saw an arm hanging below the edge of the canvas cover at the rear of the cart, and when he tugged the cover aside he was horrified to behold six or seven corpses lying jumbled in the cart. Immediately he hurried through to the main building and found the innkeeper in the rear parlour but before he could tell of his ghastly discovery there was a commotion from outside. By the time he and others dashed outside there were only the sounds of the cart and horse receding northwards up the Red Road. Pursuit in the pitch dark was out of the question and in the morning there was little in the way of wheel marks after the heavy showers that had passed over the land earlier.

The rider's demeanour was frank and undramatic, and his tale was uncomfortably convincing. Such that when she visited the next tavern, the Five Kings, and heard the tale of a ghostly witch disappearing before a crowded alehouse, she decided that she had heard enough.

Tashil hurried away from the riverside quarter, heading north and mostly uphill towards the College district. The chambers where she lived lay behind her little ink and paper shop on the top floor of a high-peaked, three-storey house, itself halfway up Gryff Path, a narrow street running along the rear of several imposing trade buildings. As she turned a corner into Gryff Path she came face to face with a scrawny street dog. In an instant her memory of last night's encounter leaped to mind, causing her to halt abruptly and instinctively begin a defensive thought-canto, but the dog, which had been pawing at a discarded, mouldy half-loaf, quickly scurried away, tail between its legs. Relieved, Tashil breathed out and crossed the street, feeling annoyed at herself for panicking so readily.

Moments later she was passing beneath the wicker archway with its twining strands of dogthorn, then climbing the iron-framed stairs that clung to the street-facing side of her building. At the third and topmost floor she paused to check that her assistant, Maut, had closed up the shop properly, then hastened along the length of the walkway to her supposed main door, which she only used when the shop was shut.

An intricate key opened the lock and she slipped inside . . . and immediately felt that there was someone or something else in the house. She stood stock still for a moment and listened through her undersenses . . . heard the faint rustle of cloth against cloth . . . breathing that was quicker than normal, nervous or anxious

. . . not coming from her bedroom or her study, but futher down the narrow hall, from the day-room next to her little kitchen . . .

In her mind she prepared the thought-canto Entwine as she slipped out of her low boots and crept barefoot along the hall. All her undersenses told her that the intruder possessed no sorcerous aura, yet that was no comfort in the light of recent events.

She stopped before the day-room, pushed it open and stepped back, the Entwine spell spinning in her thoughts, ready for release. The room was dark with shadows.

'Whoever you are,' Tashil said loudly, 'come out here where I can see you.'

For a moment there was nothing, then a tall figure in a long cloak emerged from the gloom.

'You've a strange way of greeting visitors, 'Sheel,' said a voice that was familiar. Then the figure came into the light and she saw that it was her brother, Atemor, but there was a hollow, haunted look to him.

'Atti,' she said, relaxing her guard and letting the Entwine spell dissipate. 'What are you doing here? Wait, is our father . . . is he . . . ?'

'No, 'Sheel, Old Man Akri lives yet,' he said. 'He's even taken himself a new wife so we can expect another brother or sister by next year.'

Such news was irritating for Tashil, but it was like the ache of an old wound.

'I do not think that you came to tell me of Father's latest acquisition,' she said, ushering him back into the day-room, where she parted the drapes to let in light. 'So why are you here?'

'Father has decided to make the pilgrimage to the Isle of Besh-Darok,' said Atemor, looking around him at the piles of books that cluttered chairs and shelves. 'He made it a point of duty for all of us to accompany him.'

'And my mother?' she said levelly. 'Did she come too?'

Atemor gave a wry smile. 'She refused. Said she would make his life a misery if he forced her to go.'

'But the others came?' Tashil said.

'Wives, brothers, sisters, even the granfers and a couple of the greatfathers . . .'

He mentioned a string of names, her half-brothers and half-sisters, as well as a short but sad list of those taken by death since the last contact she had, which was with one of her uncles. Listening to all this was like being engulfed by the meaning and essence of Family, the very thing she had striven to escape with her voluntary exile. Yet instead of feeling smothered, she found that she was enjoying hearing about all her many relatives in the sprawling Akri family.

But then Atemor seemed to grow weary or run out of gossip or both, which returned Tashil to the most puzzling question of all.

'And did the family arrive safely at Besh-Darok?' she said.

'Yes, we found a fine camping spot to the north of the city.'

'So tell me – if they are camped at Besh-Darok, why are you here?'

Atemor was silent for a long moment and when he finally looked straight at her, she could see fear and desperation written starkly in his face. Her unease flared into dread.

'I was walking sentry last night,' he said. 'Everything was quiet, apart from the buzz of krezziks off in the bushes. Then I started to hear . . . these voices, whispering at first, then getting louder, telling me to come to Sejeend, to leave everything and come, no pause, no delay!' His voice shook as he spoke. 'I thought that I was being attacked by a spirit of madness, like the old tree hermits of Gulmaegorn – then I thought perhaps it was the voices of the gods, maybe even the Grey Lord himself.

'But then the next thing I remember is riding my horse south from one of the bridges, with the voices filling my head, like a cloud of pain that I could not fight against. I had no control over my body . . . then I blacked out again and when I awoke I was entering Sejeend, but I also had my body back and the cloud of pain had gone. I remembered where you lived and came here, got in through a window in your shop.'

Distress overwhelmed him and he sank to his knees.

'The voices are still there, 'Sheel, calling, calling, on and on and on! You have to help me – have I been cursed or possessed? You must help me, I beg you – when I woke there was blood on my dagger—'

With outward calm, Tashil took his hands and got him back on his feet. 'I don't know how to help you, Atti, but I know someone who can.'

Inwardly, however, she was racked by horror and panic. *And if Calabos can't help you, what will we do with you then?*

Chapter Eight

Such a trap of honeyed poison,
The court of this malign king,
Where words of virtue,
Mask greed and hate,
Where arrogance calls itself valour,
And foundations decay unnoticed.

Jedhessa Gant, *A King In Alvergost*, Act I, Sc. ii, ll 6–11

The noise of some two hundred or more conversations filled the pillared audience hall of the Daykeep, a continuous surging, swirl of babble. This was the sound of the empire's aristocracy making itself heard, with old ties reaffirmed, old enmities cordially expressed, pecking orders strictly applied, insults covert and overt loosed, and flattery delivered with or without irony. And since the rigidities of palace etiquette demanded formal masquering, the potential for misidentification and misunderstanding was considerable. Indeed, to an aloof observer the assembled throng might resemble an exotic herd of jewelled and gilded wildlife.

To the Countess Ayoni, standing by her husband amid the opulent multitude, there was a certain exciting edge to not being completely sure who you might be talking to. In the early years of his reign, Emperor Magramon apparently moved through similar gatherings, disguised in an innocuous mask devised by his costumiers. The stern Ilgarion, on the other hand, would by all accounts be very unlikely to take risks with what he regarded as his dignity.

Which did not lessen Ayoni's enjoyment in guessing who lay behind which mask while keeping her eyes open for those she knew to be close allies of Ilgarion.

All the nobility had full face-masks while their attendants wore half-masks that were as plain or distinctive as their masters decided. Some masks were modelled after the blazon beasts of noble houses, like the Earl of Rovali's moorcat or the stormcrow of the barons of Ashryn Hold. Others had clearly been created to whim and fancy, resulting in a gallimaufry of images: Bull listened and nodded to Salamander, Glintmoth shared a joke with Stag, while Dog tried to cold-shoulder Crab. Ayoni's mask depicted a vixen, which derived from her own family's crest, while her husband Jarryc's was the bear of the counts of Harcas. At that moment, Count Jarryc was engaged in a muttered exchange with two of his closest allies, Baron Klayse of the Rukangfell and Margrave Tergalis of Westershore: the former was masked as a boar, the latter as a greathound.

'Did you notice dor-Fandresk?' Klayse murmured.

'With dor-Gaemos over at the Fathertree tapestry?' said Tergalis. 'Could they be ready to declare for Ilgarion, I wonder?'

Beneath his bear mask, Count Jarryc laughed quietly.

'While it's wise to entertain the possibility of darker motives, milords, facts are usually vital to any appraisal.' He turned to Ayoni. 'Mayhap my lady wife knows a mite more than we?'

Ayoni met his gaze and smiled. 'My lord husband honours me,' she said. 'I do know that Lord Fandresk's second cousin has asked for the hand of Lord Gaemos' great-niece . . . or they could be discussing the missive which they and all of Magramon's old supporters received this morning from Ilgarion's chamber steward . . .'

The Baron and the Margrave stared at her for an astonished moment while the Count chuckled.

'Gentlemen,' he said in a low voice. 'Before consenting most graciously to become my wife, the Countess was for several years one of Queen Darlia's ladies-in-waiting, many of whom married into high nobility yet maintained their interwoven friendships.'

'Intriguing,' said Margrave Tergalis. 'Milady, perchance do you know what was in this letter?'

'Sadly no, my lord,' she said. 'The messengers would only deliver it unto the nobles themselves.'

'Knowing Ilgarion,' said Baron Klayse, 'it would be either a bribe or a threat.'

The Margrave had just begun to say something about bribes needing subtlety when the general hubbub around them died down and all eyes turned to the main entrance before which three figures stood. Two were spear guards in ring mail and red cloaks; they flanked a tall man in a silver-inlaid leather hauberk and long black cloak. Ayoni recognized him as Duke Mendalse, High Minister of Night and master of the Nightkeep. Odd, she thought, that there had been no sign of Byrceyn, who was the master of the Daykeep.

Impassively regarding the glittering crowd, he cleared his throat.

'My lords and ladies, I must inform you all that the caudal audience of His Royal Highness will now take place in the Grand Hall. If you will follow me, this will entail but a short walk along the Sun Corridor.'

And so saying, the High Minister of Night turned and strode through the entrance. There were several indignant protests but the Minister seemed not to notice as he walked from the chamber with a stately pace, accompanied by his guards. Arguments broke out between noble family members and the attendants serving refreshments attracted petty reproaches. But Ayoni heard little of it, having urged her husband and his cronies and their own retainers into swift pursuit of High Minister Mendalse.

Soon the entire mass of nobility was in motion along the Sun Corridor. It was a broad, enclosed colonnade that cut through one of the imperial gardens, joining the Daykeep to the main buildings of the palace. Its floor was tiled in rose and dove-grey, and was brilliantly lit by a profusion of hanging lanterns and wall lamps fashioned in gold and brass. The white walls were decorated with a large number of acid-etched pictorial mirrors which were interspersed with small niches occupied by exquisite paintings or figurines carved in pale wood.

Before long the corridor ended at another known as the Coronal, which encircled the Grand Hall, the side doors to which stood agape.

The Grand Hall was oval in shape, narrower towards one end

where the vacant imperial throne sat atop a semicircular dais approached by a dozen or more girdling steps of pale blue marble. The throne itself was a high-back piece crafted in black ironwood, silver and various crystals and gems, and was fashioned in the form of a stylized tree, the ancient symbol of the Khatrimantine emperors. This was the focus of the Grand Hall, the seat of power, and everything – the sweeping buttresses of the high arched ceiling, the supporting columns, the placing of lamps – helped to draw the eye to it.

Of Ilgarion, however, Ayoni saw no sign as she and the Count and his companions entered and proceeded towards the dais as part of the vanguard of the nobility. There were others already present – Duke Byrceyn, the High Minister of Day, and a large retinue; the earls Broha and Narlaq, both long-time allies of Ilgarion; a group of men and women in sombre brown attire and blue three-quarter masks, whom her undersenses told her were mages; another large group wearing silver half-masks and grey or black robes marked with the book-and-keys sigil of the Imperial Academy. In addition, there were more guards posted at intervals around the hall, and a cluster of court officials murmuring among themselves. Finally, off to one side there was a knot of some six or seven affluent-looking men in rich red or green garments, their dark grey masks and skullcaps proclaiming their status as merchants.

Then she noticed that one of the women in Duke Byrceyn's retinue wore a distinctive butterfly mask and was sure that this was his wife, the Lady Fyndil, who was an old friend. Thinking that she might learn more about this gathering, or even the mysterious letter, she told her husband where she would be and set off through the growing crowd. But she was barely halfway to her goal when a tall, blue-masked figure appeared beside her, laid a hand on her shoulder and steered her out to the fringes of the throng.

It was the Archmage Tangaroth, which she knew instantly from her undersenses, realizing that this encounter would have to be handled carefully.

'Countess,' the Archmage began smoothly. 'I beg your indulgence for this unseemly intrusion, but I mean only to preserve the good-natured calm of this occasion. Which I fear might be disturbed were you to attempt to approach Duke Byrceyn.'

Maintaining an amused demeanour, she glanced past him to where the High Minister of Day's retinue was gathered and noticed details missed before. What she had taken for servants in a neutral brown livery she could now see were swordsmen who stood in a barrier between the Duke's people and the other attending nobles. The Duke himself was dressed in black and grey with a gold silk mask vestigial enough to reveal his mouth, which was set in a grim line.

'Well, the Duke certainly has a glum look about him,' she said lightly. 'And yet you would prefer me not to go over and bid him good day – why ever not?'

'Grave matters of state, my lady.'

'Oh, you mean that the poor Duke has earned his Royal Highness' enmity in some way. Is he under arrest? Will his punishment be a lesson to us all?'

Masked, the Archmage's features were unreadable but Ayoni could sense his contempt.

'Given your family history and your upbringing, Countess,' he said, 'it is disappointing that you do not show more decorum and loyalty—'

'I weary of this, Archmage. I fully intend to go and talk to Duke Byrceyn . . .'

Tangaroth moved to block her path. 'I would strongly advise against that, Countess. I am quite capable of inducing sleep in you and making it resemble a faint.'

Ayoni stepped angrily to one side. 'You must do what you see fit, ser, as must I!'

The Archmage faced her, bare hands empty at his side, and was about to speak when a man in a garish flamebird mask, laughing drunkenly and looking over his shoulder, careered into him. The contents of a large goblet sloshed forth to drench Tangaroth's midriff and sluice down into his leggings and boots. There were mutual cries of surprise, of which the Archmage's was by far the louder.

'Oh, good ser!' said the unsteady culprit. 'I am so terribly, terribly sorry . . .'

But Tangaroth was beside himself with fury.

'You half-witted *imbecile*! You've ruined this coat . . . no, stay away from me!'

This last he shouted as the man in the flamebird mask tried to use his own dangling sleeves to mop the spillage from the Archmage's garments. Then, for a moment, the man's eyes met Ayoni's – and he winked.

She stepped smartly around Tangaroth and wove a path back into the crowd. But before she could get close to Byrceyn's party, horns blared and a column of guards carrying spears hurried into the hall to form a long corridor through the gathering, which neatly stopped Ayoni getting any nearer to the Duke and his wife.

The horns sounded again, softer this time, and began a pattern of notes in round fashion as Ilgarion and his retinue entered the Grand Hall.

Two attendants in trailing, blue robes led the way, carrying between them a small casket of some kind covered in a white shroud. Then came Ilgarion and his wife, the Lady Gesaul, their hands joined and held at waist level. The son had his father's solid build and full head of black hair, now well streaked with silver, but where Magramon had possessed a certain warmth and approachability, Ilgarion glanced at the massed nobility with cold, pale eyes that betrayed only mistrust.

Behind him strode a veiled priestess of the Earthmother temple, her white robes edged with carmine suggesting someone of high rank, possibly the Abbess herself. After her came Shumond, Lord Commander of the Iron Guard, flanked by four of his senior officers, all wearing golden, open-faced helms surmounted by drakken emblems, and dark blue cloaks trimmed with wolf fur.

Following at the rear were more servants carrying a variety of wrapped bundles under arms or on shoulders. As they filed off to one side of the dais, Ilgarion – accompanied by the Lord Commander Shumond and High Minister Mendalse – climbed the dais steps but stopped halfway up and faced the wondering nobles.

During the procession, Ayoni had worked her way forward to where she could see both Ilgarion and his audience. Then, to her surprise, it was Mendalse who raised his hands for silence.

'Behold!' he said. 'The High Keepers!'

A sense of stunned amazement passed through the nobles and in its wake came whispers, shaken heads and exchanges of wide-eyed looks. Ayoni was no less shaken, realizing that Ilgarion had somehow persuaded the Conclave of Rods to disregard the Low Coronation and to hold the High Coronation now and within the palace precincts rather than by the sea's edge as was traditional. This would, she knew, be deeply unpopular with the citizenry yet it was clear that the assembled nobility were prepared to accept and endorse this sidestepping of obligation without protest.

Then she remembered Duke Byrceyn's predicament. *Perhaps the acquiescence of the aristocracy is not quite unanimous*, she thought.

Along the guard-lined corridor came two figures cloaked and hooded in pale blue, each carrying a long, sigil-topped staff in the right hand and a cloth-wrapped object in the left. By the time they reached the foot of the dais, the other servants had unpacked their burdens to assemble pole lamps, slender wooden frames draped in ceremonial banners and placed either side of the throne, little tables and plinths on which sacred relics and ritual lamps were set. Perfumed odours soon began to filter through the hall but nothing could obscure the fact that these hasty preparation were a shabby, shameful travesty of the time-honoured coronation traditions.

The High Keepers had laid down their staffs and doffed their hoods, revealing the faces of elderly men, both of whom were holy brothers of the Earthmother temple appointed by the Conclave of Rods for this specific task. Each held the object he had brought, now unwrapped, replicas of the Motherseed and the Crystal Eye, the ancient heirlooms that had been lost in the great Shadowking war.

The coronation ritual commenced in a strange dead calm, broken by occasional coughs and the rustle of garments. The Earthmother priestess unveiled herself – it was indeed the Abbess

– then began a declamatory exchange with the High Keepers, addressing first one then the other, after which they replied in unison, and all in the intricate phrasing and intonation of formal Mantinoran since the Khatrimantine emperors traced the line of succession back to the kings of Mantinor. Ayoni had never witnessed an imperial coronation but knew from historical accounts that this was a drastically truncated interpretation of an ancient ceremony which had often taken two, even three days to complete.

She had read of massed choirs singing and chanting, the tolling of bells and the sweet voice of drawn kulesti. But when the High Keepers handed the imperial replies to the Abbess it was amid an eerie silence. The priestess looked somewhat stone-faced as she turned and climbed the dais steps to where Ilgarion stood. Halting to stare up at him, she recited further lines on the sacred duty of kingship then offered up the relics. Ilgarion bowed, took them from her then mounted the last couple of steps, took two paces to the throne – now draped in a pale, shimmering material – and sat down. Two figures clad in white robes emerged from behind the throne bearing a sword, a mace and a crown, all wound in filmy gauze. Wearing pale, jewelled masks, the pair represented the Earthmother and the divine Tauric, whose conferral of the instruments of kingship was meant to symbolize the link between the throne and the land and the unseen powers.

But this performance felt like a hollow shell, empty of dignity or meaning.

Finally it drew to an end as the symbolic figures between them lowered the crown onto Ilgarion's head then fastened a clasp across his throat. As they withdrew Ilgarion stood, holding the mace of law in one hand and the sword of state in the other. The shimmering material rose with him, proving to be a long trailing cloak which was sky blue on its outside.

Someone near the front of the crowd suddenly shouted – 'The emperor is dead – long live Emperor Ilgarion!' As growing numbers of nobles began chanting his name, Ayoni found herself filled with contempt for them.

'Such a stirring moment, is it not?' murmured a voice nearby.

She turned to see her deliverer from the Archmage, the mysterious man in the flamebird mask. She could make out only his eyes and his mouth, which was smiling sardonically.

'Much about our new emperor is of a singular nature,' she said. 'I am Ayoni Feldaru, Countess of Harcas — you have my thanks for rescuing me earlier.'

The man inclined his head. 'Just occasionally, blundering carelessness brings benefits. Ah, yes, and I am Lord Kerlo of Northmarch.'

Ayoni frowned. 'Northmarch — I don't believe I've heard of it.'

'Oh, 'tis but a small and relatively unimportant part of the northern border with the Mogaun League. Pelts from the northern Rukangs, my lady, are one of our more lucrative exports . . .'

And as she listened she got a vague sense of familiarity from his voice but before she could question him further the crowd's chanting faded and Ilgarion spoke.

'This empire has stood for long centuries against the hate and schemes of evil enemies,' he said. 'And it is from the constancy, courage and loyalty of you and your forebears that our mighty empire has drawn its strength. Yet even amongst our closest and most trusted custodians, the seeds of weakness and betrayal may take root and when such banes come to light it is our duty to tear them out!'

Ayoni felt a weight of dread as Ilgarion's voice turned venomous and he looked round at the High Minister of Day, Duke Byrceyn.

'Lord Commander Shumond — the Duke Byrceyn has committed deadly treason against the crown, thus I adjure you to carry out your duty by arresting and confining him.'

The circle of swordsmen parted as Shumond and two of his officers moved in. As rope was brought out to bind Byrceyn's hands, his wife let out a cry of anguish, threw aside her mask and tried to reach for her husband.

'Confine the Lady Fyndil as well,' added Ilgarion.

'No, damn you—' was all that Byrceyn could say before a gauntleted fist cuffed him into silence.

Watching this, Ayoni felt her outrage reach the point where she had to act, and she moved straight through the gathered nobles, thinking only to stop this vile injustice. A babble of voices rose at this sight but she was unaware of it, focussed only on her friend Lady Fyndil struggling in the hand of the Iron Guard officers.

She was but a few paces away when she was struck by a wave of dizziness. The floor and the nearby dais seemed to tilt slightly and she stumbled, slowed and stopped, breathing in deeply to clear her head. But then a terrible debility flowed into her legs and as she sank to the floor amid raised voices, she just heard Tangaroth's amused voice in her head, – *Well done, my lady. You faint most beautifully* – before unconsciousness took her.

The moment Countess Ayoni set off across the hall, Corlek knew that he had to distance himself from her and sidled into a more densely occupied part of the floor. He also began to wish that his mask was modelled on something rather less distinctive than the mythological flamebird.

Then the Countess stumbled in her progress, swayed and crumpled to the floor. There were gasps and voices shouting as her husband, Count Jarryc, barrelled through the crowd. Amid the gaudy press of nobles gathered around the fallen Countess, Corlek recognized the tall, dark-blue figure of Archmage Tangaroth who was pushed aside by the Count.

Tangaroth was one of the people that Agasklin and Qothan had impressed upon him to take notice of. From where he stood he could also see Ilgarion upon his dais, coolly observing the enforced removal of Duke Byrceyn and his wife while Count Jarryc carried his own spouse from the hall in his arms. Corlek also knew that one of the four officers attending Lord Commander Shumond was Vorik dor-Galyn, but was not sure which of them he was. Then there was the one named Jumil, a dark and deadly sorcerer according to Agasklin.

'Note who he speaks to,' Agasklin had said. 'But avoid attracting his attention and keep a good distance from him.'

At that moment, Jumil was part of a group of officials and academics situated off to the right of the dais some yards along from a cluster of merchants who were watching Ilgarion closely. Jumil was slightly taller and noticeably thinner than the rest, who

were noticeably well fed. During a brief exchange with one of
the academy officials on the way back from the nearby privy, he
had learned which one Jumil was after spurious claims of being
related to someone on the academy staff.

Shifting his mask slightly, Corlek was able to glance over at
Jumil while appearing to be studying Ilgarion atop the dais. The
sorcerer was standing apart from his companions and looked
vaguely bored as he regarded the proceedings. At that moment,
one of the Iron Guard officers who had escorted Byrceyn and his
wife outside entered from a nearby side door, paused and removed
his helm. Corlek caught his breath – it was Vorik dor-Galyn, and
as he watched he saw dor-Galyn share a quick look and perhaps
the faintest of nods with Jumil, then brushed back his hair and
donned his helm once more. Corlek gritted his teeth as the object
of his enmity strode across to the dais to stand by Lord Commander
Shumond, facing out at the anxious, muttering mass of aristocrats.

Then Ilgarion began to speak again. His voice was calm, his
tones measured, almost reasonable, and the things he was saying
were broad, generalized praises for the virtues of the Khatrimantine
Empire, and the necessity of heartfelt valour when called to defend
these immemorial virtues and traditions.

Some of the nobles seemed puzzled at this almost reassuring
homily but behind his mask Corlek smiled. He had seen this kind
of demagoguery before, a soothing recital of normalcy followed
by darkness and menace.

And sure enough, in the next breath Ilgarion began to lay out
the threats that the empire faced, from the Carver fanatics to the
west and north, from the ambitious generals of Mantinor, and from
the savage pirates who ranged up and down the coasts of Cabringa.

'And the sad truth which I must reveal to you all now is that
any enemy who would cast a hungry eye over our empire would
find us ill-prepared to withstand a determined invasion. The great
hosts of our armies are under-strength and lacking in even the
essentials of weapons and armour. Our cavalry battalions make do
with inferior steeds while the imperial navy has taken delivery of
just two new ships in the last ten years. So as we become gradually weaker, those who wish us ill grow stronger.

'But I know that this empire is not doomed to be crushed by an onslaught of evil, as happened once before. No, our destiny is clear, strong and blessed and our most glorious age is yet to come, but we will have to reach for it. We shall drive our will and our purpose out across the lands, confront those who worship at the altars of evil, and embrace a new world where peace and prosperity reign.'

There was some applause from the noble gathering, a polite, restrained response Corlek noted, but Ilgarion seemed undeterred and continued.

'Our first step in the renewal of the empire will be the reinvigoration of the nobility . . .'

He paused and looked to the left where a pale yellow-gowned attendant ascended the steps, bowed and handed Ilgarion a slender, plain circlet adorned with a single blue stone. At the same time, two other attendants brought one of the soberly attired merchanters to the dais from the right and led him up to Ilgarion. The man went down on hands and knees and pressed his forehead on the dais tiles. There were indignant mutters from some parts of the crowd but they subsided when the Iron Guard officers stared outwards, trying to identify those responsible.

To Corlek, however, Ilgarion's aims were very clear. Rebuilding an army or a navy takes a great deal of money and Corlek had no doubt that each of those being called one by one to receive the title and circlet of a noble represented a subtantial amount of hard cash. Of course, history was rife with instances where an aristocracy had turned on its liege lord out of fear for its power, and here Ilgarion seemed to be moving to bolster the foundations of his own position, namely the army and the navy.

But if a scandal involving the Iron Guard and a dark sorcerer comes out into the open, he thought, *that would alter the pieces on the board and who knows what might happen to Ilgarion then?*

The atmosphere of the ceremony grew dreary and sullen, and as Corlek watched the slow procession of new-made nobles he noticed Tangaroth looking on, nodding occasionally. Dor-Galyn still stood on one of the dais' lower steps, staring out at the crowd, while off to the right the enigmatic Jumil was a motionless figure by the rear wall's heavy amber drapes.

The second-last merchant had just felt the touch of the circlet upon his brow when the sounds of a commotion could be heard from outside the northern doors, by which the nobles had first entered. Voices could be heard shouting, muffled at first then becoming clearer, men shouting — 'Alarum! Fire!' Then the doors flew open and a court steward rushed in accompanied by half a dozen scribes and attendants.

'Your imperial majesty,' he said. 'I beg forgiveness for hasty and unannounced instrusion upon—'

'Enough of that!' Ilgarion snapped. 'What is this about?'

'Fire, majesty!' the steward said in a voice full of horror. 'The Keep of Day is ablaze from top to bottom!'

Ilgarion stared at the man for a long moment, then gave a sharp nod.

'Very well, steward — gather every able-bodied servant and evacuate all chambers adjoining the Keep. Lord Commander Shumond — turn out the Guard and open every well in the gardens. Duke Mendalse and Archmage Tangaroth — give me your counsel as we hasten to behold this tragedy.'

Amid a growing uproar, the crowd of nobles was already making for the exits, with a large number heading towards the Sun Corridor. Corlek was almost struck with a panic of indecision as he watched dor-Galyn receive orders from the Lord Commander then dash off through a door on the other side of the dais. Then he turned to look at Jumil — but saw nothing but amber wall drapes swaying beside a half-open door. He paused for a moment then darted across to it and through.

Beyond it, a wide passage curved off in either direction from a furnished vestibule. There, an ornate, bannistered staircase rose from its centre and Corlek just glimpsed Jumil hurrying up to the next floor. But as he made to follow, a voice spoke from along to his left.

'Here now — you're not supposed to be in this part of the palace!' said a young spear guard who was hurrying towards him.

Corlek shrugged and, putting on a slurred voice, said; "'S a big place, eh? Y' can't tell one damn corridor from 'nother . . . so where's this fire, then . . . ?'

'Never mind that, m'lord. You just come along with me, see, and I'll help find your friends . . .'

'No, no, young fellow,' he said, wagging a finger. 'I'm qui' happy here, y'see.' He danced a haphazard jig then stumbled against the young guard. 'Oh, ah, sorry, sorry – hey, ain't that your commander?'

And as the young guard looked round, Corlek swung at his jaw with his gauntleted left hand. There was a sharp sound and a gasp as the guard spun from the blow and went down.

'Sorry, laddie,' Corlek murmured as he looted a dagger and short sword from the unconscious form. 'But you'll learn to keep your distance in future, won't you?'

Quickly, he hid the spear guard in a curtained alcove shrine then glanced behind and ahead before dashing up the stairs.

At the next floor a short, unlit passage led forward to join a corridor which was angled towards the northern wall of the palace. The corridor was cold and deserted with only a few lowlit lamps burning, but Corlek strove to tread softly on the tiled floor. The chambers along here were very likely vacant, he guessed, yet up ahead he noticed a yellow, fiery glow as he came to a stretch where several windows looked out at the cityward sections of the palace.

The sight of the burning Keep of Day stopped him in his tracks. He took off his mask and let it fall to the floor. At nine storeys, the Keep overtopped the ceremonial flag and bell tower which sat atop the crown of the Grand Hall. There were windows in every storey, and every opening was a mass of flame. To a calmer part of his thoughts, it struck him as odd that the conflagration could become so all-encompassing in so short a space of time.

In the gardens below, chains of people were desperately passing buckets of water forward to try and douse the blaze. But it was clearly hopeless – the fires were too widespread and too fierce.

Almost as if it had been arranged that way.

He spotted movement in a darker part of the gardens, close to the inner wall: a tall figure in robes skulking along a pathway hidden from the fire-fighters by thick bushes. Corlek knew that it had to be the sorcerer Jumil, and continued along the corridor, quickly coming to a square-turning stair leading down.

Descending, he heard voices from further along the ground floor passageway but swiftly found a small anteroom with an already-ajar door that led out to the gardens.

Outside, the air was warm and stank of smoke. The keep was burning like a gigantic torch, drenching everything in a harsh, molten glare. But he was drawn onwards by a glimpse of Jumil climbing stone stairs up the inner wall to a buttressed walkway and making for an arched door at the end. And someone else was with him – a shorter, hooded figure hurrying along at his side. Corlek gave chase.

Up on the walkway, planks creaked underfoot as he headed for the archway. The blazing keep was straight ahead and through the rushing roar of the flames he could hear the crash of falling timbers and the screams of those trapped inside. Then he made out angry shouts coming from below and saw several figures appear on one of the keep's balconies. Even from this distance he could see that their garments, and even their hair, seemed charred and smoking. Then two of them manhandled a long object onto the balcony rail, held onto some part of it and let the rest of it fall over the edge, unfurling. It was a banner decorated with a single red device, an ordinary craftsman's knife, the symbol of the Carver creed.

Even as the banner caught fire, the shouts from the gardens became a mass of voices bellowing in anger. The figures on the balcony only pointed wordlessly down for a moment or two before running back inside, giving themselves to the flames.

Corlek was stunned by this, finding himself scarcely able to grasp the implications, yet he forced himself onwards, determined to lay hands on this Jumil, be he sorcerer or no. But he was no more than a few paces from the archway when a dark, stalwart figure emerged to face him and unsheath an efficient-looking broadsword.

'The disgraced scion of a spent house,' a mocking voice said. 'Killing you would be butcher's work, yet it must be done.'

Against the raging inferno of the Keep of Day, Vorik dor-Galyn was a dark form with only a few details visible, dull gleams on the iron fastenings of his leather harness, on a belt buckle, on a small ring in one ear, in the unwinking eyes that stared at Corlek.

'Come now,' Corlek said, tightening his grip on the hilt of his short sword. 'Surely butchery would be an upward step for the likes of you.'

Dor-Galyn just grinned and stepped smartly forward, aiming a slashing cut at Corlek's neck. Corlek had seen the move coming and lunged with a straight-armed thrust at dor-Galyn's upper chest. But there was no shock in hand and arm of the swordpoint punching through leather and skin, no resistance, nothing. Suddenly, between one instant and the next, there was no Vorik dor-Galyn. Corlek gasped in surprise, stumbled a few feet past the archway, then looked wildly about him.

And heard someone clapping from beyond the arch. Fear and dread assailed him but he held his blade point forward at waist level and made himself step warily through the opening. Beyond, a few steps led up to a square enclosure open to the sky and surrounded by crenellated battlements. Barrels and heavy wooden chests were stacked at the enclosure's rear, to either side of another set of steps descending into the interior. This, Corlek realized, was an internal fortification, a strongpoint which would stymie any invader who made it past the gates.

It was not deserted. Vorik dor-Galyn stood off to the right, lounging against a barrel, grinning unpleasantly as he ceased applauding.

'Did you enjoy our little mirage, Ondene?' he said. 'I thought my voice was very good, if a tad too deep, though I would never have made such a blundering swing as that.'

'I told you, guard man,' came a hoarse woman's voice from Corlek's left, 'I know naught of swords.'

The enclosure faced the gardens, with the Sun Corridor directly ahead and the Keep burning at its northern end, now fully sheathed in fire. The fierce, tower blaze threw sharp, notched shadows of the battlement onto the enclosure's flagstones, and outlined a short, hunched form standing at the wall's midpoint. The woman raised a hand to point at the flat roof of the keep and just then a figure came into view there, holding aloft a Carver banner. Then she pointed at a balcony halfway up and figures in blackened garments stepped out to dance and cavort amid a thousand tongues of flame.

The woman looked round, revealing an elderly face shiny with perspiration and wearing an unbalanced smile.

'My feather folk,' she said. 'My fine, fiery, flighty feather folk . . .' Then her gaze slid back to the burning keep.

'Do you understand yet, Ondene?' said dor-Galyn. 'Have you the wit to see?'

Corlek nodded. The sight of Carver zealots seemingly instrumental in the Keep's destruction would make every Carver follower in Sejeend a target for revenge.

'An illusion,' he said.

'More than that, Ondene. Fuel for an anger that will tear down the old and make way for the new.' There was the solid iron hiss of a sword being drawn. 'The fire, however, is very real.'

Corlek turned to face him. Agasklin's advice to watch over Jumil seemed irrelevant now. Standing there, motionless, his gaze locked with dor-Galyn's, he could sense the heat of the blood in his head and the thud of his heart in his chest. Dor-Galyn was holding his sword with its point sitting on the flagstones and his hand resting almost carelessly on its pommel.

'Will you die in silence, I wonder,' he said. 'Or will you scream out your last breath?'

He then affected to yawn languidly, one hand raised to his mouth. But Corlek was watching the other hand take a proper grip on the sword's hilt, pushing the blade across – then whipping it up in an arc of reflected golden light as he slashed at Corlek's neck. It was all he could do to twist aside from the blow but still it caught him on the shoulder, cutting through his embroidered jerkin and the shirt beneath. He hissed at the sting, although the wound was a shallow one. Dor-Galyn laughed and drew the blade back for another hack.

But Corlek darted to one side and kicked the nearby barrel towards dor-Galyn, forcing him to stagger back.

'Craven dog!' dor-Galyn snarled as he surged forward in a flurry of thrusts and cuts.

Dor-Galyn was noticeably taller and broader at the shoulder than Corlek and it was all he could do to stay on the edge of the man's longer reach. Forced back among the chests and barrels, he had to parry and dodge with all his skill as dor–Galyn was an excellent swordsman.

Retreating from chest to barrel, he sidestepped a vicious waist-level thrust and felt his foot knock against something. There was a solid wooden rattle and from the corner of his eye he saw an ordinary guardsman's spear. He parried a hammering downstroke with his shortsword then dived to snatch up the spear and leaped over a long storage chest. Swiftly, he couched the spear haft over one shoulder in the Dalbari stave-fighting style, and turned to face his adversary.

This time the advantage was with Corlek. He feinted at dor–Galyn's face with the point of the spear only to have it hacked off. In the next instant, he aimed a swordthrust at the man's vitals. The Iron Guard captain saw the blow coming and brought his broadsword arcing back down in a desperate parry. At the same time, Corlek spun the truncated spear in his other hand and the haft swung round to bludgeon into dor–Galyn's unprotected neck.

The man gave a choked cry as he staggered to one side, lost his footing and sprawled on the flagstones, his blade clattering nearby. Filled with anger and a triumphant loathing, Corlek went to stand over him, sword in hand.

'The time has come,' he said, breathing heavily, 'for *your* family to know loss and grief!'

'I think not,' said a voice close by.

Startled he glanced round to see the one called Jumil standing less than a yard away, his mask hanging by its ties from one hand. Corlek went to bring his sword round but found to his horror that his limbs, his very muscles, were frozen in place.

'Only I punish my servants,' Jumil went on. 'In any case, this particular shadowplay is almost done . . .' He glanced in the direction of the burning Keep and Corlek heard the rumble and crash of collapsing walls, followed by a mad giggling from the illusionist woman. Nearby, dor–Galyn groaned.

Jumil regarded Corlek with dark, cruel eyes. The raging glow of the consumed Keep cast a dark shadow across his narrow features, a dividing line that curved from brown eyes down a sharp nose and over smiling lips to a small, rounded chin. Corlek's sword was only a short thrust from the man's heart, but the sorcerous immobility was like webs of razor steel burning in his flesh as he fought to move.

'You have proved to be a nuisance, albeit a resourceful one to have got this far,' Jumil said. 'And I was of a mind to fulfil my servant's desire by taking your life. But I've thought of an interesting way for you to serve my purpose.'

'I will . . . never . . . serve you . . . !' Corlek managed to whisper.

'An empty vow,' Jumil said. 'From an empty vessel, but soon you will be full.'

Then he made a slight gesture, and the icy web within Corlek's body flashed through his limbs, body and head like a whip of white fire, consuming his mind and every last fading thought.

Chapter Nine

Night's dread bears down upon us,
Like a ghastly ship with a ghastly cargo.

Ralgar Morth, *The Watchman's Journal*, Ch. 2

The Amatellis Retreat of the Carver Faithful was a former ware-house on the south bank of the Valewater, out to the west of Sejeend. Its tall, mortared walls were cracked and flaking and stained with years of rainwater runnels, yet they had been sturdily built and provided a sense of security for its occupants and those to whom it gave shelter. After dark, its high walls took on the aspect of a stronghold with a couple of torches burning over the big entrance doors, near a row of small windows where sentries could be seen from time to time.

Inside, in a long, high chamber which had once been the main loading yard, the dull yellow glow of a few rushlights revealed the rows of blanket-wrapped forms lying on pallets on the cold, cobbled floor. In accordance with the Carver's teachings, the Retreat offered such succour to travellers and pilgrims, as well as the unfortunate, the troubled and the destitute. Halos of heat came from a few wrought-iron braziers and a big fire burning in a massive hearth at the far end of the great chamber.

It was near there, between two long tables, that Sounek lay, vainly trying to find a comfortable position atop his thinly stuffed pallet. Dressed in threadbare garments, worn-out boots and an empty rapier scabbard, with a silk-lined cape as his purported last valuable possession, it had not been hard to portray himself as a penniless aristocrat who had lost estates, wife and all dignity. He told his story to a Carver monk called Lemker who listened

sympathetically then brought him into the warm hall and gave
him a small bowl of hot, meaty soup. Sounek later discovered
that Lemker was a Manualer, the lowest monk in the Carver hier-
archy. He knew little of the actual Carver theology, beyond a
restricted canon of parables, but the next highest monks were the
Iterants who were permitted to study the Outer Books of the
faith. There was only a handful of them in the Amatellis Retreat
and they answered to Litanist Tyorzin who was apparently in
charge. The Litanists were allowed to study the mysterious Inner
Books, along with various other holy writings, and when Lemker
spoke of Tyorzin it was in hushed tones.

So Sounek and several others had listened to Lemker recite a
parable of the Carver while munching on bread and soup, in
common with those at the other tables. At the same time, Sounek
had maintained a farspeech thread with Inryk who was then
creeping across the ledges and watercourses of the Retreat's stepped
roof.

Now, as Sounek shifted on his lumpy pallet, he was conducting
an exchange with his fellow-Watcher, who had just withdrawn
from one of the monks' chambers, after a careful search.

(. . . *and found nothing of interest*) Inryk was saying. (*A few parchments with copied-out catechisms and the like, but no pens or even so
much as a charstick.*)

There must be a scripter room somewhere, Sounek said in farspeech.
But yes — that one sounds like an Iterant.

(*A what?*)

*Iterant, a low-ranking monk. What you need to find is a chamber with
plenty of books and scrolls, that'll be the one used by the Litanist. But
try not to disturb him.*

(*You don't say. Well, I've checked all the casements on this side so it
must be on the other . . . hmmph, liable to fall and break my neck.*)

Please don't. Cleaning up the mess would be a chore.

(*Mmm, funny. And if I find nothing incriminating in this Litanist's
den?*)

*Then we'll have to carry out the same tactic at one of the other Carver
retreats.*

('*S goin' to be a long night.*)

Then the farspeech thread fell silent within Sounek's head, leaving him to his uneven bedding on the cold, cobbled floor. From where he lay, propped up on one elbow, he had a wide view of the big hall, seen from beneath one of the long tables. It was as quiet as such an improvised dormitory could be — a susurrus of slumberous breathing, with a snore here and there, someone muttering briefly in their sleep, a cough, a whimpered conversation. Over by the fire, one of the female Manualers was comforting a weeping child, all of which set off a coil of thought in his mind, the observation that these Carver followers seemed more interested in providing unconditional help and solace to the worst off than indulging in zealous browbeating.

But such observations were irrelevant to the likes of Archmage Tangaroth and Ilgarion — they had already decided who the enemy was and now it was the Watchers' task to provide the proof, that much was clear.

He was lying back, considering the curious matter of Corlek Ondene, when farspeech words stirred in his mind like another's thoughts . . .

(*'M at the other side of the roof*) said Inryk. (*There's three windows so shouldn't take long . . .*)

Is there light in any of them?

(*Not a glimmer . . . but there's some kind of glow coming from back in the centre of town. Thought I saw something earlier but it's brighter now — must be a big fire, but I can't see past the cliffs and the tree.*)

If its important, Sounek said, *we'll know soon enough.*

(*Huh . . . right, now for the first.*)

The farspeech thread dissolved, leaving Sounek to the quiet, dark hall and the flickering fireside shadows. After a while, resting there in the dimness, he thought he could hear a faint rushing sound from outside, as if strong winds were blowing around the building. As it grew louder he realized that it was coming from the street outside the front of the warehouse. Pushing himself up on his elbows he noticed other raised heads just as Inryk's voice bloomed in his mind.

(*This don't look so good, Sounek.*)

What is it?

(*Big angry crowd gathering across the road*) he said. (*A lot of torches and spears . . . they seem to waiting for something though . . .*)

Sounek heard footsteps approaching and looked round to see a worried Lemker quickly waking all nearby sleepers. Elsewhere, other Manualers were rousing the rest.

'Only some noisy drunks out in the street,' Lemker said to them. 'But just for safety's sake, we'd like you to move to the repose chambers upstairs . . .'

(*Ah, they've been waiting for a ram . . .*)

Moments later, something struck the outside of the doors with a heavy thud that reverberated around the hall. There were cries of alarm and the calm procession towards the stairs at the rear turned into a rush. There was another thud, louder than the first, and a simultaneous crack. Struggling free of the panicking crush, Sounek had just staggered against the rough stone wall at the side of the great hearth when there was a third impact which broke the wooden locking bars and sent the great doors crashing open. With a roar, the mob surged into the hall.

(*They've just broke down the doors*) said Inryk. (*Where are you?*)

Nowhere safe, Sounek said, suddenly wishing he'd let himself be carried along with the stampede. Out in the middle of the hall a handful of guards and Manualers armed with battle staves had managed to slow the intruders but they were only moments from being overwhelmed. Sounek dashed across to the right-hand set of stairs just as it began to swing upwards, lifted by heavy hawsers lashed to stanchions jutting from the bottom step. He leaped for the rising edge, caught it and dragged himself over. As helping hands pulled him up onto a landing, he could hear the attackers furiously arguing among themselves while some shouted the word 'Murderers!' over and over.

(*Where are you, Sounek? . . . damn you, answer . . .*)

Gasping with the physical effort, Sounek followed other fearful-looking guests of the Retreat up another flight of stairs, while struggling to get a coherent thought out to Inryk.

I'm . . . out of danger for the moment.

(*Good — I'm on the third floor, so find your way up and we can get out the way I came in.*)

Very well.

At the head of the stairs dozens of frightened people were arguing with some of the monks who were trying to usher them along a narrow passageway. Sounek tried to squeeze past them as they slowly moved into a chamber off one side of the passage; the other side had a series of wooden-framed openings which looked down into the hall. Gazing at one point, he saw that the mob were starting to climb the supports to get at the protruding framework of the upper floor. There was also a worrying, regular thud from directly below.

There were others hurrying along from the far end, where more stairs led up, and as Sounek reached them he heard a clattering bang from just behind him. Glancing round, he saw the black iron claws of a grappling hook embedded in one of the window frames. There was another bang as a second grapple flew through the next window and slid back to dig its claws into the wood. At first Sounek thought they were going to try and climb up to get at the monks, but then there was a deep, wooden cracking sound and he felt the floor jerk and tremble underfoot.

Mother's name! he thought. *They're trying to bring down this floor!*

He leaped towards the next set of steps and was halfway up when something finally gave way with a long creaking groan. Beams twisted and snapped in gouts of splinters and Sounek watched in horror as the passageway tore away from the building's main wall, then dropped suddenly from Sounek's end and crashed onto the floor of the main hall. People fell screaming down the tilting slope or over its jagged edge while others held on to jutting joists laid bare by the manmade destruction.

(Sounek — what's happening?)

Madness — he tried to find words — *They've destroyed half the first floor.*

(Get up here, now!)

But before Sounek could answer, hands grabbed him from behind and hurled him up the last few steps to sprawl on the half-landing. A wild-haired figure drew near and bent over him.

'I was called . . . and he told me that you have to die, you and the other one . . .'

The man was red-eyed and staring and his face was covered in

scratches while blood oozed from his battered ears. His clothing
was in tatters and to Sounek's undersenses he bore the stench of
a malign power. Sounek had the thought-canto Brace ready to
shield himself from attack but before the man could reach for him
someone else descended from the next flight of stairs behind
Sounek, crying out:

'Brigand scum – you defile our retreat!'

Sounek looked up to see a robed form charge at the scratched
man, spearpoint leading. The spear caught him square in the chest,
ran him through and slammed him against the stairway wall, pinning
him there, such was the force of the charge. The scratched man let
out an agonized bellow and struck at the jutting spear shaft with
one hand. With the other he lunged at the robed monk, grabbed
him by the shoulder and with a brute strength hauled him in close.

The terrified monk was striking at his captor with his fists but
to no avail. The scratched man glanced once at Sounek, grinned,
then pulled the monk closer still and bit out his throat. The monk's
scream dissolved into a ghastly, wet crunching sound as Sounek
scrambled to his feet and ran for the steps.

On the second floor was a T-junction with a short doorless
corridor, and from round either corner he could hear the sobs of
children and the raised voices of panicking adults. But the stairs
to the third floor began directly ahead so without pause he hurried
up them two at a time and was relieved to see Inryk emerge from
the shadows near the top.

'Finally,' he muttered. 'Why the delay?'

'An unexpected guest,' said Sounek, panting. 'He has some quite
forceful opinions . . .'

Shouts from below interrupted him, followed by a tormented
scream.

'Ah, that should be him now.'

Together they gazed down to see a nightmarish figure lurch
into view at the foot of the stairs. Blood covered the man's face
and drenched the front of his ragged clothes, while only the splintered stump of the spear now protruded from his chest. He stared
up at them and smiled horribly.

'You both have to die,' he said. 'He told me . . .'

With an agile swiftness that took Sounek and Inryk by surprise, he bounded up the stairs. Sounek jerked backwards in reflex but Inryk held his ground and despatched three fireballs in quick succession. But as they struck the impaled man they broke apart one after another, casting sprays and cascades of flamelets across nearby woodwork and down onto the stairs. Seeing this, Sounek stepped forward and cast the thought-canto Ram, sending a swift fist of air straight at their adversary. The invisible force struck him high in the chest, knocking him off his feet. As he toppled and careened down the steps, roaring in fury, Sounek looked at Inryk.

'To the roof, I think.'

'This way,' Inryk said, hurrying along to an open door to the right of the stairwell. The room within was dark and smelled of incense. A window's shutters stood agape, framing a square of night sky strewn with rags of cloud, dusted with stars. Inryk hauled himself through with the ease of long practice, and Sounek had just swung one leg over the windowsill when he heard the heavy thud of running feet. When he glanced at the door the meagre light beyond was suddenly blotted out by a dark figure which barely paused before charging across the room.

Uttering an incoherent cry he threw himself out onto the narrow slate ledge between the window and the building's low coping stones. The impaled man lunged out after him, making a grab for his legs. For a moment Sounek felt fingers closing on the heel of his boot but Inryk was already dragging him away and pulling him upright. Their pursuer gave a low, rasping snarl and cumbersomely climbed out onto the roof as well.

'Persistent, is he not?' muttered Inryk.

Sounek nodded. 'It's not a trait I care for in hired servants. Gets them into trouble.'

They sidled along the ledge as quickly as they could with the Retreat's sloping, slate roof on one side and a sixty-foot drop on the other. The impaled man almost lost his balance once and thereafter crouched with one hand leaning on the roof as he came after them. Soon they reached the corner of the roof where Inryk halted.

'The knotted rope is here,' he said. 'We'll never get to the bottom before he reaches the ropelash.' He indicated where the heavy rope was tied to an iron lug.

'We'll have to stop him. Or go round and round this damned roof until we fall off!'

Inryk nodded and together they unleashed a barrage of thought-canto spells – arrowfire, burning clouds and jagged webs of lightning. They slowed him down, and Sounek could smell the sharp odour of burnt hair, but still he edged closer and closer. Smoke was rising from the man's disintegrating clothing and the charred spear stump jutting from his chest.

'There is a way,' Inryk said bluntly. 'I'll charge at him and knock him over the edge. He'll probably take me with him, but at least—'

'No, wait, Inryk,' said Sounek with a grim smile, indicating the broken-off spear. 'We've missed the obvious. Listen . . .'

Tashil and Atemor were a street away from the Watchers' lodge when her brother suffered another brief mind-absence, the third since leaving her shop. As before, his gait slowed, his feet dragging, and he became confused, looking groggily about him and muttering to himself. Luckily, the roads in this district were usually deserted at this time of night so she steered him over towards a low wall. He tried to resist but his efforts were weak and uncoordinated and she was able to get him to sit down on the wall.

She began talking to Atemor, speaking his name repeatedly, trying to call him back to himself. It was a terrible thing to behold, this enigmatic spirit which had lodged itself in Atemor's being and was trying to displace him. His face was slack and his eyes were like blank hollows while his lips kept moving, framing words in an unknown tongue, sometimes audible, sometimes not. Once he straightened and looked round to the south, towards the other side of Sejeend, and the tone of his voice changed as if he were asking questions of an unseen presence.

But still Tashil persisted, repeating his name, brushing the pale hair back from his face, stroking his hands, till at last the light of awareness returned to his eyes, as did recognition and an inner dread. He drew a shuddering breath.

'As bad as before?' Tashil said, wiping tears from her face.

'Like . . . like drowning in voices, 'Sheel! – like being hunted by the dead . . .' His voice faltered in horror and he grasped her hands tightly. 'Every time it gets clearer and stronger. I can smell the dust in their breath and feel the touch of their hands . . .' He let go of her hands and covered his face, trembling. 'Help me, 'Sheel, I beg you.'

Knowing she had to be strong, she held back her own emotions and urged him to get to his feet.

'Come – we're nearly there.'

A short while later, with a cold breeze rushing through the trees and raindrops pattering on the bushes, they arrived at the portico entrance to the Watchers' lodge. A lamp burned in a niche by the door, before which stood one of Calabos' burly guards who nodded and let her pass. There were another three guards in the gloomy hall, along with the elderly lodge steward, Enklar. The balding attendant immediately saw how cold and wet they were and beckoned them to follow him.

'The great fire is lit in the common room, my lady,' he said. 'It should be a warming comfort for you both.'

'My thanks, Enklar. And this is my brother, Atemor.'

The old steward glanced round with a smile and a small bow of the head. 'It is an honour, ser.'

But Atemor was grim-faced and gave only the briefest of nods in reply.

'Enklar – am I right in thinking that both Calabos and Dardan are absent?' she said.

'Indeed, my lady. They both departed shortly after yourselves earlier.'

'Did they give any indication of when they might return?'

'Oh no, my lady,' Enklar said. 'Master Calabos did however partake of a cold platter before they left. It may be that he was preparing for a lengthy sojourn.'

The common room was well lit and stuffily warm with the heat of the fire. There was also someone else waiting, a small man in travel-stained monk's robes. Enklar introduced him as Brother Graas, then indicated a side table bearing jugs of ale and water and beakers before leaving the room. Tashil helped her brother out of his damp cloak and leather harness, draping them over a nearby wooden frame along with her own long coat. As she did so, she introduced herself and Atemor to Brother Graas then asked which order he belonged to.

'I am of the Healers' Chapter, milady,' he said. 'I bear a message for Ser Calabos from Bishop Daguval of Hekanseh, which only he must hear.' He paused. 'Pardon my asking, milady, but do you know aught of the fire at the palace?'

She stared in surprise. 'What fire is this?'

Brother Graas looked almost apologetic. 'Well, when I was approaching this part of Sejeend from the north, not too long before your good selves, I chanced to exchange greetings with a herbman who was bound for Adranoth. He told me that Carver zealots had set fire to one of the keeps of the palace, trapping many inside. Everyone burned to death, the Carvers included . . .'

Appalled at this news, Tashil shook her head. 'I didn't know, nor did I notice anything – my mind has been on other matters . . .' Then she remembered the audience called at Ilgarion's behest. *Ayoni will be there now . . . unless she's been hurt – no, we would have known if she was injured or worse . . .*

She glanced at her brother but he was sitting glowering into the fire. How quickly the ordered rhythm of her life, of all their lives, had cracked and fallen apart. Her only hope was that Calabos would know how to expel the presence which was rooting itself in Atemor's soul, without harming him. She had read very little about the discerption rite, and even that had been clear on the mental damage suffered by those who survived such a trial.

But if Enklar was right, he might not return for hours . . . yet it was also possible that awareness of the fire at the palace would prompt him to return here . . .

Sighing, she went over to the side table to pour a drink. The ale had an appealing aroma but she opted instead for the water which gave off the delicate fragrance of imil petals. Brother Graas was already provided with a beaker so she poured out two and was handing one of them to Atemor when she heard a door open in the corridor outside. There were footsteps and muttered voices but it was Sounek and Inryk who entered, not Calabos and Dardan.

Both looked haggard and tense and as Inryk descended upon the ale jug, Sounek fell into a padded chair, a picture of fatigue.

'Calabos?' he asked hoarsely.

'Out in the city somewhere,' Tashil said. 'No word from him, nor from Ayoni.'

'You know about the fire?' Inryk said. Having drained one beaker of ale, he was refilling it. 'On our way back here, we passed a couple of good vantage points and got a good look with my spyglass. The Keep of Day is now just a pile of smoking rubble with only a few blackened sections of the lower walls still standing.' He paused, frowning, and glanced at Atemor who was listening impassively.

'My brother, Atemor,' Tashil explained quickly. 'And this is Brother Graas – he heard a rumour that Carver fanatics are behind the fire – is it true?'

'A lot of city folk certainly think so,' said Sounek. 'Mobs have been burning Carver shrines and Carver-owned shops.' He shared a look with Inryk. 'In fact, we became embroiled in a riot in the west bank district . . .'

He went on to describe his and Inryk's clandestine activity at the Amatellis Retreat and how an angry mob broke down the doors and stormed in. The tale of his escape to the floor above the hall was gripping enough but when he spoke of the impaled man and his seeming immunity to Lesser Power spells, Tashil's blood ran cold as she recalled the hellish hound which had attacked her and Dardan.

In Sounek's account, their inexorable adversary had pursued them up onto the roof and along its edge, impervious to every thought-canto attack.

'And that is when the solution came to me,' Sounek said. 'The Lesser Power was useless against him, but physical attacks worked – after all, he had a piece of spear run through him. So I knew that we needed to hit him while staying out of reach—'

'Roof tiles,' Inryk cut in impatiently. 'We loosened dozens of slates then used Cast to throw them at 'im.' He gave a bleak smile. 'Chopped him up good, they did. Took a while afore he stopped moving, though. Bit like that dog you put down.'

Tashil suddenly realized that her brother was staring at her. Glancing at him, she saw stark fear in his face, clearly provoked

by Sounek's grotesque story. She nodded slightly to him and
reached out to touch his shoulder.

'That quite neatly sums it up,' Sounek said. 'Apart from one
other interesting detail—'

But before he could continue, the sound of opening and closing
doors, footsteps and voices heralded more arrivals. This time it was
Calabos and Dardan, doffing dark cloaks which were collected by
the steward Enklar. Calabos had a dark and grim look about him
as he crossed to a large, sealed desk and unlocked it.

'I know about the fire, my friends,' he said, opening out the
desk's covers. 'We saw it from the west bay docks while we were
trying to find a suitable ferry. Has there been any message from
Ayoni?'

Heads shook and Calabos frowned. 'The city is in uproar and
it'll be impossible to get runners in and out of the palace.' He
glanced at Tashil. 'Did you pick up any useful rumours in the
alehouses? Any mention of the Carvers?'

'Some entertaining ragtalk,' she said, 'but nothing more.'

He turned to Sounek and Inryk. 'Yourselves?'

'Got caught in the middle of a riot,' Inryk said. 'Didn't have
time for much else, apart from—'

Calabos cut him off with a gesture while his other hand plucked
papers and books from the desk's crowded niches. 'We may not
have much time left to us here. With the Keep of Day reduced
to charred wreckage, the Archmage will want to know why we
were unable to prevent it—'

'*You* . . . ! I know you . . . !'

Tashil jerked with fright as her brother suddenly leaped to his
feet, face suffused with rage as he bellowed across the room at
Calabos.

'. . . and I know your face . . . why do I know you . . . ?'

Fists clenched, he tried lunge towards Calabos but Tashil and
the others grabbed him by the arms and legs and wrestled him
onto one of the long divans. By now Atemor was jabbering and
shouting in an unfamiliar language and nothing Tashil could do,
neither stroking his face nor repeating his name, could reach him.

'Who is this?' Calabos said.

'My brother, Atemor,' Tashil said, distraught. Then she quickly told him how Atemor had appeared in her house, and how he seemed have become the host for some kind of malicious spirit. 'He said he was called. What can that mean?'

'I fear that he is the victim of that wave of sorcery from the other night,' Calabos said. 'But I believe I know how to cure this particular malady. Hold him . . .'

Then he was gone, off towards the main hall.

'What . . . is this frenzy?' Dardan said, tightening his grip against Atemor's struggles.

'I think . . . I think that he might be the same as the man Sounek and Inryk fought,' Tashil admitted. 'He was waiting for me at my shop, said that he'd heard a sorcerous calling . . .'

Sounek was appalled. 'And you brought him *here*?'

'He is my brother!' Tashil said angrily.

'Do you recognize him now?' Dardan said.

She regarded Atemor and saw nothing in his eyes or his expression that was familiar. A sob threatened to break free from her throat then Calabos reappeared, carrying a long object about five feet end to end and swathed in a yellow-patterned coverlet.

'Get him to his feet,' he said, stepping round the high-backed divan to face them.

Atemor's fury was unabated and it was a physical trial to haul him upright, after binding his ankles. As his head came level with Calabos' he seemed to calm somewhat and for a long moment the two men locked gazes. Tashil saw Calabos' frown deepen and a hint of dark anger well up in his eyes. Then without looking away he reached with his free hand for the end of the wrapped object, fingers slipping beneath the folds. Was it some kind of charmed staff kept for this kind of discerption, she wondered, or some other form of talisman . . .

But Calabos' hand clenched and there was a grating hiss as he drew out a long, straight broadsword. And light shone from it, a moire radiance, rippling silver and ardent emerald, which caught and trapped the eye.

At the sight of it, a low snarl escaped Atemor's lips.

'Mother's name!' muttered Inryk. 'Isn't that . . . ?'

Suddenly fearful, Tashil said, 'Master, what are you going to—?'

'Trust me,' Calabos said, then, with an unexpectedly lithe strength, he lunged at her brother with the sword, driving it deep into his chest on the right side.

There were gasps and curses, and Tashil let out a cry of horror. But Atemor seemed frozen, rooted to the spot, his mouth half-open, his eyes staring into midair. Tashil, holding on to one of his arms, felt the muscles become locked and rigid. An awful silence gripped them all for a second. Then Calabos swiftly pulled the sword from out of Atemor's chest and Tashil could feel the maddening tension suddenly relax and saw his face grow slack . . . yet at the point where the blade had entered there was no welling forth of blood, not a drop, not a stain.

'Release him,' Calabos said. 'And stand back from him.'

They all did as he asked, with Tashil being the last to do so. The fury and the febrile air had ebbed from Atemor's features and his stance. Looking dazed, he swayed then fell to his knees and one hand, with the other holding his head.

'. . . Screaming . . .' he moaned. 'It's . . . screaming . . .'

With that he slumped over on his side to lie shaking and breathing in shuddering gasps. Wrenched with distress at the sight, Tashil took a step towards him but Calabos stopped her with a brusque gesture.

'No! Leave him be for a few moments yet.'

Even as he spoke, the side of Atemor's head began to darken as if they were watching a great bruise develop before their eyes. But then the dark patch on his skin began to seep out in grey, tenuous tendrils that bunched together, undulating, until they slowly dragged themselves free of Atemor's skull. In appearance, it was a formless ashen thing the size of an infant's hand, thready webs of blackness that writhed in a smoky veil. Tashil shivered as she watched it, feeing dread and malign danger through her under-sense. Everyone was alert and guarded except for Calabos who looked almost ill and burdened as he studied the wraith-like thing.

'Keep your places,' he said, voice low. 'Make your minds calm and—'

He broke off as the wraith rose and floated towards him. He

did not retreat or even so much as flinch, but instead brought the radiant, silver-green sword up to hold it vertically before him with the blade just inches from his own face. The wraith slowed level with his head and put forth grey, wavering tendrils which paused when they reached the bright sword. Then they moved forward again as if to slide round the obstruction, and one of the tendrils touched the metal . . .

In her mind, Tashil heard a brief howl of hate-edged anguish, and the next she knew the wraith darted across the room to pass unimpeded through the wall next to the tall windows. Calabos, his face beaded with sweat, visibly relaxed and let the shining broadsword dip to rest point-down on the floor. Tashil went down on one knee next to her brother who was weakly trying to sit up. But when she parted his shirt, just to make sure, there was not even the slightest mark upon his skin.

'What was that?' she said as she tugged away the rope bonds from Atemor's feet.

'We're eager to know as well,' Sounek, with Inryk nodding at his side. 'Especially as that's the second one we've seen this night.'

Calabos straightened and stared at them both.

'Go on.'

Sounek gave a curtailed version of his earlier account, ending with a description of an event near identical to that which they had all just witnessed.

'One such might be considered strange,' muttered Dardan. 'Two suggests something more.'

'I think you can all guess my own hypothesis,' Calabos said.

'Fragments of the Lord of Twilight,' Tashil said as she helped Atemor to stand. 'Gathering together—'

'Being gathered together,' Calabos said. 'There is a malevolent guile behind this, the one who made that sorcerous calling, which has drawn who knows how many unfortunates to Sejeend.' He turned to Atemor. 'Including our guest. How do you feel now, young man?'

Atemor glanced nervously at Tashil who gave him an encouraging smile.

'I am . . . well. I dreamed that you pierced me with that blade,

elder ser, just before the black fist took me, yet when I awoke
there was no wound.' Atemor looked down at his open shirt, then
up at Calabos. 'Is this a good thing, or an evil thing?'

'I cannot answer such a question,' Calabos said. 'But I'm sure
that you are glad to be rid of the illness in your mind.'

'That handy bodkin,' Inryk said. 'The sword of powers, ain't it?'

'That it is,' said Calabos, holding up the blade to admire its
radiant surface. 'Forged by the Archmage Bardow during the siege
of Besh-Darok, stolen during the reign of Tavalir the Fourth, recovered from baneful hands by an old friend who then passed it into
my keeping. We will have need of it in the days ahead.'

'And just what are we going to do in the days ahead?' said
Sounek. 'We know precious little about this sorcerer.'

'Could be a connection with the Carvers,' Dardan said. 'If they
did set the Keep alight like folks're saying.'

Sounek shook his head. 'It doesn't ring true to me, but we
might have known more if the Countess had bothered to contact
any of us.'

'Chellour and Dybel are also inside the palace,' Calabos said.
'Nothing has been heard from any of them since the start of that
audience of Ilgarion's.'

Tashil chose that moment to speak. 'I could try and reach her now
with a bonding scry, Calabos – Ayoni and I do have a slight affinity.'

The elderly mage regarded her for a moment, then smiled and
nodded. Tashil sat down on a vine-patterned pale green settle,
breathed in and out steadily to calm and clear her mind. Through
her undersenses she could discern everyone nearby but knew she
had to focus her perceptions and push them out, further out,
further still . . .

The walls of Sejeend became ghostly barriers, a city of smoke
and glass through which her senses drifted. Amongst the feeble
glows of thousands of minds she wandered, listening and searching
for the familiar hue-taste of Ayoni's presence . . . and saw/felt it
from a landmark she knew, the imperial palace. But as she
approached it she quickly became aware of other, stronger minds
who were guarding the vicinity. None seemed to notice her
snooping on the fringes so she floated nearer . . . until suddenly

she felt a swift and harsh regard sweep over her and stop for a moment before moving on. For an instant she found herself scrutinized by a dark and pitiless intellect which scarcely bothered to conceal its withering contempt for her.

The encounter shook her to the core, disrupting her focus, and suddenly she was back in the common room, seated on the settle with a trembling in her limbs. Everyone, she realized, was waiting for her to speak.

'Ayoni is still at the palace,' Tashil said. 'But she's confined, by mage guards as well as the ordinary kind.'

'Dybel and Chellour?' Calabos said.

'I found no sign of them,' she said, 'but someone else at the palace spotted me so I had to return before I could search for them properly.'

Calabos' eyes narrowed. 'You were careful?'

'As careful as I could be, being stealthy and masking my thoughts,' she said. 'But this person saw through me immediately.' She shivered. 'An unpleasant mind.'

Dardan gave a dry chuckle. 'The august Archmage?'

Calabos frowned. 'I wouldn't have thought Tangaroth capable of such quickness of mind but with Ayoni in his custody we'll have to assume the worst, that he and his subordinate will be coming for the rest of us.'

'Could the Archmage be in league with our adversary, this dark sorcerer?' Tashil said.

'There is a possibility . . .' Calabos considered it for a moment then shook his head. 'No, my instincts tell me that he's following schemes of his own devising. But still it comes down to not knowing exactly what happened at the palace and being unable to contact the Countess.'

'I do not know if it would be of service,' said a hesitant voice, 'but the High Sister at the imperial palace is a friend of mine.'

As all eyes turned to regard the speaker, recollection leaped into Tashil's thoughts.

'My deepest apologies, ser, for having neglected you,' she said to the Healer monk who had been sitting patiently by the wall. 'Master Calabos – this is Brother Graas from Hekanseh.'

'From the House of Seclusion,' Graas added as he stood and came over to Calabos and gave a small bow.

'Brother Graas,' he said, features uncertain. 'Your offer to act as our intermediary is most welcome, but I imagine that you are here for quite a different reason.'

'Indeed, ser. I bear a message from Bishop Daguval but it is for your ears alone.'

'Does it concern my cousin?'

'It does.'

'You may speak your message openly,' Calabos said. 'Everyone here is trustworthy.'

'As you wish,' Graas said. 'The Bishop's message is – "Tell the honourable Calabos that his cousin has taken it upon himself to depart our House, but we are conducting a widening search for him." That is the whole of it.'

Calabos' frown deepened and he was quiet for a long moment. Tashil had not known that a cousin of Calabos had been living so close to Sejeend. She thought to ask Calabos who he was then remembered that Houses of Seclusion were dedicated to the study and remedy of derangement and decided to stay silent.

'Thank you for bringing me this sad news, Brother Graas,' he said at last, then addressed all those present. 'My poor cousin Gurric was sent to my charge by the family elders but the Healers at Hekanseh have had little success in improving his condition.' He looked at Brother Graas once more. 'When you return, you must convey to the bishop my deepest thanks for all his efforts but before you depart from Sejeend might it be possible for you to call upon your friend at the palace and pass on a message for the Countess Ayoni?'

'I would be willing to try, ser,' Brother Graas said. 'Provided my own mission is not placed in peril.'

'I understand your duty, brother. Our duty commands that we now abandon this lodge and seek refuge beyond the city – this is the knowledge that I wish passed on the Countess.'

'Am I to go with you?' said Atemor suddenly, looking from Calabos to Tashil. 'Are you making me your prisoner?'

'Atti,' she said. 'There is danger everywhere—'

'And the sorcerer who drew you to this city now knows of you,' Calabos said sternly. 'And he knows that you have encountered us, thus were you to fall into his hands you would be but a morsel for his hunger; stay with us and fate may be kinder. The choice is yours.'

Atemor looked burdened and uncertain and Tashil leaned in close to him.

'Come with us, Atti – it will be safer.'

Her brother gave a rueful smile. 'Our father will have much to say when he learns of this.'

'If you live to hear it,' Tashil said, 'he can say what he likes.'

Calabos smiled at them both. 'Good – that's settled.'

He gathered everyone closer and doled out a series of orders, items and supplies that each person was to bring to the hall, and brought the steward Enklar in to help. As Tashil and her brother hurried off in search of blankets and waterproof cloaks, she glanced back to see Calabos and the Healer monk move over to the fire.

'Now, Brother Graas – this message for the Countess . . .'

It had been a long, strange night for Coireg Mazaret, a disconnected series of lucid moments strung out through the shadows and streets of the city. At the start there had been glimpses of the countryside around Hekanseh, then vague impressions of a ride in a wooden cart, snatches of cobbled roads and the inky black openings of lightless alleyways. Other sights had also imprinted themselves upon his memory – that of a great fire burning at the palace up on the clifftop, like tongues and sheets of lurid flame rushing upwards into the funereal night. Or of an angry mob brandishing clubs and spears and striding purposefully through the town. Or fleeing stone-throwing beggar children and having to hide in a small, wooded park west of the centre of the city, on a rise near the base of the cliffs.

It was there that Coireg regained his sanity for a long blessed moment which, to his surprise, continued uninterrupted. Surroundings slowly made sense and he realized that he was on his knees in long, wet grass, crouching in a curled-up position. Gingerly he raised his head, eyed the darkness, then licked his dry, cracked lips and sat up straighter. The grass before him was strewn with various small roots, tubers and mushrooms, and as the long moment went by he grew aware of a bitter, gritty taste in his mouth. A shaky chuckle escaped his lips – clearly his insane other self had been trying to concoct a potion for some malefic purpose. Instead, it seemed to have subdued him in some way, put him to sleep perhaps.

He leaned back on his hands, let his head loll on his neck, then inhaled the cool, green moistness of the park and breathed out slowly. And still he was himself. A seedling feeling of elation threatened to burst forth but he kept an iron control over his emotions, remembering innumerable similar instances across the three centuries of this erratic life. Like the previous night when, as now, he had been enjoying an extended period of calm in his shabby, lamplit room, pottering happily with a pen and ink, writing a few notes in a small journal. Then he began to hear a vague susurrus, like a faint breeze, which steadily grew to a trickle of whispers, than a babbling clamour of tongues riding above a deep, wide voice intoning a ceaseless flow of syllables. It tore through his mind like a storm, uprooting his thoughts, stripping away every vestige of hope, leaving him clinging to awareness out of raw, reflexive desperation.

Then his insane self had stirred, tossed Coireg aside and embraced the thunderous torrent of eldritch power. And answered its call by escaping from the House of Seclusion and embarking on a wild quest through the night which led to this untended, dilapidated park overlooking the docks.

Coireg relaxed, taking in the peacefulness of the trees and bushes, noticing the tiny rustles of small creatures in the foliage above and the weed-choked flower beds just a few feet away. Yet there was an underlying tension to his state of mind, an inner watchfulness that stemmed from the burden of the past, an expectation of a return to emptiness.

'Waiting for oblivion,' he whispered to the darkness.

'It may be some time coming,' said a deep voice from beyond the vine-entangled trees. 'The dose he took should keep him submerged in your mind for a few hours yet. But when it wears off, he will be unlikely to partake of that particular combination of ingredients again.'

Coireg felt at once alarmed and resigned.

'How do you . . . how *can* you know the ways of my torment? Who are you that you can see such things?'

'My people are possessed of certain unusual talents, including eyes that can pierce the skin of life, thus exposing a little of the bones that lie beneath.'

The shadows around the trees were a mingling of vague shapes and outlines which betrayed no clues as to the observer's identity.

'So what lies beneath my skin?' Coireg said bleakly.

'A mind divided against itself,' was the reply. 'And in every crack and gash resides the embers of an ancient power. Thy appearance is that of a man in his fifth decade yet I can see that thou art much, much older . . .'

Feeling the onset of panic, Coireg got to his feet.

'Why that's . . . ridiculous,' he said. 'Fool's talk.'

'There is no need to be alarmed,' the other said. 'There are none but you and me in this little wood, and if you decide to leave I shall not try to prevent it. If you do, however, you may be assured that your darker image will reawake and consign you to oblivion once more. But if you return with me to my ship, our apothecary will know how to prepare a draught that will keep your other self from surfacing.'

Uncertainty and fear swung round into a fierce hope which he strove to master. Unsure whether or not to trust the offer, he paused and regarded the darkened trees.

'How do I know that I can believe you?' he said. 'Why do you not show yourself?'

There was no immediate reply, but he heard foliage rustle and snap as a tall figure emerged from the shadows. By now the first glimmers of pre-dawn were lightening one side of the sky and Coireg saw long-jawed, gaunt features beneath unkempt hair. The man wore a long, dark coat and his empty hands hung loosely at his sides.

'What is your name?' said Coireg.

'I am called Qothan. And you?'

'Coireg . . . Coireg Mazaret!' he said defiantly.

'That would explain a great deal,' the man said.

Coireg stared at him. 'Will your apothecary give me a potion which could still this monster in my head for good?'

'I have seen him concoct such a remedy in the past, yes.'

'Then I will go with you to your ship.'

As he said the words, Coireg had the sense that he was fated to do this. Fear and uncertainty still churned in his thoughts and he felt a stab of guilt at not having sought out Calabos first, but he had chosen his course and would hold to it. Qothan beckoned him to follow and Coireg hurried across the grassy clearing. A path led to a gate in the hedgerow which enclosed the park, and outside a cobbled street led downhill to the docks and a forest of masts and spars.

'You said that your people possess unusual talents,' Coireg said. 'What tribe or clan are they?'

Qothan was silent for a moment as they walked, then said: 'In all our travels along these and other coasts we have both assumed and been given several names. New names come with new loyalties which is good since time and tide have ground the old ones away to dust.' He seemed to grow impatient with his own words. 'Ser Mazaret, once we were the ones who served – once we were known as the Daemonkind.'

Part Two

Chapter Ten

> Into the grey veil of the sea
> Vast sepulchre of the world,
> We shall cast thine idols and thy bones,
> Safe in that bleak, eternal tomb,
> Trapped in those chilling depths,
> Eaten by rot in the abyss.

> Ralgar Morth, *The Floating Fortress*, canto xxiii

With every sail rigged to catch the fitful morning breeze, the *Mocker* slid slowly through the shifting banks of mist. The crew went about their duties, manning the braces, heaving the lead, sweeping the decks, yet all their activity and every word and laugh was muffled by the enclosing grey shroud. The rattle of chains, the knock of booms and spars, the creaks from the hull, all deadened. Even the slow beat of the *Mocker*'s guide bell seemed reduced to a muted clang.

Up on the helm deck, Captain Bureng lounged in a decaying wicker divan brought out from his cabin earlier. Before him, on a mildewed pillow of red silk, was the Crevalcor Codex, its yellowing pages held flat by one hand while the other periodically raised to his lips a short clay pipe from which he would suck and savour a sweet and heady smoke.

And even as his eyes traced the angular writing on those wrinkled pages, his senses were alive to the surrounding grey-veiled waters, to the great, slow mass of the *Mocker*, and to the moods and movements of his crew. This quest of his to go in search of the remains of Hanavok's fleet had stirred superstitious anxiety in them and now a web of dread held them in its toils.

Such children are these, he thought. *Even the likes of Flane and Logrum — I can see that now. I will be able to bring all of you to believe in me and my destiny, all of you, eventually.* He laughed to himself. *And long before that I plan to have the truth of my destiny laid bare, that I may understand it, and change it if need be. But first I must seize Sejeend, break it to my will and find out what is drawing me there . . .*

A whim of thirst came over him and he raised a beckoning hand. Moments later Cursed Rikken was at his shoulder with a bronze-lined wooden stoup of mulled wine. Pungent steam wreathed the vessel as Bureng accepted it. He then drew once on his pipe and expelled a feathering plume of smoke before putting the stoup to his lips and drinking deeply. The wine was a scalding runnel spilling into his stomach, sending a thrill of flavour and heat through him. Ever since that night in Umbril Cove, when he was overcome by his destiny, his senses had become more perceptive somehow, allowing him to discern the depths and levels of smells, tastes and sounds. He could even tell when someone was lying by listening to their words and smelling the taint of their skin.

Which was why conversations with Flane, captain of the *Bitter Biter*, were so aggravating for it seemed that the man was lying all the time.

Finishing off the wine, he held out the stoup for another measure . . . and with a sideways glance saw that Rikken was staring over his shoulder at the open book. Rikken gave a start and almost snatched the beaker from Bureng's hand in panic.

'Sorry, master, sorry . . . ! I never meant . . .'

'Enough of that, enough!' Bureng said, amused at the man's quivering fear. 'Betrayed by your eyes, eh, Rikken? So, d'you know aught of the old tongues of the Grey Lord?'

'N-nay, captain.'

'Then have you the wit to comprehend the glyphs of the ancient and noble Othazi script?'

A shake of the head.

Bureng smiled, aware that all those on the helm deck – the tillerman, the rig-caller, and his lieutenants – were all watching and listening. Thus he laid a splayed hand on the aged pages of the codex, then tapped the intricate designs which he had been studying, five quiet taps.

'Crevalcor knew,' he said. 'He was a sorcerer of the Well who knew how to draw power together, how to focus it, and he knew how to make the dead obey . . .'

A few feet away, the helmsman shuddered at his wheel while others muttered fragments of useless prayers under their breath or made surreptitious warding gestures. Bureng sensed all this but continued.

'His writings are clear and offer an abundance of guidance. Five metal objects must be taken from the wrecks of Hanavok's ships and once engraved with these metaglyphs they will serve us well . . .'

He paused, suddenly aware of something in the vicinity, something drawing near. He closed the book and got to his feet.

'We are *close*,' he said. 'Very close . . . *Lookout! What vantage?*'

'Port and aft – no sighting,' came a voice from atop the stern mast.

'Starboard and for'ard . . . coastline I see, 'bout five furlongs off the starboard bow!' came another.

'Sickle Bay at last,' Bureng said. 'Ringer – double the strike!'

The quickened belling rang out through the mist, a pre-arranged signal that they had reached their destination. The wind was rising now, tearing long gaps in the mist, but Bureng did not need sight or the sun to know whereabouts on the seabed Hanavok's wrecks lay mouldering. For the interleaving of his senses and his destiny led him on, as if there were some strange eye in his head which could see things hidden to others. He *knew* where those wrecks were and with the Crevalcor book under his arm he stood by his helmsman, ordering course changes and the reefing of sails until the *Mocker* reached a certain spot about half a furlong out from the bay's eastern shore.

'Drop the anchors!' he cried. 'Smartly now – we don't want to be staved in by the rocks that did for Hanavok.'

As a frenzy of action erupted down on the main deck, he stood stock still, seemingly staring out at the hillocky land beyond the shore of the bay. But his senses were taking in the depths that stretched below his ship, sinking down the few fathoms to where shadowed hulks lay motionless amid jagged stones and forktail sharks . . .

Ah yes, this is the place, he thought. *The graveyard of a thousand ships, a cold and desolate prison. Soon I will force it to give up its ghosts.*

He called his lieutenants to him and issued orders, with the last given to the man he had put in charge of the diving teams.

'Things of gold and silver are what I want most of all, Arik,' Bureng said. 'Otherwise, things of iron or bronze or copper. And I'll be calling the boats back in about two hours so your boys had better work hard and fast.'

'Aye, they will that,' said Arik, a burly, balding man known as the Bull to the rest of the crew.

'And coins,' Bureng said. 'I need a good number of smaller valuables, pearls or gems, as many as you find.'

As Bull Arik hurried off to join the divers, who were already clambering over the side, Bureng spotted Cursed Rikken still standing by the brazier where he mulled up the wine.

'Rikken,' he said, gesturing the man over. 'We'll be receiving guests soon so get you to the galley and bring up a keg of ale and cask of goldpurl, and half a dozen jacks.'

'I will, master,' Rikken said, then gathered up his various containers before hurrying below.

See how eager he is to please and how quick to fear, Bureng thought. *You could not ask for a better servant.*

As the boats of divers rowed out from the *Mocker,* the grey shapes of the other pirate vessels emerged from the veiled distance, following the tolling of the ship's bell. Their wraith-like appearance grew solid as the fitful breeze chased away the mists. Bureng paced the confines of the helm deck, still holding the Crevalcor Codex, while regularly glancing over at where the small boats were now riding the swell on their own anchor lines. And all the time he was aware of the other four captains observing the divers from their own vessels, waiting for him to run up the congering banner to invite them aboard.

Raleth spins a coin in the air, his inner perception told him. *Zanuur writes in a journal, Logrum throws daggers into a wooden bulkhead, while Flane just watches.*

The sun had slipped behind angry orange clouds by the time one of Bureng's lieutenants turned the hourglass for the second time. Bureng closed his book and nodded.

'Wave the red flag,' he said. 'Bring 'em back in.'

Seeing this, the divers ceased their explorations and when the last was onboard, the boats began rowing back to the *Mocker*. Before long, dripping sacks of plunder were being handed up to the helm deck where Bureng had ordered a weighted trestle table set out earlier. As he looked on, two of the galley boys emptied out the first of the sacks and began sorting through a variety of unrecognizable objects clogged with mud, weeds and other seabed detritus.

Periodically, Bureng's attention fastened on this or that lump which was then plunged into a large basin of water and scrubbed to reveal its details. But more often than not they turned out to be pieces of pottery, bone and skull fragments, and a couple of carven marble bulkhead ornaments. As the contents of each sack was pawed through and rejected his mood darkened while his temper grew short.

'Rubbish,' he muttered. 'Rubbish and dross!' He glanced at Bull Arik who stood at the end of the table, trying to conceal his edginess. 'Did you hear *nothing* that I said? Metal is what I need, even the meanest iron bucket – not *this* . . .' As he spoke another sack-load proved to be only a tangle of seaweed, scraps of sail, rotting leather shoes and potsherds. Bureng roundly cursed the filthy debris and was about to extend his despite to the divers gathered fearfully down on the main deck . . .

When one of the last of the sacks made a dull clanking sound as it was upended onto the table. All eyes turned as the mud-splashed galley boys dug vigorously into the noisome contents, decaying wads of cloth, frayed netting, the jawbone of a horse – and a piece of iron chain about four feet long.

May be of use, he thought, *should we uncover no coin.*

Frowning, he nodded and the chain was washed and put to one side.

After that finds came to light more readily – a round bronze shield, a plain iron helm, a bronze lantern, a brass statuette of a

bear, and a small silver hand mirror, its surface pitted by corrosion.
The last sack held more bones, disintegrating knots of rope, a few
lead playing pieces for the game Peril, and a small iron-bound,
wooden chest which rattled dully when shook. A blow from a
handaxe broke the rusted lock and a slurry of mud and sand poured
out, along with a score or more of gold and silver coins. Bureng
smiled and his smile was reflected in everyone else's face.

'Good, good,' he said, scooping up a handful of the coins and
letting them fall tinkling back into the chest. Then he spoke to
one of the galley boys: 'Get a hammer and pincers from Grezak
the ironmaster, take that chain apart and put the links in with the
coin.' He glanced at the other boy. 'Clear away the rest of this
stinking filth and wipe down the table . . . and I want it clean and
dry, hear?'

As they hastily went about their tasks, Bureng straightened and
sniffed the air. It was after sundown and the redness on the horizon
was drowning in the dark grey of rising night, and the air was
cool and damp while an inconstant breeze blew off the shore.
Colder weather was on its way, he surmised, but more likely as
fog or mist rather than rain. Then he caught sight of Cursed
Rikken standing by the deck's wooden railing on which he had
hung a closed-up wickerwork creel.

'That you ready for our guests, Rikken?' he said.

Rikken grinned then turned to open the creel, revealing the
stubby, stoppered necks of two clay kegs. 'Ready, captain.'

'Very fine, indeed. Now, someone run up the congering banner
– time to announce our most hospitable invitation . . .'

'The other ships are putting out boats already, captain,' said
Ferm, one of his lieutenants. 'One's near halfway to us.'

Bureng nodded as his inner eye widened to take in the seen
and the unseen. *Hither comes Zanuur, having written in his journal
and closed the cover. After him comes Logrum who dreams of plundering
Sejeend; third is Raleth and last is Flane, a most perilous man . . .*

He smiled at his inner thoughts, at their acute wisdom and
caution, pleased at the way some of them seemed to arise from
his mind of their own volition. Perhaps they were really the secret
voice of his destiny, watching and guiding.

Before long, the wiry, dark-complexioned figure of Zanuur climbed up onto the helm deck. A leather headband studded with semi-precious stones circled his brow, restraining long brown hair, while a faintly disdainful smile tugged at the man's lips.

'Waiting can be a burden,' he said. 'Thus here I am. And my compatriots are not far behind.'

Bureng shrugged. 'Some things cannot be hurried, Zanuur, so you'll still have to wait . . . Rikken, pour the man a drink.'

With that he went over to stand behind the trestle table, now scrubbed, wiped and covered with a ragged-edged length of sky-blue sateen on which the metal trophies were arrayed. He then carefully opened the Crevalcor Codex on the table and studied the interlocking intricacies that made up the metaglyph patterns, following the lines and loops, the repeating emblem-forms, the progressions of orthograms, all intended to channel the volatile power of the Wellsource into specific functions and effects. But only when the patterns were inscribed with a nimbus of power could they fulfil Crevalcor's intent. So Bureng took from within his long, heavy coat a jeweller's lancet, then cleared his mind to allow the sharp flux of the Wellsource to rise through him until he could taste its glassy flavour in his mouth and see its emerald glitter in his sight. When he felt it tingle in the fingers that held the diamond-tipped instrument, he bent over to study the first pattern in the codex then drew the bronze lantern closer and began.

All his will and purpose was sunk into this task, yet as he worked part of his mind could not help but be aware of his surroundings – Zanuur tasted Rikken's ale then asked for the goldpurl instead; Logrum of the *Vandal Lord* arrived and demanded a cup of each; Raleth of the *Iron Fist* was next to appear, choosing a beaker of ale; Flane was last, even though the *Bitter Biter* was moored closest to the *Mocker*.

Bureng was less than halfway through the lantern engraving when Flane appeared. He sensed the corsair captain's grim regard from the moment he stepped onto the helm deck, ignored the others and came over to stand at one end of the table. A brief moment passed, then Flane casually picked up the iron helm as if to examine it closely . . .

'Be so kind,' Bureng said levelly, 'as to leave that well alone.'

Everyone nearby seemed to hear the danger in his voice, as he had intended, and all eyes were on the two men. Flane appeared not to notice as he ran his thumbnail over dents in the helm.

'What *is* all this for?' he said.

It took sheer effort of will to keep his composure while maintaining the tightly controlled flux of Wellsource power. Lifting the gleaming tip of the lancet from the lantern's side, he looked up at Flane.

'I have already explained,' he said. 'The black sorcery of the dead – remember, captain? Each of these objects will become a talisman of great power, and you shall have one . . .' He took a sideways step and calmly plucked the helmet from Flane's unresisting hands, replacing it on the table. 'But not yet.'

Then he returned to the lantern, lancet tip poised to resume its chasing.

'I know a little magery,' came Flane's voice. 'Perhaps I might help quicken matters.'

'Your abilities would not be sufficient, captain. Be patient.'

'Well, ser, if I can render any assistance—'

'No, I need nothing from you.'

'Not even these?'

There was a soft, clinking thud as something landed on the table top. Bureng glanced up to see a fist-sized pouch lying there with gold coins spilling from its loosely tied neck.

'I sent one of my men down for a look at the wrecks,' Flane said. 'He came back with that.'

Bureng switched his gaze to Flane, and held that one-eyed stare.

A perilous man, came the thoughts of his inner eye. *He could endanger your plans and mar the shining perfection of your destiny. You must deal with him, but not straight away – in time he will provide reason enough for you to crush him utterly. For now, however, he has his uses . . .*

Bureng let a wolfish grin show, then reached for the pouch and tipped out the rest of the coins.

'Yes, these would indeed be of use. The five talismans I am trying to create will act as sources of the reviving spells, while these coins and others will be bound to the talismans and placed in the wrecks below, thus anchoring the power of the spells.' A sneer crept into his smile. 'Is your curiosity satisfied, Flane?'

'Only by the merest amount,' said the captain of the *Bitter Biter*. 'But it will do for now.'

He turned his back on Bureng, gazing out at the gloomy shore-line of Sickle Bay. Bureng stared at him for a long hate-filled moment, then forced his attention back to the task at hand.

During the next hour of waiting, Raleth swapped a series of ribald jokes with Logrum, each striving to outdo the other with obscene grotesquerie. After this, Logrum engaged Zanuur in a banter exchange that grew sarcastic and vicious, ending with Zanuur stalking off to the bows, his face like thunder. Logrum then proceeded to drink cup after cup of the goldpurl until the small cask ran dry, and was about to start on the ale when Raleth objected. Disagreement over this quickly led to raised voices that were added to by a returned Zanuur. It would have resulted in angry oaths and drawn daggers had not Flane interrupted.

'Cease this din!' he exclaimed. 'Mother's name, I've heard harbour-scolds make less noise than you bickering whelps!'

'They'd be a lot quieter if they were over the side, cooling their heads in the water,' Bureng said with an unkind smile.

'I'll open the guts of anyone what lays hands on me . . .' Then he gave Bureng a narrow-eyed look. 'You done with yer scratchin'?'

'The engravings are finished, each a perfect coil of braided spell emblems and each one made to interlock with the others.' On the table before him they lay – helm, shield, bear statuette, hand-mirror, and lantern, placed neatly around the small chest which now held all the coins and the chain links. A faint emerald radiance gleamed in the grooves of the patterns on the talismans, suffusing the metal of each.

'And now?' said Flane as he and the others approached the table.

'And now,' Bureng said, 'it is time for the word!'

And up from the dark pool in his mind came a long word of clashing, guttural syllables. Instantly, the glowing patterns on the talismans flared up in a dazzling burst of viridian light. The other four captains cursed and staggered back, shielding their eyes, Bureng just stared, delighting in the raw and lurid outrush of power. Hot, vivid light drenched the vicinity and for a moment Bureng felt as if he was connected to everything and everything was in his power.

Then the dazzling brilliance of it waned and subsided, leaving the talismans to glow like dull green embers. But he could feel, almost see, bonds and linkages which had not been there before.

'They are ready for you now,' he said and the other captains gathered round as he handed out the talismans one by one. The shield he gave to Raleth, the helm to Zanuur, the bear statuette to Logrum, and the lantern to Flane, while keeping the mirror for himself. The four captains regarded their prizes with a mixture of curiosity and wariness.

'Now what?' said Logrum, who was holding the bear figurine as if it was a cat that might try to escape.

'Now you all return to your ships and either place the talismans in your cabins or keep them on your persons,' Bureng said. 'I will tell you why later. And while you are doing this, the divers will go beneath again to carry these down to the wrecks.'

He indicated the small casket of coins and links, every piece of which now shimmered and glittered with puissance, ready to become a conduit for the powerful spells residing in the talismans.

Bureng beckoned to Bull Arik, overseer of the divers, and placed the casket in his hands.

'Go now with your men,' he said. 'Give one of these thaumaglyphs to each diver for each dive – they are to stow one in every wreck, wedged into a crack or some place where it will be held fast. When all the thaumaglyphs are gone, have the divers stripped and searched – understand?'

Grim and steady, Arik nodded. 'Aye, master.'

Soon, a flotilla of small craft began spreading from the *Mocker*, gigs returning the captains to their ships while some half a dozen skiffs took the divers out to return to the wrecks of the dead.

Soon, Bureng sang in his thoughts. *Soon*.

The early evening was sinking into dimness and a chilly breeze from the north was dying away. Mist was rising, harbinger of the night. At length the diving was done and from his vantage on the helm deck Bureng could see the boats draw together to allow Bull Arik to carry out a search for anything secreted. During which there was a brief struggle followed by a body being rolled over the side, then a solitary diver making a final descent.

When Bull Arik at last returned to the *Mocker*, Bureng was waiting on the short gantry that overlooked the main deck.

'Just one betrayer, Arik?'

'Aye, captain,' the big man said sourly. 'Gref the Honjirman – didn't think he'd be that stupid.'

'Plenty of stupidity in this world, Arik,' Bureng said. 'Who can know when it will burst forth?' He surveyed his crew. 'Now my savage brigands, prepare yourselves and stiffen your spines against mewling cowardice!'

He took the talismanic mirror from within his long coat. He had scraped most of the corrosion from its face but the metal was still dull and deeply tarnished except where the bright silver showed in the grooves of the pattern he had placed there. He stroked the curved frame, muttering the first lines of the conjoining ritual, and the intertwined spell emblem brightened and seemed to writhe. Then the threads of power began to grow from the pattern, extending from the mirror in straight lines out through the air, four stretching across the waters to the ships of his fellow captains while scores angled downwards into the bay, some passing through the woodwork of the *Mocker*. Soon the other talismans had sent their own threads into the deeps and the net of revenance was laid out before him, a web of ghostly tendrils that only he could see.

All was tense silence aboard the *Mocker* and all eyes were on Bureng. The breeze had dropped to naught, the sails hung limply on the crosstrees and the murky waters of Sickle Bay were calm and hazed by mist. Bureng smiled and spoke the next lines of the ritual.

From his and the other four talismans bright emerald motes raced along the conjoining threads and down into the waters. For a moment, nothing – then glows began to flicker in the depths, catching the attention of the crew who crowded the rails to see.

The glows brightened into flashes that streaked through the deeps like eldritch lightning. Clouds of inky darkness seemed to billow past beneath the waves and an ominous rumbling could be heard, the voice of a storm in the abyss.

A strange pressure settled over that part of the bay, over its perfectly flat, undisturbed surface. A faint but creeping odour tainted the air smelling like hot stone one moment, rank rust in the next. From his perch on the deck gantry, Bureng saw some of his men fumble for hidden amulets or mutter charms, among them Cursed Rikken, who was trembling visibly as he held on to a lanyard with both hands. Then Bureng felt something change in the web of power and switched his gaze to the waters off the starboard as the first mast broke the surface.

Then there were others, some whole, many broken, others still bearing the rotting remnants of sails and tangled skeins of rigging, and all draped in kelp and streaming water. Scores of masts were slowly rising now, blackened spars emerging from the waves as the dark storm flickered and rumbled beneath. And after the masts came the ships themselves, their hulls encrusted with barnacles and coral, holed and shattered flanks gushing with outpourings of water laden with silt, sea creatures and rotting detritus.

As the underwater storm abated, pale webs of sorcerous power danced across the decks and played about the rigging. The revenant vessels took on a faint radiance and as the gloom of evening deepened figures began to appear on their decks, advancing stiffly to the deck rails to stare mutely at the five ships of the living. Others were clambering up the decrepit flanks of the motionless hulks to swell the mouldering ranks of the undead. Even at this distance, some of the *Mocker*'s crew were grimacing at the stench of putrefaction.

Satisfied with all that he saw, Bureng took his talismanic mirror in both hands and said:

'Hanavok, admiral of the Sea Horde – come forth! I command you!'

For a long moment there was no indication that his summons had been heard. Then some way off, one large ship started to move, listlessly turning its prow towards the *Mocker* and, without so much as a breath of wind, slid through the calm waters, accompanied by the creak of sodden timbers as the ancient vessel came alongside. Bureng climbed unhurriedly back up to the helm deck as the undead ship slowed to a halt with its high sterncastle looming over the *Mocker*'s aft. With the mirror in one hand, Bureng smiled as he regarded the stern's decayed woodwork, the details of once-elaborate carvings now half-rotted, half-buried beneath oozing hanks of seagrass among which crabs and the like writhed.

A figure stepped out onto a low-railed catwalk running along the side of the sterncastle, almost level with the *Mocker*'s helm deck. The figure was that of a man, or at least the bony remains of a man, garbed in a barbaric armour of scales and spikes, now decayed and rent with gaps. A rusted, pitted helm loosely enclosed a slimy, dripping skull whose eyeless sockets turned in Bureng's direction. As Bureng met that empty gaze he knew that this had to be Hanavok, commander of the Ogucharn Sea Horde and deputy to Siggarak who had led the Pirate Princes against the empire a century ago. The reviving spells continued their work, drawing moisture and other essences from the surroundings in order to refashion the vanished flesh of these necrotic mariners.

And there were neither lips nor tongue within that lichenous jaw, yet still a thready whisper touched Bureng's awareness:

'*You have brought us back to this place – why?*'

'To complete your unfinished task, admiral,' Bureng said. 'To topple the Khatrimantine throne and lay waste to its capital.'

'*We . . . remember . . . but we no longer desire this. We have no desires . . .*'

'But I *do* desire it,' said Bureng. 'And I have laid it upon you to obey my will.'

By now a grey film had spread across the bony planes of Hanavok's skull and a single, pale membranous eye now stared from the right socket.

'*We obey . . . the will . . . what is your command?*'

'To set a course for Sejeend,' Bureng said. 'Once there, to lay siege and break its walls.'

'*It shall be done.*'

As one, the ragged ghost fleet began to move, coming about to

point their prows westward. At the same time, Bureng rapped out
a string of orders to his own crew who carried them out with
the alacrity of men glad to be distracted from the ghastly apparitions amongst which they sailed.

Seeing their fearful faces, he thought — *Be of good cheer, my lucky
lads. Should any of you fall in the battles ahead, I'm sure that Hanavok
will be keen to take on new crew.*

Chapter Eleven

Behold the Nightbarge comes,
To gather in the ghosts,
A harvest of severed dreams,
And derelict desires.

Jedhessa Gant, *The Lords Desolate*, Act II, Sc, ii

The mists of Korfaen Marsh were suffocating and minatory by
night. Strung out along the narrow dike that crossed it, the
company of Watchers had the benefit of three lanterns, borne by
Enklar the steward and Calabos' own lodge-guards, Gillat and Rog.
Yet the light they shed revealed only the Watchers themselves and
the stony path along which they trudged, while the cold and
endless dark hemmed them in on all sides.

It had been nearly six hours since the Watchers had fled Sejeend
and half of that time had been spent crossing Korfaen Marsh, after
a brief discussion of possible routes.

Leading the company on horseback through the uninhabited
wetlands, Calabos was well aware of the others' tensions and
depressed spirits but knew they were hardy enough for this venture.
Then he smiled wryly to himself as Gillat, walking nearby with
his pole-lantern slanted over one shoulder, grumbled under his
breath about the cold and his sore feet.

'Won't be long now, Gillat,' he said. 'We're not far from the
southern edge of the marsh, then it's a short climb to the abandoned tower where we'll bed down for the rest of the night.'

'Abandoned tower, master?' the guard said with an uneasy look.

Calabos chuckled. 'Be at ease, lad – the only thing haunting it
will be our hidden hoard of supplies.'

'If you say so, master.'

True to Calabos' reckoning, some half an hour later the stony track of the dike began to slant gently up to meet higher ground. Soon they were treading a narrow sheep track through thick, hummocky grass and passing by an occasional tangleway bush. The track curved west along a shallow gully for a few dozen paces before coming to a fork where Calabos turned left and led them up a steeper slope.

Then, sudden as the first arrow, a cry, no — two cries from the rear of the company.

Cursing, Calabos reined in his horse, tossed the leads to Gillat then dismounted and hurried past the packhorse and back down the trail. By the light of Enklar's lamp, he could see that the others were already rushing towards the edge of a rocky drop along which the path led for a short distance. Of Rog and the third lantern there was no sign but from the darkness below came grunts, snarls, sounds of struggle. Calabos made a quick tally of all in sight — Gillat was minding the horses, Sounek was alert and close by, Tashil's brother Atemor had his short blade bared but was staying near Enklar, while Tashil and Dardan were dashing beyond the glare of Enklar's lamp as they sought a way down. Which meant that it was Inryk and Rog who were facing peril.

Calabos focussed his senses through his magesight and the darkness grew pale, revealing three figures grappling on the grassy slope below. Two were upright while the third seemed to have an injured leg. Even as they were revealed, the injured one — Rog — got to his feet and with raised dagger threw himself at one of the struggling forms. The dagger punched straight through the man's neck but he seemed scarcely distracted by it and Calabos knew that it was another spirit-host, the third since leaving Sejeend.

The possessed creature was doing his best to throttle Inryk but paused to turn and deal Rog a back-handed blow that sent him flying. That seemed to give Inryk time enough to rally his defiance for in the next moment there was a bright, jagged flash which threw them apart. By then, Tashil and Dardan were able to join the fray and after a few distracting cuts aimed at the creature's legs, Dardan was in a position to decapitate it with a single stroke.

Even then, the headless man continued to writhe horribly on

the ground for another minute or more before blood loss caused it to shudder into stillness. With Dardan aiding the injured Rog, the mages drew back from the corpse and after a long moment the spirit-wraith rose from it, an ashen thing of coiling, undulant webs. It hung in the misty air as if waiting or listening, then began to drift northwards, gathering speed in its flight to Sejeend.

Calabos breathed easily once more and relaxed his grip on the sword of powers. They had dealt with another two spirit-hosts, both of whom had assailed the company within the first hour out from Sejeend. And, as with this enemy, once slain their bodies gave forth vile wraiths which likewise glided away towards Sejeend.

Where our dark adversary is gathering them, I'll wager, he thought grimly. *Some poor unfortunate is being used as a vessel for all the fragments of that mad god. Who knows what will happen if it regains some of that former strength, even if only to the magnitude of one of the Shadowkings . . .*

The rest of the company had regained the pathway and, with Enklar and Atemor, were approaching Calabos.

'How's that leg?' Calabos said to Rog.

Even with Dardan's help, the guard was limping badly.

'Gave it a hefty twist when I landed, ser,' he said. 'Won't be marching anywheres for a while, reckon.'

Calabos patted his shoulder. 'We're only a short distance from our lodge for the night – when you're resting, I'll have Tashil look at that leg for you.' He looked at Dardan. 'Put him on my horse for the rest of the way.'

'Aye.'

Then Inryk drew near, looking dishevelled, his leggings mud-spattered, one hand massaging his neck which bore red marks from the attack.

'I'll live,' he said hoarsely.

'What happened?' Calabos said.

'Bastard was waiting just under the brink of that drop – must be a ledge or some kind of foothold there – and when we passed he popped up and dragged us over the edge. I was lucky enough to land in a patch of mire, unlike poor Rog, then the thing was on me and wouldn't let go.' He paused to clear his throat roughly. 'How many more of them are there?'

'A hard question to answer,' Calabos said, turning to walk beside him. 'If I'm right and they really are the shattered fragments of the Lord of Twilight, there may be scores or even hundreds of potential hosts. But how many of them were touched by that sorcerous calling, and how far out from Sejeend did its influence extend? Only time will tell.'

Inryk gave a wry smile. 'I had hoped for a more comforting reply.'

'Comfort is not exactly my stock-in-trade,' Calabos said. 'Disappointment, however, is always in plentiful supply!'

The remaining stretch of the upward path was an easy walk, apart from the last dozen or so yards which comprised a steep series of steps cut into the pebbly ground, but rounded and weedy from the passage of time. Then at last the dark outer wall of the fort came into view, a square two-storey blockhouse of rough mortared stone whose raised defensive position afforded a good lookout vantage. This had been only one of a string of towers and forts established in a curve around Sejeend by the dukes of Cabringa some two centuries ago when the city was threatened by the marauding fleets of the Dalbari during the brief but savage years of their hegemony.

At some point in the past, one of the rear corners had collapsed owing to either poor construction or enemy attack and brought down part of the upper floor with it. The fallen rubble was now a mossy, grassy mound past which the company wearily filed as they entered the dark fort. The lanterns shed some light on the interior, and the torches were lit and sat in a few rusted wall brackets. Calabos ordered the detritus of cracked bones and discarded birds' nests swept out, then had Dardan, Atemor and Gillat move several large rocks that were heaped in one corner. Beneath them was a trapdoor which swung up with oiled ease, revealing a few steps leading down. Spirits rose as supplies of water and ale, preserved pork and fish, lantern oil and oats were brought up from below. A fire was lit in a charred hearth against one wall and soon handfuls of grain and shredded meat were being added to a bubbling pot of water, along with vegetables and herbs from the packhorse's bags. An appetizing savouriness began to permeate

the interior, yet not all were eagerly awaiting a bowl of food —
Tashil had examined Rog's leg, applied her healing talents then
bandaged the knee and ankle before putting him to sleep under
a couple of thick blankets; meanwhile, a yawning Enklar was dragging forth from the trapdoor supplies a blanket for himself.

Calabos, wrapped in a fur-edged cloak from his own saddle-
bags, regarded them all with a strange mixture of affection and
anxiety that was all too familiar. In 300 years he had seen many
friends die in combat or in accidents, although almost never in
peaceful old age, and his concern for those present was sharpened
by the absence of others. Dybel, Chellour and the Countess Ayoni
were in Tangaroth's hands and possibly endangered by their
unknown adversary. And then there was the news of Coireg's
escape from the Hekanseh House of Seclusion, not to mention
Captain Ondene's vanishing trick.

Who else is to blame for this but me? he thought bitterly. *Three
hundred years should have taught me all I needed to know about ruthless and devious enemies, yet these have repeatedly caught me off-guard.*

He snorted in annoyance. There was no time for the luxury of
self-pity. He had to know what their next steps should be, whether
to continue south into the Kyrloc Hills and the Watchers' hidden
refuge, or to retrace their steps and pit themselves against deadly
powers and cryptic purposes. Knowledge was lacking, but there
was one way to meet that need — Spiritwing.

Solid stone stairs led up the west wall and hardly an eye turned
as he climbed up to the ramparts. Calabos pulled his cloak tighter
against the damp cold and stared out over the marshes. At this
height the mists were thinner and he could see breaks in the
clouds that veiled the sky, fleeting gaps which gave glimpses of
stars. The mist was a grey, torpid mantle whose boundaries were
engulfed by the darkness while a few trees on rocky outcrops
stood like islets in a ghostly sea.

He laid a hand on the cold, hard stone of the rampart, breathed
in deeply, then closed his eyes and breathed out slowly, a steady
exhalation which paced exactly the unfurling in his mind of his
individual Spiritwing thought-canto. As his lungs steadily emptied
he could feel the bonds joining mind to body loosen, feel his senses

come adrift, his perceptions change and broaden. The breath in his throat and the blood in his veins grew tenuous and for a moment he was seeing himself from just a few feet away, seeing past the grey hair and lined face that was his chosen mask to the silt of three centuries of experience and yet further to the cruel and savage memories that belonged to the Shadowking Byrnak . . .

Then he was away, flying across the marshy landscape. To his Spiritwing senses there was no day or night, only the manifestations of life and the history of life's consequences, all of which was laid out before him. For as far as he could see, the land was an immense web of intertwined causes, potentials and hungers, all struggling or diverging, flowing from one place to another or petering out to nothing. Forests were like ancient, mighty creatures holding on to the land with an inexorable grip. Mountains were the vast thoughts of the earth made solid and thrust up to pose a challenge to everything that lived on and around them. Streams were sweet songs coursing through the land, rivers uttered rich braids of melody, while in the distance the boundless choir of the ocean gave forth an eternal euphony.

And through it all ran the gleaming tracery of the Lesser Power, which the ancients knew as the Godriver. When compared with the long-vanished Rootpower, or the sundered Wellsource, it seemed feeble and unwieldy yet its all-pervasive nature conferred a certain balance, a tendency towards harmony.

But there were other minor powers lurking across the land, like little knots of darkness hanging in a many-coloured web. Sometimes it was a particular place, like a stagnant pool or a standing stone, or a crossroads; sometimes it was some living thing, an old, solitary tree, an insect hive or a rats' nest. While not allied to the Watchers' adversaries, they could only be considered as a danger. Calabos sensed them from time to time as he soared overhead, noticing them notice him and feeling a dull, brutal regard, but only fleetingly.

Then suddenly he was nearing the outskirts of Sejeend, its buildings looming like walls and towers of frozen smoke and silvery ice. With a thought he brought his spirit-form to a halt in sight of the imperial palace, then wrapped himself in serenity, sinking down to the darkened ground as he cleared his mind. The city that lay before him was a ferment of vivid, spectral images, the ephemeral outpourings from thousands of dreaming townsfolk, and Calabos focussed on an inner core of waiting stillness around which he envisaged the Spiritwing thought-canto . . .

And the inner waiting stillness changed, became an opening, a gate into the plunging infinity of the Void, a way through . . . but only for thoughts and words.

Ayoni, he said firmly.

At once his spirit-form began to glide forward, passing through the grey, glassy hues of the city, down into the dense shadows of the soil and rock of the ground atop the cliffs. The Spiritwing was carrying him away from the palace and north across the Valewater, keeping to those districts nearest the bay and moving steadily parallel with the shore. He remembered what lay there even as the heavily fortified walls came into view, sheer curtains of ashen translucence along whose ramparts the glows of soldiers patrolled in pairs. This was Hubranda Lock, one of Sejeend's three main garrisons. Calabos could sense Ayoni's presence somewhere within, along with others that he knew – Tangaroth and his senior mages, a score of dukes and barons, Shumond, Lord Commander of the Iron Guard. As his perceptions widened he realized that well over a thousand men were quartered in the barracks while other columns of troops, both cavalry and infantry, were hurrying through the streets towards this place. This was an army in the making, and he knew that Ilgarion must have all but emptied the other two garrisons, Dremari and Kanoth, in order to assemble it.

A slight change in the focus of his senses told him that Chellour was also being held with the bastion, but of Dybel there seemed to be no sign.

What is Ilgarion going to do with this army, he wondered. If this was a response to the burning of the Daykeep then it would be a retribution attack, but the main strength of the Carver theocrats lay in southern Anghatan and western Honjir, and in order to strike at that distance he would require a much larger host, complete with long and vulnerable resupply routes. There was no evidence of that kind of preparation, therefore the object of his retaliation had to be much nearer and smaller . . . like the pilgrims gathering at Besh-Darok.

Yes, Calabos reasoned, *that fits neatly into Ilgarion's petty, self-centred view of the world. But what does he want with Chellour and the Countess? And then there's Dybel . . .*

He cleared his mind once more, and as his inner gate to the Void hesitantly reopened he focussed his perceptions upon one name:

Dybel, he said.

Suddenly he was in motion again, whirling through the ghostly edifices of the city, translucent walls and roofs that flickered past in a torrent of pearly shadows. And out of the tumult loomed the sheer mass of the cliffs west of the Valewater, which the Spiritwing swooped past in a graceful westerly curve, rising gently over the rooftops. But even as he turned along the Gronanvel he felt a presence react to his passing, felt a startled gaze fall upon him followed by a lance of blackest hate which lasted only an instant. Yet it was long enough for Calabos to recognize the taint of that presence from the sorcerous calling of the previous night.

Still further on the Spiritwing took him, slowing as he flew past districts dominated by weavers, wineries and tanners. Through opalescent buildings he swept, drawn ever closer to the foot of the cliffs, gliding in the direction of several sheds and workshops that were clustered near the foot of the Melvio Stairs, a long stairway which led up the cliff face to the very top. Then drifting towards one particular shed, through it to a dark, overgrown gap at the rear where drops and trickles of water fell from the cracked heights of the cliffs, and where a figure sat on a crate, bent over in pain, clutching his side.

Dybel, he said, speaking to the man's thoughts.

The head lifted to show the familiar big-jawed face looking pale and tormented. Water had plastered his brown hair to his skull and strands of it straggled across a furrowed brow, above eyes which betrayed flickers of hope through the anguish.

'Calabos . . . I hear you, but different from farspeech some- how . . .'

I'm right beside you, on the Spiritwing — how bad is the wound?

With eyes tightly closed, Dybel did not answer for a moment, then he opened them and let out a shuddering gasp.

'Double-barbed marksman's arrow, iron-tipped,' he said. 'Caught it in the side while escaping the palace . . .' He paused a moment then went on. 'The point is right up against one of my vitals — can't push it through, and I'm doing all I can to dull the pain and stay awake . . . I haven't the talent for serious healing . . .'

I will send some of the others to get you out of here . . .

'Please, yes, that would be most . . . acceptable, but listen, Ayoni and Chellour—'

Are being held in Hubranda Lock, I know, and I've seen Ilgarion's army.

'But Ayoni is being held hostage against Count Jarryc's good behaviour and agreement to lead Ilgarion's cavalry . . . when they march north in the morning. She and Chellour will be going too as Tangaroth's special . . . guests . . .'

Has anyone from the palace been following your trail, that you know of?

'Don't think so — I feinted tracks eastwards along the clifftop before doubling back to the Kala then slipping through the south-bank streets till I found this resting place . . . Calabos? You still here . . . ?'

But Calabos had become aware of something drawing near, some kind of spirit form radiating a turbulent malice.

Dybel! Flee this place! I've been seen by a hostile presence and it is heading this way. But be near the foot of the Melvio Stairs in two hours' time . . .

Dybel gave no reply save a raised hand as he lurched to his feet and staggered off. Calabos watched him go for a moment then ascended into the air well above the rooftops to meet the approaching menace. While near-invisible to any ordinary observer, to Calabos' eyes it looked like a roiling cluster of lightning-cracked clouds amid which there flew a creature out of legend, a drakken. It was wingless, which indicated that it was the river or lake-inhabiting variety, but its claws were large and powerful-looking as were the fangs in its gaping jaws. A trifurcated tongue writhed in that fiery throat while vapour the colour of bile trailed from flaring nostrils and crimson eyes glared with an unquenchable wrath. Soon Calabos and the drakken were facing each other in midair with only a few cart-lengths between them.

*You*must*die!* were the drakken's first words.

Begone, vermin — it is not yet my time, Calabos said.

*You*dare*to*insult*one*such*as*I?*Your*death*will*be*a*long *masterpiece*of*agony!*

Why should I bandy words with a mere lackey? Enough talking — either prepare for blows or scurry back to your master!

The only reply to this was a bellow of insensate rage as the drakken lunged forward, jaws agape. But Calabos was prepared for this onslaught; he had refined and strengthened the properties of his spirit-form down the many years of his life, and with a word transformed his upper arms into long, flashing blades with which he faced the oncoming monster. Glittering razor-edges cut and slashed and the very form of the drakken seemed to lose coherence as it veered away with the glowing clouds burgeoning around it, concealing.

A suspicion was already forming in Calabos' mind, confirmed when the boiling mass of coruscating clouds subsided and a new shape emerged. It was another mythic creature, the heavily muscled forequarters and snarling visage of a Horncat. But this time Calabos was first to attack, diving in with blade-arms swinging — the Horncat struck out at him with long, gleaming claws but Calabos just severed the forelimb and sliced it to pieces which faded in the darkness. And after several ruthless slashes the Horncat fragmented and dissolved away to reveal a twisted, shrivelled creature whose body was a grotesque amalgam of horse and wolf. As Calabos pressed home his attack the strange being dodged and ducked, uttering a dry screech as it tried to escape. But Calabos was faster and cut it down with surgical blows that left it drifting in several pieces which slowly melted into vapour.

From his reading of folk tale and myth Calabos recognized it as a comavyle, an evil leeching spirit which preyed on the sick and the elderly and was able to cloak itself in different shapes in order to reach its victims. But Calabos was neither sick nor enfeebled, so it was not immediately apparent why it had come for him. Then he gave a grim smile as a familiar, webby amorphous thing emerged from the comavyle's disintegrating remains.

Our unknown adversary has more skill than I imagined, he thought. *To be able to ensnare one of the primal spirits and command it thus . . . he will be a formidable foe.*

As the spirit-wraith glided away across the pale roofs of Sejeend, Calabos turned his gaze inward and envisaged the thought-canto Spiritwing spinning there, a perfect circle of all his self-chosen elements. It took the merest thought to pluck out just one of them, breaking the circle, ending the spell . . .

There was a sudden inrush of vertigo and weight, the twin sensations of returning to the solidity of his body which was being kept steady by the hand which still held onto the stonework. He gasped, then drew a long breath, cold misty air laced with faint odours of mud and marsh.

'So what did you find out?' came a voice from further along the rampart. Dardan.

'They're holding Chellour and the Countess at Hubranda Lock,' Calabos said, going on to relate all that had happened. As he spoke his eyes grew used to the darkness and he was able to make out Dardan's lean face.

'Curious,' Dardan said once he had finished. 'Heard of the comavyles before, but never seen one. Once saw a lickslay by moonlight . . . so who's going back for Dybel?'

'You and Tashil,' he said. 'When you find him, see to his wounds as best you can but don't delay – get him to Murstig with all despatch. It's a small village just past the city boundary along Gronanvel, which is where the rest of us shall meet you.'

'If Dybel is in a bad way,' Dardan said, 'we might have to hire a cart or a boat, though stealing'd be safer. Question is, why Murstig?'

'If Tangaroth is taking his most skilled mages on Ilgarion's punitive expedition, then those left behind would be unlikely to confront us, so we should have a free hand to deal with this master of wraiths.'

Dardan nodded thoughtfully. 'Bring him down now before he gets any stronger.'

'Exactly, which is why I want you and Tashil to leave now. Take my horse – she'll get you both back to the city quickly if you ride double.' Calabos frowned. 'Are you happy to take Tashil or would you prefer one of the others?'

'I've no qualms,' Dardan said, moving towards the stairs. 'She's a good companion and a worthy talent.'

'Fine, but remember to exercise caution and watchfulness . . .' Calabos said.

'Aye, we will, as long as you tell me your Spiritwing secret when next we meet.'

'What do you mean?'

Dardan offered a half-smile. 'My few experiences of Spiritwing left me feeling weak as a kitten in the aftermath, yet you manage to speak and stand up at the same time!'

Inwardly, Calabos cursed this lapse in his outward demeanour while making a dismissive gesture.

'Merely the benefit of my advanced years coupled with the ability to appear more alert than might otherwise be the case!'

The two men laughed, Dardan shaking his head.

'Very well, keep your secrets,' he said, starting down the steps. 'May the light guide you, brother.'

'And you,' said Calabos.

Alone on the ramparts once more, he sniffed the air and frowned as his thoughts returned to Coireg Mazaret and Captain Ondene.

I was unable to protect them, he thought sourly. *May the powers protect them now*. Then, hearing Dardan's voice from below, he hastened to descend the steps, wishing to bid Dardan and Tashil a proper farewell.

There were voices in his head, a ceaseless swirl of whispers, mutters, screams, imprecations, discussions, hysterical weeping, cruel empty laughter, inexorable catechisms, guttural chanting, and a bestial howling. If he concentrated amid this cacophony he could remember when the first of those floating wraith-things had seeped into his head, guided by that evil warlock, Jumil, who had frozen him with a touch. Then, afterwards, he had felt no difference in his mind, no obvious change, until he began hearing brief whispers in an unknown language, then a spoken word or two.

A short while later another wraith-thing appeared and was again led to its new perch within his skull, then another, and another. Soon his very thoughts were drowning in a maelstrom of babble and now, much as he cowered in the recesses of his own over-crowded mind, he cowered on the rug-strewn floor of a dimly lit chamber in an unused wing of the palace. Iron shackles gripped his wrists and ankles but he was scarcely aware of them as he struggled to hold his inner barricades against the torrent of inva-sion, to hold on to himself.

'My name . . . is Corlek Ondene, son of the Baron Arnos Ondene,' he murmured, 'lately returned from . . . the Stormbreaker Isles . . .'

Approaching footsteps and subdued voices made him fall into silence while continuing to mouth the words.

'. . . so when will this coalescence take place?' said one voice he recognized as Vorik dor-Galyn. 'How full of these scintillae will he have to be?'

'This is not easy to determine since this process has never been attempted before,' came a second voice. Haughty and malefic, the sorcerer Jumil. 'But when it comes the change will be dramatic, and you will behold something of the grandeur and might that once walked in these lands!'

'I am . . . humbled by the prospect, master,' was dor-Galyn's flat reply. 'But I merely seek reassurance that this fragment of the Broken One will aid our plans rather than obstruct them.'

'Like speaks unto like, Vorik. Understanding shall become mutual, as will the aims.'

A quiet chuckling came from somewhere, quiet and mad, and Ondene was shocked to realize that it was coming from his own lips.

'The brave captain mocks us,' Vorik said menacingly and his heavy footsteps came nearer. 'Perhaps a punishment is in order.'

'That is not Ondene, fool,' said Jumil, 'but one of his passen-gers. A promising sign . . . and now another arrives! Good, I've been expecting it . . .'

'Expecting?'

'Yes – one of those Watchers has been flitting about the city in spirit-form so I sent a scintilla-bound comavyle after him. It might have been Calabos himself, but in any case the encounter has freed another splinter of the Broken One . . . and there it goes, sinking into its new home . . .'

And Ondene felt nothing, saw nothing, heard nothing different in the clamour that bore down on the last remaining stronghold of himself.

'How many more of these things are there?' said Vorik.

'How many?' Jumil's voice dripped disdain. 'How many cupfuls would make an ocean? How many grains of sand do the beaches contain? How may one measure the essence of a god? No, you would have been better to ask how many might have been touched by my great calling.'

'Master – consider my negligent question suitably modified.'

'Scores upon scores, Vorik. Perhaps even hundreds. But enough of that for now – I must needs discuss the other NightKin Flocks. We must settle upon the final details of their despatch, so that all is ready when the time comes . . .'

Their voices faded as they walked from the room, yet Corlek Ondene lay in the same position as before with an unending malign chuckle spilling from his mouth. But his eyes wept.

It was late morning beneath a grey, unsettled sky by the time Tashil and Dardan came to the Silver Keys, an inn perched on the cliff's edge close to the head of the Melvio Stairs. During the ride from Korfaen Marsh, Tashil had tried several times to reach Dybel with farspeech but only once got anything like a reply – a wordless acknowledgement. This made her wonder if Dybel was too badly injured to move, even after healing. She said as much to Dardan as they dismounted in the courtyard of the Silver Keys.

'Which is why I'll be scouting for a boat while you mend his wounds,' he said before seeking out one of the ostlers to pay for stabling for Calabos' horse.

As they hurried from the inn, Tashil pointed out the difficulties she might face in helping Dybel. 'Extracting a barbed arrow is major surgery,' she said. 'It's not like binding cuts, and it'll leave him and me weakened.'

'Ifs and buts, Tash – let's cross the ford when we come to it.'

Now they were following a gravel path along the cliff edge which had a solid wooden fence to keep children and animals from falling to certain death. On the other side of the path was the ragged, bushy fringe of a wood which extended some way in either direction, broken by the Silver Keys' clearing and a gap beyond the Melvio Stairs where the path forked. And as they came to the head of that long rack of stone steps, Tashil narrowed the focus of her undersenses and spoke in farspeech:

Dybel – we are here. Can you meet us?

(*Come quick . . . they follow . . .*)

She and Dardan exchanged a look of alarm and rushed to dash down the stairs, risking two or three at a time, despite the wear and tear of four centuries of traversing feet as well as innumerable repairs. There were very few people on the stairs and they paid little heed to the two Watchers as they plunged past.

Tashil heard nothing more from Dybel, but about two-thirds of the way down she could see a figure crawling up the side of the steps. A suspicion grew in her mind and when they got to within a score of steps she became certain, and sure enough the person stirred and Dybel's pale face looked up at them, smiling weakly.

'There were guards . . .' he said hoarsely. 'Started searching buildings up the street about . . . an hour ago – had to move . . .'

'I don't see any now,' Dardan said, peering over the balustrade.

Tashil was squatting next to Dybel, examining the wound – a broken arrow shaft was protruding from his side, just below the ribcage. She carefully pulled aside a wad of red-soaked cloth and saw dark edges around the puncture and a lot of discoloured flesh. She frowned and spoke to Dardan.

'He needs treatment now, but we can't take the chance of travelling along the bankside – we'll have to go by the cliff road.'

'Shall we put him on Calabos' horse?'

She shook her head. 'Not for the half dozen miles or whatever it is to Murstig. It would kill him.' She glanced apologetically at Dybel. 'Be very risky, really . . .'

'The top of the stairs,' Dybel muttered, 'would be . . . a better place for this conversation, yes?'

Tashil and Dardan muttered agreement and together helped him to stand, and after about twenty minutes and several rests they reached the head of the Melvio Stairs. Across the path from the stairs' flagstone landing was a large speckled granite boulder which had been carved into a travellers' bench. They eased Dybel onto it and Tashil sat beside him while Dardan hurried off to the Silver Keys to retrieve their horse.

'Calabos told me about this army of Ilgarion's,' Tashil said. 'Does he really intend to attack the pilgrims gathering at Besh-Darok?'

'It's true enough,' said Dybel. 'I overheard some of the officers from his own household and it almost . . . sounds as if they've been hoping for an excuse to attack the Mogaun for some time, and the burning of the Daykeep was more than adequate.'

Tashil thought anxiously of her father and the rest of the Akri family and tried not to imagine them as victims of Khatrimantine troops.

'Our new Emperor is quick to judge,' she said. 'And even swifter to punish. Yet I'm sure I've heard that there is a blood tie between Ilgarion's line and one of the old Mogaun clans.'

'Which may be why he hates them so much,' Dybel said.

Tashil was about to reply but paused when figures appeared further along the cliff road, a man leading a horse and another man walking beside him. As they drew near she could see that the newcomer wore a drover's coat and heavy boots as well as a floppy hat with a torn brim. When they stopped at the bench, Dardan made the introductions.

'Tashil, Dybel – this is Egbir. He was in the taproom of the inn and overheard me haggling with the 'keeper – man has a perfectly good cart but refuses to hire or sell it. But Egbir here's a waggoner up from Harcas and is willing to help get Dybel to Murstig, for a fee.'

'Yeh, good wagon,' said Egbir in a rasping voice. He was tall and broad-shouldered but walked with a stoop. Tufts of corn-gold hair protruded from under his hat and his lopsided grin revealed yellow teeth with one or two gaps. 'Take you to Murstig, take you anywhere, just say!'

'Murstig is fine,' Tashil said. 'So where is your wagon, back at the inn?'

Egbir directed a look of contempt back along the path. 'Huh – his toll too much, I not pay, I keep wagon in trees. We go along a-ways, yes?'

Tashil shrugged, then nodded. She and Dardan helped Dybel back onto his feet and with the waggoner Egbir in front, leading Calabos' horse, they made slow progress along the road. There was no one else in view, only a greenwing perched on the cliff edge fencing, eyeing their approach for several moments before leaping into the air with a blur of wings and darting up and over the dense wood. Egbir led them past the main turn-off for another dozen yards or so before pausing to point at a viny curtain of fleshy leaves beyond the undergrowth.

'Hid wagon back there,' he said. 'Old steading.'

Sure enough, Tashil could see a few fenceposts amid the bushy foliage and wheel ruts of crushed vegetation as they followed him into the wood's edge. Beyond was green-tinged dimness and an over-grown track that led to a decrepit, doorless stable whose roof had long since fallen in. Inside, a grey mare stood patiently in the traces of a low-sided, canvas-covered wagon. Calabos' horse, however, seemed restless and as they approached Tashil caught a whiff of decay, like rotting meat. When she sniffed and grimaced, Egbir nodded.

'Dead dog in there – food for rats now.' He grinned nastily and paused to tie the horse to a thick, waist-high post. Then he looked at Dardan.

'You help with wagon? Lift cover, make place for sick friend, yes?'

Dardan gave him a hard look for a moment. 'As you like,' he said, leaving Dybel's burden for Tashil to shoulder.

As the two men made their way around the wagon, Dybel shook his head.

'Something's wrong here,' he said. 'That smell . . .'

'I know,' Tashil said. 'Reminds me of something I heard recently—'

Then she remembered an instant before she heard a thud and

gasp from behind the wagon, followed by a flare of red radiance and a cry of pain and rage.

'Dardan!' she cried.

Then Dybel pushed himself away from her, waving her off.

'It's one of those spirit-hosts,' he said. 'Get you gone while there's time . . .'

'I'll not abandon you,' Tashil said angrily. 'Never . . .'

The sounds of struggle ended with a muffled crack and a grunt, and a moment later the waggoner Egbir leaped into view, holding a heavy club despite the smoke trailing from one charred shoulder. Dybel raised his hand and cast a Firedagger bolt, a knot of flame that flew straight at the waggoner's head. But instead of ducking, Egbir let it strike him full in the face. Tashil was horrified to see him grinning as the Firedagger burst across his features, wreathing him in flames that seared away eyebrows and hair but left his skin untouched. Seeing this, Dybel staggered back but Egbir lunged forward and struck him to the ground with his club. Then he turned to stare at Tashil.

'I know your spirit,' he said. 'Dark master gave me a taste, tells me – "kill her, add her to the rest" . . .'

The club lashed out but she had seen the turn of the gripping hand and the lifted forearm and was able to sidestep the blow then dive forward, chopping at his exposed neck with a spell-bright hand. But even as the silver web of power danced and clawed at her foe, she remembered the fight with the hound and felt the onset of desperation as Egbir laughed off her attack and rounded on her again.

She thought frantically as she dodged the waggoner's blows and darted around the small clearing, striving to recall the details of previous encounters with the spirit-hosts. Ducking round trees and crossing and recrossing the overgrown cart track, she brushed against one of the old fenceposts – and cursed herself for missing the obvious. Quickly she kicked at the post and jerked it from side to side, dislodging it enough to wrench it out of the ground before Egbir could reach her. His brutal club swung and missed, just, and she retaliated with the earth-clogged end of the fencepost, dealing him a buffeting blow to the head that sent him flying.

As he struggled to get back on his feet, Tashil spoke her keyword for the Cast thought-canto, with which she seized the fencepost, held it in midair for a second then hurled it straight at Egbir. It caught him high in the chest, on the left, just as he was rising, and smashed him back down, lancing through him to impale him to the ground.

The waggoner let out a bestial bellowing which quickly ratcheted up in loudness and fury with every new uprooted fencepost which she used to stake him down. Ignoring the deafening cacophony, she retrieved Dybel's short sword, after checking his pulse and breathing, and went over to the pinioned spirit-host. The prevalent stench in the clearing told her exactly what was in the back of the wagon, and her own fury was like a cold armour enclosing her. Disregarding the clutching hands, she quickly stepped in close and with two hard, hammering cuts struck off his head.

Once the blood had ceased gouting, the impaled body's movements grew weaker and slower, the fingers ceasing to grasp the air, the limbs finally subsiding to a fitful twitching, then . . . stillness. Trembling from shock and effort, Tashil slumped to sit on the ground nearby and stare and wait.

'That was . . . done well.'

She glanced round to see Dardan grabbing hold of one of the wagon's wheels and hauling himself upright. Suddenly worried, she got up and went over.

'You look bad,' she said bluntly. 'How do you feel?'

'Head pounding, nausea, sense of balance gone awry,' he said. 'The bastard clouted me on the temple and managed to put all his weight behind it.' Dardan tightly closed his eyes for a moment. 'Foul headache . . . ah, now comes the possessing spirit – look!'

As Tashil had seen before, a coiling, smoky web was exuding from the headless body, tenuous tendrils undulating gently as it pulled itself free. For long seconds it hung writhing in midair before moving in what Tashil knew was the direction of the centre of Sejeend. Then it slowed and changed course, heading on a more easterly path. Tashil and Dardan exchanged a puzzled look.

'Follow it,' Dardan said. 'But keep your distance.'

She nodded and set off after it, wending her way through the trees. She tracked it across the turn-off track and on into the wood again, finally giving up some ten minutes later when it floated over a fast-running stream and away. Quickly she retraced her footsteps to the ruined stable where she found Dardan tending to a barely conscious Dybel.

'East,' she said. 'Wherever it's going, it's not Sejeend.'

Dardan grimaced. 'Another mystery to add to the myriad we already have. We had better repair to Murstig with all speed, but I may not be able to help you very much.' He gritted his teeth. 'We need the cart but it is full of bodies.'

'I understand,' said Tashil stoically. 'I'm sure I can find a way to clear it out.'

Like using the thought-canto Cast.

Chapter Twelve

When Night stares from his eyes,
Skies will darken,
Rivers will run dry,
Crops will fail,
Children will sicken,
Towers will fall,
And kings will go mad,
When Night stares from his eyes.

Gilly Cordale, *The Pageant of the Destructions*, Ch. 5

From the *Mocker's* aft quarterdeck came the sound of the ship's bell tolling eight. Cursed Rikken, on lookout in the prow, sighed with relief. His watch was done and he could go below to find a bunk in the darkness warm enough to thaw the raw chill which had settled into his limbs, despite the heavy cloak he wore. Just as soon as someone arrived to take his place.

Glancing over his shoulder he saw no one approaching so he went back to staring off into the grey shrouds of mist ahead. For all that it was noon, the veil of mist remained as heavy and icy as it had during the night, neither thinning nor breaking apart but keeping constant pace with the great silent fleet as it sailed unswervingly westwards. Rikken turned his gaze to starboard, peering through the swirling haze at the shadowy lines of one of the ships of the undead, the flagship of Hanavok, admiral of the Ogucharn pirate princes. An hour ago the courses of both ships had by chance converged close enough for Rikken to see that the crew of that deathly vessel appeared to have gained the semblance of flesh on what had earlier been no more than weed-draped, clacking bones. Now, though, he could make out only a few dim figures, yet still he shivered from cold remembrance . . .

A hand came down on his shoulder and he jerked with startlement. It was the relief lookout, Girzi, a scrawny Calegman who wore a sneering grin as Rikken doffed the cloak and handed it over. Suddenly feeling how cold it truly was, he hurried down from the prow and aft to the main hatch.

Below, the corridor was narrow and dimly lit by small bulkhead lamps smothered by protective cressets made of cow horn gone a dirty amber with years of heat and fumes. That smell of burning tallow laced the air, mingling with the odours of sweat and recent cooking. Suddenly hungry, Rikken hurried along for'ard, imagining in detail a bowl of hot stew and maybe a wedge of black bread to go with it. But just as he got to the galley's curtained entrance, the bald, sweat-beaded head of Erdzic the cook popped out, saw him and laughed.

''Bout time! Cap'n's been asking for yer.' Erdzic glanced over his shoulder for a second, then his hand came into view holding a swinging tray, its lid firmly in place. 'There – Cap'n's cabin right away!'

He ducked back inside, leaving Rikken facing the grubby curtain for a moment before he turned and trudged back along the way he had come. The captain's cabin lay aft, on the port side, and the easiest way there was down into the hold, across to the port ladder, then up to the stern deck, a pace or two and you were there. But when Rikken reached the captain's door he found it slightly ajar.

'Captain?' he said. 'You there?'

Above the creaks and knocks of the ship he heard nothing, so hesitantly he pushed the door open wide enough to see inside. The cabin was lit by a single, hanging lamp and was a clutter of chests and wax-sealed crates, with a boxcrib full of crumpled bedding, and a solid table covered in maps held down by conical plumb weights. Cold, dank air flowed in through the open shutters that led to the stern balcony where Rikken could see the shadow of someone standing just out of sight.

He stepped into the cabin and sidled round the table, thinking to get Captain Bureng's attention from closer. As he reached the other end of the cabin he could see that the captain was leaning on the balcony rail, staring off to one side. Rikken was about so speak but then froze as that which the Captain was regarding drifted into view. It looked like a knotted cluster of ash-grey, feather tendrils, all squirming slowly as it floated at head-height towards Bureng.

Rikken's first thought was that it had come from one of Hanavok's ships but before he could utter the merest sound of warning, the tendril-thing suddenly surged forward onto the captain's face. As Bureng gasped and reeled backwards, Rikken cried out — and Bureng whirled round, half his face covered with that writhing monstrosity, the other half twisted with murderous rage and a single burning, pitiless eye.

In a single swift movement he lunged through the open shutters and snatched fistfuls of Rikken's thin jerkin. Transfixed by terror, Rikken went limp in that furious grip.

'You spy on me!'

'No, Cap'n, no — I just brought your—'

'An enemy, then? Are you an enemy?'

But before Rikken could reply, Bureng's grip slackened as he moaned and slumped to his knees. The writhing tendril-thing was sinking into his face, passing through the skin like the ghost of one of those deep-sea abominations Rikken saw discarded on fishermen's wharfs. After a long moment the last of it was gone, absorbed into the Captain's features, leaving it looking normal and unmarked. Rikken heard him let out a long shuddering sigh and watched him lift one hand to wipe his brow and gingerly probe the invaded side of his face. Then he raised his head to look at Rikken, and his eyes widened as if seeing him for the first time.

'Rikken, my Rikken,' he murmured. 'Did you witness . . . the joining?'

Rikken could only nod, and Bureng made a wry grimace.

'Hmm, pity that you had to behold it thus.' Then he grinned. 'But better you than any of the others, for I know that I can trust you.'

'That you can, captain,' Rikken said unflinchingly.

Bureng nodded and got to his feet, urging Rikken to follow suit. But even just the effort of that caused him to lean heavily on the map table then sit down on a stool nearby.

'Weakened me, it has,' he said. 'Still, it will pass and the body of my essence shall increase.' He glanced at Rikken. 'I have a long and strange heritage, Rikken – would you hear of it?'

Rikken felt a sense of exhilarated anticipation, as well as humility at being entrusted with such personal confidings.

'Aye, captain.'

'Then listen well – once this spirit of mine, this niggardly sliver, was part of something immeasurably greater and more powerful than all the mages combined.' He shrugged. 'Was it a god, this vast immanence? I cannot say, but I do know that it suffered some catastrophe that shattered it into a cloud of fragments that spread across this continent, lodging in the streams of families, resting there from generation to generation, a scattered legacy of majesty, and now all those wisps and splinters are awakening and seeking each other out, and gathering . . . I only knew this by stages, from that night on the strand at the cove to this post, sailing at the head of a grim and cadaverous fleet . . .'

Bureng frowned, eyes narrowed in thought. 'But there is another and he resides in Sejeend – a young man, racked with fear, unable to cope with the voices thronging through his mind. When the spirit-fragment awoke within me I knew immediately that it was to be embraced, yet he continues to fight the incoming tide, struggling against the inevitable.' He laughed. 'Poor fool – I can sense his feelings of panic, as if he's slowly drowning. But he does not realize that the joining is a beginning, not an end, when all the voices begin to speak as one . . .'

He smiled and Rikken did so too.

'So . . . there'll be more of them . . . fragment spirits, cap'n?'

'Yes, Rikken, and I'll want you by my side now that you know this secret of mine,' Bureng said. 'Hanavok's ships must shield themselves from the sun with this deadening mist, thus cutting our speed. So we will not arrive at the Straits of the Vale before tomorrow afternoon, even with the greater distance we'll cover tonight. But once near the Straits we shall still have to wait for the onset of dusk before beginning the onslaught since the web of spells is stronger after sundown.'

'But how could I serve you, master?'

'You'll be with me when we break the walls of Hojamar Keep and storm the palace itself,' he said. 'And whenever a dark spirit comes to me, your help will be invaluable.'

Rikken stood straight and gave a formal bow.

'I am your servant, captain – my blade is yours.'

'Good. Now there are a few other things to tell you, but first pour me a jack of goldpurl from that small chest over there . . .'

The Countess Ayoni heard the rear door of the confinement carriage open and booted feet climb inside. There was a muttered exchange with the guard at the end of the short passage and a moment later he appeared at the barred window as he unlocked the door.

'Visitor, your ladyship.'

He stepped aside to be replaced by Ayoni's husband, the Count Jarryc. On seeing his beloved face, she felt her carefully and rigidly maintained composure begin to crumble, and she rose quickly to be enfolded in his arms. They stood there for several moments, murmuring comforts to each other as Ayoni felt the sting of tears on her face.

'Damn them,' the Count said. 'This box isn't fit for a dog!'

'Well, I do have my little wall lamp, and a volume of Roharkan devotional verse, kindly provided by the Archmage,' she said, dabbing at her eyes with a kerchief. 'Just think how much worse it could be – I might be in one of old Magramon's verminous dungeons, and you might be facing *real* danger.'

He gave a sour smile at that. 'A day out of Sejeend and not a sign, not a breath of the "Mogaun threat" – why am I not surprised? Yet still I have to endure Ilgarion's staff meetings and his inane orders which I must accept without question since Tangaroth holds you and Chellour in this wheeled cage.' He curled his lip and glanced momentarily up at the low carriage ceiling. 'I saw your jailers as I was brought here.'

Ayoni knew that he was referring to the three experienced battle mages posted by the Archmage atop the prison carriage to keep a close eye on both her and Chellour, ready to subdue them at the first sign of any mageworking.

'I never imagined that your Watcher obligations would lead you here,' he said with a sad smile.

'I'm so sorry, my love,' she said. 'But seeing the way that they treated poor Fyndil and the Duke, I just lost my head . . .'

She laid a hand against his chest and bowed her head, and moments later felt his hand stroke her hair.

'You've nothing to be sorry for, my sweet,' he said. 'There are others who must answer for a greater burden of dishonour than any you or I might acquire.'

A throat-clearing sound came from outside the open cell door.

'Sorry, your grace, visiting is not to be very long, by order of the Archmage.'

The Count gave the guard a cold look, then held his wife close. She reached up to his neck, their lips touched for a gentle moment full of yearning and sorrow and farewell since she knew that fate or chance might deliver a measure of cruelty into their lives. Then they drew apart, hands joined as they gazed into each other's eyes, then their fingers slid apart and Jarryc turned, stepped outside her cell and was gone. As her door thudded shut and the bar fell back into place, she heard his footsteps recede and vanish.

She sat down on her low box crib, cushioned only with a straw pallet, and fought not to be engulfed by despair.

'Are you well, Ayoni?' said Chellour loudly from the adjoining cell.

'Here, quiet now. No talking . . .'

Ayoni's despair shifted into anger. She stood and went over to the door and after a moment said:

'Couldn't be better, dear Chellour, and how are you this fine evening?'

'Ah, you know how it is. Too much good wine and choice viands. A fellow could get quite spoiled by this bounty—'

The guard was suddenly there in front of her door which he rapped with a short stave.

'That'll do from the both of you! You know the rules – there will be no speaking or conversing, none, for the duration of your confinement.' He sneered. 'Or shall I ask the Archmage's men to send you to sleep again?'

Ayoni shook her head and silently went back to sit on her crib. She knew that the carriage had several Lesser Power charms embedded in its structure which allowed Tangaroth's mages to send any captives into involuntary slumber, and to wake them, as and when they saw fit. She and Chellour had already undergone this awful enforced oblivion twice, a dreamless and empty gap between one moment and the next. She had no desire to repeat the experience but she lay back on the straw pallet and tried to put her worries about Jarryc aside, seeking natural sleep.

After a while her awareness of the cell began to fade as sleep descended, and several dream threads offered themselves, each one leading to a vivid patchwork of the familiar and the improbable. But before she could make a choice, something strange happened – the hazy play of interweaving shimmers and shadows grew dim and she heard someone whispering in an elderly, raspy voice, whispering a prayer or a chant in a language that seemed vaguely familiar . . .

Then the wall of sleep thinned and melted away and she found that she was sitting on the edge of her crib in darkness, her wall lamp having burnt out the last of its meagre amount of tallow. Except that this was a strange kind of darkness where a faint nimbus glowed about everything, like a dusting of jewelled radiance. Ayoni looked slowly from side to side . . . and gasped as she saw a form lying on the crib behind her, a figure with her own face. Startled she jumped up, leaning on the cell wall for support—

—and found herself staggering through into the other cell where Chellour was examining his own sleeping image. Surprised, he straightened and grinned.

'Greetings, Countess. Are we in each other's dreams, I wonder, or someone else's?'

'Whatever's happened, it's escaped our keepers' notice,' she said.

'I haven't ventured outside yet, though,' Chellour said, stretching one hand out to and through the wall of his cell which was also the side of the prison carriage.

'There is no outside,' said a rasping voice behind them.

Together they turned to see an old, balding man wearing a grubby assemblage of furs and a patched tunic with a long string of beads and charms and bones wrapped around neck and armpits and across his chest. Ayoni knew that this was a Mogaun shaman, perhaps even a seer; she also noticed that he was hovering about a foot above the floor.

'There's no outside?' Chellour echoed.

'No outside,' the old Mogaun said. 'No inside either, where we are.'

'So, honoured one, where are we?' said Ayoni.

The old shaman gave her a thoughful smile.

'Ghostland, the Domain of Undeath, the Painless Sea, the Forsakening,' he said. 'Had to bring it to you to hide you from prying eyes.' He paused to look upwards, cocking his head as if listening, then shrugged and beckoned. 'Now I bring you to them – come.'

He turned, still hovering over the floor, and walked off through the closed door of the cell. Ayoni shared a puzzled look with Chellour but before she could speak they both began to glide smoothly after the departed shaman. The walls of the carriage flicked past and then they were outside in the night, floating away in the shaman's wake, steadily gaining height.

Ayoni found that she could alter her perspective just by trying to twist her head and shoulders round, and was thus able to look down at the imperial army's encampment, which had been pitched across two outcrops of higher ground, part of the irregular line of worn bluffs and broken ridges that followed the outer bank of the Great Canal. This mighty waterway, nearly half a mile across in places, encircled the ancient demesne of Besh-Darok and joined with the waters of the Gulf of Brykon several miles north and south of the city itself. Ayoni knew, of course, that three centuries ago there had been no waterway but a long curve of craggy peaks, the Girdle Hills, which the Shadowkings in their cruelty and hate had transformed into a long, black fortified wall and the twin dark citadels, Gorla and Keshada. When the Lord of Twilight was defeated, that terrible wall and its citadels had collapsed into the depths, down into the undercaves of the world, thus opening an immense channel to the sea. A sorcerous, underground highway known as the Great Aisle had also linked the two citadels to Rauthaz in the north, and its destruction also created another monstrous trough which reached all the way to the Gulf of Noriel.

In the evening's deepening gloom, the Great Canal became a curving sweep of blackness over which Ayoni and Chellour flew, as if towed by the old Mogaun shaman. The lights of the imperial camp were receding to distant glows and were gone by the time they crossed over the opposite bank. Then they caught sight of another, larger cluster of bright pinpoints a few miles further round the Great Canal, spread out on the inner bank.

'That is Belkiol, the thousand-tent city,' said the old Mogaun. 'The last resting place for pilgrims before they walk the final stage to Besh-Darok. There, they will perform the three privations, the five songs, the six prayers, and the ten farewells.'

On they flew with their guide wordlessly pointing to bands of pilgrims moving on from or returning to Belkiol, their pole-lamps carried over their shoulders. And there, just a few miles to the east, were the pale walls of Besh-Darok. Ayoni had visited the ancient, mostly deserted city just once, in her youth, when she had accompanied her father on a journey to visit relatives in southern Mantinor. Their small ship had docked at one of the few piers still safe to use – old wrecks littered the waters by most of the wharfs – and they had spent the night at an inn on the front without straying any further into the ruined city. She smiled at the irony of it. Although she had been keen the next morning to go and explore the abandoned streets, her father refused out of respect for the dead and whatever spirits might walk the walls and towers, yet here she was returning to Besh-Darok as a disembodied spirit . . .

Through the darkening sky they rushed, feeling no sensation. Before long they were swooping down low over the crumbling battlements of the city and the caved-in, derelict buildings beyond, all of which possessed the same tenuous darkling radiance, a faintly turquoise nimbus. The dilapidation of the centuries and the incursion of plantlife of every kind was plain to see – tumbled masonry swathed in moss and grasses, bushes and climbing vines half-concealing doors and windows, broken pillars wreathed in dog-ivy or wallthorn, entire trees grown up from the centre of buildings, branches pushing aside walls while their roots burst through the floors and burrowed outside.

Their elderly Mogaun guide angled their course towards a huge oval building enclosed by the remains of a diamond-shaped fortification with a large, round keep at either end. From its nearness to the city wall Ayoni suddenly realized that this had to be the old imperial palace, on which the palace at Sejeend had been modelled in part. She had seen drawings and paintings of how it had once looked, but at some point after the great Shadowking War the graceful High Spire had toppled to leave huge overgrown mounds extending north from the central stronghold across the curtain wall and the city wall, both clearly breached by the tower's fall.

Inside the palace walls, more wild undergrowth had smothered the evidence of ruin and the age-old ravages of battle. The old Mogaun brought them to alight on a weed-choked stretch of cracked flagstone before a tall arched entrance which once would have been barred by heavy timber doors. As the shaman led them towards it, Ayoni thought that she saw a pale, almost misty figure pass behind one of the upper windows, just for a moment. Chellour frowned as she hurried to catch up but shook her head and stepped smartly in front of the old shaman, turning to face him.

'What is your purpose in bringing us here, honourable one?' she said. 'Who sent you to get us?'

'I am not *sent* by anyone,' the Mogaun said sharply as he sidestepped her. 'It was and is necessary to bring you here to ask, to answer and to witness . . .'

They were walking through a devastated great main hall, much of its area filled with rubble, sections of lichen-encrusted masonry and long shards of pillars. Once a wide staircase had risen from the middle of the floor and a portion of it still jutted above the mossy wreckage, broken-off steps visible against the purpling night sky. The old Mogaun strode on through, leading them to a wide chamber off the hall, its floor littered with more grass-fringed rubble, massive shattered pieces of stone from the ceiling which was open to the outside. The pale, opaque form of a young woman sat on one of the pieces, gazing out a tall narrow window. She looked round as they entered, and smiled.

'Why, Atroc – you've brought guests!'

'For a short time only, Alael,' the Mogaun named Atroc said. 'And theirs is a serious task.'

The woman called Alael nodded as she approached. 'This must be about the newcomers,' she said to Ayoni and Chellour. 'They've set up camp in the Keep of Day and Bardow is very worried.'

'Where is the master mage now, lady?' said Atroc.

'A little while ago I saw him up on the Silver Aggor, talking with Yasgur,' said Alael.

'Hmph, didn't see him. Perhaps he is at the Keep of Night,' Atroc said. 'I thank you, lady.'

The young woman smiled brightly then wandered off through the wrecked chamber. As she left, Ayoni exchanged a wide-eyed look with Chellour.

'Was that really . . . Queen Alael?' he said.

'Queen Alael's ghost?' Ayoni suggested, trying to reconcile the slender young woman with the images of Queen Alael that she had grown up with, those of a stern, commanding woman always pictured wearing the imperial crown and sharing the frame with a sword or a shield or some other implement of war. Crowned in the aftermath of the Shadowking War, Alael had been faced with widespread chaos and upheaval from which marauders and freebooters had sprouted like vicious weeds, and in which several determined would-be rivals sought to challenge her for the throne. The first twenty years of her reign had almost been one continuous military campaign aimed at reuniting the former territories of the Khatrimantine Empire, a campaign that left succeeding generations with the enduring image of Alael, the warrior queen.

Yet here she was in this city of ghosts, looking as youthful and relatively burdenless as she might have been before her coronation. And there had been mention of other names from history, the Archmage Bardow, and Yasgur, the Mogaun prince who had been made a Lord Regent during the war. And their guide had to be the Mogaun seer Atroc, who had been Yasgur's closest advisor and the man who had befriended Gilly Cordale and kept him from harm.

'We could be meeting Chael Bardow,' she muttered to Chellour as they followed Atroc from the chamber by stepping through the wall.

Chellour frowned. 'Something is wrong here – why would the ghost of Queen Alael be young rather than old? Does she even remember being queen, I wonder . . .'

The seer Atroc led them through the violet darkness of an outer pathway choked with dying bushes and saplings to a wider gap between the palatial stronghold and the inner wall. Out here, where the light was plentiful during the day, all was a profusion of foliage, flower and berry-laden bushes, great iron-wood and torwood trees pressing against the stones of the inner wall, the branches decorated with hanging masses of litrilu blooms, all wreathed in subdued, many-coloured auras. Amid all this, Atroc paused to point along to the dark mass of the Keep of Night.

'Bardow awaits us,' he said. 'Ask him what you will but be assured that you will have more questions at the end than you did at the beginning!'

'He is not there,' said a voice.

The translucent figure of a tall, bearded man in half-mail and a cloak emerged from the gloomy mass of greenery. His face was sombre, perhaps even a little weary, Ayoni thought, but his dark eyes were steady and alert.

'So, milord,' Atroc said. 'Where might we find him?'

'The imperial barracks, Atroc. Up in the observatory.'

'Again? Reading the stars?' Atroc snorted. 'Be as well to try and read the ripples on the bay for all the good it will do. If the end is almost upon us then how can we prevent it by this gazing?'

Then the newcomer seemed to notice Ayoni and Chellour for the first time, regarding them with a stony distrust.

'Perhaps that is why Bardow asked you to look for witnesses,' he said. 'Lady, ser – I am Ikarno Mazaret, former Lord Regent of this sad and withered place. I do not know why a party of strangers has come here but I fear the worst, thus any and all aid would be most welcome.' He turned back to Atroc. 'I will be in the gardens, watching . . .'

The old Mogaun sketched a stiff bow. 'Of course, lord.'

Ikarno Mazaret, Ayoni thought as she watched the tall, spectral man stalk off along an overgrown path. *Who survived the final battle in the Lord of Twilight's realm, according to the sagasongs.*

'Come,' said Atroc. 'We shall take a direct course.'

As he spoke, they all rose into the air along a curve that swept up and through the palace battlements to emerge within a large building outwith them, then ascended past empty broken floors to the loft where birds perched on rusting iron joists and the stumps of buttresses standing stark against the sky. At one end of the long, roofless attic, a pale figure stood staring up at something on a crumbling section of wall. As they approached, Ayoni could see the stocky figure of a man peering through one of several tube-like contrivances jutting from the wall.

'Ah, good,' the man said without looking round. 'Thank you, Atroc, for bringing such noble guests to our regrettably ramshackle abode.' He gave them a sideways glance and smiled. 'I'm glad you are here and I hope that, as mages, you might be able to shed some light on the mysterious visitors who arrived here by sea several hours before that army of Ilgarion's set up camp.' He straightened, turned and clasped his hands. 'But firstly, introductions. This is Atroc, shaman and seer, as you may already know, and I am Chael Bardow, former Archmage to his imperial majesty Tauric the First, and you are . . . ?'

'Ayoni, Countess of Harcas, and bound by oath and duty to the Order of Watchers,' she said.

'Nyls Chellour of Adnagaur,' Chellour said sardonically. 'Likewise of the Order of Watchers.'

'Excellent,' Bardow said. 'And the fact that you are currently imprisoned by that fool Ilgarion speaks volumes to me about your character.'

'Pardon my asking, Archmage,' Ayoni said. 'But do you know much of what happens in Sejeend?'

'Not specifically,' Bardow said. 'We pick up a few useful details about recent events from the pilgrims who travel to and from the city, although the more worthwhile comments come from others: traders, sailors and the like.'

'When they can be bothered actually talking about such matters among themselves,' Atroc said sourly.

'But occasionally I also come up here,' Bardow went on. 'Not all of these neareye tubes are for looking up at the stars. But enough of these pleasantries – perhaps we should now proceed to the Keep of Day and see if they've let slip any revealing details.' He looked at Atroc. 'Is Yasgur still on duty there?'

'Gilly has the watch now.'

'Good, and I am finished here for now . . .'

Ayoni smiled at him. 'Archmage, I confess to being puzzled by both our and your presence here and in these forms. Forgive me, but are you all ghosts and if so, then what of Chellour and myself?'

Bardow nodded as she spoke. 'I likewise admit uncertainty, Countess. We seem ghostlike and are invisible to all the pilgrims and the few city residents, as well as to most animals. We seem to inhabit an empty place congruent to this world, thus we are able to pass through solid objects since they are absent from where we truly are. Yet when people sleep and dream they take on a new form which is how Atroc was able to bring you here.

'But are we ghosts? That implies that we died and these pale shades are our spiritual residues – certainly I do remember my death in the realm of the Lord of Twilight, how I was cut down by those reptile-riders with their scythes, and how I later found myself wandering through the streets of Besh-Darok as singing, cheering crowds celebrated the fall of the Shadowkings and the collapse of their reign – yet none could see or hear me. Soon after, I encountered Ikarno Mazaret, his form as pallid as misty as my own, and his last recollection was the awful climax of that battle in the Lord of Twilight's realm. Others like he and I arrived in Besh-Darok in the days and weeks following the end of the war, and every one had a similar tale to tell.'

'Who were they?' Ayoni said. 'And where are they now?'

'They were mostly mages of one kind or another, or those who had been directly touched by either the Lesser Power or the Wellsource. The great majority of them simply moved on while we few stayed out of a sense of familiarity or attachment, or perhaps because we hope that one day long-lost faces will eventually show up, passing through.' There was a palpable sadness in his words. 'But I do not think we are ghosts. More than a week after the phantom-like Ikarno Mazaret arrived here, he and I were to see the flesh and blood Mazaret ride in through the city gates. The same happened with Alael and Gilly, although our Gilly stayed here while the real one left for Cabringa.'

Chellour was intrigued. 'So does that mean that Lord Mazaret watched himself . . . grow old?'

'He was there in the Court of the Morning when his beloved Suviel Hantika appeared amid a bed of flowers,' Bardow said. 'And while his real self greeted her he could only stand there watching in silence.'

'How sad,' Ayoni murmured. *So that's why he said he would be in the gardens.*

'Alael had a similar experience, watching herself be crowned, then finding her way into the role of queen, ruling, commanding, weighing problems and crises, judging and punishing, or rewarding.'

'That must have been difficult for her,' said Ayoni.

The Archmage smiled faintly. 'At some point I think she decided that this other Alael was just another, different person and her interest became less encompassing. But when the real Ikarno Mazaret passed away, at a crotchety eighty-two, there were two Alaels mourning by his deathbed. Our Mazaret avoided it, and the burial ceremonies.'

'Understandable,' Chellour said drily.

'So, ser Bardow, if you are not ghosts then what are you?' Ayoni said.

The Archmage glanced up at the sky for a moment, smiling enigmatically, then said, 'I think that we are the echoes of our true selves. Something colossal happened when Suviel and Tauric confronted the Lord of Twilight in the Void, something which affected certain people and cast reflections of them into this dream-place.'

'I don't feel like an echo,' Atroc said gruffly.

'Yet we have been trapped in this ageless bodiless existence for three hundred years or more,' Bardow said. 'Well, we may at some point find an answer to the enigma, but for now let us employ our ethereal nature to our advantage in the Keep of Day.'

Then as one they rose into the air, heading north, and moments later passed through the outside of the Keep of Day, the great cylindrical bastion which oversaw the inner and outer parade grounds. Most of the flat roof had fallen in and parts of the outer wall lay in grassy mounds of rubble at the base. Lightless yet still visible to their eyes, the interior was a muddle of caved-in floors, cracked pillars and stairwells choked with shattered masonry. As they descended through the floors, it seemed that the lowest had escaped the worst of the structural ruin. Then they arrived at the ground level, in a large circular chamber plentifully lit by torches and where a wide ring of ten small, conical candles sat burning in the middle of the floor. Before each candle a cowled figure sat facing out, and the moment the four spectral mages entered the chambers the nearest candle flames flared and tilted in their direction.

'Master!' cried out the men nearest their entry point. 'Another intruding presence, over here!'

At the centre of the circle of ten was an eleventh who sat straighter then pushed back the heavy cowl to reveal a handsome, fine-featured face whose dark eyes gleamed with arrogance. Ayoni stared at him in surprised recognition.

'Mother's name,' she said to Chellour. 'It's Lymbor cul-Mayr!'

Chellour stared a moment then nodded. 'The threadbare lordling himself, and I'll bet that's his flock of NightKin . . . ah, I'm not sure what he's doing but perhaps we should back off a-ways . . .'

Cul-Mayr had taken a small blowpipe from within his robe and was calmly slipping a little red-feathered dart into the mouthpiece. The four quickly retreated beyond the wall of the chamber to a dark, curving corridor along which another man, translucent, bearded and grinning, was strolling.

'Wondered how long it would take,' he said. 'Did he spit one of his darts at you?'

'We didn't wait to see, Gilly,' said Bardow, turning to Ayoni. 'You know the leader of those men? He is familiar to you?'

She regarded the newcomer for a moment, certain that he had

to be Gilly Cordale, then nodded, saying; 'He is a penniless noble who lost almost all his family's estates and riches through trade debt and gambling. We've been sure for a while that cul-Mayr was involved with a malefic sect called the NightKin but solid proof has evaded us — until now.'

'Is there any connection between these cultists and that army camped on the other side of the Great Canal?' said Bardow.

'We know that certain members of the nobility as well as senior military officers have some involvement,' Ayoni said. 'But we know almost nothing about their motives or their goals so it's difficult to make sense of their actions . . .'

'Well,' Gilly Cordale said, 'it so happens that there's an open doorway along this passage from which we can watch without signalling our presence.'

All agreed to this and as they proceeded round the curve the Archmage formally introduced Gilly and Ayoni and Chellour.

'I miss Sejeend very much,' Gilly said. 'Even as the overcrowded city that it's become.'

'So why are you here rather than there?' Chellour said.

Gilly Cordale smiled bleakly. 'The one thing worse than being a disembodied spirit is being one in a place you think of as home.'

When they reached the open doorway they gathered on its threshold to watch. The leader, the noble Lymbor cul-Mayr, was still seated at the centre of his NightKin flock, and from a casket was producing several small golden emblems which he placed on the floor all around him, ten in total. To Ayoni's eyes each one possessed a strange ash-grey nimbus. Cul-Mayr smiled an unpleasant smile as he placed the last one, then surveyed the NightKin.

'Brothers,' he said. 'The blessed vulsors.'

Hands dipped into pockets or delved within robes and brought ten pendants, all identical — a flattened copper ring with a greenish stone at its centre and glyphs inscribed all around it. As the NightKin hung them about their necks, Ayoni noticed that they possessed the same flickering grey aura. There was nervous, quiet laughter, exchanged looks, dry lips licked, hands restlessly moving or tensely clasped. Cul-Mayr nodded in satisfaction.

'Now the orisons.'

The ten began a low-pitched chant in old High Mantinoran, archaic syllables that Ayoni could just about understand as imprecations for an entity called the Great Shadow, pleading for its intercession. As the NightKin repeated their chant, cul-Mayr began to declaim in Yularian:

'Hear thy servant, Great Shadow of the age – the foes of Holy Night are weak and scattered and our lands lie fallow, awaiting thy plough, thy seed, thy scythe. The towns and the cities will cast down their walls before thee and thy eternal word shall become the very arbiter of life and death. Open the fount of thy will and wisdom, we pray, that we might further perfect and strengthen our purpose. Open the well of thy powers that these poor servants of thine may offer themselves up as truly worthy vessels of thy inexorable might . . .'

Cul-Mayr continued in this vein for a short while before lapsing into silence. But this was only a brief pause before he started again, introducing a string of servile oaths and vows, promises to pursue the Great Shadow's enemies and exterminate them down to the last. When he paused for a second time, Bardow turned to Atroc and said, 'Do you recognize any of that, I wonder?'

The old Mogaun grunted. 'Before the tribes came to this land, the Acolytes of Twilight often walked among us, trying to teach us their prayers. While many shamans were swayed, the seers remained wary, always seeking to avoid cages for the mind. The doggerel that this one is spewing is a corruption of those ancient devotions.'

'So this is a ritual for invoking the Lord of Twilight?' Bardow said.

Atroc shook his head. 'Such a ritual would be more than just words; it demands all thought, all belief, all of love and hate. No – you should look at the charms they are wearing and the ones he put on the floor around him. There is something darker coming.'

Bardow looked Ayoni and Chellour. 'In three hundred years all of us have borne witness to innumerable groups of zealots, mystics and self-proclaimed prophets in this place, so something may transpire, or it may not.'

'And yet the Carver came here and ascended,' said Chellour. 'Did any of you witness it?'

'Only Nerek saw it,' Atroc said. 'And she said very little save that the Carver's body became wholly like ours before he disappeared.'

'Is that what these are attempting?' said Gilly. 'Ascension of some kind?'

'No, my friend,' said Bardow. 'Real power in the here and now is their goal, power to use for their own self-aggrandizement, power as a way of gaining more power . . .'

'Something's happening,' said Ayoni.

As she watched, the restless grey auras around the ten floor emblems had begun to expand, slowly but noticeably. Now they were extending upwards, wavering like tongues of ashen flame that encircled cul-Mayr, who spoke on and on with eyes closed. At the same time, the pendants worn by the NightKin began to pulse with the same grey radiance while their wearers sat still and chanted, oblivious as each nimbus extruded a hazy tendril towards the corresponding emblem on the floor next to Lymbor cul-Mayr. Suddenly, all the ghostly tendrils lanced forward to join with the auras surrounding the floor emblems and as one the NightKin acolytes froze in mid-chant, mouths open, lips trembling as they strove to speak or even scream. Seeing this, the seated cul-Mayr smiled.

'Master, hear me,' he said. 'My flock is trammelled and I am ready to begin the Bloodgate ceremony.'

Then another voice was heard in the great empty chamber, a sibilant rushing voice.

'*You have done well . . . prepare now for your reward!*'

Then the upward trailing tongues of ash-grey flame swirled and swiftly coiled around cul-Mayr, embracing him from crossed legs to the crown of his head. A look of utmost horror came to his face and his throat gave forth only gasps as he fought against the spectral bonds. But his struggles quickly slowed and his eyes became glazed and vacant. The ten NightKin jerked where they sat, small convulsions that preceded a darkening of the grey tendrils that bound them to cul-Mayr. Then the darkness grew red and flowed down towards the golden emblems encircling cul-Mayr and before long a crimson flush spread up through the greyness that entwined him. Ayoni felt sick as she watched, knowing that all of these fools had been betrayed by their master, condemned to be sacrifices in a vile act of blood sorcery.

One by one the NightKin slumped or toppled lifeless to the floor as their veins were exhausted. The grey weave enclosing cul–Mayr changed to a dark, mottled scarlet which also began to suffuse his own flesh and garments. By the time the last of his flock finally lay sprawled and dead, cul–Mayr was fully cloaked, encased in a dully gleaming red caul in which the features of his face were only vaguely discernible. Its surface wept shimmering droplets and a heavy vapour drifted down its flanks as it took on a slight glow. The glow brightened through shades of red until it became the unwatchable, burning fury of the furnace. Ayoni and the others averted their gaze as the brightness obscured all and filled the chamber.

Soon it subsided and faded away. When Ayoni looked again she saw that all the lamps and torches had gone out, leaving only the faint, glimmering radiance of the dream-realm to challenge the darkness. As they entered the chamber, she realized that there was a strange blotch of greyness in the middle of the floor exactly where Lymbor cul–Mayr had been sitting. Drawing near, she saw that it was an irregular patch of some neutral blue-greyness, like a mould. It was perhaps four or five yards across and had a foot-high mound at its centre and ten tapering protrusions.

'Nobody touch it,' said Bardow. 'This is the result of necro-mantia, which usually means deadly peril.'

'I am relieved,' said Gilly with a grin as he rose into midair, and floated over the greyness. 'I thought it might be really dangerous.'

Bardow frowned and shook his head. 'If you choose not to listen . . .'

But Gilly had reached the centre of the greyness and was hovering a yard or so above the mound.

'The surface of it is finely textured and very even,' he reported. 'There seem to be vague shapes beneath, however . . . not sure what they are – ah!'

'What?' Bardow snapped.

'Er, a pair of eyes just opened in the top of this mound and they're staring up at me.'

'Move away from it, now,' Bardow said. 'Everyone else get back.'

Gaining height, Gilly twisted away from the grey mound but then the surface bulged and put forth a thin, flat-tipped tentacle which thrust upwards to wrap itself around his legs. Gilly let out a cry of shock and fought as other grey coils lunged up at him, engulfing his legs.

'Bardow, what can we do?' Ayoni said.

'What can the disembodied do?' he retorted angrily.

'Perhaps nothing,' Atroc said. 'Perhaps something.'

At first the Archmage shook his head, then he shrugged and together he and the old Mogaun flew over to Gilly who was being drawn inexorably down. But the rippling greyness beneath him bulged again and, in an abrupt transformation, became the head and shoulders of a pair of hooded figures, both as grey as the thing blighting the floor. These deathly forms rose suddenly on thick curved columns, hands outstretched. Ayoni and Chellour shouted warnings and although Atroc managed to evade the snatching grey hands Bardow was caught. Then the hooded figures' outlines melted and flowed, engulfing the Archmage up to his chest.

'Send them . . . back, Atroc!' he cried as he was pulled down towards the roiling greyness which was clearly growing in size. Just behind him, Gilly's still-struggling form was sinking into it.

The seer Atroc swerved past more tentacles and flailing figures as Ayoni and Chellour backed out of the chamber's wide entrance. Atroc was grim-faced as he reached them.

'A terrible way to die,' said Chellour.

'We do not live,' the Mogaun said bitterly. 'How can we die? But remember what you have seen here, for any good that it will do . . .'

He muttered a swift string of words and made a cutting gesture. Ayoni's last sight of that place was Atroc turning to face one of the monstrous tentacle-forms as it lunged through doorway at him—

The transition back to the physical reality of her own body was like being dropped into a cold river. Gasping and trembling from the sudden surge of sensations, it was several moments before Ayoni realized that the prison wagon was in motion. From the way it was jolting and swaying it was clearly being driven at speed, but by whom?

And her cell door was open, she saw, with lamplight coming from the passage outside. As she sat up on her boxcrib, Chellour staggered into view, holding on to the door frame, and a moment later a bearded man in leather and mail armour joined him from the other end of the passage.

'Are you well, ser?'

Chellour gave a dry laugh. 'Nothing that a month of rest and fine wine wouldn't remedy!'

Disorientated, Ayoni spotted the crest of a boar on the man's chest at the same time as she recognized him as one of her husband's closest allies, Baron Klayse, and her heart leapt.

'My dear baron,' she said. 'It is most gratifying to see you. I assume that we are escaping.'

'Indeed we are, countess,' Klayse said with a grin. 'Your recovery will please your illustrious husband almost as much as I.'

'Where is Jarryc, baron?'

'Driving this wagon, lady. Our destination is a small port near the southern mouth of the Great Canal and thence to the port of Besh-Darok. From there, a ship will take us east to Margrave Tergalis' coastal estates in far-off Cabringa!'

Ayoni exchanged a look with Chellour who then said, 'How did you cope with the mage guards?'

Klayse grinned. 'Had one of Tergalis' hedge wizards decoy them with a fireball and while they were preparing to focus on that, a squad of my archers let fly.' He chuckled. 'Tangaroth must have had a fit.'

Chellour was grinning too. 'I wouldn't be at all surprised!'

'Well, lady and ser – if you try to find some comfort in this rattling box, we should soon reach the Great Canal where we can have a happy reunion and the sharing of stories.

And hopefully the chance to persuade my beloved husband to avoid Besh-Darok! Ayoni thought as she and Chellour dragged their pallets outside their cells so that they could sit on the passage floor and chat amiably with the baron while the wagon jounced on through the night.

*   *   *

High on the westerly side of Hojamar Keep, Vorik dor-Galyn shivered in an icy dawn wind as he sat out on an exposed balcony, keeping vigil while his master Jumil, voice of the Great Shadow, sat a few feet away, deep wrapt in a mind-journey . . .

The Iron Guard had the exclusive use of the top two floors of the Keep, and since most of the Guard was riding north with the Emperor, Hojamar Keep was now mostly uninhabited, apart from the wardens. Which to Jumil made it perfect for the planning and execution of his unfolding strategy.

Jumil sat cross-legged on the balcony's stone floor with eyes closed as the freezing north wind ruffled his short hair, thin shirt and troos. Vorik was bundled up in several layers of clothing and a heavy jerkin over all and he could still feel the wind cutting through to the skin. The shivering came over him in waves, and he was toying with the idea of standing up to let circulation return to his legs, when Jumil suddenly let out a long sigh. Looking up he saw that his master's eyes were open and staring out at the hazy, distant mountains. Then he smiled and, without altering his posture in the slightest, glanced sideways at Vorik.

'The flock at Besh-Darok has succeeded in its task,' he said. 'The first Shatterseed has taken root, and the seeding shroud is starting to expand.'

Despite the cold, Vorik chuckled. 'Poor Lymbor,' he said sardonically. 'So what now, master?'

'The next NightKin flock to reach its destination should be Rugilo's at Oumetra, followed by Skotan at Alvergost, and then Amaj at Adnagaur.'

Vorik nodded. All were well-populated and would provide the sustenance and forms necessary for the seeding shrouds to grow well.

'Lastly, of course, will be your own flock and your own version of the Shatterseed rite.' Jumil's smile never faltered. 'Soon, you will be invested with the powers of the Wellsource and able to share the joys and burdens of mastery. In the meantime, take yourself indoors and pay the good captain a visit. Question him a little, see what progress he is making. I have to return to oversee the early stages of the Shatterseed burgeoning at Besh-Darok.'

'As you will it, master,' Vorik said, clambering to his feet and ducking through the heavy drapes that hung across the balcony door. Inside it was warm and full of gold lamplight and he doffed his heavy robes and gauntlets and loosened his quilted jerkin before stepping through a shadowy arch to where stone steps wound up to the top floor. He pondered Jumil's words of assurance as he climbed, feeling certain that all the promises of sharing power were as empty as the man's heart and that he meant for Vorik to share Lymbor's fate.

Oh no, my master, that will never do, he thought. *Which is why I have made other arrangements for my own Shatterseed rite . . .*

As he reached the top of the stairs he could hear the voices coming from the storeroom which they had refurnished to hold Captain Ondene. He unlocked the door and entered, closing and locking it behind him.

'Comes the jailer,' said a voice, nasal and sneering.

'Jailer, mailer, sailor, failer, whaler, tailor,' rambled another, low and slurred.

'Do you think he wants to paint our portrait?'

'What would it resemble, o cretinous one? A smashed plate with a face on every piece maybe?'

'Will he, will he, will he . . .'

'Fire burns the words, makes them smoke and curl . . .'

'Does he know? Does he know? Does he know? . . .'

'Know what?' Vorik said abruptly.

Ondene stared at him with head tilted and his face askew, one eye wide and bright with malice, one side of his mouth smiling wolfishly. Whatever remained of Corlek Ondene was now buried under the throng of spirit-fragments that were crammed into his head. Which was a source of satisfaction that went some way to countering the unease he felt whenever had to speak to this jabbering semblance of a man.

'Do you know the harmonies of the languid night?' came a familiar, harsh voice that Vorik thought of as the Priest. It was usually the Priest, or sometimes the Brigand, that he found himself conversing with.

'Do you know the boundaries of the deathless realm?' the Priest went on.

'Should I?' Vorik said mockingly.

'I see its boundaries in your eye,' the Priest said. 'In the stones of this fortress and in the river outside.'

'My master has a master,' Vorik said. 'Only *his* realm will matter in the end.'

'Your master, that dark prince . . .'

Then the voice cracked as a succession of others struggled to speak.

'I know that cur, that glorious vermin . . .'

'. . . and gave my face to him, to her, to them all, my lovely face . . .'

'But does he guard his flank? Should always allow for the unexpected . . .'

'. . . fleeting words of pain, a graceless farewell . . .'

'Watch the boy – he has the look of nemesis about him . . .'

'. . . To charge with spears . . . arms outstretched, I pray . . . all the things we desire . . . a fallen, bygone time . . . banished, I close all doors . . . the anger of fools . . .'

The stuttering jumble of voices seemed to exhaust him and his head lolled forward for a moment. Then he straightened and looked directly at Vorik who felt a cold trickle down his neck as he met that level, bitter regard.

'What torment you've caused,' said Corlek Ondene. 'What a festival of horrors. Had I the use of my body I would be at your throat.'

'So says the honourable captain,' Vorik sneered. 'Indulge such fancies as you wish but your fate is to be consumed by your betters!'

'Vermin!' Ondene said in a choking voice, face reddening with exertion as he forced himself to his feet. 'There will be retribution, I swear it . . .'

But before he could even take the first step, a spirit-wraith came floating through the wall and struck him in the side of the head. He gasped, fell shaking to his knees then keeled over with the writhing thing sinking into his skull. Smiling, Vorik leaned against the wall to watch, even though he had witnessed this several times before. As before, Ondene ceased his convulsions and became relaxed, lying full-length on the floor. Then the spirits began fighting for control of his voice again, which Vorik knew would usually result in the more dominant fragments taking charge of it for a time before exhaustion sent him off to sleep.

But not this time. Instead of a rising, throat-tearing cresendo of voices, they suddenly subsided to a strange little chant which then tailed off into silence. For a brief moment, nothing, stillness, then Ondene calmly got to his feet, facing away from Vorik, raised his hands and brushed his hair back, fingers running through it.

'The deathless realm . . . awaits,' the man said. 'Tell your master that I would speak with him.'

'Indeed?' Vorik said. 'Why?'

The man he knew as Corlek Ondene turned to face him and immediately Vorik saw the change in him, the unyielding composure, the sense of deadly menace. And there was nothing of Captain Ondene in those penetrating eyes.

'The coalescence has come, Vorik,' he said. 'Tell Jumil that a Shadowking is here, and tell him that I am not the only one!'

Chapter Thirteen

In dark and vasty caverns,
The bones of ancient powers,
Await the eager flesh of greed.

Gundal, *Siege of Stones*, Ch. 3

Aboard the *Stormclaw*, Qothan answered the summons to the auracle chamber and found Prince Agasklin sitting in one of the visuran chairs.

'Peril is upon us, Qothan,' he said. 'The vicious wiles and machinations of the dark sorcerer Jumil have finally borne fruit.'

Qothan nodded. 'Almost the entire crew has felt it.' He shuddered. 'All those fragments of the Grey Lord have merged, and created . . . something terrible.'

'Few of those still alive among us remember the Shadowkings,' Agasklin said, 'but now another of them walks the world again, thus we must make every effort to conceal ourselves from his hungry gaze. We have vital work ahead.'

'I understand, master, but will it suffice to plan an attack on Jumil's forces here when the first Shatterseed has taken root in Besh-Darok?'

'Jumil is the linchpin, the guiding will behind the way the Shatterseeds develop,' Agasklin said. 'Without him, they will be far less dangerous, which is why we are alert to his purposes in Sejeend. Yet he and this new Shadowking he has brought into being are not our only worries – all the ship's chieftains held an ingather here not long ago and we received disturbing news from the auracle aboard our sister ship, the *Seafang*, that someone has raised a fleet of ships from the seabed and set a course for Sejeend.'

'A fleet of the undead?' Qothan said, aghast.

'Just so.'

'Forgive me, master, but am I right to say the Sleeping God says nothing of this in the Vortex narratives? I have only studied the summations, thus I may not know of relevant passages.'

Agasklin gave a bleak smile. 'The Book of the Vortex makes no mention at all; the Sleeping God may have been correct on many things but such a fleet makes no appearance in any of the stanzas.'

There was a long moment of silent reflection. The Book of the Vortex was considered near-holy writ by almost all the Daemonkind: its pages contained dialogues between the first High Captains of the Daemonkind and a strange divinity called the Sleeping God. This encounter had taken place just a few years after the end of the Shadowking War, far out to sea on a storm-wracked, rocky islet called Nydratha. From this islet craggy towers of natural stone rose more than a hundred feet into the air, enclosed by a perpetual raging vortex of winds. The highest of these towers had a spiral of steps hewn into its core and when the four High Captains climbed to the very top they came face to face with a mysterious presence calling itself the Sleeping God. From several long encounters, the captains' scribes compiled many scrolls of dialogues, monologues and prophecies in which the Daemonkind themselves appeared. And now that some of those auguries were coming true, closer attention was being paid to everything in the Book of the Vortex with the consequence that any significant event not anticipated in its pages took on a kind of heretical menace.

'Coireg's role has become clearer,' said Agasklin. 'This new Shadowking might well be the weapon to use against the Great Shadow. However, if this revenant fleet attacks by this evening as the clade chiefs aboard *Seafang* suggest, we may have to put Coireg ashore quite soon before raising anchor and sailing north to find shelter between here and Adranoth.'

'What of Calabos and the Watchers?' Qothan said.

'They've returned to Gronanvel and are poised to re-enter the city,' Agasklin said. 'Compared to Jumil, their powers are weak yet they are resourceful and determined and their leader Calabos is deep and enigmatic. They may prove to be a useful diversion when

Coireg Mazaret is despatched.' He smiled at Qothan. 'Of course, he will not be alone.'

Qothan gave a slight bow. 'It is an honour and a pleasure to serve as an outrider, master. Will any accompany me in this?'

'Another two besides yourself will be appointed – our captain, the illustrious Pericogal, has ordered that it be so.'

This was a measure of how serious matters had become, that the captain would take an active part in these deliberations. Pericogalteraninor was the last surviving Daemonkind leader out of the four who had spoken directly with the Sleeping God. Old when the fall of the Shadowkings condemned the Daemonkind to exile, Pericogal had endured and surpassed storms, battles and betrayals on a hundred coastlines between here and the other side of the world and found that the only foe he could not defeat was old age. Thus he resided in his own secluded chamber at the heart of the *Stormclaw*, shielded by locked doors, guarded night and day by elite sentries. Qothan had seen the captain perhaps three times in the last ten years, and not at all in the last two. Yet his presence informed the entire vessel as if, despite the dreams he dreamed and the long meditations he undertook, some part of his mind remained in watchful attendance.

'Then so shall it be,' Qothan said. 'Yet could you also consider waiting until the last moment before putting Coireg and ourselves ashore? My concern is that we need to know as much as possible about this revenant fleet, and if we have to conceal ourselves from this new Shadowking then we will be unable to use the long voice to converse with you after you depart. Also, I wonder if we might be able to prevail upon the good will of the High Steward to provide safe passage for the Watchers in exchange for our aid in the coming struggle.'

'Such a scheme has merit – very well, I shall share this and your concerns with the other chieftains,' Agasklin said. 'And perhaps we can persuade our brothers aboard the *Seafang* to discover more details about this approaching threat.'

'I am gratified by the wisdom of this course,' Qothan said.

'Then retire to your quarters and prepare for your next outriding,' Agasklin said, getting to his feet. 'The names of your companions will be decided on shortly, whereupon you will be informed.'

He brought both hands together, signifying the end of the meeting. Qothan gave a stiff, measured bow and left the auracle chamber, wondering who his companions might be and if this was the last day he would spend on board the *Stormclaw*.

The *Merry Meddler* was a thirty-foot, single-masted riverboat which had carried too many cargoes of vegetables in its time, resulting in a lingering odour of rotten cabbage which made Tashil wish she had a less well-developed sense of smell. When she muttered about this to Sounek he came back with the suggestion that their captain had 'seen the inside of too many tankards of ale'. And indeed, Captain Jodec was a pot-bellied riverman with a toper's nose and watery eyes. He also had food fragments in his beard and dried gravy spots on his doublet, yet his hand seemed steady enough when he shook on the ferrying deal with Calabos and took his money.

Thus on the day after Dybel's rescue, and three since the rushed flight from Sejeend, here they all were returning to face who knew what kind of strife. The *Merry Meddler's* long deckhouse was a timber shelter roofed with heavy canvas over its rear half, and the Watchers were resting within, sitting either side of a narrow fixed table. Tashil was half-listening to Calabos as he outlined his plans to Dardan and Sounek, who were visibly unconvinced, to Inryk who seemed willing to hear it all first, and Tashil who knew that they had to act, even if only to gather more information.

Yet her attention was divided as she glanced over to where Dybel was keeping the steward Enklar and the guards Rog and Gillat occupied with tales and anecdotes. Her brother Atemor was sitting nearby, trying to appear uninterested, yet Tashil knew her brother well enough to spot when he was taking notice of something and just then Dybel was retelling the story of how the boy-emperor was smuggled into Oumetra on a canal boat.

Tashil smiled to herself. *Yes, that's really what we could do with now – a lost heir to the throne who can wield devastating powers. Sadly, they seem a little thin on the ground in this age . . .*

Then her attention was pulled back to Calabos' discussion when
Dardan spoke up.

'No, Calabos, this is an invitation to disaster,' he said. 'We agreed
last night that it would be you, me and Sounek who would track
down the dark sorcerer's lair, together. Dividing us would be folly.'

'I am thinking only of your safety and the Watchers' long-term
survival,' Calabos said gravely.

'Yet together we would present a tough obstacle for our adversary,' Sounek said.

'You must understand that he will focus his attacks on me,'
Calabos said. 'And if I fail, how long might either of you then
survive?'

Dardan glowered at this but Sounek smiled.

'Ah, but my dear Calabos, if he has to go through us to get to
you, think how weakened he may become.'

Calabos sighed and shook his head. 'You are both stubborn,
stubborn men!'

'Indeed,' said Dardan.

'And whatever I say, you'll still foist yourselves upon my company
when I go ashore at Yared's Wharf, yes?'

'Just so,' Sounek said.

'Then it seems that I must yield to your impetuous demands.
Perhaps you should decide between yourselves who should be first
to face our enemy's ruthless power.'

'Naturally, we hope that events will not develop in such an
unfortunate way,' Sounek said.

'Yet we shall be prepared,' answered Dardan.

For a moment all three men smiled. Inryk laughed.

'Then it's settled,' he said. 'We put you three ashore at Yared's
Wharf, then the rest of us sail down to the bay then along to this
safe house on the south shore at . . . what's the village called again?'

'Rishtu,' Dardan said.

'You should hear from us by the time you reach the house,'
Calabos said. 'If you hear nothing from us by, say, an hour after
nightfall you should assume the worst. The papers of the Order,
including a full list of all secret caches, houses and assets, I have
placed in a sealed casket in my shouldersack which I'm leaving

with you, thus you can decide what course of action to follow, in the event of . . .'

'What a dismal summary,' said Sounek.

'The facts of our situation must be faced, I'm afraid,' Calabos said as he stood stiffly with the aid of a stick. 'It won't be long before we reach Yared's so I must go aft to let Captain Jodec know who's going and who's staying.'

Tashil sat forward as he sidled past and climbed a narrow set of steps to the cockpit where Jodec and his helmsman sat. Like the rest of the Watchers, Calabos wore ordinary townsfolk attire, in his case a heavy red doublet over a light green tunic and plain brown troos with a soft, brimless hat of some dark grey material, yet he somehow contrived to look commanding or even kingly. As she watched him ascend the steps it occurred to her that she had never been seized with worries about his safety, until that encounter with the Archmage Tangaroth a couple of days ago. When Calabos passed out and fell to the floor before them all, it had been a shock to realize that he was vulnerable and mortal. Yet it was something that she knew Dardan had already been aware of, and in discussions last night she had volunteered to go with Calabos in search of the adversary's lair. But the ensuing vigorous argument (of which this discussion was merely the aftermath) put paid to her playing such a part. She had been full of anger and resentment but rumination and a good night's sleep had done away with such self-centredness. As her old mentor Tregaylis once said, 'No matter where we are, we are in the right place', which led her to wonder if she was there for the right reason.

Standing, she left Inryk, Sounek and Dardan talking tactics and went along to the for'ard end of the deckhouse, where she could sit and gaze over the side at the rippling waters or the sights on the riverbank.

Hearing someone approach she turned to see her brother Atemor sitting down next to her. He gave her a faint smile and for a moment or two said nothing as he stared over at the crofts and stable of the riverbank. But she knew he would not be silent long.

''Sheel,' he said. 'How long must I stay with you and your

friends? I have to return to our family and warn them about your mad emperor.'

'I'm sorry, Atti,' she said. 'I'm not sure but I'll speak to Calabos to see if we can spare money to buy you passage back to Besh-Darok when we reach Rishtu.'

Atemor frowned. 'How long could that be? Several days? Could you not put me ashore somewhere along the north bank with enough coin for a new horse?'

'It's a good plan,' she said. 'But we'll have to get Calabos' agreement. I'll ask him before he leaves us.'

They did not have long to wait. Some minutes later, the *Merry Meddler* rounded a sheer-sided promontory to where a limb of land jutted from the south bank into the Valewater. Among the bushes and stunted trees was a collection of cabins and animal pens clustered near a rudimentary L-shaped pier which had to be Yared's Wharf. The riverboat came in slow enough for Jodec's deckhands to jump onto the pier and lash the fore and aft hawsers, during which Calabos emerged from the deckhouse with Dardan and Sounek. Tashil caught his attention and outlined Atemor's discontent and his proposal to which Calabos readily agreed.

'I am sad that you'll be leaving us,' Calabos told him, clasping his hand. 'It may be just as dangerous for you near Besh-Darok as here, but I wish you the best that fate has to offer, Atemor. It has been refreshing and most pleasing to meet one of my colleague's relatives. Fare you well, ser.'

Then he turned to Tashil and Inryk. 'I'm going to say to you what I've already told Dybel and the others – we may be going to face our doom . . . The next hour, day, or week is not written, thus we will not say goodbye except to say – may the light be with you when you walk in dark places.'

The *Merry Meddler* rocked as the three mounted and crossed a short gantry onto the pier. Calabos paused to look back and give a nod to Captain Jodec who then ordered his deckhands to cast off and very soon the boat was drifting back into the main flow of the river as once more the sail was rigged.

Tashil stayed by the side, looking back, even though the three Watchers themselves were swift to leave Yared's Wharf behind. She could not avoid the sense of loss she felt but was determined not to give in to despair, so she set herself to thinking about the practicalities of what lay ahead, whether or not they should stay out of sight as they neared the centre of Sejeend, what to do if river wardens stopped them, and just where to put Atemor ashore.

The outskirts of the city began just beyond Yared's Wharf, larger buildings and storerooms for the grain and meat that was gathered from the western districts of Roharka prior to shipping to the main markets. Denser rows of houses, fewer farmsteads, more lumber yards, tanneries and forges. The afternoon, however, was nearing its end and with the sinking sun and the arrival of grey clouds some lamps were being lit, ashore as well as on board. The riverside roads became busier as some people headed for home and the carts of bakers and brewers rattled off to the city's inns and taverns. Once, Tashil saw a wagon on an open stretch of road, speeding citywards in the shadow of the cliffs with three passengers, two of whom sat in the back while the third shared the driver's bench, a man who was wearing a red jerkin and a shapeless grey hat . . .

But before she could say anything, the road took the wagon away from the bank and out of sight beyond houses and trees. Then she realized that drawing attention to themselves and what might have been Calabos and the others would not have been entirely wise.

Further on, the *Merry Meddler* sailed with the sun dipping ever lower and a sharp coldness creeping into the breeze at their backs. The cliffs south of the Valewater pushed closer to the bank and soon the Melvio Stairs came into view, its long rack of steps made visible in the deepening shadow by torches that burned at intervals all the way up. As they passed it by, Tashil glanced back at Dybel who was stretched out on one of the benches, asleep beneath a cloak. He was still frail from the healing last night at the inn at Murstig, and it would be more than a week before he regained something like his former vitality. Tashil had suggested that he should stay in Murstig to recuperate but Dybel had argued vehemently for accompanying them, and Calabos had agreed. Such were the dangers from the spirit-hosts, he argued, that Dybel would be safer with the rest of the Watchers than by himself. The sense in that was obvious so Tashil gave her assent.

With the Melvio Stairs sliding away behind them, the Valewater curved slightly to reveal a densely wooded hillock in front of which was a tall warehouse with a blackened, burnt-out roof. She glanced round at Inryk, who was sitting further inside the deck-house, peering out a gap in the canvas.

'I think we're passing the Amatellis Retreat,' she said. 'Do you see it?'

He turned away from the canvas, grimacing. 'I'll forgo the pleasure if you don't mind,' he said darkly. 'Not a place I want to be reminded of.'

Grey cloud had been crossing the sky in tails and patches that grew into an unbroken shroud, even as the sun slipped towards the horizon. There was no rain and as the light faded the surround-ings seemed to lose a little colour, becoming vaguely grainy in appearance. The riverboat was approaching the centre of Sejeend now, and the air of tension on board was rising as they passed river warden boats heading upriver, or attracted the brief atten-tion of guards patrolling the bridges or standing sentry on either bank. Tashil had already discussed this part of the journey with Captain Jodec who said that if stopped he would claim he was heading to Norshen to pick up a load of timber and had taken on a few passengers along the way.

The nearer they got to the mouth of the Valewater, the more the city's sea defences became visible. Where the Valewater spilled into the bay, two immense gates stood open yet ready to be winched shut with hawsers and chains at first sight of a seaborne attack. In addition, massive walls stretched along the north bank to a bastion linked to the garrison of Hubranda Lock, and south to meet a series of lesser walls that led straight up to the sheer cliffs and cut off the docks from the rest of Sejeend. And over-seeing it all was Hojamar Keep, a straight-sided, circular fortress of pale stone.

As the *Merry Meddler* drew nearer to the sea gates, Tashil gazed up at the Keep, wondering how many troops remained to defend Sejeend now. A huge banner bearing the regal crown-and-tree

device of the Khatrimantine Empire flew from the battlements.
Several yards along from it, looking almost dwarfed, was a solitary
cloaked figure standing with both hands resting on the crenella-
tions. Intrigued, she focussed her perception through her magesight which brought the figure closer in her vision, but annoyingly
just as he turned and took a step or two away. Tashil was about to
shrug and give it up when the man came back to assume the same
posture, his features now clearly apparent. It was Corlek Ondene.

'Mother's name!' she gasped.

And even as the shock of recognition jolted through her, Ondene
snapped round to look straight at her and his face seemed lit from
within by a malefic glee. In reflex she broke out of the magesight
as she staggered back and would have tripped on a coil of rope
had Inryk not been close enough to steady her.

'What is it?' he said.

'I saw Ondene at the top of the Keep,' she said. 'He looked
. . . possessed, and he saw me!'

Inryk nodded, face grim as he leaned on the wooden rail and
stared across at Hojamar Keep. Then he looked quickly at the
dockside and the wharfs, before glancing at the seagates and the
bay beyond.

'There's trouble coming.'

Almost as soon as he spoke, Tashil spotted the squad of soldiers
emerging from the Keep's main doors and running down towards
the wharfs, with some splitting off to head for the seagates. With
a glance she gauged the speed of the *Merry Meddler* against that
of the running soldiers and realized that they were not going to
make it.

She whirled and dashed through the deckhouse past a surprised
Atemor and Enklar, leaped up the steps to the cockpit and came
face to face with Jodec just as he was uncorking a leather bottle.

'Later for that, captain,' she said and swiftly outlined their
predicament. Jodec's expression went from annoyed though puzzled
to panicky in short order.

'This weren't what I agreed ter,' he said. 'Trouble with the river
wardens'd bankrupt me! I should drop anchor and wait for them
to take you . . .'

'Come now, Jodec,' she said. 'You're already implicated, so you better put on every scrap of sail and pray that we don't get captured. Because if we do, we'll tell them that you're one of us and have been for years . . .'

'Mother damn you!' he spluttered.

'Spare me the histrionics,' she said. 'Just get us through the gates before they close.'

Leaving Jodec cursing and stamping, she hurried back down to the deckhouse where Inryk was explaining the situation to Dybel, Enklar, Rog and Gillat. The two guards were already donning armour and helms, even as a volley of arrows struck the boat from the south bank, prompting another burst of invective from the captain. As everyone retreated to the wholly wooden part of the deckhouse, Dybel drew Tashil's attention back to Hojamar Keep which he was observing through a small, slatted porthole. When she looked and saw that the regal banner had been replaced by several smaller coloured pennons, she groaned and dashed forward to see what was happening at the mouth of the Valewater. And sure enough, the gates were starting to close.

A black sense of angry despair welled up within. Then a couple of arrows clattered on the deck nearby while a third struck the planking an inch from her foot and jutted there, vibrating. Quickly she dived back under cover then craned her head out to look back the way they had come but saw three river warden boats starting out from a jetty a hundred yards upriver.

And the gates are closer than that, she thought, and closing fast. We'll have to turn about – there's no other choice.

Then a hand on her shoulder brought her back in to face Dybel.

'Keep going,' he said, indicating Inryk who was balancing a short spear in one hand, face full of concentration. Tashil stared for a moment, then said, 'Cast?'

Dybel smiled, and she nodded and hurried aft to the covered cockpit where the captain was cowering on the floor, cursing them all.

"I'm turning back!' Jodec wailed. 'We can't . . .'

'You'll hold this course,' she said menacingly at the fearful young helmsman grasping the tiller. He met her gaze for just a moment before nodding.

'Good,' she said, then looked round in time to see Inryk standing outside the deckhouse, amidships as he drew back the spear and smoothly threw it straight towards the fortified chain house that sat on the right of the seagates. Tashil followed its flight, a graceful, undeviating, flat curve through the air. The chains that were hauling on the massive gates were being winched in by a stepped series of huge cogs driven by falling weight mechanisms in two squat towers either side of the gates. She knew that the only vulnerability in the entire assembly was where the great chain passed between two heavy cogs before being wound onto its drum. In the greyness of sundown and the faint mist that was starting to rise, the spear fell into the shadows by the harbour battlements.

Tashil thought she could still see some figures running around the gantries near the cog sheds, and for a moment there was nothing as their riverboat sailed on towards the still-closing gates. Then there was a loud sharp crack which reverberated along the dockside. She had no explanation for it, but she could see that the right-hand gate had stopped moving altogether . . . then her fierce exultation faded as Inryk cried out and slumped to the deck with an arrow in his shoulder. Tashil had Rog and Gillat venture forth to carry him back to the deckhouse.

'Got it right into one of the chain links,' he said, smiling despite his wound.

'We'll take care of that properly once we're through,' Tashil said. 'We're a bit busy just now . . .'

They were less than fifty yards from the gate, and infuriated guards along the wharfs were firing volley after volley of arrows onto the *Merry Meddler*. They were also in range of the archers along the gates themselves and as they approached they attracted a steady rain of bolts, slingstones and arrows. The distance shrank and when they were less than a dozen yards away Tashil could at last see that one of the great winch chains had snapped and one of the twin cogs had been wrenched out of its mountings.

Then they were drawing level with the tall, heavy gates themselves, passing through the open one, and out into the darkening bay.

'We did it,' Dybel said, shaking his head.

'I'm afraid we're not quite in the clear yet,' Tashil said, peering round the side of the deckhouse at the river warden boat which was just emerging from between the gates. These were small craft driven by three pairs of oarsmen and usually carrying about half a dozen wardens. As it pointed its prow at the *Merry Meddler*, another three glided out into the encroaching dusk.

'This could get interesing,' Tashil said. 'A Firedagger might be enough to discourage them, but if it doesn't we may need more than I can provide. Do you feel up to lending a hand?'

When Dybel gave no reply, Tashil turned to see him staring forward at the increasingly hazy gloom.

'This mist is curious, don't you think?' he said.

'Sorry?'

'Well, our sail is still filled with a westerly breeze, but this mist is moving in from the east.' He sniffed the air and breathed in deep. 'Don't like this in the least . . .'

There was a bright flash and a jagged line of argent struck the deckhouse's canvas covering and lanced through it to stitch a charred and smoking wound in the woodwork.

'So they've brought a mage with them,' Tashil said with gritted teeth. 'How clever . . .'

Suddenly the riverboat lurched as if it had struck something below the waterline. Tashil heard Jodec spit a curse, and then noticed that the boat had come to a complete halt. Atemor and the two guards were readying weapons as Tashil glanced back at their pursuers who also seemed to have faltered in their course. The boat rocked again and a Mogaun battlecry brought Tashil round to see her brother hacking at a drenched-looking man who was in the act of clambering up from the waters. Then there were a dozen pairs of hands lunging up to haul and drag aboard . . . men who were men no more, only cadavers returned to motion and a ghastly semblance of life.

Horror was writ starkly in the faces of Atemor, Rog and Gillat yet they drew their swords and leaped into the fray. Dybel, his face armoured in an icy calm, raised hands wreathed in tiny crimson flames and sent a pair of bolts into the chests of two of the boarders. Fire ripped through their torsos as they were flung back into the waters, but there were others to take their place. The stench of decay was vile.

Tashil called on every last shred of her strength, using the thought-cantos Shock and Ram, striving to clear the deck of these gruesome attackers. She heard other sounds of conflict from further away, and during a brief pause while preparing another spell she chanced to glance to one side. A score of yards away, half visible in the gathering mist, the river wardens were in similar difficulties with one boat sunk, another listing badly and the other two filled with scenes of desperate combat.

Then suddenly the last of the undead had been hacked down, and everyone else was still standing, if bruised, cut or scratched. Once the unnatural life went out of the revenants, however, their cadavers suddenly began disintegrating into a disgusting heap of ichorous flesh and blackened bones, which were hastily tipped over the side with hooks and shovels. Then Tashil noticed that their boat was wallowing in the swell, its sail flapping uselessly, the lines hanging adrift.

'Jodec,' she shouted. 'We have to get under way . . .'

'Captain's dead,' said someone up in the cockpit, the young helmsman, looking pale and frightened. The other two deckhands were emerging from the aft hatch but before Tashil could start issuing orders she heard her brother Atemor curse behind and she looked round.

Coming through the mist towards them was the tall dark form of a ship, its masts reefed with the tattered remnants of sails that scarcely stirred in the erratic westerly breeze. Yet on it came, steadily, inexorably, its hull and forecastle becoming clearer, blacker, encrusted with barnacles and rotting kelp. And even as Tashil yelled for the *Merry Meddler*'s sails to be brought round, cadaverous figures began dropping from the ship's flank into the water to swim towards them.

When the riverboat was just nearing the centre of Sejeend, Calabos, Dardan and Sounek were hurrying past the high outer wall of

Hojamar Keep's courtyard. All three wore hooded cloaks brought from Murstig and tried to adopt the demeanour of devout pilgrims as Calabos led them towards the Kala and its leafy dale. This was as far as he had got on the night of the sorcerous calling, but this time he should be able to track down the lair of their dark adversary without interruption. The memory of that vile invocation was still fresh, seemingly seared into his mind and providing a certain sense of direction.

Past a couple of junctions, they came to a street with a row of prosperous-looking townhouses along the left and a head-height wall along the right. The wall's coping was decorated with leaves and berries, and tall trees were visible beyond, patches of their foliage illuminated by lamps hanging further down. This was a burial grove and the closer they came to its entrance, the stronger was Calabos' feeling that they were on the right track.

'It's somewhere near here,' he muttered as they kept walking.

'There are guards watching from these houses,' said Sounek.

'As long as they're not chasing us or shouting for aid,' Calabos said, 'they can watch as much as they like.'

Although sundown was bathing the rest of the city in a rosy glow, an evening gloom already held sway here in the shadow of the cliffs. The lamps in the trees brightened the shadowy paths and tombs while the interleaving branches concealed much of the grove from the guards across the street. As they entered the arched gateway, Calabos immediately felt a change in the air and also in the ground beneath his feet. Once, while travelling through northern Yularia, he had chanced upon a long valley whose villagers and steadings had been recently been devastated by an earthquake. Amid the awful quiet he had felt a disturbing sensation from the ground there, hints of instability or deep, unseen blight as if the ancient supports of the world had somehow been dislodged or damaged. It was very similar to what he sensed now, walking through the burial grove, a faint but insistent sign that a violation of the earth had taken place.

The burial grove was bounded by high walls on three sides and the sheer grey face of the cliff itself on the fourth. The closer Calabos strayed towards the cliff, the stronger the feeling of wrongness and the greater his wish that the others had heeded his warnings. But all his arguments had proved useless against their companionship and their steadfast sense of loyalty towards him.

Perhaps that's not such a bad thing, he thought, his smile hidden within his capacious cowl.

Before long he had traced the dark sorcerous aura to a sepulchre built at the foot of the cliff, a large ornate affair which had been made to resemble a military palisade. Then he found that a glamour had been cast over a small section of the cliff face behind the sepulchre, which he dispelled to reveal a rusty iron door. Calabos exchanged wary looks with Dardan and Sounek but it was the work of a minute to unlock it.

Inside, a dark, roughly hewn stairway curved downwards. Dardan produced a small tallow lamp from one of his pouches and by its yellow glow they made their descent. The stairs turned to the left, then right, then became long and shallow before emerging at one end of an oval chamber. Crude symbols had been daubed on the walls long ago in paint that was faded and flaking, just as a variety of aged wood-and-cloth charms hung on corroded nails, decayed and desiccated, or lay crumbling into dust on the rough floor. Once upon a time, Calabos guessed, this had been the secret shrine from some cult of spirit-worshippers and then fell into disuse until their adversary found a use for it.

Calabos could smell the afterpresence of Wellsource use throughout the chamber, but especially at the centre where a mound of cracked, baked clay several feet wide sat upon the stone floor. Whatever function it had served was not immediately apparent.

'Is this the place?' said Sounek who was holding Dardan's lamp higher.

Calabos shook his head. 'There have been some kind of vile rituals conducted here . . .' With the toe of his boot he nudged a broken skull on the floor, 'but the invocation didn't . . . emanate from here.'

'There's another door,' Dardan said from the other end of the chamber. 'Didn't see it till I was right next to it.'

A narrow opening led to a wider passage of strangely smooth, contoured stone the surface of which gleamed dully in the lamplight. The passage sloped down for a short while then up towards the entrance to another chamber, an uneven doorway that framed a pale radiance. Calabos was in the lead, closely followed by Sounek with Dardan a few yards back. He had just stepped through the doorway when he heard a series of cracks from above and a grinding sound. Without hesitation he turned, grabbed Sounek by the shoulder and hauled him up out of the entrance.

There was a rumbling crash and a spreading cloud of dust. When the rockfall stopped, Calabos and Sounek rose coughing to their feet and surveyed the collapsed doorway and passage, now buried under tons of rubble. Of Dardan there was no sign or sound and shouting his name produced no response, likewise using farspeech. But when they both fell silent, fearing the worst, another menacing voice spoke from the chamber behind them.

'*Welcome to your new prison!*'

An ominous chill passed through Calabos as he turned to see who addressed them. Sounek let out a startled gasp but Calabos maintained his composure.

Hanging in midair a few yards away was a tall, slender man dressed in the plain yellow attire of a minor functionary or a tenured scholar. A few pale blue ribbons and tassels floated freely, much like the wide sleeves and voluminous troos which undulated slowly as if from faint, languid breezes. The man scarcely glanced at Sounek, reserving his full attention for Calabos.

'*Such an honour,*' the man said, '*To finally meet the great Beltran Calabos — yet not the first time, perhaps . . .*'

The man's voice was sibilant and distorted and his form, Calabos noted, was slightly opaque which meant that this was a spirit presence, another sign of powerful abilities.

'I do not know you, ser,' he said. 'Your face, however, is vaguely familiar.'

'*Ah, this face. Once it belonged to our servant, Jumil, but then it came into my possession, just as you have.*'

'So you are not who you seem to be,' Calabos said with a shrug. 'A thief, then — just like your master.'

The man's eyes darkened with anger and hate, and he drifted a little closer. Calabos met his gaze and crossed his arms.

'*This world was our ancient legacy and it became ours again by right of conquest, only for our strategy to be thwarted by lies and trickery . . . and the perfidy of turncoats, o great lord! But it shall be ours again, remade forever in reflection of the Great Shadow's will.*'

In that moment, as Calabos stared unflinchingly up at the cruel face, a shocking certainty bloomed in his thoughts – *Mother's name, he knows who I am! But then who is he?*

The dark sorcerer smiled.

'*I can feel your desire for knowledge*, Calabos,' he said. '*Know this, then – my name is Xabo and know also that a Shadowking is here in Sejeend, yes. You may speculate upon these morsels as you will in the time that is left to you, for this chamber has denizens who are jealous of those who have flesh. The phrase "the living rock" has real meaning here.*

'*Of course, if you somehow contrive to escape then we shall merely wait for you to come to us, as we know you must. And once the Shadowking has met you, we can bring your overlong tale to an end!*' He laughed, a rushing evil sound. '*May you die in agony.*'

Laughing and smiling, the man called Xabo began to fade, his translucent features becoming transparent and finally disappearing altogether. By which time Calabos and Sounek were thoroughly occupied by the monstrous change which came over the walls of the chamber. The previously solid-looking rock had begun to move, at first slowly bulging and rippling, all accompanied by grating whispers and moans. Then more definite shapes became visible, the unmistakable contours of bones, the joints of knees, elbows, shoulders, the ridges of ribcages and the gaping jaws of skulls, yet all coated in rough greyness as if the surface of the rock had become a kind of malleable membrane. Several of them half-emerged to stare across at Calabos and Sounek with grotesque, stone-grey sockets while skeletal hands made grasping motions.

Then to the two mages' horror, the bony shapes flowed down the wall and began writhing across the floor towards them on all sides. Calabos hurled a fireball at one group while Sounek flung a shock-charge dagger at some others – both charred the flexing stone but did nothing to stop the things beneath.

'I'm sure there's a way to escape this doom,' Sounek said. 'Yet my mind seems curiously blank.'

Calabos' thoughts were hectically spinning as he eyed the encroaching encirclement. Then a solution presented itself to him and he almost cursed himself aloud for not seeing it sooner.

'The rubble,' he said, pointing over at the collapsed entrance. 'It might offer protection from these horrors if we climb up on it.'

'So we just need to cross about twenty feet of squirming, deadly stone,' Sounek said drily. 'Right, let's go!'

With that he was off, leaping over a cluster of grey, clutching skeletal hands amid a rising din of rasping, sawing sounds. Calabos grinned and followed suit, choosing a different route across the restless floor as it heaved with skeletons in various stages of completeness, a bizarre, twitching garden of bones. Calabos' hooded robes were wrenched from him and ripped to shreds and the sole of one boot was half torn-off but he kept going and reached the sloping mound of rubble ahead of Sounek, who was no more than a stride or two away when he stumbled and pitched forward. At once he tried to scramble up towards the rubble but half a dozen grey hands emerged from the stone and grabbed his ankles just as he linked his own hand with Calabos'. Calabos attempted to pull Sounek free but he was fighting the strength of stone and could see that the man's legs were being engulfed by the surging greyness.

'I think I can get you out of it,' Calabos said. 'But it won't be pleasant.'

Sounek's face was drawn in fear and pain. 'Matters not — just try!'

Calabos called on the Lesser Power with the thought-canto Iceweb turning in his mind. A pale, glittering blueness appeared about his hands with which he reached down to touch the restless, bony floor. A hard white frost sprang up and spread about a foot or two across the stone surface, stilling it in mid-undulation. A few more touches froze all the bone-infested floor that encased Sounek's legs and all it took was several sharp blows with a dagger hilt to shatter it enough to allow him to crawl shivering up onto the rubble.

Skeletal limbs reached for them but could not get closer than

the edge of the broken rock and gravel. Then, as they sat atop the
rubble slope, Calabos felt a presaging tickle in his thoughts, then,
faintly . . .

(. . . *speak to me, damn you . . . ! do you hear . . .*)

He shared a smile with Sounek – *Yes, we live and hear you well,
Dardan. Forgive the lack of communication. We were otherwise occupied.*

(*Good to know. Remain where you are and we'll have you free very
soon.*)

Sounek gave Calabos a puzzled look. 'We?'

Calabos shrugged, and they waited, still keeping an eye on the
monstrous cave of bones whose restless manifestations had subsided
somewhat. As they sat there, Calabos noticed Sounek giving him a
sidelong glance or two and began wondering if some of the things
Xabo had said had caught Sounek's interest. And then there was his
physical exertions which scarcely matched his purported age.

As for Xabo – well, that malign spirit could only be Obax, the
senior Acolyte who had advised Byrnak the Shadowking. And he
had claimed to have brought one of them back – how could that
be? Was it possible that Xabo/Obax had gathered all those spirit-
wraiths together in some host, some doomed unfortunate, for such
a purpose? What could be going through the mind of such a creature, and how dangerous would it be? He sighed and tried to put
his worries aside until they were out of danger.

Soon they heard the muffled knock and rattle of stones being
shifted and several minutes later the rubble at the top was lifted
away piece by piece till there was enough space for them to crawl
through. The first face Calabos saw in the dusty lamplight was
that of a dirt-smeared Dardan who gave a sardonic smile and
clapped him on the shoulder before turning to help Sounek.

The next he saw was Coireg Mazaret, looking alert and in good
spirits.

'I'll wager you've a tale to tell,' Calabos said.

'Ah, at least one, my friend!' said Coireg. 'But they'll have to
wait – we've hard work ahead of us, upstairs.'

'Why – what's been happening?'

'While we were potholing around down here,' Dardan said,
'Sejeend has been paid a visit, a very unfriendly visit.'

Chapter Fourteen

Thou shalt become,
A fortress of life,
Amidst a desert of death.

Keldon Gant, *Orosiada:*
A Masque, Act III, Sc. i

The night was full of burning. All along the Silver Landings,
Sejeend's busiest docks, innumerable sheds, godowns and even the
lesser wooden jetties were aflame. Bureng had also ordered
Hanavok's cadaverous crew to set fire to everything flammable
near the great defensive walls which separated the quays from the
rest of the city, with the result that clouds of dense, choking smoke
were now engulfing the ramparts. When Bureng's invaders, both
living and undead, had poured off his ships onto the quays, the
defenders had sent a hail of rocks, arrows and bolts down upon
them. Now, scarcely any missiles were being fired, much less aimed.

The smoke was also an ideal cover for the squads he had sent
up the walls with orders to unlock either or both of the immense
timber and iron gates which were keeping his part of the host
trapped on the docks. And all the time, the other captains were
making much more headway than was he. It was not until he and
his men had stormed ashore that he learned that the immense sea
gates of Sejeend were open when Flane and Raleth's vessels reached
them. His cursing had been vitriolic and inventive and strayed
more than once into more ancient tongues.

Yet it seemed that the mouth of the Valewater soon became the
focus of stiff resistance and many fires were burning there too,
looking like the molten glow of a gigantic forge through the

smoke and the mist. It was a reflection of the furnace of desire and impatience that filled Bureng's mind, colouring every thought and impulse in shades of need. He no longer seemed entirely certain of his goal, whether it really was the plunder to be had from the houses of the wealthy and the palace of the emperor, or if it really was all about finding the source of that awakening call. Or if it was that dark and powerful presence which drew him on, an incarnation of powers so like his own and so equally certain of itself that it did not bother to cloak its glittering aura.

He was standing at the side of a stone custom-house, accompanied by his lieutenants and Gont and Reshik, captains of the _Hound_ and the _Snake_. The crews of all three of his ships were gathered in clusters flanking both of the great dock gates, yet they were almost lost in the mass of dead men who were spread all along the wharf in their hundreds, standing near-motionless, exchanging not a word, and utterly unaffected by the smoke from the burning timbers and debris. Bureng could see the grey-pallored Hanavok off to one side by himself, his head turning this way and that as he shifted his stare from the smoke-swathed battlements to the fires at the sea gates, then to the dark outlines of his ships crowding the long piers of the Silver Landings.

What nameless thoughts were filtering through the sluggish mind of the undead admiral, Bureng wondered, while being certain that impatience was not one of them.

He cursed and kicked a barrel off the edge of the dock. As it splashed heavily into the unseen waters, he rounded on Bull Arik.

'So where are they?' he snarled. 'Why are the gates still sealed?'

'Captain, we sent eight squads over the wall,' Arik said, eyes wide with fear. 'You'd've thought that at least one'd get through—'

'Send more over.'

'But they'll be expecting . . .'

'Do it – or I'll cut out your tongue!'

Shoulders slumped, Bull Arik walked over to a group of crewmen standing by the wall. But before he could issue any orders, a ragged cheer went up from the further of the massive gates, which began to swing open. At once Bureng shouted at Hanavok to get the revenant pirates moving through to the city.

For a moment the admiral looked at him with black, unreadable eyes, pits of distilled emptiness, then raised aloft a corroded sword and stalked over to the widening gates. Corpse eyes stirred and decayed feet began trudging as if to some silent battle cry.

Bureng followed close behind, one hand grasping the mirror talisman, and at his side trotted Rikken, faithful, doglike Cursed Rikken who was secretly carrying the Crevalcor Codex in a locked leather satchel slung across his shoulders. Bureng had not dared leave it aboard the *Mocker*, yet felt that its bulk would be too encumbering so he decided to entrust it to Rikken whose loyalty he knew was beyond question.

As his lieutenants and chosen guards forced a way through the press of dead shuffling men, he felt a rising sense of anticipation, excitement, hunger. He had received four more spirit-wraiths during the slow voyage to Sejeend and the memory of their absorption into his mind led him to savour from afar this other presence, this counterpart who also regarded him with a similar rapacity.

Such a celebration of pleasure it will be, he thought, *to crush your defiance then devour the very stuff of your making, piece by piece, power by power. Then I will be greater than you or any of those scurrying magelings, and I will build an empire that will never fall!*

Then they were through, part of a great surge of invaders pouring into the streets of Sejeend. There were a few defensive points, not much more than a few packing crates heaped with sandbags or an overturned cart, whose handfuls of soldiers either fled or were quickly overwhelmed. There were other soldiers and archers on rooftops and balconies from where a mounting hail of fire was coming, but Bureng now had only one prize in mind:

'To the Keep!' he bellowed.

A gusting breeze made the signal banners up on the Keep's roof snap while torches flickered wildly in their niches on the brick walls of the square storage bunker. A dozen and a half archers, mostly imperial army men, were at the walls watching for any likely-looking shapes in the streets below. There were also another half dozen engineers manning the two arc-throwers, war machines designed to hurl heavy, weighted arrows. Just then, however, there were no invaders in sight or in range so a good deal of joke-telling and barrack gossip was being exchanged as well as murmured speculation about the Iron Guard officer and his two companions who stood across the other side of the keep's roof.

But for all that they kept their voices low enough to avoid their serjeant's attention, the Shadowking still heard all that they said, each and every word as clear as those spoken by Jumil and Vorik nearby.

'. . . but if Ilgarion had not stripped the city of all his seasoned troops, we wouldn't be in this situation,' Jumil was saying irritably.

'If we had known what this Shadowking was capable of, I might have been able to persuade Shumond to keep an entire company of the Iron Guard here,' Vorik said. 'As it is, High Steward Roldur and his officers are struggling with the Cabringan levies and there's few enough of them.'

'I've told you already that the crafting of great powers is not a discipline of exact measurement,' Jumil snapped. 'The Wellsource resists detailed alignment or neatness – it wants to be used, not constricted, set loose not marshalled. A Wellsource mage needs a mighty strength of purpose and will, qualities that this *other* clearly must possess in order to have concealed himself and his campaign for so long . . .'

The Shadowking smiled to himself at that. His rival was scarcely capable of controlling his base and inchoate desires, never mind consciously adopting a clandestine scheme. The Shadowking could see that the situation was deteriorating with the line at the Valewater wharfs starting to collapse while one of the Silver Landings gates was now open. Soon . . .

A runner emerged from the main stairs and hurried to whisper a message to Vorik who nodded and dismissed him. Then he looked at Jumil.

'About two hundred of these pirates have outflanked the water-front defences near the Valewater,' he said, standing. 'Some made for the Melvio Stairs but the bulk of them are headed this way. The waterfront line is in tatters as well, with more raiders spreading through the streets with no particular formation. But the best news is that they've broken through at the Silver Landings.' He smiled sourly. 'Perhaps the time for the crafting of great powers is upon us. Excuse me, master, but I must give the serjeant and his men new orders.'

As Vorik strode across the keep roof, the Shadowking watched Jumil stare off to the north and could feel him trying to extend his senses as if seeking to verify what had been told.

'It is true,' the Shadowking said casually. 'All of it.'

The Wellsource mage regarded him coldly. 'Your powers reach far and deep,' he said. 'How easily can you draw upon the Wellsource?'

The Shadowking ignored the question and turned to lean on the stone crenellation of the battlement, leaning out to inhale hints of smoke.

'You call your master the Great Shadow,' he said. 'Who or what is he?'

'You know him well,' Jumil said.

'I know what all the parts of me once knew,' he said. 'Taken together they say that I am still only a part of the godhead that was broken, splintered and scattered at the end of the Shadowking War. Are you saying that there is yet another of we half-blind remnants, a third Shadowkinglet vying for whatever trickles of power still find their way to the Realm Between? Answer!'

Jumil smiled calmly. 'Like calls unto like and it is not necessary to exhibit every line of influence, every armature of intent for powers to follow their nature and thus work in concert.'

'It is of interest to me, do you understand? Why should I submit to the schemes of one who may be no more than an equal, if that?'

'He is both less than that and more,' Jumil said. 'Further I cannot say — you will just have to trust to his plans and to me.'

The Shadowking laughed. 'Why trust when I can squeeze the truth out of you?'

Unruffled, Jumil met his gaze. 'You could try.'

With unthinking instinct, the Shadowking reached out with his mind, seeking purchase and openings . . . but found only a perfect, intractable barrier. The closer he examined it and what lay behind it, the better he came to understand the futility of coercion, for although he was able to break down that defence, Jumil would undoubtedly abandon his physical frame rather than disclose what he knew.

'You see how pointless it would be,' Jumil said. 'How my passing would wreck our plans for a new realm here. That is what the NightKin and the Shatterseed are for, to prepare this world for a new beginning.' He glanced over at the soldiers. 'However, these raiders are drawing near and I see that most of them have been raised from death . . . interesting too, that their unlife is sustained by spell-infused charms. I fear that they may be too much for the Keep's troops to cope with – perhaps you could go down and lend assistance?'

The Shadowking nodded and grinned, marvelling at the way Jumil had turned his weakness into a strength. Clearly, he himself still had much to learn.

'Give death to the undead?' he said. 'Why not?'

Saying no more, he rose and walked across the gloomy roof to the wide, downward steps. He was still wearing the long, dun cloak given to him just after the coalescence but he doffed it and threw it into a corner as he descended. Beneath he had on heavy quilted troos and an old, dyed-red leather harness, all scuffed, cracked and scored but still serviceable. He also had a long, horn-handled dagger in a sheath at his side but he knew that he would have no need of it. The floors of the Keep were mostly deserted, some unlit apart from the lamps of the square stairwell, and he passed no one on the way down.

At the first floor he decided to leave by one of the large windows rather than go out the main door. Using a whisper of Wellsource he jumped the twenty feet or so, landing lightly on his feet. He then loped swiftly and silently across the cobbled side-court to a stairway that rose to the top of the thirty-foot courtyard wall. The sentries on the ramparts were watching the group of figures gathering to the west, across a tree-adorned square and a wide road beyond, so he was able to drop down to the street outside unnoticed.

He then soundlessly threaded his way through the shadows towards the other side of the square. Hearing voices he scaled the side of a shop and padded along a recessed sloping roof then onto a balcony which ran along to an alleyway and round the building's corner. There, below, a crowd of undead raiders was gathering, accompanied by a small number of living brigands. Some kind of argument was developing.

'You better be getting across there to fight them ironcaps,' one of the brigands was saying. 'Captain Raleth don't take kindly to them as disobeys orders . . .'

'This . . . was not his . . . command,' came the wheezing voice of one of the revenant pirates. 'This is . . . not . . . our desire . . . we wish only . . . a final ending . . .'

'Curse your rotten mouth! Move, I say!'

'You do not . . . hold the shield . . . your words . . . mean nothing . . .'

There was the metallic hiss of a sword drawn forth.

'We . . . would welcome the edge . . . of your blade, we . . . crave death's return . . .'

'What's this?' said a new voice. 'Gaf, put up your sword!'

The Shadowking smiled in the dark. He had felt the aura of the talisman and its bearer, felt the webs of power shift and contract even before he saw the newcomer approach at the head of a band of pirates and carrying an iron shield. To the living, it would seem to be no more than an unremarkable, battered buckler but to the Shadowking's eye it was a semi-living thing crawling with Wellsource power which pulsed from the intricate symbol scribed upon its face.

'These carrion ain't attacking, captain!'

The man with the shield, Raleth, glared at the massed crowd of the undead.

'Why do you hold back?' he said.

'It is . . . not our . . . desire . . .' said the hoarse spokesman. 'But . . . you have the . . . talisman . . . what is . . . your will . . . ?'

Raleth pointed across the square at Hojamar Keep. 'There is the stronghold of our enemies. I want everyone inside slain . . .'

The Shadowking decided that now was the moment and with one lithe movement leaped over the balcony, landing softly at the crowd's edge.

'No one,' he said, 'is going to attack that keep.'

Heads turned and the crowd parted as Raleth came towards him, pausing a few yards away, suspicion and contempt in his face.

'Really?' he sneered. 'No one? Well, begging your pardon, your lordship, but I have other plans and plundering yonder fort is top o' my list!'

The Shadowking ignored his words. 'Not only is no one going to attack the keep, but you're going to give me that shield of yours.'

Raleth laughed. 'A merry jape, fool, but I have no time for this . . .'

The Shadowking took a single stride towards the nearest of Raleth's undead pirates and reached out to lightly stroke his forehead. The blank-eyed, stiff-faced revenant lurched back a step, swayed there for a second, then fell apart in a cascade of desiccated skin, dust and bones. There were curses from the living and silence from the dead as Raleth bellowed, 'Protect me!'

Scores of the grey, impassive revenants converged on the Shadowking with a strange alacrity as it they were sleepwalkers eager to awake. As with the first, he had only to sever the invisible threads of power that bound them to the talismanic shield and thus to that dry, empty unlife. One by one he dealt with them, like a priest bestowing a benediction, his touch released them from servitude. Then, as the ranks of the undead began to thin, he came face to face with one of Raleth's own pirates who snarled as he brought a long axe arcing down towards the Shadowking's head.

He swept up one arm, a blur of motion, and grabbed the haft of the axe just below the blade. Then he wrenched it from the hands of the surprised pirate and struck him in the face with the leather-bound grip. As he went down, the Shadowking spun the axe in one hand to gain a proper grasp, sent a few more undead assailants to oblivion with the other hand, then turned to seek out Raleth in the darkness of the alley. The pirate was backing away towards a side wynd while a section of his raiders were advancing across the square.

He vigorously laid about him with the axe then leaped across the heaps of bone and dusty, torn garments in pursuit of Raleth who had broken into a run. In only a few strides he was within arm's length of the man, and chose to tap him on the side of the head with the flat of the axe. Raleth cried out as he went down, losing the shield as he rolled across the filthy ground to sprawl motionless by a brick wall. As the Shadowking picked up the shield, Raleth's undead pirates as well as his own brigands were moving towards him from either end of the alleyway, dark figures dimly lit by lamplight from a high window. Among the dead men, the living ones bared their teeth and readied their blades . . .

Regarding them, he raised the shield, focussed his mind on the scribed symbol it bore and let Wellsource power pour into it. In seconds the symbol began to glow red, then yellow, then white before it melted and ran in rivulets down the shield. By then, all the undead were turning on the living in their midst and the Shadowking tossed the shield aside as he walked untouched through the furious battle to the wider alley then out to the tree-darkened square.

The shield talisman was a source of control rather than the means of maintaining the revenant spell. He could see other threads of power trailing off to the coast, to the main docks. As he started in that direction, leaving the clashes and cries behind, a voice came to him, a low sinuous voice:

Ah, so you're the one. Destroying one of my talismans will avail you little.

'You should give up this siege,' he replied. 'Surrender yourself, for it matters not which of us triumphs – the aggregate will be the same, will be a greater whole.'

I see, then you would have no objection to surrendering yourself to me.

'I think not.'

An amusing dilemma.

'But not an unfamiliar one.'

It will be resolved soon, one way or another.

'I can sense your goal,' he said. 'Be careful not to get killed before I reach you.'

I shall be waiting. Bring all of your skill.

The Shadowking laughed and set off at a leisurely run.

*   *   *

After their escape from the underground chamber of bones, Coireg gave Calabos an account of his experiences while leading them along a tortuously secretive route to the dale of the Kala.

'What's their name again?' Calabos said, frowning.

'The Ushralanti,' said Coireg. 'They're a clan of traders and hard-ened sea travellers, as well as talented potion-mixers.'

Calabos smiled, glad beyond words to see his old friend freed from the demon in his mind.

'You wear your sanity well,' he said.

Coireg Mazaret laughed quietly and nodded. 'It confers an entirely new perspective on life – I've not had the chance to reflect upon the past . . . for quite some time.'

A look passed between them, unseen by Dardan and Sounek who followed behind as they all slipped through a shadowy alley. Calabos was sticking to the story he had concocted back at the lodge a few days ago, and had let Coireg know with swift whispers during the hasty ascent from Jumil's lair. And now Coireg was enjoying the benefits of his fortuitous encounter with these Ushralanti who, it seemed, were keen to meet Calabos and discuss matters of moment with him. This made him wonder if Coireg's encounter with them had been less a matter of chance than it seemed.

A narrow, stone-walled passage between two buildings led to a small, flagstoned courtyard where rats scurried away from a barrel overflowing with stinking rubbish. Wrinkling his nose, Coireg indi-cated a door beneath a guttering niche lamp and they hurried after him. Inside, they found themselves wandering through a coaching inn empty of guests and staff alike, a very recent depar-ture going by the still-steaming tankards of mulled wine resting on the counter. From the latticed window Calabos could see that they were now on the north side of the spot where the Kala river dipped into a masonried culvert and vanished beneath the city. When he followed it back through the gloom he could see that a rough barrier of upturned carts and barrels had been thrown across the mouth of the Kala dale.

'You see the barricade?' Coireg said. 'It's manned by troops from the palace and the academy, as well as the few mages Tangaroth left behind – they're expecting us.'

'Hold a moment,' said Dardan abruptly. 'Do you mean to trap us?'

'Mother's name, no!' Coireg said, surprised. 'No, listen – because the Ushralanti are highly valued by the Throne and Sejeend's merchanters, they were able to persuade Roldur, the High Steward, to guarantee the Watchers safe passage in exchange for helping to repulse this invasion.'

'Do you trust them?' Calabos said.

'I was there when Qothan, the senior Ushralanti outrider, came to terms with Roldur's adjudicant,' Coireg said, looking at all three. 'Yes, I do trust them and with reason.'

Dardan was dubious. 'This does not sound favourable to me.'

'But if I had intended to trick you all into some trap,' said Coireg, 'why would I mention the mages at all? Why not just lead you into their clutches?'

Sounek laughed drily. 'Good point. I think we should go on.'

'So do I,' said Calabos.

'But if it is as you say,' Dardan said, 'then why are we skulking about like this?'

'Because the few Iron Guard squads left in Sejeend, along with some imperial army patrols, have been ordered to arrest and confine all the Watchers on sight. Hence all this hugger-mugger.'

'I'm satisfied,' Calabos said. 'Let us waste no more time.'

The four men were spotted almost immediately. Tense moments stretched out as Coireg went forward to the barricade to negotiate, during which time Calabos could make out far-off noises, individual cries and the shouts of many in unison. But it was yet distant. Then Coireg emerged from the barricade and waved them forward. There were perhaps thirty or more soldiers manning the barrier with only about a third of them armed with bows, and a small group of dark-robed men who glared as Calabos, Dardan and Sounek were helped over the compacted wall of crates, barrels, furniture and assorted timbers. Calabos, recognizing one or two as Tangaroth's mages, smiled brightly at them.

A stern, grey-bearded man in blue-patterned formal robes and headwear came forward, flanked and followed by assistants and lesser officials. Calabos knew this to be Roldur dor-Mar, High Steward of Sejeend, and gave a solemn bow, prompting the others to do likewise.

'Ser Calabos,' the High Steward said evenly. 'The circumstances of your appearance are certainly quite singular. In recent days I have learned that the Watchers, whom I had thought to be no more than a city legend, do actually exist, and then discovered that at their head is the renowned dramatist, Beltran Calabos. But then Archmage Tangaroth declared them a danger to the throne and before his departure with the Emperor, he ordered that they be taken into custody.' A faint smile tugged at the corners of his mouth. 'Then, a mere hour ago, I received a visit from emissaries of the honoured Ushralanti, offering their counsel and aid against this dire invasion — if I can guarantee a safe passage and amnesty for you and your Watchers. It seems a small price for such valuable assistance so be welcome Calabos, at the crux of these cryptic times.'

'All our lives are but threads in the great tapestry of the world, High Steward,' Calabos said. 'We thank you for your kindness.'

'Tapestry, hmm? I am tempted to wonder if such as yourselves are the weavers or the weft . . . but come, time wastes and the Ushralanti emissaries await you further along the dale. Ser Coireg will guide you.'

Then with a slight nod, they were dismissed as the High Steward turned to speak to his functionaries. Coireg beckoned and Calabos and the others followed him along the footpath to a little taproom, a single-storey building sitting on low stilts and having a peaked roof, a hearth flue leaking grey smoke, and coloured lamps in its tiny windows. As they reached the few steps leading up to its porch, Coireg paused and turned to Dardan and Sounek.

'For just now, sers, the Ushralanti have asked to speak with Calabos alone.'

Dardan scowled and Sounek raised an eyebrow. Calabos laughed softly.

'Be patient, gentlemen,' he said as he climbed the porch steps. 'If you grow bored, you have my permission to talk about me behind my back!'

With that he pushed open the lodge door and entered, and straight away felt an air of tension and an undercurrent of something like fear.

Inside were several tables, all deserted except one where three imposing figures sat. All wore some variety of grey or earth-brown coat, voluminous garments that could conceal even sizeable blades, while their faces were equally impassive, even severe. As he regarded them he had a rising sense of familiarity, tenuous and inexplicable. For a moment they only gazed wordlessly back as he walked across the room, then the one in the middle spoke.

'Ser Calabos – I am Qothan, outrider of the clansboat *Stormclaw*, and these are my companions Viras and Yostil. Please – be welcome at our table.'

Calabos took the empty fourth chair, placed it round beside the Ushralanti and sat down. This forced them to look to one side rather than bring their attention to bear on him, as if he were some kind of supplicant.

'So, ser Qothan,' Calabos said. 'What I have heard about you from my friend Coireg intrigues me as does his remarkable recovery from a mind-malady, resulting from an elixir made by yourselves. Then it transpires that you wished to meet me, which served to sharpen my fascination with your people, the Ushralanti, whose name is a mystery to me.'

The one named Qothan gave a faint smile.

'We have gone under many names,' he said. 'But our essence remains as it was . . . as it was when you knew us.'

The vague feelings suddenly came into focus and Calabos' thoughts came under pressure as a nameless panic took hold.

Do they know who I am? How could they?

'Your words confuse me, friend Qothan,' he said amiably. 'If we had met in the past, I would have remembered without a doubt.'

'Trust to your mage sense, Calabos,' Qothan said. 'We shall diminish the mask of our seeming for a short time that you may behold and understand.'

Calabos started to say 'wait' but then the small lamps in the rest of the room began to darken and the three figures appeared to shrink slightly, their faces blurred and shadowed. At the same time, the ghostly outline of much larger forms took shape around them, wavering and transparent, becoming more definite, more detailed. There were broad torsos, massive shoulders, great, narrow, reptilian heads, claws and hooked wings.

Calabos drew a shuddering breath, for recognition was unavoidable.

The Daemonkind, first and mightiest of the Lord of Twilight's servants, whose ancient true name was the Israganthir.

Calabos' first impulse was to assume the worst and call on the hardiest of his defensive thought-cantos as he started to rise from the table. But then the fearsome shapes faded, leaving just the three austere men, and Qothan extending a calming hand.

'Friend Calabos, I beg you to have no fear. None of us bears you any ill will nor intends any harm.'

'Easy words to say, Qothan,' Calabos said.

'Then judge us by our actions – we have remedied the disarray of your friend Coireg's mind, and thereby helped him to aid your escape from the sorcerer Jumil's trap. And very shortly we intend to go forth into the chaos of the lower city to find and destroy the Wellsource-driven relics which are sustaining the undead army.'

There was silence between them as Calabos sat back in his chair, mulling this over.

'You know who I once was,' he stated, hardly believing that he was admitting it openly.

'In truth, the man we see before us is far removed from the dread presence our forebears knew as Byrnak the Shadowking. Just as our loyalties and purposes have become altered, first broken in the forge of defeat then recast by time and experience and hard-gained shreds of wisdom.'

'So you know that He is trying to return . . . or rather this Jumil is gathering in the everlasting fragments of His evil essence,' Calabos said bitterly. 'And something has happened earlier today, hasn't it? I have been sensing for some hours another dark presence in the city, somewhere not far from here . . .'

'Jumil has managed to create a Shadowking, Calabos,' Qothan said. 'Nor is it alone – a second, lesser one is leading this attack of the revenants on Sejeend. Neither is as powerful as the original Shadowkings were individually, but there seems to be some concealed process of change at work. We also felt the sorcerous calling sent forth by Jumil, and we are certain that it is still playing a part.'

A Shadowking, Calabos thought, feeling a shiver go through him.

'Yet, by all this,' he said, 'I am driven to wonder at your reason for involving yourselves in this dark drama, and why I have gained your interest.'

It was Qothan's turn to pause and frown thoughtfully for a moment. At last he said:

'We are a people caught on the bridge of prophecy,' he said, and went on to tell of how the shipborne Daemonkind fled into the eastern seas after the defeat of the Lord of Twilight, where they found an island of jagged towers and its eternal roaring vortex. At its heart, he said, they encountered a strange deity called the Sleeping God which issued a string of prophecies, some of which were now starting to come true.

'But by their very nature,' Qothan went on, 'most prophecies are limited and uncertain, with no mention of what seems important in the crux, which leaves us halted on the bridge of prophecy with mist all around . . .'

'Uncertain which side to approach,' Calabos said, completing the conundrum. 'And myself?'

'The auguries in the Book of the Vortex speak of the Prince of Change, who will be the one to face the rising shadow and defeat him.' Qothan grimaced. 'Unfortunately, there are several possible candidates who possess the kind of qualities described in the prophecies . . . *"No mother, no father, but torn from the earth"* one of the verses says – also *"Broken and remade is he, buried and unveiled, cherished and abandoned"* . . .'

'And you think that I could be this Prince of Change,' Calabos said sceptically.

'Perhaps, or he could be your companion, Coireg Mazaret,' Qothan said. 'He came to our attention on the night of Jumil's calling, which accentuated the divisions in his mind and provoked him into fleeing the House of Seclusion. With subtle far-voice whispers we were able to draw him in the direction of the Silver

Landings where we took him under our protection and offered him the calmative. He has a strange ability to reach what remains of the Wellsource, but it is an unpredictable skill that is rooted in the deranged part of his mind.'

Calabos shook his head, not quite knowing what to make of this view of his old friend.

'You said there were "several" candidates for this heroic position,' he said. 'Whom else is there? – Please tell me that it's not Tangaroth or Ilgarion . . .'

'Neither,' said Qothan. 'However, you do know him – Corlek Ondene.'

'The errant captain?' Calabos was nonplussed for a moment, then realization struck. 'It was one of you who spirited him out of that courtyard.'

Qothan inclined his head. 'It was I – it was the end of a long journey we had taken in the captain's wake. Owing to various visions and portents down the years we had know about him for some time although we were not certain that he was the one we sought.'

'So is he aboard your ship?'

'No . . .' The Daemonkind's face became grave. 'Through our own lack of foresight as well as unfortunate circumstances, he fell into the hands of the dark sorcerer, Jumil. He has been using Corlek as a receptacle for the spirit-wraiths of the Lord of Twilight, those deathless shreds of his essence, and it was their coalescence at Hojamar Keep which you sensed earlier.'

It was an old crawling fear that Calabos felt, a sharp dread which had haunted countless dreams, that horror at the possibility of the Lord of Twilight's return. And now those shadowy nightmares were distilling into reality. He looked down at his hands, expecting to see his inner tumult mirrored in trembling fingers. Yet they were calm and he gradually realized that this was an echo of Byrnak's fear of obliteration by the Lord of Twilight's convergence, heightened by the malign presence of the god-fragment that he had carried within. Imprinted in his thoughts, it tried to spread its cold grasp throughout his mind yet now he could look directly at it and know it for what it was.

He breathed in deeply, relaxing with the exhalation. 'So – an unfortunate situation,' he said. 'Complicated by this eldritch attack of the undead, which you intend to stand against, yes?'

'We must challenge Jumil and the possessed Captain Ondene,' Qothan said. 'But we have to deal with the revenant invaders first, not least because it would be useful to capture their leader, the one who raised them, rather than allowing him to be slain. Deprived of its host, the fragment of the Lord of Twilight he carries may then seek out another, most probably Ondene, thus strengthening that which rides in his mind.'

'Be assured that the Watchers will do all they can to aid you in this,' Calabos said. 'What action do you propose?'

'To take three parties composed of soldiers, yourselves and Tangaroth's mages, with one of us in each,' Qothan said. 'Then to sally forth with the aim of turning aside the undead and seizing their leader.'

'A laudably straightforward plan,' Calabos said. 'Assuming that we are able to make this man our prisoner – what then?'

Qothan gave him a wintry smile. 'Much will depend on the circumstances of his capture – it may be that our ship will return and provide the necessary aid.'

All four stood, and Calabos turned to face the Daemonkind squarely.

'I am honoured by your decision to take me into your confidence,' he said. 'Although I am not Byrnak, the echoes of his life still reverberate in my mind. Tonight, however, they have grown quieter.'

'The honour is ours, long-lived Calabos,' said Qothan. 'We are still the ones who serve, but we now follow a duty higher than the black ambitions of a broken god.' He tilted his head. 'We are done here, sers. Let us go forth.'

Outside, a persistent rain was falling and the leaves of bushes and trees gleamed in the light of the footpath lamps. Archers and spearmen were hurrying past in twos and threes, heading for the barricade which had grown in the interim and was now defended by a hundred or more.

As the four emerged from the alehouse, Calabos saw Dardan and Sounek deep in conversation which ceased abruptly when they saw him. For a moment Calabos thought he saw a look of uncertainty in Dardan's face then Coireg approached, his bare head soaked, hair matted to his skull.

'We cannot wait much longer,' he said. 'Tangaroth's people say that there are at least three groups of invaders heading this way.'

Sounek and Dardan had joined them and Calabos glanced their way for confirmation. Sounek nodded.

'An accurate summary,' he said. 'Focus through your undersenses and you can feel the talismans their leaders carry – they're like three burning jewels in the night. And you should also know that we've had word from Tashil – she and the others are safely ashore, at the Silver Landings of all places.'

'I heard nothing from her,' Calabos said, turning to Qothan with a frown.

'We habitually veil our thoughts from any possible spies,' said the tall Daemonkind. 'Your closeness to us may have prevented such farspeech reaching you. But we must delay no longer – various powers are moving into concurrence.'

Calabos nodded and looked at his companions. 'Three parties it shall be then, and with the help of Tashil and the others we may stand a better chance of taking the invaders' leader alive. Listen . . .'

Down in the sloping, rain-lashed street, a horde of the undead were charging uphill towards a shaky barricade where barely a score of city guardsmen waited. Axe and sword blades shone wetly in the fitful light of guttering torches while a limping serjeant tried to snarl some courage into his men – go for the wrists before the ankles, he was saying, and the ankles before the head. Use your bucklers offensively, guard your companion's back, and hearken to my orders . . .

Then the first wave struck. A section of the barricade gave way and the decayed attackers surged towards the breach to meet the guardsmen's axes . . .

From a third-floor window back along the street, Tashil watched the ensuing battle while keeping a weather eye on the main body of invaders, both alive and dead, who were massing about twenty yards from the fight at the barrier. Yet while this transpired, her thoughts were full of farspeech as she and Inryk settled on a plan with Calabos.

(. . . *follow them up to the Onwyc Parade*) Calabos was saying, (*And when they start across it, you launch your first attack — Firedagger should suffice to begin with — and once you've got their attention, we'll strike from their rear.*)

Master, the buildings on the north side of the parade are only covered stalls and two-storey workshops, Tashil said. *There's nowhere for us to take a stand.*

(*While our main group is striking their rear, a second group led by Dardan will be heading for your position, enough to keep you from being overwhelmed*) Calabos said. (*By then, hopefully, the revenants will have ceased to be a problem.*)

If that's the plan, then let us proceed, Inryk said. *The enemy shows no sign of flagging.*

Which was true enough — down in the street, a mere handful of surviving guards were fleeing uphill through the pouring rain towards another torchlit barricade. Beyond that, Tashil knew, was tree-lined Onwyc Parade which ran west and curved south past the main gates of Hojamar Keep where it met the square there. Where this Jumil and another powerful sorcerer were ensconced, according to Calabos.

If it's absolutely necessary to capture the invaders' leader, she said, *then this seems as good a plan as any.*

(*It is necessary, I assure you.*)

Then let us press onward, she said. *Just tell Dardan not to be late!*

She caught a flash of the old man's humour, then the presence of his thoughts faded, leaving her in the cold, dim room with the others. By the light of a solitary hooded lamp she could see that her brother was studiously sharpening his sword while Rog and Gillat were chewing on dried beef and hard biscuit which they had looted from an abandoned guardpost near the docks. Inryk stood by the other window, smiling sadly, and she wished briefly that Dybel was with them. But he had been utterly exhausted by the fight out on the bay and was in no fit state to continue: when they moored at the Silver Landings, hard on the heels of the undead ships, the steward Enklar had volunteered to stay aboard the *Merry Meddler* and mind Dybel, to which the rest agreed.

Atemor looked up and met her gaze. 'Are we to join the battle, 'Sheel?'

'After a fashion,' she said and outlined Calabos' plan. Rog and Gillat shrugged and nodded, while Atemor frowned.

'A perilous tactic,' he said. 'If your friend and his fighters are too late, we die.'

'When we find the right place from which to launch our attack,' Inryk said, 'we could survey the vicinity for possible escape routes . . .' He glanced out the window. 'And the sooner we leave the longer we'll have.'

Down in the street, the mob of invaders had swollen in number, now looking to be several hundred strong as they strode uphill. As one, the five companions rose and made for the stairs with Tashil in the lead, employing her magesight while the lamp was with Gillat who brought up the rear. Outside, they dashed across the cobbled road and clambered over a log wall which blocked a narrow alleyway. While the main streets in this part of Sejeend ran straight, the back streets were a maze of alleyways, passages, private yards, gardens, and improvised walls. This would have been risky territory for any invading force, crammed with ideal ambush points and avenues of escape both above and below ground.

It was a higher path that they were taking, a route that lay along courtyard walls, the flat roofs of decrepit sheds and crumbling middens, balconies and gantries, much of it slippery from the rain. The townsfolk were much more in evidence here than out on the main streets, and the five attracted catcalls and curses as they hurried past open windows and doors. Once, as they traversed an angled roof, a gang of gutter urchins starting throwing stones at them from a nearby low wall until Inryk sent a spray of ice needles their way, forcing them to duck out of sight.

An intermittent fence of rotten planking marked the boundary between the back streets and the properties that faced onto Onwyc Parade. As they dropped from a rickety balcony down into a muddy lane, Tashil risked a brief sending in farspeech.

Calabos, she thought. *We're almost in position.*

For a moment there was no reply, then:

(*We've got problems . . . more of the enemy here than we thought so*

*we're taking another way towards Onwyc — let me know when the main
group reaches the parade . . .)*

She began to agree but he was gone. All was utterly dark in
the lane and for a second she thought that the others had abandoned her, until she caught Inryk's presence nearby. He was just
round the corner of a two-storey building, probably one of the
workshops.

'Atemor and the guards have gone inside to scout,' he said as
she joined him. He was standing beneath the dripping lintel of a
double-doored entrance. 'This place is much like the others along
this part of the parade. Once the invaders break through the barricade at the top of Beehive Street they'll have to come past here,
whether they're heading for Kala dale or the Keep . . .'

He paused as Rog appeared in the darkened doorway to mutter
an all-clear, then lead them along a short passage and up stone
steps to a lightless second floor. Gillat was standing over by another
set of steps with the hooded lamp, its muffled glow showing up
rows of wooden shelves crammed with what looked like pottery.
These stairs led up to the roof, emerging beneath a sloping, unsteady
wattle-and-canvas canopy which sheltered some small barrels and
an open crate half-full of shattered crockery. A knee-high mortared
wall enclosed the roof and Atemor was squatting near one of the
front-facing corners, staring out at the wide road. Tashil went over
to crouch by him, ignoring the rain which was now gusting heavily
along Onwyc Parade, rushing through the trees.

'Sometimes these cities feel more dangerous than the swamps
of Gulmaegorn,' Atemor murmured.

Tashil smiled wryly, knowing the truth in his words. She was
about to mention some of the perils of life in their father's house
when a couple of figures dashed into view along the road, close
to where Beehive Street began. Sure enough, moments later
ragged-looking men came stalking forth in ones and twos at first,
then a dense mass of them poured into Onwyc Parade, then
wheeled round to march in the direction of Hojamar Keep.

Swiftly, Tashil went within to focus her farspeech, seeking
Calabos — *They've reached the parade! They're here . . .*

Again, a long empty moment.

(*We can't . . . we're hemmed in on an upper floor but our serjeant thinks there's a way out . . . Tashil, you must delay them . . . Dardan will be with you soon . . . have to . . .*)

As his thought-aura faded, Tashil came back to the cold wet night to see Inryk crouching beside her, a half-smile on his lips.

'He's been held up, but we still have to attack, yes?'

'That's right,' she said.

'It's going to be a like twisting a moortiger's tail,' he said. 'So – firedaggers in the middle of a downpour . . . hm, might work . . .'

A glittering, roseate radiance bloomed around his hands and he smiled. Tashil laughed softly and looked back out at the enemy host as it approached. The sight was unnerving – only a few carried torches, living pirates probably, and they were grouped near the leading rows, clustered around someone who had to be their mysterious leader. The rest comprised a great shuffling mass numbering in the hundreds, their forms barely discernible as they trudged on in rain-drenched darkness, their deathly presence pervading the surroundings. She could sense the dim flickering awareness of those subjugated spirits, dragged back from the Vale of Unburdening and the other realms of death to act the part in another's extravagant melodrama. Ending these pitiful existences could only be the grimmest of chores, but a necessary one.

As the host began to draw level with their position, Tashil resorted to farspeech once more.

Calabos . . . Dardan? – we shall soon be in need of your skills . . .

(*We're not far away*) came Dardan's irascible response (*Just run into a little trouble . . . carry on . . .*)

And he was gone. Inryk chuckled.

'Time to light up the night, methinks.'

She glanced at the dark host of the undead, whose crowded centre was passing by, and suppressed the fear that gnawed at her resolve. She made a 'hold' gesture, waited for the trailing edge to straggle by, then nodded. Together, the mages stood, their hands ablaze, and hurled a volley of firedaggers into the central mass of the undead invaders. Hissing like knots of burning snakes, the blazing bolts struck and spread over several forms. Gouts of steam erupted and a few angry cries went up from the living. The dead, though, merely halted and turned to look up at Tashil and the others on the workshop roof, all clearly following the overarching regard of their master. For a frozen moment, Tashil almost felt the eerie pressure of hundreds of dead gazes focussed unwinkingly on those who had dared to assail them. Then the mass of sodden figures moved as one towards the workshop.

Almost immediately, Tashil heard a shout and sounds of fighting from over by the steps – Rog and Gillat were hacking and kicking at figures trying to climb up to the roof while Atemor was rolling two barrels over from the other end of the shelter.

'They're not part of the crowd at the front,' Tashil yelled. 'Where have they come from?'

As Atemor steered the barrels one after another into the open stair hatch, Tashil gritted her teeth and turned back to the street before the workshop. As the undead crowded in close to the walls, she and Inryk sent repeated barrages of firedaggers down into the press but with little obvious effect.

Dardan! she thought in farspeech. *Now would be a very good time . . .*

(*Wait . . . just hold for a bit longer . . .*)

I wish we could, she thought as a sopping wet figure hauled itself up over the wall to her left and lunged at her. In savage reflex she called on the thought-canto Barb and as those shrivelled hands grabbed at her she delivered a back-handed blow with a fist wreathed in lightning. For a second she saw the unleashed power flare through the revenant's mock flesh, turning it patchily translucent and showing up age-browned and bitten bones – then it opened its mouth as if to scream but instead burst apart in a cascade of rotten, desiccated bones and soaked rags.

But there were now others following his example, clawing up the outside of the workshop, clambering up over each other to reach the roof.

Are we going to die here? she thought to herself. *Is this how I touch my fate?*

Atemor was still fighting furiously to clear the side wall and the canopy while Rog and Gillat wrestled a long object from

behind the barrels, a heavy ladder which they then hauled over
to the wall – and flung out to span the gap between their workshop and the next.

Tashil felt a surge of something like optimism and tapped Inryk
on the shoulder.

'On to the next bastion!' she cried above the noise.

Pausing to toss another firedagger into the half-skeletal face of
a giant undead brigand, he followed her to the improvised bridge.
Tashil strove to keep her feet on the rungs as she hurried across,
and when she got to the other side she urged the others to do
the same. Gillat was the last over and he had to fight off two
undead assailants and one of the living raiders before he was able
to step onto the horizontal ladder. A yard or two from salvation
his footing slipped but he held on and crawled the rest of the way
on hands and knees. Once he was safe, the rest dragged the ladder
across too, dislodging a couple of the enemy down into the milling
crowd.

Tashil had a desperate plan – to use the ladder in a similar
fashion to bridge the gap between this workshop and the fence
that ran along the back lane and thus escape back into the maze
of alleys. She quickly explained this to the others and they were
about to manhandle the ladder over to the roof's rear wall when
a man carrying a small silver object leaped up over the wall and
landed nimbly on the roof before them.

'Time to pay the price for your folly,' he said, gesturing at the
ladder which promptly burst into flames. There were fearful, angry
cries as the ladder fell clattering on the rain-puddled roof. The
man studied them as he strolled over and casually rested one booted
foot on the low wall, grinning as a stream of his undead servants
emerged from the stair hatch behind him.

'Who are you?' Tashil said, angry in her despair.

'Captain Bureng is my name, fair swordmistress,' he said.
'Although when this is over I may have to take on a title more
befitting my new standing . . .'

'Your new standing?' Tashil said. 'Please, Captain, explain further.'
And in her thoughts she said – *Dardan, we need you!*

Bureng laughed while holding up the silver thing he held, which she realized was a mirror and also the heart of the Wellsource spell that was maintaining the host of the undead. To Tashil's eye, it was like the burning core of a web of threads extending in every direction and she knew that only its destruction could ensure the invaders' defeat.

'Your friend cannot answer because very likely he is fighting for his life,' Bureng said, glancing at the dozens of black-eyed revenants now gathered on the rooftop. 'As for my new standing . . . well – as I look around me, I see an empire badly in need of leadership, a throne without an emperor . . .'

'Actually, we already have one,' Inryk said. 'Admittedly, he's not too bright, but at least he has the virtue of moderate sanity.'

Bureng gave him a look of deadly glee. 'I think I'll kill you first,' he said and took a step forward, his free hand raised and burning with emerald fire.

There was a bright burst of light and a loud thud as a sorcerous bolt of power struck the edge of the roof where Bureng had just been standing. The dazzling flash lit up the rain-whipped rooftop in a brief instant of startled reactions, then Bureng heedlessly stepped up to the smoking, shattered hole in the stonework and waved his fist at one of the tall buildings on the other side of Onwyc Parade.

'Come now, brother!' he bawled against the rush of the wind and the rain. 'Why so timid? Meet me face to face—'

A second bolt lanced out of the darkness and crashed into the crowd of revenants, destroying several, knocking many more off their feet or over the side of the roof. As Bureng ranted and railed at his unseen adversary, Tashil turned to the others.

'If we take him by surprise, we could get hold of that mirror,' she said. 'That's where the power over the undead resides.'

There were nods all round and as one they charged at him, but a short scrawny man standing nearby yelled a warning and Bureng turned to meet their attack. He brought the mirror round blazing with power and gave Gillat a mighty blow which threw him off to the side, then landed a fist squarely in Inryk's chest. But Atemor managed to wheel behind him and wrap his arms around the man's throat while Rog went for a sliding kick at his legs.

They all went down in a tangled heap of grunts and roars of fury. Tashil had got hold of the upper part of the mirror and was trying to tug it away but Bureng was holding on for dear life, his voice taking on an eerie, sawing quality that grew louder while apparently emanating from his body. Suddenly, a terrible heat invaded her hands and arms as she wrestled and fought for the mirror, a hot buzzing stabbing at ears and eyes. A kind of animal panic took hold and she had to let go and get away from that burning vibration, as did the others apart from Atemor who held on to Bureng's neck with grim determination. But Bureng was possessed with eldritch power and dragged Atemor with him as he got to his feet then reached round for the young warrior. Tashil was about to throw herself at him again when a tall, gaunt figure dived between them and dealt Bureng a blow to the face that brought blood from his nose and sent him reeling.

The newcomer then swiftly seized the hand grasping the mirror and wrenched it free. Still struggling against Atemor, Bureng bellowed in rage as the tall man held the mirror out in one hand and stared at it. All around was a scene of mayhem, Rog and Gillat fighting like madmen against the mob of dead brigands, Inryk regaining his feet and loosing firedaggers at them while sheets of rain swept over them all.

The tall stranger seemed to shut it all out as he gazed at the mirror. Then the complex, interwoven pattern on the mirror began to glow a dirty orange, then ruby red then brightened to the colour of gold in a forge . . . all the undead brigands ceased their fighting and clawing and pushing, and turned to regard the mirror. The pattern upon it was white hot now and as it slowly sagged and melted, the hundreds of revenants on and around the workshops and everywhere across the city of Sejeend uttered a collective, mournful moan and broke apart, every shrivelled, rag-clad form collapsing into a heap of bones and crumbling, dusty matter into which streams of water ran.

As the stranger tossed the buckled remains of the mirror down into the street, where it clinked on the cobbles, Bureng let out a howl of fury and twisted his shoulders, trying to dislodge Atemor. As he did, a blazing bolt flew down from the high buildings opposite and struck the roof nearby, engulfing them both in a deafening eruption of chaotic brilliance amid which shadowy figures went flying. When Tashil's eyesight recovered she found that she and the others were crouched on a rooftop strewn with heaps of wet bones. Smoke and vapour rose from a charred hole where the bolt had struck and near the centre of it a figure was sprawled. As she stumbled over she saw that it was not Bureng, who had vanished, but her brother.

Atemor lay on his side, still and unbreathing. An awful quivering fear gripped her as she crouched down beside him. Some of his hair was missing and there was a ghastly, dark red wound high on his neck, beneath one ear, yet his rain-beaded face seemed calm, the eyes half-open as he was about to fall asleep or had just woken . . .

Tashil could hear Dardan's voice nearby and sense Calabos' farspeech calling to her on the fringes of her mind. But all she could think about was how her father would blame her for Atemor's death, how she had failed to protect him . . .

The tears and the rain ran down Rikken's face into his sobbing mouth or down his neck as hauled the small, two-wheeled cart containing Captain Bureng along a sidestreet. Everything had gone wrong – the talisman mirror had been wrecked, the undead army had been unmade, the *Mocker*'s crew were either dead or scattered, and the Captain had scarcely seemed alive when Rikken had dragged his scorched, inert form out of the filthy alley after his fall off that roof. He had been lucky enough to find the rudimentary handcart in a small shed not far along the back lane. But finding a safe route back to the pier where the *Mocker* was moored was proving a stern test.

Many buildings were afire and some citizens had banded together to protect their shops and houses while gangs of drunken looters and roughs roamed freely from street to street. Of the army and the city guard there was no sign except for overheard rumours that there were running battles over at the wharfs by the sea gates. There were, however, enough people out and about to make Rikken fear the chance of being stopped so he snatched a discarded piece of sacking from a backyard midden and draped it over Bureng's unconscious form.

Then it was a maniacal progress through the rainy streets, trying to avoid anyone by steering the cart along alleys and through back courts. Those who accosted him were usually dissuaded by the story that he was taking his dead dog across town to the apothecary, then letting drop that the dog had died from the black yaws. Which was usually enough to have them wide-eyed and clasping a hand over nose and mouth while making tracks to the other side of the road.

At last the tall gates of to the Silver Landings came into view as he pushed Bureng out from a muddy side alley. As he crossed the wide street he imagined that hundreds of eyes were watching his every move and it was an effort of will to try and appear relaxed and unhurried, as if this was something he had done every day for years. Moments later he was through the gates and pushing the cart quickly north along the quayside, eyes eager to find the *Mocker*'s lines in the darkness.

But instead of dozens of dark, decayed ships moored along the wharfs and quays, there were clusters of slanted masts jutting from waters clogged with broken timbers, tangled rigging and ragged pieces of sailcloth. Rikken slowed in amazement, uncomprehending for a moment until the slow realization came upon him that the destruction of the mirror talisman had brought about the sinking of Hanavok's fleet as well as the disintegration of his undead army.

And as he splashed along the dockside, weaving around heaps of bones and dead bodies, a sense of mortal fear and loss grew in him when he saw that the *Mocker*'s berth at one of the main piers was empty. He could just make out the lamps of a ship about half a mile out and heading for open sea, and he thought he recognized the lines of the *Mocker* as it faded into the rainy night.

'Gone,' he whispered. 'It's gone 'n' left us . . .'

Then he noticed movement along the now-vacant pier, a sprawled figure trying to rise quite near to one of the few hanging lamps still alight. Pulling the cart and the captain, he hurried along towards it and was startled to see that it was Captain Logrum, who brought out a dagger as he drew near. Then Logrum saw who it was and let his dagger hand fall.

'Bureng's underling,' he said and laughed, but the laugh turned into a deep, hacking cough which etched pain into his features. His hair was matted to his skull and the steady rain had soaked him through, and as Rikken crouched beside him he saw blood pooling beneath legs clad in slashed breeks.

'Hamstrung me and threw me on the pier,' Logrum said.

'Who?'

Anger flared in Logrum's eyes and water dripped from his beard. 'Flane,' he said. 'Shadow-cursed, red-eyed bastard! And he left me another little gift before he sailed . . .' The big man pulled aside a fold of his shirt to reveal the broken stump of an arrow sticking out of his chest. 'Barbed arrow,' he said, voice wheezing. 'Flane did it by hand to make sure it went into the lung, just so I'll take a while to die . . .' He paused for another bout of agonized coughing that left him pale and trembling.

'Have you seen aught of Raleth?' he said.

'Nothing,' Rikken said.

'Wonder if he ran into one of 'em tall bastards . . . don't know who they was but they were after them talismans. I saw one of 'em leap into the middle of Zanuur's mob of walking corpses and suddenly they're turning on Zanuur and his men, tearing them apart, ripping off heads and arms. Same thing happened to me, got jumped by one of 'em tall 'uns, grabbed my bear statue – don't know what he did but next thing I know everything went mad . . . lucky for me there was an open window nearby . . .'

He paused to glance with narrow eyes at the handcart and its covered cargo. 'What's on the cart?'

Rikken froze with uncertainty, then reasoned that Logrum was incapable of being a threat.

'My captain,' he said.

Logrum smiled sourly. 'So Bureng's still alive, eh? Don't look too lively to me . . .' He stopped as a spasm of pain forced a groan from his lips, '. . . too much, devil's pain . . .' He stared at Rikken. 'Take my dagger, push it into my heart—'

'No,' said Rikken, backing away. 'No, I couldn't . . .'

Logrum cursed and spat at him. 'Crawl away then, you worm!
Leave me . . . have to do it myself . . .'

Rikken grabbed the cart's handles and pushed it back along the
pier, pausing on the stone dock to look back. He was just in time
to see the half-raised Logrum fall forward onto his face. Through
the hiss of the rain he heard a grunt and knew that the captain
of the *Vandal Lord* was dead. Rikken's feelings of isolation swelled
and he crouched down beside the handcart, and leaned his head
against the wet wood, fighting tears, not knowing what to do.

Then one idea forced its way into his thoughts – *Hide.*

Yes, that was it. He would find somewhere safe for them both
to hide, and where he could tend to the captain's wounds. And
when he was strong, his master would come out from his hiding
place and crush all his enemies!

Leaping to his feet, he took hold of the cart with its motionless, covered passenger, and started back along the dock. A new
certainty was flowing through him now, and another word came
to him – *Food.* Yes, there would be plenty of unattended shops
and stalls in the area, so getting food should be easy.

. . . *Weapons* – ah, plenty of bodies lying around who won't be
needing their blades no more . . .

. . . *Money* – probably get that from the same place, or abandoned houses . . .

Chapter Fifteen

Spirits fly in darkness,
O'er wrathful gulfs of sleep.
Spirits fly in darkness,
On errands foul and deep.

Tazay, *Prekine Poems*

The rain and the wind came out of the raw blackness of the ocean's nightbound realm to batter and claw at the buildings and godowns all along Besh-Darok's waterfront. Countess Ayoni watched the storm from the near-empty common room of a dock-side inn called the Yardarm, looking out of a small, latticed window which she had wedged open. The occasional gusty draught brought sprinklings of droplets and made the flames flutter in her table's ornate lamp.

Ayoni's mood was dark and tight with anxiety. A short while ago, in her room upstairs, she had had a detailed and disturbing farspeech conversation with Calabos during which he let her know that the rest of the Watchers were still alive then went on to tell her about the dark sorcerer Jumil and the unfortunate Captain Ondene, and to warn her about the spirit-hosts. She in turn gave a brief account of the grotesque ritual she and Chellour had witnessed in the ruined palace, the grey blight that had resulted, and told of their escape from Ilgarion's camp and subsequent arrival in Besh-Darok, where they were waiting for a ship that was not due for at least another day.

And then all dialogue came to a halt when Calabos said that Tashil was in danger from an invading army of the undead, and he had to venture forth into the city. As the farspeech bond faded she was left with a growing determination to persuade Chellour, Jarryc and Klayse that they should return to Sejeend to lend aid to Calabos and the others. When she came downstairs, however, none of the men were there and when she asked the innmaster about them he only shrugged and said something about 'the slipway market'. But sallying forth in such vile weather was unappealing so she opted for sitting by the window and sipping from a beaker of silverpurl while contemplating the haze of wind-driven spray flying in from the waves crashing against the long quays.

She did not have too long to wait before the first, Chellour, returned, entering with rainwater streaming from his drenched cloak and leggings. Seeing Ayoni, he grinned as he doffed the cloak and hung it over a high-backed chair near her table. Brushing soaked hair out of his eyes, he sat down opposite her.

Ayoni related the main details of her dialogue with Calabos, ending with her change of mind on their destination. Hearing this, Chellour sat back, face thoughtful.

'I must admit that I was quite looking forward to seeing Margrave Tergalis' estates, but yes, we should be ready to help our fellow-Watchers in any way we can.' He glanced out the window. 'If only we could get to Sejeend. There's also the matter of persuading your esteemed husband and the baron.'

'I'm sure that I can get Jarryc to hear me out,' she said, 'which would be half the battle.'

A pair of hooded figures, hunched against the driving rain, came hurrying along the quayside towards the Yardarm. Noticing them, Chellour gave Ayoni an amused look.

'I think we're about to find out how persuasive you can be.'

She adopted a mock disdain. 'Ser, I am replete with confidence in my arguments!'

Moments later the inn door flew open to admit the two men along with a blast of rain-laden wind. Laughing, Jarryc, Count of Harcas, and Baron Klayse quickly closed the door, hung a box lantern on a hook, then pulled off their dripping cloaks and tossed them across the table next to Ayoni's.

'Now that,' the Count said, 'is what I call a storm!'

'Indeed, my lord,' Ayoni said. 'Venturing forth into its inclemency certainly appears to be a manly thing to do.'

Jarryc gave her a sideways, narrow-eyed half smile, and she strove to keep her own smile somewhere between innocent and enigmatic.

'My dear lady wife, you are of course quite correct – it is a buffeting storm of outstanding vigour and dampness, especially when experienced from the old battlements on the headland.'

'And did you espy much of interest from this vantage?'

Jarryc and the baron exchanged a look and a smile.

'Well, there were those branches flying through the rain,' he said.

'Don't forget the clothes,' said the baron. 'A monk's robes, I saw, amongst others, just flapping along—'

'And those fish . . .'

'. . . and that basket of vegetables . . .'

'. . . and the mouse!' Jarryc paused to frown. 'Or was it a cat from a distance . . . like the snake which turned out to be a worm?'

'Quite so, m'lord.'

By now, Ayoni and Chellour were openly laughing at this succession of storm-borne fancies. Jarryc's grin held a certain cunning, and Ayoni knew that there was more.

'. . . And of course,' he said, 'we beheld with our own eyes the decklamps of a ship headed this way.'

Ayoni and Chellour sat straighter at this news.

'Really?' said Chellour.

Baron Klayse laughed. 'No word of a lie or whimsy, ser,' he said. 'The ship itself is invisible against the night and the sea but its stormlights we saw repeatedly, and it certainly appeared to be on course for Besh-Darok. Excluding mishap, they should dock within the hour.'

'Good news, in truth,' Ayoni said.

'Tergalis has his own brewery on his estates,' Klayse went on. 'Their finest is a sweet ale that's a joy to the tongue. Wait till you taste it . . .'

'You paint a pretty picture,' Chellour said, glancing at Ayoni. 'Our destination sounds better all the time.'

Ayoni sighed, knowing it was now or never.

'My lord husband,' she said, standing. 'May I speak with you?' She looked over to one side to indicate the wish for words alone. He frowned for a second but the smile remained.

'Gentle sers,' he said to Chellour and Klayse, then they both crossed the common room to an empty corner where he turned to her and spread his hands.

'My dear lady wife, I am at your disposal.'

She matched his smile and began to relate again the main points of her farspeech exchange with Calabos, and explained her wish to return to Sejeend. As she spoke his face became grave and his eyes troubled.

'There's been no further messages from him?' Jarryc asked.

'None, from him or the others.'

Jarryc nodded thoughtfully. 'An army of the dead,' he murmured. 'And if this terrible host has triumphed, what point would there be in sailing to Sejeend?'

'I just don't believe that could happen,' Ayoni said. 'The nobles and garrison troops from the outlying demesnes will be hurrying there now – no invader can succeed for long.'

'And I feel the same, Ayoni, but if they do have mastery over the city then the docks are the last place we should think of approaching. However, if you do hear from any of the Watchers between times, and whatever vessel we take passage on reaches the waters south of Adranoth, and the news is favourable, I'll convince the captain to put in at Sejeend, with gold if necessary. Is that agreeable?'

'Both agreeable and sensible, o wise count!'

'I knew there was a reason why you married me!'

Once they had rejoined Klayse and Chellour, Jarryc outlined the possible courses they might take and there was sombre consent all round. Then to while away the time as they awaited the unknown ship, they took turns to relate an anecdote or a story or a joke.

It was Klayse who first noticed the vessel drawing near and the others gathered by the small window to stare out. A couple of swaying storm lamps were visible through the storm's gusting veils of rain and after a moment Ayoni could make out the form of a ship, a three-master with all but its lesser sails reefed and secured. A handful of harbourmen in heavy cloaks were already out on the longest of the jetties and as the ship rocked and pitched through the swell a few figures clambered up on the raised prow. Then weighted lines were hurled forth, most falling short while the necessary two or three reached the jetty to be caught by gauntleted hands and hauled on to bring in the heavier hawsers.

Soon the ship was securely berthed, its fore and aft mooring ropes lashed to ironbound posts, and a broad gantry was being manhandled out from the main deck to rest on the jetty's planks.

'We need to speak with the captain,' Jarryc said. 'Should we wait to see if he comes in here, or go outside to get his sooner attention?'

'The latter, I'd say,' Baron Klayse said. 'He may have decided on another inn altogether.'

Agreeing on this, all four donned their capes and cloaks and left the inn. Outside, the downpour had abated somewhat but Ayoni could still feel the dampness working its way through at the neck and shoulder seams. As they splashed across the dockside, a procession of passengers were already disembarking, tall people bulkily attired it seemed in voluminous cloaks and furs, some of them carrying pole-arms and spears. Intrigued by this, Ayoni did not notice the small group of men hurrying towards them from along the dock until Klayse spoke up.

'What can these fellows want of us?' he said.

There were five of them, two quite short in stature, and all wore long, cowled cloaks. As they approached one of the taller ones, a dusky, small-featured man, smiled and brought out empty hands, spreading them.

'Greetings, friends! We wish to make your acquaintance and put a proposal to you.'

'What kind of proposal?' Ayoni said, frowning.

'Oh, quite an involved one, yet it is certain to be of great profit,' he said, raising one hand to rub his neck.

Everything seemed to happen at once. The two shorter strangers parted their cloaks and cast clusters of filmy, beaded tendrils at

Ayoni and Chellour. Jarryc and Klayse reacted in sudden fury, both
glancing momentarily at the two mages and in that instant the
other two assailants had moved in close to press the points of
daggers against exposed throats. Ayoni and Chellour fought against
the fine entangling meshes but to no avail, and when she called
on the Firedagger thought-canto nothing happened. The
interlocking symbols of the spell turned in her mind but of the
Lesser Power she felt nothing; even her undersenses were bereft
of all the nuances and invisible currents that comprised the
bedrock of mage perception.

The man who had spoken was now holding a pair of slender
sabres, one pointing at Ayoni's throat, the other at Chellour's.

'The both of you,' he said, 'are now blind. Be still.'

'What is the meaning of this?' Ayoni said angrily. 'What harm
have we done to you?'

'It is not our well-being that matters,' said one of the shorter
men in a Mogaun accent. He still held the other end of the webby
tendrils which enfolded Ayoni who was suddenly convinced that
these two were Mogaun shamans. The two daggermen meanwhile
relieved Jarryc and Klayse of their blades.

'Hold your tongue,' the first said. 'Our master approaches.'

Neither blades nor eyes wavered yet there was an air of
expectancy. Reluctant to move, Ayoni tilted her head slightly and
looked sideways to see the ship's former passengers drawing near,
led by one tall imposing man garbed in a long hooded cloak of
wolf fur fringed with gaily coloured tassels and adorned here and
there with gold and silver symbols. Beneath he wore a quilted
leather doublet a couple of sizes too small and gaping open to
reveal a fine chain-mail shirt. Battered, grey-brown leather leggings
were armoured with small iron squares, yet the feet were shod in
light sandals. He had a long mane of hair, most of which was dry
beneath the hood, and dark intense eyes that betrayed no hint of
pity or compassion.

'Are these the ones?' the man said in a hard voice.

'Trussed and defanged, elder brother,' said the ambush leader.

The big man gave no reply, instead turning his harsh regard on
the four prisoners, appraising them one by one and ending with

Ayoni. Feeling almost nakedly vulnerable without the Lesser Power, she avoided meeting his gaze while striving to force her mind to break through the sorcerous barrier created by the strange fine webs. Not even an echo of the Lesser Power came to her but she did sense a menacing pressure on the edge of her thoughts, a hunger for secrets . . . and a realization crept over her.

This man looks like a Mogaun chieftain – is he a shaman as well?

Then the man turned his attention to one of the shorter Mogaun and the pressure vanished.

'What of the grey blight?'

'Still it grows, lord,' the shaman said. 'But slowly.'

Then it was back to the ambush leader. 'And the ardour of my host at Belkiol – how do they fare? Are the rafts finished?'

'All is ready, elder brother. They eagerly await your arrival.'

The chieftain nodded. 'I want to see the blight first. Bring *them* with us.'

As all four had their wrists bound, Klayse and Jarryc struggled and were cuffed into submission by the Mogaun who had arrived with their chieftain. Ayoni cried out in fear for her husband and was warned into silence by the sabre held by the chieftain's brother. Racked with terror and utterly helpless, Ayoni averted her face from the hovering swordpoint. Soon they were being roughly urged into the back of a covered wagon along with half a dozen tribesmen armed with axes and clubs. Then the wagon set off through the rainy darkness, wheels banging and jolting over the decrepit roadways.

Before long the road began to slope upwards slightly and when the wagon came to a halt she knew that they were near the old imperial palace. Lamps were lit as the prisoners were hustled out into the rain again then guided through the grassy, roofless remains of an imposing entrance. Ahead was only a murk out of which sodden mossy heaps of tumbled masonry emerged as the halo of their lamps moved ahead of them. The chieftain walked in the lead, guided by one of the shamans while the second followed close on Ayoni and Chellour's heels with the trailing threads of their clinging, entangling webs in his hands. Ayoni knew that they had to be within the confines of the palace but their location was a mystery until they turned along a short, narrow passage between two ruined buildings and at the end passed through a massively built arch and stopped. Everyone stared in silence at what they saw.

When Ayoni and Chellour had last seen the deathly greyness it had occupied most of the ground floor chamber of the ruined Keep of Day. Now the Keep was gone and the blight had spread out into the overgrown, weed-choked courtyard and up to the main wall of the palace itself. The nearest edge of it was just several yards from where they stood. The greyness also gave off a faint, pale radiance which by night gave it the appearance of a blanket of ashen snow. But when she stared towards the centre of it, that spot where the ritual had been conducted, the blight darkened into pitch blackness.

A pair of lamp glows came bobbing out of the gloom to their left, resolving into a small group of Mogaun, more shamans, Ayoni guessed, from their fur-clad scrawniness.

'Hail to thee, son of Krahel,' said one as they bowed.

'Greetings, Masjig,' the Mogaun chief said. 'My voices speak well of you.'

'We serve with hand and blood, o prince, and hold to the old ways.'

The chieftain indicated the blight. 'And is this the work of the Grey Lord? Should we welcome it or be wary of it?'

The shamans glanced at each other.

'It remains beyond our understanding for now – we can say what it does but not why.'

'Then show me what it does.'

The shamans' spokesman nodded, then beckoned over his shoulder. One of the others came forward leading a small dog which he and the spokesman picked up between them, carried to within a yard of the blight's edge and hurled it in. The dog yelped as it landed, legs scrambling, but before it could gain purchase to run back, a solid wave surged up out of the greyness and rushed over it. Ayoni felt sick as she watched the struggling outline of the poor creature grow still and sink down until there was only flat, dead grey.

The chieftain turned suddenly and took three swift strides towards Ayoni. Looming over her, he said:

'Your emperor has laid siege to west Belkiol and he builds war machines, thinking to batter down its walls. I want you to tell him that the town is empty, that everyone has fled over the crossing to east Belkiol.' His glare was like focussed black fury. 'Do this or your friends will follow the dog.'

He was close enough for her to smell his rank breath and the wet stink of his fur cloak.

'They won't believe me,' she said, desperate to convince him. 'We've already escaped from the imperial camp, a day ago – why would they trust anything I have to say?'

'You must make them listen and make them believe,' he said. 'Find a way, or . . .'

Ayoni felt as if her mind was caught in a drakken's jaws and she had to battle the despair which threatened to overwhelm her. She bowed her head to blink away tears, striving to calm the tumult of her thoughts, then she looked up to meet his gaze.

'I will do as you ask,' she said stonily. 'There is one thing I wish to know from you.'

'What?'

'Who are you?'

For the first time, he smiled, and it was a bare-toothed thing of malice.

'I am the warrior with a hundred faces,' he said. 'The words and thoughts of the ancestor spirits flow in my thoughts, awoken by the voice of the Grey Lord himself only days ago. His essence awaits me in that sewer-midden of a city named Sejeend – my first essence is named Huzur Marag, and that will suffice for your degenerate emperor!'

Then he turned away, calling for horses. As she was dragged off towards the archway, she looked around for Jarryc and met his angry, desperate gaze through the press of figures. His lips moved as if he were about to speak, but then she was through the arch and off into the darkness.

With impatience gnawing at his composure, Vorik dor-Galyn stood at his window and stared out at the city of Sejeend as a slow, grey dawn drew back the veils of night. The fighting and chaos of the night had left wounds on the city, yet it had fared worse in the past.

Such matters were only fleetingly on Vorik's mind which was instead occupied with doubts and worries concerning Jumil, the forthcoming Shatterseed ritual and his own place in it.

Where is that thrice-damned sorcerer? he fumed. *He should have been here half an hour ago.*

He thought about his flock, the NightKin that he had personally selected – they would be making their way up to the palace even now . . . assuming that all of them survived the convulsions of last night. That thought stabbed at him, sending his thoughts spinning in the grip of a sharper anxiety.

What was keeping Jumil? Then he wondered if he was talking with the Shadowking, who had reportedly returned an hour before dawn after having disappeared into the battle-torn streets at the height of the fighting. Vorik stepped away from the window, back into the golden warmth of his chamber and the pervading fragrance that emanated from the hearth where oiled logs burned. He poured himself a goblet of sweet Roharkan wine, turned to study an antique Dalbari tapestry for a moment or two, then crossed to the bookshelves and picked out a volume of Rootway aphorisms. Opening it at random, he read a couple of pages, seemingly engrossed . . . then uttered an oath, slammed the book down on a nearby table and wrenched open the door to the main corridor.

A pair of weary-looking archers gave him a startled look as he burst forth and stormed past. Paying them no heed, he strode the short distance to the sorcerer's door which he rapped hastily as he pushed through and entered.

'Master, the hours waste away thus, shrinking the leeway for our plans . . .'

He paused, suddenly aware of a tension in the room and the familiar copper tang of Wellsource power. Jumil and the possessed Ondene were standing either side of a heavy ornate table whose polished surface bore several scorch marks. In the grip of the Shadowking's spirit, Ondene was enfolded in a faint viridian nimbus which served to accentuate the look of frustrated anger

on his face. Jumil, on the other hand, seemed relaxed, his gaze
steady and amused although Vorik did notice a gleam of sweat on
his smooth pate.

He stepped forward, letting the door close behind him.

'Forgive me, sers, if I am interrupting . . .'

The Ondene-Shadowking gave him a poisonous stare. 'I have
questions I want answered – perhaps you can be more helpful
than your master.'

Vorik smiled coldly. 'It is unlikely that the student would know
more than the master.'

'I'm more interested in how willing you'll be.'

Vorik glanced at Jumil who was smiling enigmatically as he
watched the exchange. There was no concern or even a hint of
a warning in his countenance, so Vorik decided to see what the
boundaries of his knowledge were.

'Very well,' he said, crossing his arms. 'Ask your questions.'

'To whom do you and your master answer?' the Ondene-
Shadowking said. 'Whose plan are you fulfilling?'

'The Great Shadow.'

'And is he the Lord of Twilight?'

'Yes,' said Vorik. 'I think so . . . perhaps he is the major part of
that godhead.'

The Ondene-Shadowking moved towards him, something
dark and unreadable in his face. 'But I can feel the essence of
the Lord of Twilight in my mind, in my blood and my bones.
Your master has already hinted that this Great Shadow and I
are but fragments of a greater whole – do you believe that to
be so?'

The intensity of his regard was a pressure on Vorik's thoughts.

'It may be so,' he said. 'But I do not know enough to be sure.
Might it not be that the Grey Lord and the Great Shadow come
from . . . the same place . . .'

He was fumbling for some kind of explanation but at this Jumil's
eyes widened.

'This Nightrealm?' the Ondene-Shadowking went on. 'Is that
another name for the Realm of Dusk? Well, I've seen it, I've
looked into that realm or what's left of it, and I saw no trace of

a great power.' He sneered. 'So what is he, this Great Shadow – a homeless god?'

'The domain of holy, deathless night,' Jumil said suddenly, 'is every bit as real as this existence, this Realm Between. He waits there in all his glittering majesty, waits for the Shatterseeds to take root and begin the inexorable conquering of all these lands.' The sorcerer's smile had the steady brightness of unshakeable conviction. 'There will be high places for both of you in the grand pantheon which will rule this world.'

'Colourful words and lavish promises,' the Shadowking retorted. 'Baubles for children! I will not be a servant and I will not submit!'

With that he strode over to the door and gave it a casual knock with his knuckles. There was a sharp cracking sound as the door came apart in a shower of fragments and splinters that flew out into the corridor. Scarcely breaking step, he carried on through and was gone, even as some wooden slivers were falling to the floor in his wake.

'What is he going to do?' Vorik asked.

'Join with us,' Jumil said. 'Eventually.' Then he took up a carven staff and came over to Vorik. 'Now, the time is nearly upon us.'

Vorik straightened, feeling a surge of anticipation. 'My NightKin flock will be gathering at the appointed place very soon, master.'

'Good, good – let us be on our way.'

Pausing only to fill a small sack with several items – small figurines of gold and silver, herb bundles, a tinder box, a wad of parchment strips – Jumil then calmly led the way. Out in the corridor Vorik paused to speak with one of the Keep's master artisans who had already come to assess the damage, and asked him to replace the door as soon as possible, citing the variable moods of mages as the prime cause. Then he had to hasten to catch up with Jumil who had strode vigorously on ahead.

From one of the Keep's upper floors a bridge spanned the short distance to the top of the nearby cliffs. Once, a graceful mage-wrought stone bridge had cross that gap but the unrest and sporadic rebellions during the reign of Tauric IV had led to its collapse. Now a solidly built wooden one was in its place, constructed in the first years of Magramon's reign. With the rising sun, the cloud cover was starting to break and rush across the sky, letting shafts and glimpses of sunlight through to brighten the city and the waters of the bay.

At the other end of the bridge they were met by guards and a plain two-horse carriage, clearly pre-arranged by Jumil. Once they were moving through the affluent, clifftop districts, Vorik's thoughts turned wholly to the coming ritual. He had witnessed the reassuring lies that Jumil had given to the other Flock leaders and also had some idea of the abominable fate that each had embraced in the last day or two, first Lymbor at Besh-Darok, then Rugilo at Adnagaur, Skotan at Oumetra, and Amaj at Alvergost. Each one had unknowingly allowed themselves to be used as receptacles for the life essences of their Flocks, which helped transform them into living gates between this world and the Nightrealm of the Great Shadow.

Vorik had also received assurances, that he was by far the most valuable of all of Jumil's disciples, that for him the ritual would be quite different and that by its end the powers of the Wellsource would be engraved in his spirit. None of which he believed, so he had taken steps to learn as much as he could about the ceremony from what Jumil let slip, as well as copying what cantrips he could understand from the sorcerer's own books. What Jumil said about engraving the powers of the Wellsource into his spirit turned out to be quite feasible, provided there was an intense flux of it present, as would be during the Shatterseed ritual. For Vorik the problem was how to be in the vicinity of the Wellsource flux without becoming the sacrificial vessel. The solution he had arrived at involved having one of his Flock secretly don the real Well Amulet while he would wear a well-wrought duplicate.

As the carriage rattled across one of the Kala bridges, he shifted his arms slightly into a more comfortable position and could feel the shape of the fake amulet in a pocket beneath his cloak and doublet. Looking out at the foliage-masked dale, he smiled.

'Resist the illusion of over-confidence, Vorik,' said Jumil. 'Until the ritual is complete, all we have are mere plans and pieces – a failure is always total.'

'Both true and wise, master,' Vorik said, trying to sound humbled while keeping his resentment below the surface of his thoughts.

Before long their carriage passed between the gates of a large townhouse located very near to the boundary wall of the imperial palace. Its owner, a fleshy, jowl-faced man called Lusad, emerged from the main entrance to welcome them, closely followed by the rest of Vorik's NightKin flock. The greetings were grave and formal with Vorik and almost servile with Jumil. When Vorik shook hands with Lusad they exchanged a look, for it was he who would be wearing the real amulet under his shirt.

Vorik then took a moment to study his flock and was pleased to see that they were all properly attired as novitiates and aspirants of the Earthmother temple, seven men and three women robed and cowled in shades of brown.

'Brothers and sisters,' he said. 'Onward to our great task.'

So saying, he and Jumil led them from the townhouse and out through the gates. It was a short walk past a ceremonial garden where statues of heroes stood amid masses of bushes in bloom or by peaceful, tree-shaded ponds where insects buzzed and feathertails scurried amongst the branches. Everyone was cowled by the time the path brought them to the small postern gate in the palace's south wall. Two guards stood yawning in front while a third regarded their approach from a peaked tower over the gate. But as the hooded procession drew near, Jumil paused, frowning, and glanced back towards the city.

'Is anything wrong, master?' Vorik said.

Jumil shook his head, thoughtfully at first then dismissively.

'Just our Shadowking friend – he's up to something but it doesn't seem threatening.'

Vorik shrugged then led the group the last dozen yards to the gate. The guards knew him well and on the strength of his authority as an Iron Guard officer, all the NightKin were admitted, along with Jumil who was posing as an official recording scribe sent by the Academy. Once they were all through, Vorik glanced over his shoulder as the gate swung shut.

When I pass this way again, he thought, *the world will be a very different place.*

Almost two hours before Vorik and Jumil departed Hojamar Keep,

Calabos and Coireg Mazaret were navigating the polished wooden passageways of the Daemonkind ship, *Stormclaw*, seeking out a chamber called the auracle where a grave conferral was to take place. After the battles and terrors of the night's chaos, Qothan had announced that the *Stormclaw* had returned to Sejeend and the clade chiefs were preparing to offer the Watchers sanctuary in accordance with the safe passage guaranteed by High Steward Roldur. Everyone gratefully agreed to this proposal but firstly they had to find a shrouder who would prepare the body of Tashil's brother, Atemor, for a Mogaun burial. Then they collected Dybel and Enklar from the storehouse where they had sought refuge the previous night, after which they hastened along to the lesser quays beyond the Silver Landings where the *Stormclaw* and other vessels were forced to berth.

Everything about the ship was a surprise to Calabos, who could still recall the fragments of Byrnak's knowledge of the Daemonkind. They had been the first and mightiest of the Lord of Twilight's servants, raised out of darkness and the mindlessness of beasthood, bestowed with an unshakeable sense of honour and duty and gifted with their own source of powers, their own conduit to the primal forces of the Void. But the defeat of their master at the end of the Shadowking war had both exiled them from their home, the Realm of Ruin, and diminished their powers. So when they chose to leave the continent Toluveras, they decided to take on human form as a disguise to avoid and evade suspicion and retribution. Calabos had actually picked up a few thin rumours suggesting this years after the extravagant conflict, when he and Coireg had sought seclusion in northern Ebro'Heth to rest and forget.

Now, as he walked these corridors, he marvelled at the quality of the expressive workmanship he saw, having never suspected that these former servants could be capable of such skill. He had not known what to expect from the *Stormclaw* – which had apparently been some kind of trading dromond beforehand – but the Daemonkind had made it wholly their own.

The lines of door frames and ceiling beams had all been pared down to graceful curves and although polished carvings were visible everywhere there was no sense of overpowering ornamentation. The images of wings and winged creatures had been worked into panel borders and wallposts or were the subjects of bulkhead mosaics in mother-of-pearl. Occasionally, he saw in the centre of wall panels or on decorative ceiling roundels the image of a curled-up and sleeping figure.

The Sleeping God.

At last Coireg came to a halt before a red wood door bearing an odd device, a ring of twelve eyes inlaid in silver and mother-of-pearl. He knocked sharply three times then entered, with Calabos following.

'Greetings, friends Calabos and Coireg.'

Qothan was standing at the centre of an oval chamber, next to four inward-facing ceremonial chairs. In one of them was a bearded man in black and grey robes, who watched the newcomers with impassive eyes.

'Ser Calabos,' Qothan continued, 'Permit me to introduce you to my chieftain, Prince Agasklin.'

Agasklin rose to meet Calabos who looked him steadily in the eye, trying to discern the Daemonkind behind the appearance. For neither man gave ground, then a brittle smile crept across Agasklin's features as he extended a large hand which Calabos grasped.

'It is an honour to meet the author of *The Great Shadowking War*,' Agasklin said.

Calabos hesitated to respond for a moment, wondering if the chieftain meant himself or, more sardonically, Byrnak. Then he decided that no pointed ambiguity was intended and gave a nod of acknowledgement.

'You are too kind,' he said. 'It was my first prose work of ambition, thus I'm always surprised when it garners approval – were I writing it today, certain aspects would be executed in an entirely different manner.'

'A natural sentiment, friend Calabos,' Agasklin said. 'All the works of hand and mind appear flawed in hindsight. Our own actions, for example, have been intended to constrain the scope and harmfulness of the dark sorcerer, Jumil, yet they have instead served to complicate matters.'

'This is undoubtedly true,' Calabos said. 'But it is also the case that we are hampered by a lack of knowledge or understanding of Jumil's motives.'

'This is what we hope to address now,' Qothan said. 'This auracle chamber has certain properties which will allow us to conduct a conferral with the chieftains of our sister-ship, the *Seafang*. In the course of which we shall attempt to speak with deeper forces in the Void and elsewhere, to see if we can learn more about this ritual that one of your Watchers witnessed in Besh-Darok.'

Agasklin nodded in confirmation. 'To that end we have decided to invite you both to take part in the conferral, a privilege very rarely granted to those outside the crews.'

Calabos glanced at Coireg and saw a troubled frown on his face. 'Would this be difficult for you?' he said.

Coireg shrugged. 'I'm worried about how it might affect the unstable part of my mind.'

'You will not experience any disruption,' said Qothan. 'The calmative elixir works on the flows in the brain, at a level which is untouched by the group thoughts of the conferral.'

Coireg seemed interested in this yet the tension in him did not ease. 'If I were to display any signs of reversion to that derangement . . . would you be able to help in some way?'

'Isolating you from the conferral would be easy to do,' Qothan said. 'Do not worry, friend Coireg.'

'Very well, I would be pleased and honoured to be part of this ceremony,' Coireg said, visibly determined.

Yet Calabos could still tell how uneasy he was and could entirely understand the fear of losing himself to a pitiless devouring thing in the mind.

When I first saw those spirit-wraiths, he thought, *my terror was like a coiling fog which threatened to choke my every rational thought. The mere memory of the presence which had once sat enthroned in my head is still enough to cast a pall across the senses — how much worse must it be for Coireg who still carries a monster within, for all that it's locked away.*

'Then we shall commence,' Agasklin said, indicating for Calabos and Coireg to sit in two of the four central chairs, with the fourth taken by Qothan. At the same time, other Daemonkind began entering the room, eight in all who found places among the twelve

chairs spaced around the wall of the oval chamber. Calabos noticed
the twelve painted divisions on the ceiling and the elaborate floor
tiling which mirrored them, and the dark smoothness of his chair's
armrests, and the ochre bees embroidered on the dark green cushioning, and the cloudy, crystalline stones set into the carven, high
backs. And the stern looks, some disapproving, which he got from
Agasklin's fellow chieftains as they settled into their seats.

All gradually fell silent and an air of sombre expectancy took
hold. After a moment Agasklin began to recite some kind of
rhythmic verse in a tongue that Calabos at first did not recognize, then Qothan joined in, followed a verse later by one of the
chieftains and so on until they were all intoning an intricate interwoven pattern of words. As a faint pearliness grew in the air,
touching everything with a softening aura, Calabos felt the hairs
on his arms rise, a sure sign of gathering power.

Then ghostly outlines began to appear, wavering shapes of figures
seated in chairs similar to the four at the centre only positioned
between them, thus giving the impression of eight chairs facing
inwards. And outwith them was another spectral circle of chairs
occupied by the opaque forms of Daemonkind chieftains.

'I bid you welcome to this conferral, brothers and sisters,' said
Agasklin. 'How fares the *Seafang* and her crew?'

'Our sails spread wide,' said one of the ghostly chieftains in the
inner circle, an elderly looking man with grey wipsy hair. 'And
our hull flies over the waves. And the *Stormclaw*?'

'Tight-drawn is the glamour that conceals our nature, Sunyoril,'
Agasklin said. 'And full-ready with weapons is our crew, for the
enemy must now suspect our existence after we moved against
the talisman bearers of the undead host.'

'The enemy Jumil is difficult to fathom,' said Sunyoril. 'The
burning of the tower at the palace, the attack of that vile revenant
fleet, the re-creation of a Shadowking, and now the disturbing rites
that his agents are undertaking – all part of something, but what?'

Calabos straightened, suddenly intent.

'Ser, forgive my interruption,' he said. 'We have thus far known
of only one ritual, in the ruined palace at Besh-Darok – do you
know of others?'

The chieftain Sunyoril looked at him with opaque eyes that considered him for a tense moment.

'Ser Calabos,' he said. 'We welcome your presence here. Be aware that another three of these rituals have been completed in the last day and a half – one south-west of Sejeend, perhaps on the Ramyr peninsula but more likely in Adnagaur itself; one far to the south, somewhere near Oumetra; and a fourth to the west, in Alvergost.'

Calabos sat back, stunned, suddenly recalling Jumil's dread words in the bone cave – '*It shall be ours again, remade for ever in reflection of the Great Shadow's will*'. He quickly related what Ayoni had told him about the rite in Besh-Darok and the resulting grey blight. Stern faces became grim, even angry.

'How long would it take for these patches of devouring grey to spread across the land?' said a frowning Agasklin.

'Who can tell?' Calabos said. 'Slowly if they are isolated or fenced off, faster if living creatures are trapped by them. But then, for all we know, there may be more rituals to come that could accelerate the process . . .'

'We have to put a stop to this abomination,' said one of the chieftains.

'Four sites, scattered across the western half of the continent?' said another. 'Both our crews combined would not be enough to tackle such a task.'

'We cannot stand by and do nothing.'

'It is not our concern – there are other lands across the seas . . .'

'Face it now or face it in a year, two years – that's the real choice.'

'There must be some way of neutralizing it.'

Then out of the babble a single voice spoke forth.

'There is a way – seize the sorcerer Jumil and force him to reverse the effects of the rites,' said Coireg Mazaret, who was now standing. 'If he refuses – slay him.'

Calabos looked at his old friend, saw the iron resolve born of centuries of mental torment and knew that he was right.

'Yet Jumil is very powerful,' Calabos said. 'I don't think that he has yet exerted even a quarter of his full might.'

Coireg met his gaze and nodded sombrely. 'It would be an arduous undertaking against mundane foes as well as sorcerous ones, and we may have to face the Ondene-Shadowking as well. But this Jumil is the source of all the woes and catastrophes that have afflicted Sejeend and now other unfortunate places . . .' He glanced about him, looking suddenly nervous at being the focus of attention. 'Thus if we remove him from the picture, our situation can only improve. Thank you for listening to me, honoured chieftains . . .'

Words trailing off, he quickly sat down but just as quickly voices were raised in approval and to urge action. Yet not all were in favour and about three separate arguments were going on around the auracle chamber. Agasklin and Qothan were having an animated discussion with the translucent Sunyoril and Calabos was about to break in when he noticed a sudden lessening in the babble and looked up to see two more ghostly figures standing on either side of the inner circle of chairs. Both resembled old men carrying staffs and both were attired in jewelled, ceremonial armour, fine silver chain mail for one, golden, overlapping scale mail for the other. Confused, Calabos turned to Qothan who murmured, 'The captains!'

As a respectful hush settled on all, Calabos looked from one apparition to the other, wondering which was Pericogal, captain of the *Stormclaw*.

'*Such a secret enemy is this Jumil,*' said the one in gold, his agitated voice overlaid with strange sighing echoes. '*He has seeded the land with spores of corruption which will eat out the heart of the world if unchecked. Ruin beckons! To refuse to act is to condemn all to destruction!*'

Then the one clad in silver spoke;

'*In all the centuries of our long exile,*' he said, '*caution and stealth have been our watchwords, which have served us well even during our sojourn in the lands of Araphel and Ogreina. But the danger we now face is unlike any of the other perils that we encountered on our travels – the fate of peoples and nations is at stake and it is our fate to play a pivotal role.*' He paused to survey his audience for a moment. '*And yet this is not new – we have been in this position before.*'

There were murmurs of disquiet.

'*I think you know of what I speak,*' he went on. '*Three centuries*

*ago, the Israganthir allowed themselves to be used in the Shadowkings'
schemes, blinded by ancient ties of loyalty and trust to a godhead which
had been perverted by an incautious transformation. I am now almost the
only one left who witnessed it all, from the vaunting greed of unrestrained
ambition to the ignominy of utter defeat. And when we, your forebears,
set out on our exiles' voyage, we swore that we would serve only out of
a duty to the well-being of all.'* He then looked at Calabos. *'Honoured
Calabos, you are living proof that the past need not become a burden of
madness and death for the future. Therefore we shall stand with you in
this struggle and follow the suggestion of friend Mazaret. Jumil is the one
responsible, therefore we shall move to take him prisoner.'*

Calabos stood and bowed to the one he now knew was
Pericogal, the *Stormclaw*'s captain, then to Immalarin, captain of
the *Seafang*.

'Sers, we are honoured by the kindness and help you have
already lent us so your declaration to further our cause is a boon
that can be repaid only with the defeat of our common enemy.
May this prove to be so . . .'

This cannot be so.

The voice seemed to come from every direction and everyone
in the chamber was startled and wide-eyed. A cold trickle of unease
passed through Calabos in that moment as old memories stirred.

Agasklin was openly angry. 'Who speaks? Who dares to disrupt
this assembly?'

'Be calm, Agasklin,' said Captain Pericogal. *'We have been honoured
by the presence of that one whose words and auguries fill our most precious
of books.'*

Agasklin and Qothan, as well as the others, looked almost incredulous. A whisper rippled round the chamber – 'the Sleeping God!'
– and Calabos felt his unease confirmed. Glancing over at Coireg,
he saw that his friend looked pale and ill and imediately knew
why, knew that he too feared the pitiless touch of gods.

'Why have you come amongst us?' Pericogal said aloud. *'Why do
you say that we cannot defeat our enemy?'*

The air above the inner circle of chairs darkened into a large,
roiling knot of shadows which coalesced into a strange representa-
tion of a dense mass of leaves, sprigs, fronds and berries that were all

murkily translucent as if fashioned from smoky glass. Then the mass of eldritch foliage parted and a great face emerged, pale and opaque in the likeness of a woman sculpted from stone – the perfect, blank eyes, the positioned hair, the classic line of cheek and chin and the skin unmarred by the slightest blemish, all elements of a sublime ideal.

The immense face stared at Pericogal for a moment before speaking in a voice like the torrents of a waterfall.

Your enemy is not who you think, and your scheme could never defeat him. The one named Jumil has already directed the seedings of four Shattergates and he will shortly go to the palace to conduct a fifth . . .

'Even more reason to gather our forces and attack them now!' cried Coireg.

No! Such a plan would waste your strength and the opportunity that presents itself to you now. Forget the Shattergates – that damage is already done.

'What opportunity do you mean?' Calabos said.

The opaque face turned to look down at him and its appearance changed, losing some of its female character and becoming more male.

The deliverance of the Prince of Change.

There was a stunned silence. Calabos knew that the Prince of Change was a mythic figure central to the prophecies proclaimed by the Sleeping God to the first exile captains of the Daemonkind.

'And who is he?' he said, fervently hoping that it was not himself.

The unfathomable eyes regarded him.

You know him well . . . Corlek Ondene is his name.

There were sighs, quietly excited mutters.

'He has been utterly possessed by fragments of the Lord of Twilight,' Calabos said. 'Jumil has used him as a vessel for all those spirit-wraiths which have found some kind of unity. We cannot be certain that anything of Ondene remains . . .'

Coireg smiled sadly at him. 'It's not impossible, Calabos. I was locked away in my own mind by usurping spirits during the Shadowking war, yet I survived.'

Not even I am able to perceive all ends, thus the identity of the Prince of Change was hidden from me until

very recently. Now I am certain – I have seen the branching possibilities . . .

Calabos remained unconvinced.

'Yet this is not simply Corlek Ondene who we must capture but a Shadowking, a living piece of the Lord of Twilight – he can tap into powers that dwarf our own.'

I had thought you more dauntless than this, poet. With the aid of guile and the potion concocted for your friend here, might not you be able to subdue a deranged god's remnant?

Calabos was about further pursue that line of query when Qothan spoke.

'Your pardon, divinity, but will the calmative elixir have the desired effect? Our friend Coireg suffers from a deep schism of the mind whereas Captain Ondene has been wholly possessed by a hostile spirit.'

The god-face turned to look down at him.

The potion suppresses those flaws in the mind that disturb or run counter to its natural balance, be they caused by an underlying schism or an intruding spirit. The principle is the same although the man Ondene may require a more concentrated dose.

Qothan nodded thoughtfully, but Calabos regarded the godlike manifestation above them with growing resentment. Coireg's proposal may have been impulsive and angry but at least it had the merit of being directly concerned with the person who lay at the root of the entire crisis, Jumil. He could see that Agasklin also harboured doubts from the sombre frown creasing his brow, yet he seemed reluctant to speak. So Calabos decided to voice his own.

'I feel compelled, divine one, to ask you this – assuming that we successfully entrap Ondene and subdue the Shadowking within him, what do we do with him?'

The great face altered as it looked back at him, blurring oddly between male and female. Then, unexpectedly, a cold smile passed across its features.

I want the man Ondene brought to my island Nydratha, to me, and if you accompany him, Calabos, you will learn

much that has been hidden from you. The face of the Sleeping God surveyed all present. **Know that this man Ondene is the key to a final triumph over the deathly shadow which has marred the essence of this world down all the long ages. I ask you for your trust and for every last shred of resolve and audacity that you can muster – I shall await you at Nydratha, amid its storm**.

With that the god-face closed its pale, translucent eyes and sank back into the grey, glassy foliage which in turn folded in on itself until there was only a swirl of ashen haze fading above their heads. As assenting voices rose all about them, Calabos looked over to see Coireg gazing at him.

'What will you do?' he said.

Calabos shook his head. 'Should we resign ourselves to the plans of gods? Should I?'

But after half an hour of intense discussion with Agasklin and Qothan and others, Calabos found that only he was left playing the role of sceptic, for the Sleeping God had persuaded the captains of both ships and their chieftains. But in the end it was the prospect of freeing Corlek Ondene from a harsh domination that swayed him. Soon, Calabos found himself in the company of Qothan and seven other Daemonkind crew from the *Stormclaw* as they descended the gantry to the quayside under a leaden sky. His frame of mind was a mixture of trepidation and wry humour at the irony of the role he would soon be playing, that of the bait. True, he had himself suggested this as a ploy to draw the Ondene-Shadowking out of Hojamar Keep but he had half-expected that another scheme would be adopted.

Coireg Mazaret had been appalled, but when it became apparent that no other equally plausible or workable plan was on the table, he withdrew his objections. As Calabos stepped onto the quayside he glanced back to see his friend watching him from the main deck, standing alongside Agasklin. Hands were raised in farewell and Calabos strode off, lengthening his pace to keep up with Qothan and the others, most of whom were carrying long, cloth-wrapped bundles slung over their shoulders. During their earlier discussions, the tall outrider had hinted at some kind of sorcerous veil that would allow them to travel into the centre of the city undetected. Now, as Calabos followed the Daemonkind up from the wharfs, uphill past the godowns, smokeries and livestock pens, his curiosity began to gnaw at him. When Qothan led them into a wooded bluff off the main road curiosity was fast becoming puzzlement. Puzzlement turned into confusion when Qothan halted in a small clearing where his companions unpacked their bundles and began to assemble a small platform on the grassy ground.

Calabos could not help smiling as he said, 'An interesting place, friend Qothan, but what is our purpose, here?'

Qothan did not smile, instead picking out a few articles of clothing from one of the unpacked bundles, a heavy woollen cloak, holed in places and fraying along its edge, and a pair of fur-lined boots.

'You will need these, ser Calabos,' he said, holding them out.

'In summer?' Calabos said. 'Even as mild a one as this?'

'Be assured, you will have need of them.'

A glance around him showed that the others looked intently serious. He shrugged, accepted the garments and put them on. Immediately he could feel himself starting to sweat.

Moments later the platform was finished, consisting of not much more than a couple of yard-long planks atop an iron framework about two feet high. It creaked as Qothan stepped up onto it then beckoned Calabos to do the same, giving him a hand up as he did so. Qothan then regarded his fellow crewmen.

'Have a care as you approach the vicinity of the Keep, brothers. When the moment for you to descend comes, our signal will be unmistakable.' Then he turned to Calabos. 'Ser, now you must close your eyes and bend your knees a little.'

'Is this the sorcerous veil you mentioned?' Calabos said. 'What does it do?'

Qothan's voice, like his grip on Calabos' arm, was iron.

'It takes us into the pit of Time. Now, close your eyes . . .'

Calabos squeezed shut his eyes and almost at once felt a knot of nausea start to uncoil in his vitals. He suppressed the discomfort but it changed into a feeling of dizzy hollowness which surged slowly up into his chest. Qothan's hand was still tight on his upper arm but his legs felt rubbery and in his effort to keep his equilibrium his eyes cracked open . . .

A dark vista of rushing vastness flew towards him and away from him and around him, from the height of a hundred sheer mountain faces to the plunging, abyssal depths of a thousand oceans piled one upon another. An instant of shattering immensity, and in the next instant it parted and poured away, dissolving into dazzling whiteness.

And a startling jolt in his legs as he fell a short distance onto softness, white, cold softness . . .

'Snow,' he muttered.

'Indeed, ser Calabos,' came Qothan's deep voice as he helped Calabos to his feet. Calabos blinked as the whiteness began to blur into shadowy shapes, then swiftly recalled the thought-canto Cleareye and applied its restorative quality to himself. At once his vision sprang into focus, revealing that he stood in the same bluff as before, except that the bushes were many and the trees were few, and all were leafless, spidery and smothered in snow. An icy peace held sway and it was near sundown, yet the light was evenly suffused beneath a blue-grey sky.

'We're still in Sejeend,' he said. 'But not our Sejeend . . . and it's winter.'

'Very good, ser,' Qothan said. 'Captain Ondene took much longer to reach that assessment. Now come – we must make haste, for when we left our time, I heard from Agasklin that Jumil and Vorik have been seen departing the Keep.'

So saying, he set off down the snowy slope towards the centre of Sejeend. Wrapping the heavy cloak tighter against the needling cold, Calabos plunged after him, his mind full to bursting with questions. As they made their way along the deserted bay road, past a few fisher huts and their flimsy jetties, he managed to glean a few meagre snippets of knowledge from the big outrider. Yes, this was how Ondene had been spirited away from the courtyard; this was the past . . . yet it was not. The Daemonkind exiles had been severed for ever from returning to their shattered realm, and it had been some time before any had the courage or despair to attempt it. It was two malfeasors who had done so, but this had been at sea, and neither of them returned. Only after the exiles' ships had returned to these waters did some other daring crew member try to cross over to their ancestral home . . . and found himself in this snowbound world.

'Yet it is a world that seems locked in its time – whenever we come here it is alway winter, always the same day, and our presence here is always limited,' Qothan said as they trudged up a road where carts and horses had turned the snow into slush. 'After about an hour we will be pulled back to the world of our time, like bubbles returning inevitably to the surface – although we can also cause the return voluntarily. When that happens, I plan for you to be very close to Hojamar Keep . . .'

'Which should be enough to get the Shadowking's attention,' Calabos said with a smile. 'I wondered how we were going to do that.'

'Once he knows of your presence,' Qothan went on, 'it will be up to you to find a way of tricking him down from the Keep and outside its perimeter wall. Once that is accomplished, my brothers and I will finish the task.'

Which meant, Calabos knew, bringing him back here. 'I just hope that he is surprised and confused enough for you to administer the potion. But tell me, does this time-journeying not lead to you encountering yourselves or others?'

'Never,' said Qothan. 'Once we return to our time, all trace of our presence here is erased, which leads to the conclusion that if this is a real point in the past then it is also some kind of pocket into which we can repeatedly delve. Perhaps further time-walking undertaken in other locations will reveal more about this anomaly, but for now we shall put it to good use.'

Before long they came to the rough wall that marked the boundary of this historical Sejeend, less a city than a town and military garrison. The crumbling arched gate was unmanned and as they made their way up through the snowy streets, Calabos noticed between the buildings a procession of refugees crossing a bridge across the Valewater estuary north of the town. Further, they came within sight of the great cliffs but only dense woods were visible along the top of them. The formidable edifice of

Hojamar Keep still dominated the town, however, although the courtyard wall was lower than Calabos knew. Guards stood sentry in squat, timber towers either side of the courtyard gates, yawning white breath in the deepening cold. Qothan steered Calabos along a slush-choked cobbled pavement across the square outside the gates before halting by a narrow, flagstoned passageway.

'This part of the road remains unchanged for the next three hundred years,' Qothan said. 'When I leave your side and walk away, you will be pulled back to our time and the Shadowking will become aware of you. Have you thought about what to say?'

Calabos stroked his chin. 'Any workable deceit demands the inclusion of something true – I will tell who I was and offer to meet him, perhaps claim to have knowledge that he lacks.'

The tall outrider cracked a thin smile. 'Good – by the time he reaches you, the rest of us will be moving in.' He turned and began to walk away, back up to the main road, pausing at the corner to say, 'And ser Calabos – keep your eyes closed.' Then he was gone from sight, leaving behind only drifting wisps of his breath.

Almost immediately Calabos felt the start of the same nausea surge as before, only this time he had a stone wall to lean against as he closed his eyes tightly. After another drawn-out succession of delirium-provoking physical sensations, his body calmed itself, all agitation dissolving into the pulse of breathing and the blood in his veins. He opened his eyes on an empty street bare of snow and slush, and an early morning sky brightening from the east. He let out the breath he had been holding in a long, relieved sigh and started back up to the main road.

In the few moments it took him to get there, his undersenses told him that a powerful regard had narrowed and focussed upon him. Once round the corner and looking across at the Keep, he composed his mind and marshalled his thoughts, then channelled his words into farspeech.

Greetings, friend.

There were impressions of arrogance and disdain. (*Who are you? This is my domain – what are you doing here?*)

I was once like the one who carries you – I too once played host to the might of a god.

Shock mingled with a craving for knowledge, then doubt and hate. (*Lies! You stink of lies! What could you know of this glory?*)

Calabos paused a moment then said,

Byrnak was my name when I and my brothers held all these lands in thrall. Look within — you will see that it is true.

The craving returned, and a new wariness. (*Parts of me know that name — we — I remember it . . .*)

But how much do you remember?

(*Not nearly enough! They are keeping secrets from me, those vermin — I must know more!*)

Calabos inserted a degree of humorous contempt — *Meet me face to face down here and perhaps I will be able to fill the gaps in your knowledge. And waste no time — I'm a busy man.*

He broke the link, shielding his thoughts against the rage-fuelled probing brought on by his final remarks. Then it ceased abruptly, leaving him alone at the street corner, leaning against the stonework as he gazed across at the Keep's tall courtyard wall. All was peaceful in the brightening morning light with only a few people visible over by some shopfronts and a barrel wagon crossing a junction further along. Then suddenly he was aware of someone approaching and looked over to see a cloaked man striding towards him from the direction of the Keep. It was Corlek Ondene and Calabos felt his spirits rise a little, for all that he knew that other intelligence was enthroned in that form.

As he drew near, Calabos could see the smouldering fury in the face and the clenched fists swinging by his side, and realized what danger he was in. He could feel the man's intense focus of Wellsource power through his undersenses and for a moment he wished he had the sword of powers with him, but freeing the Shadowking from Ondene's body would only make matters worse — now was the time to rely on his own wits and hope that Qothan and the other Daemonkind would be timely.

The Ondene-Shadowking came to a halt a couple of yards away and sneered.

'How can an old man have been the host of the Grey Lord?'

Calabos smiled, shook his head. 'Looks are deceptive — this appearance is a convenience, nothing more. And I was host to only a fifth of the Lord of Twilight, which is still a greater fraction that the remnant that you are.'

A sullen anger showed in Ondene's face as he glanced down at the rest of the city and the lands beyond. 'This is true – I can feel other parts of him, of me, out there, killing, stealing, maiming, burning. If they were with me, I would have the strength to master that toad, Jumil.'

'You said he keeps secrets from you.'

'Yes, like the true nature of this Great Shadow,' the Shadowking said, scowling. 'Is he just another fragment, like that pirate Bureng? Why should I bend the knee and follow his orders? When I find a way to this Nightrealm of his, I think I'll just kill him and add his fragment to my own.' He looked round at Calabos with a malign glee in his features. 'Yes, that sounds like a worthwhile goal.'

'And a dangerous one,' Calabos added, wishing that Qothan would arrive. 'Would you be strong enough?'

'Strength is important,' the Shadowking conceded. 'But so is mastery of technique. And when I look at you, Byrnak, I see that you are an adept of the Lesser Power and that not a gleam of the Wellsource resides in you. Yet I can feel where it once was and I can feel how your blood and your bones still hunger for what runs freely through my flesh. But I am here to take, not to give . . .' Somehow, he was now just a foot or two away as he reached out towards Calabos' throat. 'Willingly or not, you will yield up to me everything you know, every skill, every trick, every twist, every morsel of understanding in the usages of power, and maybe then—'

He never finished the sentence. A dark shape swept in from one side and fell on him. There was a bellow of rage followed closely by a sudden flare of emerald fire from the Shadowking's hands as they tightened around his assailant's neck. Calabos had staggered back against the nearby building and recognized the battling attacker as one of the Daemonkind outriders. His hair was beginning to smoke within the wreath of green fire and the Shadowking was grinning when the second outrider joined the fray, then a third and a fourth.

And in from the left rushed Qothan, one hand gripping a clay vial which Calabos knew had to contain the mind calmative.

'Later at the ship!' was all Qothan said to Calabos before he reached into the struggling, grunting knot of bodies and grabbed one of the Ondene-Shadowking's arms.

There was an instant of blurred multiple images, then they were gone. Calabos, his pulse racing, stared at the vacant spot for a moment or two then looked up to see guards hurrying over from the keep. He quickly strode to the corner and headed down the side road, then ducked along a shady alley, seeking a labyrinthine way back to the quays.

It was a darkness of the mind so complete that it had no boundaries while giving no room for thoughts. Corlek Ondene could only feel, not think, in the smothering, limitless pit into which the usurping Shadowking had thrust him. From time to time he was aware that events were taking place but the only signs of these were far-off roars of triumph or rage and the thin whispering of many voices that came and went like fitful breezes crossing a desolation.

He had gone through anger and hate repeatedly, cycling back into self-pity and quivering fear although fear seemed to have less of a hold now. Without limbs and a body, the sensations of touch, smell and taste, there seemed to be few prompts for chaotic terror.

Until change came. First he heard the great roars, like gigantic beasts defying each other from the peaks of mountains. After a little of this, they fell silent for a short while before beginning again, an insistent yet distant bellowing that grew gleeful and decisive ... then erupted into a shattering cacophony of enraged howling. Fear did grip Ondene then and he seemed to feel a tremble pass through the imprisoning darkness. And despite the pandemonium he could still hear the many whispering voices, only now they were growing into mutters.

Then a sensation welled up to take him by surprise, a feeling of falling which turned into flying then rising ...

Then the darkness began to take on texture and solidity—

And a swirl of sounds—

And a patchwork of hot and cold—

And a veil of odours—

And the ungainly, jointed bonework of a body—

And then the darkness itself began to leach away, pursued by the cloud of muttering voices and for moment it seemed that the great shadowy murk would break apart. But it stayed whole as it sank beyond the horizon of Ondene's expanding perceptions.

Which rose into the soft light of evening and the cold ground on which he lay and the looming shapes of figures gathered around him. The icy air in his lungs he savoured, along with the wetness seeping into his clothes and the cries of stallowners somewhere along the street. As he struggled to sit up, hands grabbed his shoulder and arms and lent him support. Coughing on a rawness in his throat, he looked round to see who his helpers were, saw it was Qothan and others like him, and began to laugh. Qothan, who was holding a lidless grey vial in his other hand, glanced up at his companions for a moment, then smiled faintly.

'Are you well, ser Ondene?' he said.

'Never better, Qothan, my friend!' He noticed more about the others present and the surroundings, then realized where he was and grinned. 'Are you about to tell me that we've got to get down to the docks and without delay?'

Qothan stood and helped him to his feet.

'An accurate guess, Captain.'

'Good — give us a chance to swap tales, eh?'

'Perhaps later,' the tall man said. 'The first thing you must understand is how to cope with the passenger which you have in your head.'

Ondene's smile faltered. 'That thing . . . is still there?'

Qothan nodded. 'Suppressed by an elixir which I managed to force down his throat. But come — there will be time enough for details as we go.'

Ondene could only feel a hollow dread as they began walking, as well as a host of minor aches and bruises. As he rubbed his neck he said, 'It is your ship we're returning to, yes?'

'Yes — my captain is keen to speak with you, as is Beltran Calabos.'

That has an ominous ring to it, he thought as he followed Qothan along the northerly road. *Could there be, I wonder, more risk and peril awaiting me?*

Chapter Sixteen

We sail through the icy dark,
Towards a shore of death and blood,
Where dream armies of ironclad pain,
Fight and fall and rise to fight again.

Eshen Caredu, *Storm Voyage*, Ch. 5

Smooth and unbroken, the grey seeding shroud lay evenly in a ragged oval across the hall. From where he stood, near the centre, Jumil looked on with satisfaction as a pillar, its base eaten away, cracked loose from the ornate ceiling and toppled to crash onto the shroud. It smashed into several pieces which quickly vanished under a surge of grey as the shroud consumed them. Meanwhile, plaster and mortar was spilling from one of the walls as the shroud's edge nibbled at it, a precursor to the slowly widening hole in the wall opposite.

Cracks were starting to appear in the painted, gilded and mirrored ceiling and with increasing frequency shards of golden plaster and silvered glass fell in glittering cascades that were swiftly swallowed by the greyness. Soon, the ceiling would give way and when one of the supporting walls was gone a great collapse would begin and spread further out, bringing down more and more of the palace.

About which Jumil was unconcerned, for it was all part of his master's plan to join this realm to his own, to bridge the great abyss, to finally right the ancient wrong, invincibly, indivisibly, irrevocably.

On the spot where he stood, not far from the featureless mound in the middle, the substance of the shroud was only a hard grey surface beneath his shoes. But there was another figure upon the shroud, cloaked head to foot in its greyness, meandering to and fro, trudging nonstop around the shroud's perimeter. Jumil smiled to see Vorik's torment, especially whenever he scowled or mouthed imprecations or shook a clenched grey fist in his direction. His former mainstay had conspired with a member of his own flock to confound the consequences of the Shatterseed ritual by switching the amulet and employing cantrips cribbed from some of Jumil's own notebooks. But because the fool did not understand the very spells he was using, he ended up trapped in the seeding shroud anyway. He seemed to have considerable autonomy within its boundaries for now but sooner or later, Jumil surmised, he would be wholly devoured by it.

Yet Vorik was only a minor distraction – Jumil's attention was actually split into five, his senses taking in sights and sounds from the other four Shattergate locations as well as this one. From Adnagaur and Oumetra came images of guards patrolling the surroundings of the grey shroud, in both cases amid areas of closely built houses and warehouses, the former amid gloomy mist, the latter under bright sunshine. In Alvergost, the ruined citadel in the far south of Khatris, rain was falling on the seeding shroud which had gnawed its way past the confines of a tumbledown house and was already demolishing those around it while a ragged crowd gazed fearfully from flimsy shelters.

In Besh-Darok he caught glimpses of the Mogaun he had noticed earlier, a peculiar development coming so soon after those four intrusive ghost-things which he had ruthlessly dealt with, obliterating all but one of them. But these Mogaun – he was sure that they were shamans from the slightness of their stature and from their apparent ability to know when he was watching, resulting in a brisk scurrying out of sight. Were they taking part in the pilgrimage to the Carver's shrine, or were they perhaps members of some chief's retinue? But if that were so, why were they still nearby?

Then he smiled to himself, secure in the knowledge that nothing they were capable of doing could stop or slow the inevitable advance of the seeding shrouds. Indeed, before long he would be ready to commence the next stage of the Shatterseed ritual which would allow the shrouds to expand at a faster rate. Seizing a greater breadth of territory, along with all that it held, would provide all the raw matter necessary for the correct forming of the Shattergates and once they were complete, the conquest could truly begin.

An arrow came flying into the collapsing room and was snatched out of midair by a grey meshlike limb which shot up from the shroud. Others followed, some in Jumil's direction, some at Vorik who was waving his arms and ranting silently at some archers gathered by the gap in the wall. Every missile which struck him was absorbed into his grey form, almost without his noticing.

Soon, Jumil thought as the archers hurriedly retreated from a cascade of tumbling masonry. *Soon, the kingdom!*

Bound hand and foot, Ayoni had been first slung over the shoulder of a hulking and malodorous Mogaun warrior then carried out of the palace and down to an overgrown, bush-flanked gap in the city's crumbling wall. There she had been unceremoniously dumped into the back of a small cart to which a mule was harnessed, and had a damp, moth-eaten fur cloak thrown over her. The strange gossamer mesh was still wound tightly about her and isolating her from the Lesser Power, with a smothering glamour which defied every attempt to break through.

She eventually had to admit defeat and tried to relax as the cart bumped and rattled its way towards Belkiol on the banks of the Great Canal. But when Ayoni began thinking about what she could say to Tangaroth or Ilgarion that might persuade them to attack the mainland part of Belkiol, a kind of panic set in. The faces of Jarryc and Chellour and Klayse kept coming back to her and her thoughts turned into a frantic whirl of possible stories, possible opening words, what to emphasize and when to do so . . .

But by the time the cart came to a halt near the bushy banks of the canal, her mind was no clearer on what tactic to employ. When the fur cloak was tugged away she could see that it was now well into the morning, with only brief moments of sunlight slipping past the shifting tapestry of clouds that was unrolling across the sky. She could also see that they were about half a mile along from Belkiol, visible beyond rocky hills by virtue of its camp fires. Then her captors, two leering Mogaun fighters and a scrawny shaman, cut the bonds on her ankles then steered her roughly down a pebbly track to where a timber landing poked out from the bank. In a flat-bottomed boat moored at the end, a man in a grubby brown shoreman's smock looked up at their approach, his face turning surly when he saw who it was.

'Took yer time,' he said.

' We pay for your boat,' the shaman said, 'not for your comfort.'

The boatman seemed about to give a biting reply, then eyed the warriors and shrugged.

'Right . . . well, put 'er in my boat and I'll take 'er over.'

Ayoni was lifted by the arms and none too gently deposited in the little craft's stern. The boatman then looked up at the shaman and held out his hand. The two men glared at each other for a moment before the shaman dropped some coins in the outstretched hand. Once the money was counted and pocketed, the boatman took out a long, rust-spotted dagger and cut the rope binding Ayoni's wrists.

'Thanks,' she said in surprise, massaging feeling back into her hands.

'Oars,' the boatman said, gesturing with the dagger.

If her upbringing had been as cosseted as most of the ladies of the court, she would probably have been reduced to tears by now. Instead, she calmly picked up the oars, fitting one then the other into the rowlocks; when they were set and done he merely pointed out across the canal with the daggerpoint. As she bent to the oars and the boat moved away from the landing, the boatman gave the three Mogaun a despising smile.

'Pleasure doin' business with yer . . .'

It was a long and tiring row, for all that there were no currents to battle nor serious waves to contend with. As she pushed on with the rhythm of it, she could still see the figures of the Mogaun standing on the jetty, watching.

'I knows yer a mage,' the boatman said unexpectedly. 'And I knows that them webby strings keeps you harmless.' There was

something greedy in his eyes. 'If'n cut them off, you could do me
some favours, on your oath . . .'

She met his gaze. 'Such as?'

'Well, see this pig-sticker?' He held up the dagger. 'Be nice
if it were silver and had a few jewels on it . . . or if I had rich
robes . . .'

'I don't do that kind of sorcery.'

Anger showed in his face. 'They don't mean ter let you go, I
heard 'em. That thing'll stay on and when the empire soldiers
come you'll be as helpless as a lamb – but if you give me your
word to help me, I'll cut it off . . .'

There was a faint crackling sound and as Ayoni leaned forward
and pulled back, the glittering meshes around her midriff broke
apart and fell into her lap and the bottom of the boat. At once
Ayoni felt a surge of sensations as her mage perceptions made
contact with the Lesser Power. She allowed herself to feel a certain
measure of satisfaction as the boatman's attitude altered radically
– she could almost see the fear filling him up to the brim. She
ceased rowing and angled the oars towards him.

'Your turn, I believe,' she said brightly while calling up the
thought-canto Barb, which wreathed her hand in a web of
lightning.

When the boat bumped up against a sagging, half-submerged
log jetty, she forced herself to be relaxed as she rose and stepped
onto the slippery timbers. And before she could utter so much as
a sardonic word of farewell, the boatman had pushed off from the
jetty and was already rowing strenuously away. She watched him
go for a moment then stared out at the opposite bank where she
could just see three figures walking out of sight.

With that her spirits began to sink once more. She surveyed
her surroundings, trying to get her bearings as she made her way
up the decrepit and unsteady jetty to where a couple of huts
stood next to an empty livestock pen. This had to be a farmer's
crossing, she reasoned, but apparently abandoned for some time.
Looking east through the faint river haze, Ayoni could make out
clusters of buildings and innumerable trails of smoke about half
a mile away, which had to be the mainland half of Belkiol. A

town fortified against the imperial army, according to the Mogaun Huzur Marag, the very place that he wanted Ilgarion to attack.

How can I possibly ensure that our stupid emperor will follow that course? she thought. *If I try to persuade him to do so, he might take it as a bluff or even a double bluff, and if I try to persuade him to avoid it the same applies . . .*

She shook her head, knowing that her husband Jarryc and the others depended on her so she would have to do what had to be done, which now meant getting herself captured. Ayoni saw that several tracks led away from the jetty, one of which led up a hillside then along a ridge heading west in the direction of the imperial army camps. Ilgarion's scouts would surely be watching these approaches so getting their attention should not be difficult.

Her every footstep felt heavy with despair as she left the bank and began trudging uphill. The air was cool but had that fresh edge which hinted at rain to come, even though the sky was a panorama of clusters and knots of clouds all seemingly racing each other to the horizon.

There were bushes and scrawny trees all along the trail and occasionally she heard the crack and wheep of twig birds or the tiny sawing of a dogbeetle. She was concentrating on the sweet musical trill of a greenwing coming from just up ahead when she heard the rush of something flying towards her from behind. Even as she turned she knew she should be ducking, knew that the birdsong had been a lulling distraction . . .

The missile struck the side of her head and exploded in a cloud of purple dust which was inside her nose, mouth and eyes before she could react. With her first breath a jostling band of tastes cascaded across her tongue; with her second breath, the tastes and odours seemed to break from her nose and mouth and flow up into her mind; with her third breath her senses began to slip and blur and it seemed that she could see sounds and hear colours, even as her legs gave way and she sprawled on the grassy ground . . .

She was dimly aware of figures gathering around her, one of whom berated another over some misjudgement, in voices that conversed in the Mogaun tongue, she noticed. But it seemed unimportant to her as a delirium of strange beauties swamped her senses. Impressions of action filtered through, an air of urgency (silver voices muttering warnings) then movement as she was being carried somewhere near river odours (green and blue notes echoing) and a wallowing, a gentle rocking, moving along again, silence and a rising caution (black and purple hiss), then lifted and carried once more into a shadowy interior, a building perhaps . . .

Her thoughts drifted into torpor as the effects of the dust began to wear off, and a deepening drowse deadened all thought until it seemed that slumber was only the antechamber to a darker, more desirable oblivion . . .

Something cut through the smothering reverie like an axe through weeds, a shockingly strong smell that wrenched her into full alertness in just a moment or two.

'Good! You have not been crippled – the gods must approve of our plans.'

Eyes wide, Ayoni sat up and looked about her. She was in a small, dim room lit by tallow candles flickering in a couple of wall niches. She was being closely, warily watched by half a dozen scrawny, elderly Mogaun shamans, one of whom was holding a little leather pouch which she guessed was the source of that astonishing odour.

'Foxbane?' she asked.

The shaman holding the pouch nodded sharply. He was the most aged of the six, bony shoulders bent beneath a grubby hide cape, long grey hair trailing from a balding skull so pared of excess flesh that his steady dark eyes were the most vital thing about him. His smile was humorless and gap-toothed.

'A fine scour against ragbloom powder, of which you were dealt too much,' he said in a throaty, faintly sibilant voice. 'I am Pirak, twenty-seventh seer to the Ten Families, and it gives me no pleasure to have brought a mage of the Godriver into honourable Belkiol. But while other seers have given themselves over, duty still binds *us* – abomination must be torn out!'

There were agreeing nods to this and Ayoni felt a foreboding stir within her.

'What abomination?'

'You have seen him,' said Pirak. 'You have heard him speak of the voices inside him, yes?' He nodded quickly, his lips curled in disgust. 'You know of him.'

'The chieftain, Huzur Marag,' she said, suddenly reluctant to know any more.

'Yes, you know,' Pirak said. 'And we know what must be done—'

One of the other shamans interrupted, pointing off at the other side of the room. 'He comes.'

Pirak looked half-pleased, half-fearful as he turned and the gathering drew apart to admit a slight and spectral figure which drifted over to regard Ayoni with stoic humour.

It was Atroc.

'The last I saw of you,' she said, 'you were about to become food for the grey blight.'

'Heh – hard-to-catch food!' he said, grinning.

'So what am I to be?' she said. 'A sacrifice of some kind?'

He shook his head. 'We want you, countess lady, to kill Huzur Marag!'

Ayoni breathed in and out deeply, trying to stay calm.

'Pardon me, honoured Atroc,' she said. 'But you may not be aware that Huzur Marag holds my husband and two other friends prisoner against my obedience to *his* plans . . .'

'I know of this,' Atroc said. 'And they will be safe, on my oath.'

Ayoni was suddenly angry. 'Why do I find it hard to believe or trust you, seer? What accounts for your meddling in this?'

There were outraged mutters from the onlooking shamans but Atroc silenced them with an upraised hand.

'During the Blood War, which you call the Shadowking war, a great many warriors of the Mogaun were possessed by evil spirits of death,' Atroc said grimly. 'And even one of the high chieftains, my own Prince Yasgur, was usurped by the corrupted spirit of his father, Hegroun. This is why Huzur Marag must be cleansed, one way or another.'

'So who is Huzur Marag?' she said.

Atroc glanced at Pirak who seemed to steel himself before speaking.

'Huzur Marag is the third son to Krahel One-Arm, high chieftain of the Ten Families Clan, and also the clan's battle general. A
few days ago he had some kind of fit in his tent and fell into a
black slumber – when he awoke he gathered those bands and seers
loyal to him and rode south. But before he reached these lands,
a few of those close to him were angered and frightened by his
actions and by the change in him. They abandoned him and told
us all they knew, which made our duty hard but clear.'

Ayoni nodded as she listened, realizing that Huzur Marag had
to be host to several spirit-wraith fragments of the Lord of Twilight.

What a long, terrible shadow he has cast on these lands, she thought.
*But what can I do against such a creature, and how can I be sure that
Jarryc and the others will be safe?*

'Tell me how my husband and friends will be protected,' she
said to Atroc.

'They are being guarded by two shamans and a handful of
warriors,' the ghostly seer said. 'One of the shamans I have spoken
with – he hates Huzur and is ready to strike a blow against him,
so he will free the prisoners when I say.'

'And what of Huzur Marag? He stank of the Wellsource, which
makes me wonder how you expect me to be any danger to him.'

The reply to this came from Pirak. 'He is powerful, yes, but he is
undisciplined,' the old shaman said. 'We are not as powerful yet we
have more cunning so while we bind his fury to us, you will strike.
He will have no ward against the Godriver – it will be fatal to him.'

There was a pause, an expectant silence.

'You do not have to do this for us,' said the spectral Atroc. 'You
can be taken back to those foothills, if you want to try and fulfil
Huzur's malign and pointless ploy.'

'Why pointless?'

Atroc's smile was weary. 'Because neither of these raging forces
will change their courses – Huzur has quietly evacuated half of
mainland Belkiol and ferried the bulk of his troops across. Ilgarion
has been building siege machines since he reached the outskirts,
making it appear that he intends to attack the town, but unbe-
known to Huzur he has also been sending troops across to this
side, by night.'

Ayoni was surprised at this and wondered if her husband had had a hand in the planning for this tactic.

'So what will happen?' she said.

'Who can tell?' Atroc said with a dark laugh. 'Enough slaughter and madness to please the gods, perhaps? It is sure to happen later today as Huzur is going to send a band of his most brutal warriors out to raid the encampment around the nearest siege engines – Ilgarion won't allow such a sting to his pride to go unanswered.'

Again silence fell as Ayoni considered all this while the shamans stood watching her.

'I still need to know that my husband and the others will live,' she said.

Atroc drifted a little closer. 'Then when the time comes, I will myself go to Besh-Darok to where they are being held and ensure that our spy does not fail.'

'Then I will help you,' she said, looking round at the Mogaun shamans. 'I will do all that I can.'

Calabos found Corlek Ondene on the *Stormclaw*'s aft observers' deck, a wide, cramped chamber on the third stern deck through which the shaft of the ship's rudder passed. A couple of narrow windows afforded a view to the vessel's rear, the churning white wake, the seabirds wheeling in pursuit, and the shuddering moan of the strange powers that drove the ship along.

Calabos bent slightly to lean on the window's jutting ledge, right next to Ondene. The former captain of the Iron Guard had been noticeably withdrawn since Qothan and the other outriders had brought him aboard. In private shortly afterwards, Qothan had remarked to him that Ondene had been visibly disturbed to learn that the Shadowking essence still resided in the recesses of his mind. Calabos knew how such news almost inevitably led to inward brooding and had decided to seek Ondene out and see what might transpire.

For a while the two men stood there in companionable silence, watching the waters froth and swirl behind the *Stormclaw* like a long, grey tail. Then Ondene sighed.

'Is it true that you have a sword which can cut out these filthy possessing spirits?' he said, looking straight at Calabos. 'Can you free me of this thing in my head?'

Calabos did not flinch from meeting that gaze. He understood with grim clarity what was going through this young man's thoughts.

'I do possess such a sword, yes,' he said, knowing that it lay sheathed and wrapped in one of the *Stormclaw's* storerooms, along with the other baggage which had been transferred from the *Merry Meddler*. 'And yes, using it on you would very likely cause the expulsion of the Shadowking spirit, but there could be consequences that would make our predicament worse.'

Ondene remained outwardly calm but Calabos could deduce his inner tumult from the masklike blankness of his face and the dark intensity of his eyes.

'So once dislodged,' Ondene said, 'the Shadowking spirit might range away beyond our perception and find another victim to enslave, correct?'

'With the additional risk that it might split apart into who knows how many fragments,' Calabos said. 'That would make matters . . . complicated.'

Ondene frowned and rubbed his chin, now covered with the beginnings of a beard.

'Gods,' he muttered. 'Even though the broken remnants of a god can be fatal, we are bound for the lair of yet another god and our ship is being hurried across the sea by some power of the deep!' He stepped back from the window. 'I've had my fill, Calabos, can you not see that?'

Calabos nodded. 'I do, but know this – an unbearable burden can only be borne if the weakest part is either fortified or removed entirely. I place no faith in gods or their minions, but I know that there is such a thing as fate and when the burden comes to you it is usually for a reason. I know that the prospects seem grim just now, but have patience – let us see what this Sleeping God has to say.'

'This road is a hard one,' Ondene said. 'The hardest I have ever trod. I don't know, Calabos, if there is strength in me for it.'

He turned away, leaving by one of the narrow hatchways.

Watching him go, Calabos wondered if he should have been more optimistic, then gave a wry smile.

What feat of oratory could make this black trial of his appear hopeful? An account of my previous self's similar ordeals might be the thing to give him a sense of perspective, provided he didn't think me entirely mad!

He laughed ruefully and left by the other door, thinking to wend his way through below decks to the quarters which Agasklin had given over to Ondene, Coireg and himself. But he was halfway down the main spinal corridor on the second deck when he felt the familiar stir of farspeech on the fringe of his thoughts. He paused to sit on a locker beneath one of the companionways, then opened his mind to the essence-hue of Tashil.

(*Master . . . ?*)

I hear you very well, he said. *How fare you and the others?*

(*We are . . . recovering. Sounek and Dybel complain but we are making them rest. But listen — something has happened since you left . . .*)

Is it to do with Jumil? he said.

(*Just so — that grey blight Ayoni witnessed in Besh-Darok has appeared in the palace. It's spread from one of the parlour chambers and is steadily bringing down walls and the floors above. And Jumil is at the centre of it, just standing there as if waiting. High Steward Roldur has tried using archers but their arrows never reach their target. Should we move against him, probe him with a few firedaggers?*)

No — you've no way of knowing what powers he can draw on now that he has opened these gates. Avoid direct confrontation and keep him under observation for the time being.

(*The High Steward will not be pleased.*)

Calabos' heart sank. *He has already approached you? What about the mages Tangaroth left behind? Why aren't they being consulted?*

(*They've declined, citing exhaustion, the poor dears.*) There was an impression of laughter (*Which is why our assistance has been requested, less than an hour ago in fact. When we spoke with the High Steward, I got the distinct feeling that refusing would have unfortunate consequences for us.*)

And never mind the agreement of yesterday, Calabos said bitterly. *Then you'll have to baffle him with some cryptic twaddle. Talk to Dardan and work out some arcane-sounding gibberish, then go to observe the blight, throw in some impressive light and sparks, but do not launch a real attack. Once I return we shall make a thorough examination of the blight and determine how to deal with it.*

(*An interesting ploy, master. I shall enjoy putting it into practice.*)

Just be careful that none of Tangaroth's people are nearby.

(*That is certainly advisable, yes.*)

And Tashil – when this is all over, I shall see that a memorial to your brother is put up in the Kala burial grove. He was a brave man and did not deserve to die so young.

(*Thank you master. Farewell.*)

As her presence faded from his thoughts he straightened from a hunched-over seated position and saw Coireg Mazaret leaning against the side of the companionway, watching with a faint smile on his lips.

'Friend or foe?' he said. 'Good news or bad?'

Calabos uttered an amused grunt. 'Friend, and bad news which could become worse.' And he related the highlights of what he had learned from Tashil.

'So now we *do* have five of these blights,' Coireg said, frowning. 'Five? We've already seen the emergence of one Shadowking . . . you don't think . . . ?'

Calabos shrugged. 'I'm not sure what to think, but hopefully our audience with the mysterious Sleeping God will shed some light where there is none at the moment.'

'We live in an esoteric world,' Coireg said. 'Or at least one where real understanding lies behind veils of lore. Real people and events from the past become symbolic to later generations and that just obscures our understanding even more – understanding of the present as well as of the past.'

Calabos chuckled, knowing what people and events he was referring to. 'Perhaps history should be put on the pyre, yes? Stick to the oldest myths?'

'No, for that would turn the possibility of repeating past mistakes into a certainty. What is missing is the uncluttered understanding of those distant myths, the hoary origins of this deadly conflict in which we're trapped.'

'An uncluttered understanding . . .' Then Calabos snapped his fingers. 'Ah, what you mean is the ancients' own comprehension of the primal myths but in your own terms!'

Coireg was still for a moment, then he grinned.

'Yes, that's close.' He nodded. 'Then we could grasp the reasons why we are being harried by gods and the remnants of gods, and what drives them to involve themselves in the business of mortals. The powers that are hurling us across the sea at such a pace – are they truly gods of the deep or are they godlike spirits?'

Calabos smiled. 'Have you asked Qothan or Prince Agasklin this?'

'I did and was told that the ancient analects of the Israganthir have much to say about the gods of the deep but only the eyes of the elders are permitted to read them. Which is why I came looking for you.'

Calabos stood and sidled out from behind the companionway.

'Sorry, Coireg, but I can't be much help with such matters,' he said. 'My, ah, predecessor's knowledge of primal origins was sketchy at best, and was also received knowledge – he had no under-standing of the roots of events and thus no context for the tumult of images and half-memories . . .' Calabos glanced either way, then lowered his voice. 'Which anyway were the Lord of Twilight's, not Byrnak's.'

'So nothing remains? At all?'

He shrugged. 'Scraps, names and little more – Tethost, Uzlat, Mozals the Many, Grath the Unbounded . . . I'm sure I overheard Agasklin mention "Mozals" to Qothan just before we left Sejeend, so that may be who or what is pushing us across the sea.'

Coireg nodded thoughtfully. 'Perhaps questioning Qothan and Agasklin together was a mistake – I wonder if Qothan would be more forthcoming on his own?'

'It shouldn't do any harm,' Calabos said. 'Provided you don't overstep the mark.'

'Ah, you mean knowing when to let go of a question,' Coireg said. 'Wise advice – I just hope I keep it in mind.'

Laughing, they parted, Coireg climbing the companionway to the main deck where Qothan usually was , while Calabos continued for'ard. His earlier exchange with Ondene had came back to him during the chat with Coireg and he had a niggling urge to check on the sword of powers, to be assured that, if all else failed, there was still one way to deal a telling blow.

Coireg climbed the companionway some half a dozen steps then paused to glance back at Calabos' receding form, studying his gait and his appearance for a moment before smiling. Yes, the change was becoming visible – Calabos was altering his physical attributes, shedding the frailness that had been the unavoidable part of adopting the guise of an old man. Now his bearing was straighter and an air of vigour was beginning to emerge, which was much more like his old self.

But what was not familiar was his decision to admit to Qothan and Agasklin his former identity. In all their long wandering years together, Coireg had only ever heard Calabos mention Byrnak when he was very drunk and then only rarely. Perhaps at last the old names and memories were starting to lose their deadly potency for him. Perhaps a new life beckoned for him – once the current difficulties were attended to.

Smiling, he resumed his ascent.

The journey from the shamans' hideout in Belkiol to the bank of the Great Canal and thence over to the island of Besh-Darok was fraught with the fear of discovery. As well as the troop and supply boats that were moving back and forth across the strait, there were other boats with archers which were patrolling for a couple of miles in either direction. By the time Ayoni and the shamans reached the opposite bank, nearly three hours had elapsed since she had been brought of the induced stupor.

From the cover of a weedy, bush-enclosed overhang, they climbed a steep set of stairs crudely hewn into the side of huge, jutting rock. Once up on level ground, they followed a track through trees wound with dog-ivy, and emerged momentarily on a rocky ledge on the flank of a broken-backed mountain. The ledge afforded a magnificent view of the rolling fields and lush wild orchards which lay between the canal and the city of Besh-Darok, its pale walls just visible in the hazy distance. Under the clouded sun of early afternoon, a kind of slumbering tranquillity hung over the scene, accentuated by the small flock of belltails which swooped up and away from a wood below.

The track led back into the undergrowth and twisted and turned down through a maze of fallen trunks and mossy stone boulders as big as houses. A dry streambed turned into a steep gully masked by interlaced, overhanging torwood trees where the air was warm and moist and the light had a distinctly green tinge. The foliage thinned away to nothing when the gully reached an abrupt and sheer drop which must have been a waterfall, Ayoni guessed. But they had taken a side path just before the drop, which led through dense, spiny bushes to the edge of what at first looked like a wide clearing where they beheld an encampment. The camp was in turmoil.

As Ayoni took in more details she realized that she was looking along a sizeable saddle ridge between the wooded hill and the harsh, rocky slope of a small mountain. Amid a din of voices, Mogaun warriors were milling around, snatching up weapons and vaulting onto the backs of their horses. Feathery flags and small, embroidered pennons fluttered from thin poles by every curved tent while a large red banner bearing a wolf's head hung from a crosspiece jutting above a larger tent at the centre. Before its draped entrance stood a tall, fur-clad figure issuing orders with every breath – the chieftain Huzur Marag.

The shaman Pirak listened for a moment, then turned to Ayoni.

'Ilgarion's secret incursion is a secret no more – they've been spotted some three miles to the south so the warriors are riding to meet them.'

'Why not hold their positions here?' Ayoni said. 'They could repulse any attack . . .'

'Because on the other side of this ridge is the eastern portion of Belkiol, the tent city of the pilgrims, which is now swollen by evacuees from across the canal.' Pirak shook his head. 'Huzur cannot take the chance that Ilgarion will outflank him by marching round the mountain to attack the tent city from the north, thus he hopes to stop him on the open ground.'

Ayoni nodded, wishing privately that Atroc was still with them

– but only for moment. She knew that he was away in the palace at Besh-Darok, watching over her husband, Chellour and Baron Klayse, a steadying knowledge.

At length the last of the riders was gone with a shout as he guided his mount down the southern slope of the ridge, leaving behind a nearly empty camp. Huzur Marag stood before his tent conversing vigorously with a bone-adorned underling while half a dozen warriors with blade and bucklers stood guard nearby. There were a few other figures moving around, boys carrying hay bales to the vacant horse pens, a few old women tending to the camp fires or refilling water kegs.

'Now we shall act,' Pirak said.

Ayoni turned to see the elder seer flanked by two of his fellow shamans, but the other three had gone.

'Where . . . ?' she began.

'Like mist across the grass, they are already moving forth among the tents,' Pirak said. 'When our struggle with that abomination begins, they will make sure his guards are muzzled. When all of us who survive join the onslaught, that will be the sign for you to strike, and strike with all your might!'

Ayoni swallowed her anxiety, feeling perspiration prickle all over her body. She nodded and Pirak smiled.

'May the gods guard your way,' he said.

'And yours, honoured seer.'

With that, the three shamans turned and walked side by side out of the greenery and through the camp towards Huzur Marag. The chieftain noticed their approach only when one of his guards gave the alert, and the furious glare which came to his face quickly turned into an unpleasant smile. Pirak led his companions to a halt several yards from him, raised his hand and spoke what sounded like a greeting, followed by a small, stiff bow. From where she waited behind a veil of foliage, Ayoni had to focus on her mage-sight to bring the scene closer in her vision. The exchange seemed polite and calm enough with Huzur Marag listening attentively and nodding occasionally.

But the tension leaped when he interrupted Pirak's oration, jabbed a forefinger to the south then the north, then made a slashing gesture to end the dialogue and turned away to his tent. Pirak raised one hand, palm outwards, and uttered an angry shout so loud that it echoed back from the mountain face beyond. For a second Huzur Marag looked as startled as Ayoni felt, then said something with a snarl and spat on the ground. Pirak's upraised hand came down to level an outstretched pointing finger at the chieftain as if what he was pronouncing was some kind of judgement. Huzur Marag just laughed and gestured his guards to move in on the shamans.

All six guards, however, took only a few steps before they all went down, choking and struggling against foggy white serpents which had appeared around their necks. At the same time a flock of similar apparitions flew from the three seers' outflung hands towards Huzur Marag. As they entangled themselves around the enraged, bellowing chief, the other shamans emerged from behind nearby tents, their hands scribing invisible patterns then making casting gestures. Misty ripples rushed through the air and struck the chieftain, throwing him back off his feet.

Ayoni suddenly realized that this was when she was supposed to play her part. Pushing out of the leafy curtain she ran across the grassy, rocky ground, keeping the tents between her and Huzur. Moments later she was behind a tent next to the small battleground but as she edged her head round to see what was happening she saw the tall figure of Huzur Marag standing again with his back to her just a few yards away. One hand was blazing with a hot emerald fire as he tore the blurry white snakes away from his face, neck and chest, while the other hand was clamped around the throat of one of Pirak's fellow seers, whose blank eyes and limp body spoke only of death.

As she called on the Lesser Power, fashioning it into a Firedagger spell, he became aware of her presence and turned. A jagged, red bolt sprang from her suddenly open hand and struck him high in the chest. His furs and hair flashed into flames and he howled in agony. Releasing the dead seer he clawed at the fire even as it took hold beneath his skin. The howling became a shattering scream and he fell writhing to the ground. Pirak came at a stumbling run with a peculiar stone dagger in his hand, fell to his knees beside the convulsing chieftain and buried it in his chest. The man's still-burning head let out a long, hoarse groan and sank back, lifeless, yet the legs twitched and kicked and the clutching hands managed to grab hold of Pirak's bony arm. Ayoni joined in the struggle to free him but moments later the rest of the body went limp. As they got to their feet, Ayoni felt a shiver of horror as what looked like dark smoke oozed out of the corpse's mouth and eyes and gathered together in a slow, undulating knot of ashen vapour, a spirit-wraith Ayoni realized, a fragment of the Lord of Twilight.

As it floated away, a second one emerged and a third and Ayoni wondered how many other people were cursed to be hosts for such vile remnants of evil.

'He mentioned his inner voices,' she said as she turned away.

'They are thirsty ghosts,' Pirak said. 'They hunger to devour the world and even that would not suffice . . .'

A fearful shout from one of the other seers made them look back, Pirak turning sufficiently to take the point of a long cleaver blade wielded by Huzur Marag as he sat up and roared. Ayoni screamed in shock as Pirak fell back with a cry to sprawl on the ground. Huzur Marag, his head and face a charred and smoking ruin, let out a bestial growl and lurched to his feet. Without hesitation, Ayoni and the other shamans launched another sorcerous assault and he went down again, blade tumbling from an insensible grip. Once more the body twitched and lay still and again a spirit-wraith drew itself out of the seared head and began to float away. But then it swung round and flew back to the corpse and into the blackened, hairless scalp. The eyes flew open, the lips parted and the chest drew breath . . .

But Ayoni snatched up the fallen sword and with all her strength hacked off the loathsome head. Blood gouted and once more the grey spirit-wraith tore itself free from the lifeless head and darted away. Ayoni watched its departure for a moment before turning to crouch beside the fatally wounded Pirak.

'A mighty blow, child of earth,' the old seer said, wheezing. One of the other shamans was trying to staunch the bleeding but it was clearly futile, and the rest were sitting nearby, quietly murmuring a dirge-like chant.

Pirak beckoned to her with trembling fingers. 'My time is . . . almost upon me, child, so hear me well – your husband and your friends are free and riding this way . . . the long voice of Atroc told me this, even as we were coming upon this camp . . .'

'You said nothing?' Ayoni said. 'Why?'

'For a dreadful thing has happened, child . . . the grey blight, which he said so much about before you came to Belkiol, it has started . . . to grow . . . !' The wheezing in his throat sounded like torment. 'It is spreading out from the old palace as fast as a running man, consuming everything in its path . . . when your companions arrive you must go with my brothers here and return across the canal . . . there is fighting around the town so you must find . . . somewhere safe . . .'

'Will the blight stop at the canal?' she said.

Pirak managed a frail smile. 'Who is to know? Only by crossing will you know . . . now, you must do me a service, child, by hurrying to the side of the ridge and looking towards the city so we may know more . . .'

'Very well, Pirak,' she said.

She got to her feet and ran over to where a natural rock platform protruded from the southern face of the ridge, and from there she gazed east. But the far-off pale walls of Besh-Darok could not be seen for a grey murk which lay across the land like a low even band of fog or smoke. As she looked closer, focussing on her magesight, she gained few more details except that the foggy murk looked denser and had the appearance of a barrier several storeys high, moving forward and engulfing fields, trees and buildings alike. It was a chilling sight. Panicking people she saw, too, fleeing on foot, horse or cart, but of three riders together she saw no sign, but knew that they could be beneath the canopy of any of the woods laid out before her. She concentrated on the panoramic view, fixing it in her mind, then dashed back to the centre of the camp.

But when she reached the little group Atroc was there, hovering near the sad, still form of Pirak, who was dead.

'He didn't want me to see him slip away,' Ayoni murmured.

Atroc nodded. 'We seers hold on to our dignity to the bitter end.'

Hearing an echo of her own sorrow in his voice, she regarded him and saw that the opacity of his spectral form was more transparent than before. He looked weary and rueful, and utterly untouched by the steady breeze that was blowing over the ridge, making the tents flap and the flags flutter and snap.

'I do not know how I and the others came to be trapped on this island,' he said. 'Trapped here like ghosts in a stoppered bottle. And now another mighty, unfathomable event has come to break the glass and let the sands pour away.' He met her gaze and smiled, kind yet resigned. 'This is my end, Countess, but I will not make you avert your eyes.'

The surviving shamans chanted softly and Atroc gradually faded into fine, gauzy outlines and a few diminishing details. The ghostly seer raised his hand in farewell to them all and seemed to close his eyes as the last of him vanished silently from sight. Ayoni wiped tears away, then stood and walked beyond the tents to look out towards the encroaching wall of the blight. The greyness was wider and noticeably nearer than before, although it would still take more than an hour to reach the hills and crags near the canal. Then as she swept the open fields and downs in the middle distance she spotted three riders moving towards the ridge at a gallop.

Chellour! she said in farspeech.

(*Ah, there you are . . .*)

How is Jarryc? And Baron Klayse?

(*Both eager to teach that Mogaun chief a lesson or two.*)

She smiled. *Tell them that won't be necessary.*

(*I see — do I detect hints of a heroic tale?*)

I'm sure you'll be able to match it.

(*Hmm, you may be right. See you soon . . .*)

As his thought-presence trailed away from her mind, she sat down on a mossy boulder to face the east and wait.

•

Chapter Seventeen

In the icy verge of twilight's hour,
We stumble through the jaws of the storm,
Behind us the ruins of an age,
Before us a defiled world.

Vosada Boroal, *The Great House of Hallebron*, Book ii, 2.12

Corlek Ondene was standing on a canopied part of the *Stormclaw's* forecastle, sheltered from the gusting rain and the spindrift, when the island of the Sleeping God hoved into view. Its name, Nydratha, meant 'lair of tempests', or so Qothan had said earlier. At first it was just a blurred darkness in the vast grey downpour but as it drew near, shadowy forms began to emerge, outlines of tall crags with something darker at the centre. Closer still, the clustered crags took on more detail and Ondene saw rearing, wind-scarred spines, twisted and serrated stone faces, bizarre columns and ridges, adorned with curves and smooth holes like the last work of a disturbed sculptor.

And at their centre, a gyring tornado whose grinding bass moan was starting to vie with the rushing roar of the rain.

He stared at the towering grey-brown-black vortex, at the tails and wisps of low cloud being dragged into the fury along with rags of mist and spray.

The home of a god, he thought sombrely. *What am I doing here? What would a god want from me?* Then he thought of the dark and hungry thing lodged in the depths of his own mind, and shuddered.

Beneath his feet the forecastle deck heeled and rocked as the ship ploughed relentlessly on through the increasingly wild waters. Great sheets of spray flew up under the impact of the prow, and a fitful crashing sound was just audible above the embracing din of the tornado. And yet, within the convulsive roar, he could just make out voices shouting somewhere behind him. Turning, he saw one of the tall, cloaked Ushralanti standing at the starboard side, arms raised as he bellowed in the face of the broken, whirling waves. And as Ondene watched him, he felt something shift within, the sense of a presence stirring and taking notice like the glitter of inimical eyes staring from far back in the night.

After a moment or two, something began to emerge from the spray, silvery outlines of huge shapes, grotesque ghost forms that rode and plunged through the spume alongside both flanks of the *Stormclaw*.

Powers of the deep, he thought as he stared. *To whom do they owe allegiance and what kind of payment do they exact?*

He was not sure whether to feel dread or awe, while wishing that he could adopt Calabos' more sceptical point of view. Yet the older man had the air of one who knew the meaning of burdens beyond the domain of ordinary living, who seemed to wholly understand the sickening fear that gnawed at Ondene's sanity. In his thoughts he sometimes imagined it as a swarm of rats or serpents threatening to spill out of the slumbering shadows at the back of his mind . . .

Behind him he heard the footsteps of someone climbing the companionway and looked over his shoulder to see Coireg Mazaret come into view. When he saw Ondene, he nodded.

'Greetings, Captain,' he said. 'We shall soon be at our destination and mysteries will start to give up their secrets!'

Ondene gave a wan smile. 'So, friend Coireg, what berth can be found in this place? It looks purposefully fashioned to be a ship-wrecker . . .'

'As I understand it,' Coireg said, joining him and pointing at the approaching isle, 'there is a clear channel through the hidden rocks and reefs to a small sheltered harbour. Prince Agasklin tells me that our powerful benefactors have agreed to bear us there, but that almost implies that we may need similar help to leave!'

'They are a strange people, the Ushralanti,' Ondene said evenly. 'Almost as strange as Calabos and yourself.'

Coireg gave a surprised smile and raised one eyebrow. 'Indeed? How so?'

He shrugged. 'You both clearly have a long shared past, even when you account for your family connections. Yet when I was younger, before my maturity, Calabos was a regular guest at my father's house and I never heard him mention you or any other of his relatives.'

An amused look passed across Coireg's face. 'Our family . . . is a singular tribe. We seldom make the effort to contact each other, and even then it is usually through odd intermediaries.'

'I would also guess that you've both seen some majestic sights and engaged in perilous ventures.'

'Occasionally,' Coireg conceded. 'Now and then. Before my unfortunate malady laid me low, of course.'

Ondene nodded sagely, knowingly. 'Calabos' help must have been a great solace to you – in truth, he spoke as little about his early life as he did about his family, yet I did learn of a peculiar blade that he possesses. Do you know of this?'

Coireg seemed puzzled for a moment, then nodded. 'Ah, you mean the trophy! I understand that it once had some kind of sorcerous potency, but that has faded with time, apparently.'

'Has he got it here on board, perhaps?' Ondene said, and was suddenly aware of the desperation in his own manner when he saw Coireg frown.

'Why do you ask? . . . Ah, wait, we are almost there – look!'

Following his outstretched arm, Ondene saw the maze of wave-thrashed reefs pass by on either side as the *Stormclaw* rode through on eldritch currents. The ship's timbers creaked and shook underfoot while great fangs and walls of rock loomed closer. The monstrous, towering funnel of the vortex filled the sky, its harsh droning near loud enough to drown all else. The gusting air snatched at loose folds of Ondene's cloak and disarranged his hair, provoking a nervous laughter, and he grabbed at the deck's balustrading for support as the ship slowed suddenly, its stern swinging round. The waters seemed to boil as the Ushralanti's

sorcerous allies guided the *Stormclaw* into the comparative calm of
a small harbour cupped in the shelter of bare, sheer crags. A jutting
tongue of stone had been crudely hewn down to serve as a jetty
and it was to this that their vessel was finally moored with several
large padded baffles of old sailcloth hung over the side to protect
the hull from damage.

Calabos and Qothan emerged from below decks and watched
the crew energetically cope with the berthing for a moment before
looking up at the forecastle and waving. Ondene called out a
greeting which was swallowed in the storm's roar, and waved back,
then Coireg tapped him on the shoulder and leaned in close.

'We shall soon go ashore,' he said loudly. 'Be prepared.'

Ondene laughed. 'Is it possible to be prepared for meeting a
god? And how would I know when I was?'

Coireg's answering laughter was muffled in the din. 'Good – I
can see that you are ready now!'

The turbulent waters subsided to the normal surge and swell
of a stormy sea. A heavy, wind-driven mist filled the air as Ondene
and Coireg Mazaret descended to join Calabos and Qothan on
the main deck, where Agasklin and the other chieftains of the ship
were also gathering. All were now wearing large, hooded robes
strangely patterned in pale brown and red – similar garments were
passed to Ondene and Coireg and as they donned them, Calabos
said:

'These are for protection against the inner and the outer conditions. Are you ready? Excellent!'

He turned to Agasklin and gave a sharp nod. The stern Ushralanti
then led them all across an open gantry to the stone jetty. Feeling
not the least bit ready, Ondene gathered up the baggy folds of his
robe and followed Coireg across and the moment his feet touched
the uneven solidity of the jetty he felt a certain uneasy tension,
the feeling that he was being observed. Walking in line with the
others he glanced about him at the rearing, weathered columns
and curved walls, all bare of any kind of vegetation, then let his
gaze rise to the vast roiling pillar of the storm. He wiped away
beads of moisture from his face with one capacious sleeve while
giving the vortex a wry smile.

Do our capers please you? he thought. *Have we played well enough our part in the masque?*

But there came no answer that he could hear.

Through flying mist the party made its trudging way along a cracked, rubble-strewn path which wound among great, shattered pieces of rock, many clearly positioned to form an irregular tunnel. Water dripped and trickled through the many gaps, forming pools and rills for feet to splash in, and the sound of the vortex was a fiendish cataract of shrieks and howls that swamped the ears.

Ondene felt the intensity of the observing presence gradually grow with every onward step, becoming stronger and more encompassing as if he were a frail toy being examined by something mighty. He was not sure how fearful he should be, caught between a known inner horror and a menacing outer mystery.

Before long, the path started to slope upwards, curved to the left then entered a rain-gouged cliff face and became a tunnel proper. A few paces in and the howling din was muffled and the air became warmer and drier. A few diamond-shaped windows had been cut in one side, letting in a dull grey light which revealed a fine dust on the tunnel floor, gathered in its many crevices and notches. The passage climbed for a short way then dipped and curved to the right, dimming as the windows grew fewer. A hazy pale light ahead resolved into a door through which the shattering roar of the vortex came, along with a dense veil of fine water droplets. Condensation had soaked the tunnel walls near the door and many streamlets were flowing back along the floor and outside to be snatched up by the fury of the storm and once more pulverized into vapour.

Beyond the doorway, a rocky bridge led straight into the raging wall of the vortex itself. Without pause or faltering footstep Agasklin and Calabos led the party out of the tunnel and into the teeth of the storm. Coireg slowed just ahead of Ondene for a moment then pressed on through the doorway with Ondene close on his heels.

The ferocity of the blast made them all adopt a crouched walk while raising an arm to shield their faces against the needling scour of tempest-driven rain. For Ondene, crossing the bridge was at once terrifying and exhilarating – not even his previous ship-borne experience of the wild gales of the Stormbreaker Isles could match this for sheer eldritch peril. He half-expected to see uprooted trees or farmyard animals go flying past, despite the desolation of the island.

Minutes after leaving the shelter of the tunnel, his vision was reduced to just a few feet in the rushing, deafening murk, such that it was a considerable surprise when a vertical rock face with a rough arched door emerged from the whirling dimness. Another couple of steps and he realized that it was no wall but the side of a huge rock pillar rising before them, its heights obscured by the vortex. Ondene recalled Qothan telling him of the origins of the Book of the Vortex and wondered what prophecies might be spoken this time.

The entire party filed into the dark archway where they rested in a cold, shadowy room, wordless in the encompassing din. In the corner a set of narrow stairs rose in a spiral and after a short time they started up them, their way lit by shuttered lamps. The spiral climb soon became an effort that got his heart beating and the sweat prickling on his skin and scalp. Then it became gruelling as his chest heaved, then punishing as aches and pains assailed his legs and feet. The leaders allowed the party only the briefest of rests before resuming the upward progress, provoking muttered curses from Ondene and Coireg. Then at last a glimmer of light from above brightened until they stepped up onto a somewhat flat area a few yards wide atop the pillar. Yet for all its exposed nature, only a mild breeze played across it as if an invisible barrier somehow excluded the rest of the vortex, as well as much of the noise.

'Not exactly a place for a dance,' Coireg said, pointing out the smooth-worn edges of the platform.

Ancient, this place, thought Ondene as he looked about him at the pillar-top then up at the swirling fury of the storm. As he stared into its heart he caught glimpses of another two similar stone towers standing amid the ceaseless gyre. *Once home to elder gods now devoured by the maw of time . . .*

He paused and frowned, puzzled at the dark turn of his thoughts. *Elder gods? How could I know that?*

But before he could delve further into the enigma, Calabos and Agasklin beckoned them all closer. The Ushralanti prince produced from within his robes a leather-bound book and opened it near the front.

'Our Captain, the honoured Pericogal, has shown me the lines whose chanting will attract the regard of the Sleeping God and . . . bring . . .'

Like the others, Ondene's attention was drawn to the centre of the vortex where outlines and vague shapes were coalescing out of the dark and misty tumult. A myriad indistinct details, a cloud of phantom fragments slowly burgeoning until a sudden clarity made plain the vast form of a tree enfolded in dense, lush foliage. Flowers unfolded in undulant perfection and clusters of gleaming berries hung heavily from firm sprigs. It would have been the very image of luxuriant fecundity but for the strange translucent hues − bruised grey, parched and pale brass.

As the entire party stood frozen and gazing up at the vast manifestation, a ripple of movement passed across the leafy surface and gathered into a single cleft which then began to part. The feeling Ondene had of being at the focus of a pitiless perception faded a little, yet another sensation seemed to be building within him, some kind of impatience or instinctive restlessness. A nervous tension made his neck muscles taut and he began to sweat all over.

Then he half-forgot the discomfort as the gigantic, numinous tree opened to reveal a pale, ivory form, its head lowered, shoulders hunched, arms wrapped across the chest as if in an attitude of sleep. A melodious note crept into the harsh song of the vortex and the great form stirred, lifting its head and very slowly turning to observe the small gathering atop the pillar.

'The gaze of a god,' Coireg whispered nearby. 'I can feel it upon me . . .'

As could Ondene. The eyes of the Sleeping God were nacreous orbs whose unwinking, unrelenting regard felt like a weight upon his mind, an irresistible scrutiny that bored into his inner thoughts . . . and something broke loose inside him, the restless impatience flaring into an angry hate he recognized only too well as the voice of the Shadowking rang in his thoughts.

Sleeping God, I know you! I know what you are!

As Ondene slumped to his knees, a certain panic seized the others. Anxious mutters were exchanged as Coireg and Calabos quickly came to Ondene's side, not knowing what he was hearing in his own thoughts. Then another voice spoke aloud with such a force that reduced the din of the vortex to a whisper.

I know you, wretched fragment of a still-more wretched whole! Fate has wrought a cage for you, this man who is the Prince of Change!

Within him, the Shadowking gained control of his mouth and spoke openly:

'*Prince of dregs!*' he said, provoking outraged cries from the *Stormclaw*'s chieftains. '*Prince of defeat, your defeat when the Lord of Twilight's aspects are once more joined together!*'

Foolish fragment – twice before has your greater self been trapped and despatched by the fateful necessity which he himself has graven upon the altar of his own essence. Just as this world cannot escape him, he cannot escape his own doom.

'*Lies, lies, god of lies! I can taste your fear of me in every false word . . . !*'

Ondene strove to hold on to his sanity as the deranged voice ranted and raved across his mind. 'Please . . .' he moaned, covering his face with his hands. 'Make it stop . . .'

Then Qothan was crouching beside him, offering a small, uncorked vial. Gratefully he accepted it and poured the contents down his throat.

Everlasting shall be my despite for you . . .

Quickly, a warmth began to spread across his chest.

Invincible my strength, unyielding my purpose . . .

The warmth became a heat that rose to his neck and up to his ears and scalp.

Tireless my onslaught . . .

A curious tingling flickered around his neck and shoulders and his anxiety began to lessen.

Implacable . . . am I . . .

And after that, a kind of peace held sway in Ondene's thoughts.

'Thank you,' he whispered to Qothan who just gave a bleak smile. Then a hand touched his shoulder in a comforting gesture and he glanced up to see Calabos looking down with eyes full of understanding and some kind of old, old pain. The grey-haired mage then offfered his hand to help and as he regained his feet the Sleeping God spoke:

Many and tangled are the threads that have brought you all here, and dark and perilous are the days that lie ahead. All of your fates now run together and strength is joined to strength, even without your knowing . . .

The Sleeping God leaned forward a little, towering over them as its pearly eyes sought out Ondene from the rest. As that colossal regard settled upon him, it was as if every corner of his spirit was laid bare and all was being judged. At the same time, he stared up at that immense countenance and tried to gain a reckoning from features which one moment seemed to bloom with every attribute of femininity and the next appeared to shift amid shadows and take on the contours of youthful maleness. But before he could even begin to make sense of this, the mighty voice spoke forth:

The thread of your fate has many twists, Corlek Ondene, and its course will test you to the heart. The muted howl of the vortex lent a mournful counterpoint to the voice of the god. **I have seen the broken shard of malice you carry and felt the edge of his wrath, yet you will be called upon to bear a still greater burden. To endure such a thing may seem to be beyond you but I have not named you the Prince of Change for naught – when change comes you will know it.**

'I only wish to be free of this burden,' Ondene said stonily. 'I did not ask for it . . .'

I could not take it from you without maiming you, said the Sleeping God. **But I do not need to do nothing** . . .

The eyes of the Sleeping God held Ondene's gaze in unbreakable thrall as they looked deep into his thoughts and for a moment he imagined that a shaft of pure sunlight shone through his body, illuminating, dazzling him completely. Then the moment passed and that encompassing presence withdrew, leaving him weak-kneed, blinking as he swayed on the spot. His vision was blurred by the brightness and as it began to return to normal he looked up and saw that there was no trace of male aspect in the Sleeping God's face. Only the glory of womanhood shone forth, making him wonder at this manifestation.

Calabos, filled with worry for him, reached out to steady him. Ondene jerked slightly at the touch as if roused from a reverie.

'What happened?' Calabos said. 'Are you well?'

'A light,' Ondene said in a stunned voice. 'Such light . . . yes, I am well – well enough . . .'

From now your lives and the lives of all hang in the balance. The Israganthir seek an end to their wandering, but your tale is not done yet and its outcome may test you.

The chieftains of the *Stormclaw* looked angry as they muttered among themselves, and Calabos thought that one or two might shout or curse. But then Prince Agasklin managed to calm them with a lowered voice and a steady gaze before turning to face the presence.

'Have we displeased you, divine one?' he said. 'Why do you lay further tasks upon us?'

The greatest weights are not hung on the weakest chain, nor is a task of fire entrusted to an adept of water. Have patience, trust to your strengths.

Then the huge countenance turned and Calabos had to force himself not to flinch as that exalted regard bore down on him.

Yours has been a long voyage, Beltran Calabos. We remember the face you once wore as well as that which once wore you. The scar was deep in you yet you have triumphed over the memories it holds and forged yourself anew. Are you now ready to behold the cause, the deadly seed which has brought about such a flowering of malice across these lands? Would you see into what has been hidden?

Calabos took a deep breath. 'I am ready.'

Then look . . .

Abruptly, the pillar-top and the moaning vortex and the Sleeping

God with its louring tree were gone. He was standing in a rock-ribbed chamber open to skies of swirling rose-grey, standing on polished viridian marble just within a rough square of twisted black pillars while at its centre was a squat conical altar atop a low dais . . .

The Wellsource, at the very heart of Hewn Mountain, in the realm of the Lord of Twilight.

The raging emerald of it flickered and flowed up like a fountain of fire, then a jumble of rods and vanes, then a boiling cloud of agonized faces. He remembered it, bit by bit recalling what had happened as he saw Byrnak's entry with Atroc, the blow aimed at Kodel, then his passage through the Wellsource with the Crystal Eye and the Motherseed in his arms, then emerging with them fused together.

Then Keren entered in Daemonkind form, bearing the Staff of the Void which Suviel joined with the other talismans. Byrnak left but Tauric arrived and Calabos saw for the first time the event which Atroc had later described, Suviel and Tauric walking hand in hand into the fury of the Wellsource.

There was a sudden dislocation and a dizzying, disembodied plunge into darkness as he followed them down through the under-realms and further down into the depths of the Void. Their plummeting descent followed the harsh emerald stem of the Wellsource and Calabos could see the wonder and fear in their faces as they fell through that conduit of coruscating power.

Eventually they slowed and slipped out of the narrowing flow to drift down towards a strange black plain of blurred and shifting features, across which cold blue webs of radiance crawled and flickered. Suviel and Tauric found themselves wading through a clinging black fog and Calabos followed as they moved away from the Wellsource's burning fumarole only to halt perhaps a dozen paces away. Suviel produced the fused talisman staff and gave it to Tauric, muttering something as she did so. The young emperor nodded and went down on his knees in the misty blackness, clasped in both hands the headpiece of the staff then raised it above his head for a brief moment before bringing it down to smash into the strange floor of the Void.

Polychromatic light burst forth from this new wound, spouting around Tauric who did not flinch amid this torrent of raw, primal energy. Then a change came over him and a many-coloured lustre began to pour through his skin, glowing from the exposed areas of face and neck and hands. Soon a single colour emerged to dominate the others, a pure violet that cast its hue in blue-tinted shades across all his form as the remnants of his garment melted away. Tauric had become a god.

Calabos stared in amazement. From all around jagged webs of blue light flashed in towards the nascent fount of Tauric's power, momentarily brightening the surroundings and allowing a glimpse of the vastness of this plain at the bottom of the Void. Suviel came over to face Tauric and said something to which he nodded, his eyes aflame. Then he turned and strode back in the direction of the Wellsource. But he was only a few paces from it when a huge figure came rushing out of the glittering shadows to stand in his way. Tauric halted and gazed up at the evil grinning visage of the Lord of Twilight, whose barbaric armour and downward-curving horned helm gleamed in the glimmering radiance of the Void. Then Tauric raised one foot and stamped – and his form grew to match his foe, then the battle of gods was joined.

It was a violent, thunderous struggle in which Tauric, for all the righteous fury of his cause, found it increasingly difficult to match the skill and practised wiles of the Lord of Twilight. It was the vigour of unschooled youth against the experienced cruelty of age, with the latter gaining the upper hand. Bolts and blades were hurled back and forth and the savage ardour of combat stirred up the black fog of the Void's lowermost plain and made its foundations tremble. And it was bitter to see Tauric reel from blows yet drag himself back to his feet to deliver weakening attacks. The Lord of Twilight had not been untouched by Tauric's attacks but the triumphant grin on his glowing face told all. With fists wreathed in viridian fire he gathered himself for an assault on the nearly defenceless Tauric – then another figure entered the fray, slender, womanly, her eyes burning with hate.

A single shock of golden force sent the Lord of Twilight flying backwards, and without pity the Earthmother rained more blows upon him. Calabos looked on as battle resumed with a savagery that spoke of an ages-long enmity. And as the Earthmother and the Lord of Twilight engaged in a shattering string of mauling attacks and flaring countersallies, Tauric regained sufficient strength to lunge back into the struggle.

Even so, it was not enough. The Lord of Twilight was still able to fend off the Earthmother's raging thrusts while dealing Tauric a blow that knocked him off his feet to lie sprawling on the dark and foggy plain. And still he forced himself to clamber upright, uttering a cry of despairing anger as he regained his feet and prepared to charge once more . . .

Then a tremor passed through the plain and several shadowy figures emerged from the turbulent black mists, converging on the conflict. There were no details to their oddly elongated and angular forms, which were wholly black.

The masters of the Void, said the Sleeping God in Calabos' thoughts.

Suddenly aware of the newcomers, the three gods ceased their violence and drew apart, all weary from the fight yet all still bright with anger.

*This*must*not*continue* said one of the Void masters. *This *vicinity*already*suffers*damage*from*your*barbarity*

'Do not stand between me and my victory!' said the Lord of Twilight.

*There*can*be*no*victory*for*you* said another.

The Lord of Twilight answered with an emerald spear of power. But the Void master caught it in midair and returned it three-fold to strike him full in the chest, throwing him to the ground.

*You*forget*where*you*are*

*You*forget*who*rules*here*

*You*forget*whence*you*came*

'I know my power,' the Lord of Twilight said with an evil grin as he got back on his feet. 'And I know yours, thus I know that I can defeat you in the end.'

*You*know*less*than*you*believe*one of the Void masters said. *But*even*if*that*were*a*possibility*the*war*would*be*a*long *drawn-out*torment*that*would*wreck*the*Void*and*all*the*realms *and*leave*both*you*and*us*diminished*beyond*recognition*You *know*this*to*be*true*

Calabos stared, hanging on every word. The Lord of Twilight glowered back at the Void master who had spoken, his silence a tacit admission that it was true.

'*I will not submit,*' he said. '*Destroying all of you would be a sweet triumph, and what matters it if I am diminished? I have regained myself before and will do so again.*'

*We*understand*this*which*is*why*we*want*to*propose*a *compromise*

At this the Earthmother stepped forward, her perfect features distorted with fury.

'*Do not make a pact with this vermin!*' she cried. '*It is in his nature to betray and kill and corrupt!*'

Beside her, Tauric nodded. '*She speaks truly — he cannot be trusted in anything.*'

The Lord of Twilight laughed. '*The bleating of the prey,*' he said, the addressed the Void masters. '*Say your piece — reveal your plan.*'

*We*propose*to*split*the*coursing*of*Time*and*thereby*create *one*world*where*you*are*defeated*and*another*in*which*you* triumph*completely*

Tauric and the Earthmother were aghast.

'*That would be an abomination,*' the Earthmother said. '*It would condemn an entire world to slavery under his will!*'

*But*in*the*other*course*of*Time*that*same*world*would*be*free *of*his*influence* the Void master said. *Free*to*make*its*own*way*

'*You would be purchasing the safety of one world by sacrificing another,*' Tauric said. '*That would be irredeemably wrong — I say no!*'

To which the Earthmother gave a nod of agreement, but the Lord of Twilight just laughed.

'*I say yes! Carry out your plan!*'

Tauric clenched his fists and violet flame wreathed them. '*I will stop you . . .*'

But he paused as another of the Void masters came into view bearing a limp form in inky black arms — it was Suviel and even Calabos could tell that she was dead.

*We*can*bring*her*back*to*life*and*return*her*to*the*realm *between*if*you*agree*to*the*division*of*Time*

'*I had forgotten how cruel you could be,*' said the Earthmother.

Or*would*you*prefer*to*contend*against*both*ourselves*and*the **Lord*of*Twilight?*It*would*not*be*a*long*battle**

Calabos almost wished that Tauric and the Earthmother would choose to resist, but they looked at each other for a long moment before Tauric said bitterly:

'*Do as you will — we shall not oppose you.*'

Suviel stirred in the cradling blackness of one of the Void masters, glancing about her, and in the next instant her bearer rose straight up and soon vanished in the upper gulfs of the Void. Then a series of tremors passed through the plain and flickers of red and gold radiance gathered around them, building until they joined together in a single dazzling flash of power. In the aftermath, the foggy murk seemed darker than before.

*It*is*done*

The three gods glanced about them then regarded the Void masters.

'*So which world is this?*' growled the Lord of Twilight. '*Along which path of Time are we passing?*'

One of the Void masters began to drift towards him.

In*splitting*the*course*of*Timeit said **certain*weaknesses*have* **occurred*thus*this*is*not*a*good*world*for*you**

At this the Earthmother let out a cry and lunged towards the Lord of Twilight, closely followed by Tauric. Calabos watched in awe as white fire clashed and clawed against blades of hot green power while Tauric sent violet whips darting in. Then the Void masters converged and called down shards of indivisible blackness from the yawning heights. As their terrible impacts struck the Lord of Twilight to the ground and hammered through his defences he bellowed—

'*I can see it! — I can see my victory . . . !*'

Then a concerted rush of attacks broke apart the last of his shielding powers and the howl of his death-agony was heard for only a moment or two before his essence shattered in a bright, abrupt wave of force which drowned everything in blinding green radiance . . .

The Void masters also attempted to close off the Wellsource, the Sleeping God said in Calabos' thoughts, **But they were only able to curtail it to a trickle**.

'And Tauric and the Earthmother,' he said. 'They joined to become you, correct?'

An admirable piece of deduction, Calabos – yes, this is what happened, a fusion made pragmatic by our greatly reduced state in the wake of the enemy's shattering.

'And what happened in the other world?' Calabos said, seeing with his returning sight a gloomy, grey-brown mist all around. 'Where the Lord of Twilight triumphed . . .' A realization came to him, 'And he became . . .'

The Great Shadow. After defeating us in that place he enslaved us to his will, combined our powers with his, then broke the Void masters before wreaking havoc throughout much of the Void, into which he dragged all the other realms.

For a moment Calabos did not grasp the full meaning of the Sleeping God's words, then the cold horror of understanding crept over him.

'All the other realms?' he said. 'He dragged them into the Void?'

Perhaps it would be more accurate to say that his wrecking of the Void's underpinnings caused the realms to collapse into it, but it was still his intention.

'The death toll must have been . . . incalculable,' Calabos murmured.

None perished, for he made himself master of all laws and could impose or prevent death according to his whim. Thus when all the lands contracted and crashed down into the sundered Void, he kept all alive, whatever their tribulations. After all, as absolute ruler of the Nightrealm he wanted servants, worshippers, and all manner of entertaining underlings. Many tried to end their own lives when they realized what had transpired, but that proved futile. There was no escape.

Calabos was grim. 'It must be a terrible place.'

Every village, town and city from every land lies side by side in the Nightrealm's tilted territories, crammed together in a single, vast expanse of buildings. Districts make war upon districts with unrestrained savagery, and

occasionally rivals form alliances to conduct assaults on the Great Shadow's own fastnesses, all to no avail. Such convulsions serve only to divert and amuse the lord of all existence. Also, his selfish, delusional activities have distorted the scales of Time between this world and the Nightrealm, such that it flows faster there than here.

'Yet he decides to turn his attention to our world with conquest in mind,' Calabos said. 'Has he become bored?'

Perhaps over-familiar with the caperings of his myriads of prisoners, but also gnawed at by the knowledge that another world exists where the memory of his power was reduced to semi-legendary tales. It could only have been a short step from hating our world to actively moving against it.

The surrounding grey-brown mist began turning into the detailed density of foliage, as if he were poised somewhere within the vast tree that had filled the vortex.

'It occurs to me,' Calabos said, 'that if no one died during the collapse of the realms, then all are still living.'

In a manner of speaking, yes.

'So what became of the other versions of the Earthmother and Tauric?'

The Great Shadow has a special prison for those who earn his deepest hate, a vast wall of ice that stretches up behind his throne and which holds them all embedded in its freezing grip. That is where he keeps the Earthmother, near at hand for whenever the need for torment takes him. As for Tauric, he succumbed to his enslavement . . .

'So those Shatterseed rituals and the expanding blights are intended to add this world to the Nightrealm, yes?' Calabos said. 'Are the Void masters here going to let this happen?'

They have done more than you suppose, and always as invisibly as possible.

Calabos managed a wry smile. 'And am I right in thinking that the thread of my fate will at some point lead me across to the Nightrealm?'

This is possible, and not just for yourself . . . The Sleeping

God's voice paused for a long moment. **And that crossing may come sooner than you think**.

The great mass of ghostly vegetation swung around him with a gliding smoothness and suddenly he was back on the pillar-top platform with the Sleeping God staring down from the parted crown of that colossal tree in the vortex. His senses were reeling from the abruptness of the transition and when someone grasped his shoulder he thought he would overbalance and pitch forward . . .

'Calabos! – It's Ondene!' came Coireg's voice. 'He's just been taken . . .'

'Ondene?' he said, trying to force alertness into his thoughts. 'By whom?'

'A spirit-wraith came flying through the outer winds of the vortex and was on him before anyone could react.' Coireg looked distraught. 'He let out a cry of such terror . . . then he scrambled away and vanished down the steps. Qothan and some of the chiefs went after him . . .'

You must follow him, Calabos.

The Sleeping God's voice thundered forth from the muffled moan of the vortex, and all eyes gazed up at that majestic countenance.

There can only be one destination for him and that is where you must go too.

The Nightrealm, Calabos thought sombrely.

Above them the Sleeping God turned, eyes closing as it withdrew into the giant tree whose foliage closed around it. Then the tree's leaves and branches blurred and dissolved into the whirling, dark roar of the storm. Calabos watched it go, then headed for the stairs.

'Are you able and well for such a chase, ser Calabos?' said Prince Agasklin.

'I will know only when I make the attempt,' he said, gathering up his robe as he descended the dark spiral of steps.

Coireg was hard on his heels with a lantern, making it easier to keep his footing during what became a hectic vertical pursuit. At last, with aching feet and scraped hands, they reached the bottom of the staircase and stumbled out into the wind-blasted stone bridge. The scuttled across it at a low stoop and gratefully entered the tunnels which led down through dry warmth to the path flanked by shattered slabs of rock. With the rushing howl of the vortex filling the air, Calabos could hear nothing else but he saw Ondene before the others, up on a boulder by the path, crouched on his knees, his head down and clasped in his hands. Of Qothan and his companions there was no sign.

He was instantly aware of Calabos' approach, head whipping up to look with eyes that stared with animal wildness from a twitching, sweat-glazed face.

'The stones . . . have no face yet they . . . *speak* to me!' Ondene cried jerkily. 'Speaking stones speaking . . . Are they the . . . stones of Gorla, stones of Keshada . . . ?'

'Corlek,' Calabos said calmly. 'Listen to my voice . . .' As he slowly advanced he tried to project his words with farspeech, hoping that he might reach Ondene. 'Listen to me, follow my voice, ignore anything else you might hear . . .'

Hate twisted Ondene's features. 'Traitorous old man! I'll feed your eyes to the eaterbeasts . . .' Then between one word and the next his voice and expression changed, '. . . Calabos, help me, I beg you, I can't fight . . .'

Then Qothan and two chieftains appeared further along the path. Ondene spotted them, leaped to his feet and clambered down the other side of the boulder, off the path. Calabos cursed and ran along until he found a gap through the shattered rock. With the others coming after, he found a way across an expanse of jumbled stone shards as he followed the manic figure of Corlek Ondene towards the shore. But rather than head for the water's edge, he mounted the flank of a weather-scored stone outcropping which lengthened into a promontory jutting out into the sea.

Ondene ran to the furthermost edge and stood there, with huge waves roaring and crashing just below and flinging up clouds and spouts of spray. As Calabos climbed onto the lower slope of the promontory, Ondene glanced back at him and laughed. Then he faced the sea, raised his hands and bellowed a string of words barely audible against the raucous noise of the waves.

For a moment there was no other sound to be heard in that din, then through it came a distant sonorous chiming, as if out in the depths a giant bell had been struck. Seconds later it sounded again, louder and nearer, and Calabos could feel reverberations in the stone beneath his feet.

The third was a deafening, jarring boom and as it assailed the ears and made the ground shake, the waters before the promontory erupted. Clusters of dark tentacles lunged up out of the waves, slender or thick or articulated or sheathed in scales or bearing collars of spines. In their thousand-strong profusion they coiled and squirmed towards the rock promontory while still more lesser tendrils writhed in the rocky shoreline surf.

Calabos felt a hand on his arm, pulling him back. It was Qothan. 'It is Grath the Unbounded! We're in great danger here . . . !'

Grath the Unbounded . . . which Calabos knew was supposedly an ancient sea god. But Qothan was clearly adamant, even nervous, about their safety and he found himself torn between that and the urge to reach Ondene who was now a mere dozen paces away. Then a deep-throated, plangent groan sounded as a vast shape reared up before the outcropping, like some immense neck down whose rugose, filth-encrusted flanks water streamed. Ondene stood before the grotesque colossus, clenched fists held before him as he continued to croon something unintelligible.

Calabos shouted at him to get back but Ondene only cast a grinning glance over his shoulder without interrupting his invocation. Then there was another massive, sepulchral groan and the end of the huge tentacular neck unfolded into a dark, glistening mouth. As it dipped to come level with the end of the promontory, Ondene uttered a cry of triumph and leaped straight into it. Calabos caught the merest glimpse of him falling into an inky gullet before the immense mouth closed in on itself. Then it leaned back, curving as it fell into the sea with a mighty crash sending long curtains of water gouting up on either side. Likewise, all the lesser tentacles and tendrils swiftly withdrew into the churning waves and in seconds the gigantic being was gone from sight.

'Mother's name!' said Coireg, who was getting to his feet nearby. 'That was Grath? So is Ondene dead?'

'No, friend Coireg,' said Qothan. 'Grath is known as the Unbounded because the appendage and extremities of his vast entwining form reach to every part of the girdling ocean, to every coast and beach. Grath is a roadway through the seas, a path made swift by the intrinsic sorcery of his nature – no matter what shore is the Ondene-Shadowking's destination, he will be there in less than an hour.'

'Sejeend,' Coireg said to Calabos who nodded.

'Which is where I should be going too,' he said. 'According to the Sleeping God.'

'Yes, this god imparts as many mysteries as answers,' muttered Coireg, as if half to himself.

Then Prince Agasklin came into view, clambering up onto the outcropping, followed by two of the younger-looking Israganthir chieftains.

'There may be a way to take you to there, Calabos,' he said, glancing at Qothan who nodded determinedly.

Calabos started to ask what he meant, then Qothan and the two newcomers began to doff their outer robes as their forms began to grow and change, torsos blurring, limbs becoming more heavily muscled, with long, hooked wings fading into solidity over their shoulders. And suddenly he understood, and laughed softly.

'Friend Agasklin,' he said. 'The efforts of you all humble me, yet I would ask a small additional boon before departing for Sejeend, namely a swift visit to the *Stormclaw* to recover a certain sword of mine.'

Agasklin gave a faint smile. 'This shall be done, then we shall send you speeding across the ocean, Calabos. May your fate be a kind one!'

Chapter Eighteen

Open the gates,
For through that monstrous mouth,
Lie all the dreams,
Where hope has died.

The Black Saga Of Culri Moal, canto xi, stanza 3

Beneath a bright, cloud-scattered morning sky the grey seeding
shroud rippled faintly, wrinkles coming and going as nutrition
from the far-off expanding edges flowed into the centre, here
where the imperial palace once stood, overlooking Sejeend. Only
the broken, grey-swathed ruins of walls remained – everything
else had collapsed into the shroud to be devoured.

At the centre of it all sat the Shattergate, a vaguely conical
outcropping with a dark, gaping door in its sloping face. Beside
it, a hooded figure sat on a block of fallen masonry which seemed
as free of the shroud as he. Yet on closer examination an observer
would have seen the greyness creeping up the block and the grey
streaks on the man's hand and legs.

Xabo-once-Jumil knew that the shroud would take him eventually, just as it had finally gnawed away at the glamour which had
sustained Vorik. *Yes*, he thought, *soon, blessed soon the seeding shroud
will eat away this false body and return my essence to the Nightrealm
and to the glittering dream-court of my master.*

It had been a great success, the campaign to absorb this world
and all its works. From yesterday afternoon and all through the
night the quick expansion of the shroud in all five locations had
taken all their enemies by surprise before it reached either its
inherent limits or natural boundaries like the Great Canal

surrounding the Isle of Besh–Darok or the Valewater which divided
Sejeend. It would not be long now before the first advance squads
of the Black Host emerged from all five Shattergates and began
preparations for the true conquest.

Yet even as Xabo relaxed into these feelings of contentment,
he became aware of a presence drawing near from the direction
of the sea. He extended his perceptions, partially employing the
sensitivities of the shroud, and noticed some activity amongst those
Watcher mages on the north bank of the Valewater. But he
dismissed that and turned his attention to the rounded, grey-
cloaked expanse of the former docks and wharfs, where the waves
lapped and few birds dared come close.

The wait was short-lived. There was a deep, resonant booming
sound and a gargantuan, lop-necked creature burst up from the
waters accompanied by squirming clusters of tendrils by the thousand. The end of the immense tentacle opened at the waterline
and from the slimy darkness a familiar figure emerged and stepped
down onto the shroud-coated strand. Whiplike extrusions rose
from the shroud and wavered towards the newcomer for a moment
before sinking back into the even greyness. Xabo smiled – the
Shadowking had returned.

A fitful shower was falling by the time he appeared at the edge
of the palace ruins and began to wend his way inwards. Xabo's
good humour persisted, stoked by the nuances of change in the
Shadowking's manner and aura, evidence of growth in that ever-
long essence coupled with new experience.

'There is purpose in you,' he said. 'Our enemies thought to trap
and diminish you, but instead they have helped you grow. Did
you know of Grath the Unbounded before this?'

'I knew,' the Shadowking said, entering the roofless chamber,
'but I did not *know* as I do now.'

Xabo smiled, feeling the skin pull taut over bone like the imper-
fect mask that it was. 'So now you are here – what do you want?
Power? Dominion? All you need do is wait here for the
Duskgeneral's marshals and captains to arrive – they will be more
than grateful to cooperate with you in the subjugation of this
world.'

The Shadowking said nothing, just glanced at him as he strolled leisurely across the grey floor towards the Shattergate.

'Or do you wish to slay me?' Xabo said. 'It would be neither a surprise nor a true death, merely a hastening of the inevitable. Kill me and my essence will travel back across to the Nightrealm and the shining dream-courts of my master who will give me another form, one more fitting to my prestige than this poor flesh.'

'I will not bend the knee,' the Shadowking said. 'I will not submit, I will not bow before the storm. Just as he would not before me.'

'Aah, then you desire it all,' Xabo said. 'My master the Great Shadow will be both eager and intrigued to see how you cope with the peculiarities of the Nightrealm. Know that in my eyes such a contest would only be a fruitful thing, for the victor will be stronger than either and thus better able to ensure the success of the conquest.'

'Your composure may be your undoing,' said the Shadowking. 'If I am victorious, my re-ordering of the Nightrealm and all its works may not be to your liking.'

'If you are victorious, lord, you will be quite different from how you are today,' Xabo said. 'As would be the case if my master the Great Shadow triumphs, which, you'll forgive me for saying, is the more likely outcome. If the essence changes so too does the outward appearance, for which I am prepared.'

The Shadowking laughed and walked up to the open black-ness of the Shattergate.

'Then be ready for a new purpose and a new realm!'

With that, he stepped through and vanished.

I am certainly ready, lord, Xabo thought. *But are you?*

More than an hour after the Ondene-Shadowking's departure, Tashil was standing on the battlements of the remaining sea-gate tower at the mouth of the Valewater, listening to Dardan and Sounek arguing.

'. . . and a huge mouth opens and a traveller emerges,' Sounek was saying. 'That's what we saw, therefore it had to be the great sea god Grath.'

'Yes, according to the milk-tales you learned at your nanny's apron-strings,' said Dardan.

'I never had a nanny,' Sounek said. 'Unlike you.'

Tashil quickly cut in. 'At least we can agree that it was Corlek Ondene who walked out of the thing.'

'With the Shadowking in charge again,' Dardan said morosely. 'Whatever happened on this Sleeping God's island, it wasn't good.'

Sounek nodded. 'And no word from Calabos, nor Dybel . . .'

Tashil shook her head as she regarded them both. *One minute they're picking away at each other, the next they're brothers in gloom. But then perhaps they have cause to be . . .*

Yesterday's desperate scramble to escape the sudden and terrifying expansion of the blight was still vivid in her mind. She and the others had been in a taproom off Brewers Way, trying to steady exhausted nerves after the recent havoc, not to mention the death of Tashil's brother . . . and they had been listening to a wounded archer tell of how he had been knifed during Ilgarion's march north to Besh-Darok, when a panicky youth burst in from the street and shouted at everyone to flee.

Outside, they had been confronted with the sight of hundreds of townsfolk rushing past on foot, horseback or in carts towards the Valewater. None would stop and explanations had seemed garbled until they spotted a guard in palace livery among the throng and hauled him out. Questioning revealed the very cause that Tashil had feared – the grey blight within the palace had started to grow and at a fearful rate, eating its way through the walls and bringing down building after building as it spread outwards at walking speed. Tashil had wanted to go and investigate but the others had strenuously argued against this, pointing out how escaping to the north bank by boat or bridge would become more difficult as time passed, not less.

Thus they had joined the hurrying crowd then, only minutes later, Dybel let out an exclamation of annoyance and reminded the rest that Enklar and the guards, Rog and Gillat were asleep in a lodging house nearby. Then, ignoring the others' pleas, he fought his way back out of the thronging people, vowing to meet them down at the wharfs. After that, they had progressed to the next corner when a shriek of terror went up some way behind them. Pausing to look round, they saw the greyness of the blight pouring over the edge of the cliff, tongues of pale grey slowly drooling down the cliff face.

Seeing this, the exodus turned into a roaring stampede, carrying Tashil, Dardan, Sounek and Inryk along in a torrent of bodies. The next hour was an unbroken spectacle of madness in which Tashil was witness to acts of both blind barbarity and selfless heroism, people trampled to death while others were dragged clear of certain peril. At one point Tashil had become separated from the rest but managed to haul herself up to a window and inside a house. Once out in the back courts she wove and skulked her way north, tracking down the others who had reached an animal-feed storehouse near the riverbank.

From the weather-worn battlements of the sea-gate tower, Tashil was able to look along at the very spot where she and the others had ventured out onto the Valewater in a flat-bottomed rowboat unearthed in one of the storehouses's sheds. Halfway across the thing had started letting in water and efforts at bailing had been hampered by swimmers attempting to board them. Somehow they stayed afloat long enough to reach the north bank, while towing some half a dozen fugitives grasping the sides and who were near frozen by then. In all the chaos of escape there had been no hope of finding Dybel, Enklar and the guards, even if they had made the crossing. So on Dardan's advice they headed for the sea gate (through which they had escaped in the *Merry Meddler* not so very long ago) and the north tower, around which there had been savage fighting during the undead invasion.

And now, from these fortifications, the south side of Sejeend was a shocking sight to behold, the heart of the imperial city destroyed, consumed by that creeping abomination which now covered every square foot of solid ground. From far along the bay to the south bank of the Valewater and all the way down, heading west, was pale, dead grey with just the low ruins of buildings jutting like broken bones beneath a clinging shroud.

Calabos, she thought despairingly. *What now for us?*

There were footsteps and Inryk, looking alert but dishevelled, climbed up onto the tower platform, glanced with distaste at an unscrubbed bloodstain on the floorboards, then regarded the three of them.

'I have news,' he said.

Dardan snorted. 'Good or bad?'

'Some is incontrovertibly good, some not so good.' He gave a dry laugh. 'In fact, depending on your mood, it might be quite bad.'

'Then please, lift our spirits with the former,' Tashil said.

'Dybel, Enklar and the guards are alive – I just had a message brought by a trader who arrived during the night then spent some hours tracking us down.'

'This is good news,' Sounek said. 'Yet no word by farspeech . . . then again, he's not at his best. And what, pray tell, is the not-so-good news?'

'His Supreme Exaltedness, the High Steward Roldur, awaits our presence in the common chamber below,' Inryk said brightly.

'Horse dung,' Dardan muttered.

'In what frame of mind is he?' said Sounek. 'Does he appear angry or calm?'

'Calm,' Inryk said, leaning forward slightly. '*Very* calm.'

Sounek shook his head and looked from Tashil to Dardan.

'He will, I think, be seeking answers from the both of you, given your doubtless convincing performances yesterday.'

Dardan glowered at Inryk. 'Does he have an escort?'

'Yes, about a dozen guards.'

'The entire north bank is in chaos,' Dardan said acidly. 'Yet he doesn't have anything better to do except harrass us!'

Sounek was peering over the cityward battlements and making tsk-tsk sounds. 'Yes, I'm afraid it looks like you'll both have to swim for it – I wonder if any of those pirate ships are still around? I'm sure they'll be taking on new recruits . . . Tashil? What is it . . . ?'

Tashil shook her head, made a hush gesture and tried to focus on her undersenses. A moment or two ago she was sure she had heard a glimmer of farspeech from someone . . .

(. . . *Tashil, Dardan* . . . *look to the east* . . .)

Her spirits leaped. *Calabos*!?

But the only reply was a silence of the mind. Still, she went to the seaward wall and stared out at the horizon, erratically visible as ragged rainfronts chased each other from north to south off in the distance. She tried to picture tiny sails emerging from the hazy curtains almost as if by doing that she could make them appear. But their steadfast absence continued and prolonged, even as she sent her call out in farspeech once more.

Dardan made a sound that was equal parts disgust and worry.

'We'd be as well wishing for Ilgarion to show up with pardons and dukedoms for us all,' he said.

'Yes, on the scale of probability,' said a well-educated voice, 'that would indeed be vanishingly small.'

Tashil exchanged resigned looks with Dardan and Sounek as they all turned to face Roldur, High Steward of Sejeend. He was immaculately attired in a pale blue and yellow gown worn open over a fine sable doublet adorned with the rose-and-key sigil of his office. His greying hair was well-groomed and his chin well-shaven, but there was no disguising the ire in those eyes.

'An explanation is required,' he said, indicating the featureless, mordant greyness blanketing the north, 'for that.'

Sounek spread his hands. 'Honoured ser, this grave tragedy could never have been foreseen. We face an enemy whose contempt for anything resembling civilized values is near-bottomless.'

'What he means if that they'll destroy us if we don't destroy them first,' Dardan said with not a scrap of deference. Tashil gritted her teeth, resisting the urge to send him an angry look.

Roldur, though, gave him a hard appraisal.

'But you, ser, and the lady here came to the palace and conducted an impressive ritual near the fringes of that vileness. Was there in truth any relevance or efficacy in that performance?'

Dardan looked him in the eye. 'In truth, ser, very little, though we did confirm that our enemies are very powerful.'

'A conclusion you chose not to share with me.'

'We did not think it wise.'

'*Wise*?'

At this, Tashil had to intervene.

'Honoured Roldur,' she said. 'Although we were highly uncertain about the enemy's true abilities, we had no reason to believe that they would allow that devouring veil to . . .'

'Enough, lady Tashil,' the High Steward said, raising a hand. 'You have nothing of substance to tell me, that much is clear. I was prepared to trust to your aid and counsel on the strength of Calabos' wisdom and association – however, it seems that this trust was misplaced, for which I blame myself.' His gaze grew cold. 'But for ineptitude and poor counsel, I blame you Watchers! I can see that Tangaroth may have been right – you should have been reined in long ago . . .'

As Roldur began to enumerate their failings, Inryk, who had been leaning sideways on the seaward wall, silently caught Tashil's eye and glanced out to sea but skywards as well. Tashil stared at him, nonplussed.

What? she said in farspeech.

Just look, will you? was the response.

Aware of the High Steward's disapproving glare, she turned to peer into the skies and saw there a black dot. She focussed on her magesight to diminish the distance . . . and the dot became larger, a dark object, then a cluster of figures, three with wings carrying a fourth who was wingless. As they came nearer, seemingly headed for the mouth of the Valewater, the High Steward abandoned his polemic and with the others gazed skywards. By the time Tashil was able to recognize the passenger as Calabos, it was also abundantly clear just who his bearers were – Daemonkind.

The three half-reptilian creatures, great wings beating, carefully set Calabos down at the corner of the tower roof, then flew over to alight on the northern part of the sea gates, which still stood partially open. Like the rest, Tashil was half-fearful, half-mesmerized by the sight of these legendary beings.

Now they stood upon the gantry which ran the length of the gate, wings folded as they regarded the blanketing greyness to the south, seemingly oblivious to the excited crowds of townsfolk who were gathering on the bank to see.

'Friends,' said Calabos. 'It gladdens my heart to see you once more.' Smiling, he clasped hands with Sounek, Dardan and Inryk, lastly taking Tashil's and giving it a brief and noble kiss. Tashil noticed that he was wearing the sword of powers slung over his back, with the hilt jutting above his shoulders. And she suddenly felt a stab of anxiety as she realized that this had all the hallmarks of a final farewell, but before she could speak he had turned to the High Steward.

'Most excellent Roldur,' he said. 'I hope that my companions have been of some assistance to you in my absence, although even if I had been here I could have done nothing to save the treasure of Sejeend.'

At these words of commiseration, the High Steward's face became a picture of sorrow. 'I cannot express the sense of loss I feel, honoured Calabos,' he said.

Calabos nodded sympathetically. 'We are faced with a careless, rapacious evil, Roldur, and it is our burden to face it, just as it was three centuries ago.'

'You say what must be said,' the High Steward said. 'Even though the Emperor and his Archmage face the foe in the north, we must needs find the courage to stand firm here. But we know little of what assails us, good Calabos, despite the . . . *efforts* of your Watchers.'

Tashil glanced uncomfortably at Dardan.

'My knowledge is equally uncertain,' Calabos said. 'But you may yet face a new danger emanating from a portal at the centre of this grey blight, invaders armed and ruthless.'

The High Steward looked appalled and suddenly seemed older. Then he visibly gathered his resolve. 'We shall have to be ready for them,' he said, moving towards the stairs. 'Thus I must go to make preparations and warn my captains. Will you be staying to lend us your skills and counsel?'

Calabos shook his head. 'My duty takes me elsewhere, to the portal I mentioned before. I, and my unusual allies . . .' he glanced at the three Daemonkind '. . .will infiltrate the enemy's domain and carry the fight to him there.'

All of Tashil's fears came together as she struggled to take in his words. 'But where is this domain?' she said, then indicated the sword he wore. 'And what manner of dangers will you face there, and

how many? Calabos, you cannot do this alone — some of us should
go with you, please . . .'

Even as the others added their voices to her argument, Calabos
halted them all with an upraised hand and sad smile.

'If I am unable to prevail against the Great Shadow on my own,
then your presence would be too much of a sacrifice . . .' He
glanced at Dardan. 'And this time it's true, old friend!' He straightened and looked over at the Daemonkind for moment, and as if
at a silent beckoning they stirred and leaped aloft on beating wings.

'Remain in Sejeend,' he said, turning to Tashil and the others.
'Although you might find Hubranda Lock a better refuge — make
yourselves ready for battle, help the High Steward as best you can,
and watch for anything untoward from west along Gronanvel —
there is another of these blights centred on Alvergost. Also, you
should prepare yourselves for grim news from Besh-Darok . . .'

The three Daemonkind were now hovering a short distance overhead, and Tashil could feel the breeze from their wings. As they
began to descend, Calabos looked at them all again, one by one.

'My fate now leads me into a dark and perilous realm and in
all honesty this may be the last time we meet in this life.' Then
he gave a flash of his old grin, all dash and cunning. 'But if I can
return, once doom is averted, be assured that I will — and then
you'll hear a tale like no other!'

He raised his arms and the Daemonkind lifted him into the air.
Tashil shouted a farewell as tears stung her eyes, and she stayed by
the battlements to watch the flying cluster of figures head south
and quickly slip out of sight beyond the grey-swathed cliffs. In
her loss she found herself thinking of her brother, Atemor, and of
her father and family. Leaning on the cold stone, she whispered a
prayer for them, directing her plea to the Earthmother yet feeling
it to be a gesture cast into the abyss.

How else do we petition the gods? she thought and went to join
the discussion of practicalities just begun by the High Steward.

A soldier was screaming in agony as attendants rushed him away
from the ravine barricades, back up to the camp. Sitting on a partly
smashed barrel, Ayoni wondered if any of the wounded were

surviving after reaching the healer tent, considering that the senior healer had died yesterday during the bloody chaos that swept the mainland shore after the crossing.

Chellour, having finished tending to the barricade troops' flesh wounds, came stumbling over to sit on the grass nearby, hanging his head in an attitude of utter weariness.

'The serjeants say we may not be able to hold them off next time,' he said. 'Especially if we don't get those troops back from the vale.'

'It was a desperate situation, Chellour,' Ayoni said. 'Jarryc's captains had to have reinforcements. Even so, it could have gone either way – we're just lucky that the Mogaun don't seem able to co-ordinate their attack.'

Chellour looked up, eyes dark from lack of sleep. 'I wonder how many of their chieftains they lost over there, after you dealt with Huzur Marag.'

She shrugged. 'Too soon to tell, but hopefully this will be as good as they can get while we grow in strength as more survivors keep arriving . . .'

'But no Ilgarion so far,' Chellour said with a wan smile.

'Hope springs eternal,' she murmured. 'Have you heard any farspeech since we came back across?'

'Before that last attack, I thought I heard fragments of something from Calabos, then not long after a response from Tashil. But I was just too tired to focus – still am.'

'Something is going on,' Ayoni said. 'I wonder if the other blights have grown in the same way . . .'

Chellour gave a bleak laugh but before he could speak, an infantry runner hurried up, saluted them both and handed Ayoni a message tablet.

'From the general, m'lady.'

Ayoni resisted the urge to grin at Jarryc's newest title and opened the tablet, swivelling the lid on its hinge. There were only a few words – *Come quickly, new arrivals* – accompanied by her husband's seal. With her thumb she smoothed the clay flat before closing the tablet and handing it back. The runner put it in a waist pouch beside some others, bowed and left at speed.

'I am needed at the the general's tent,' she said, getting to her feet.

'Tell Jarryc that we have to have those troops back,' Chellour said.

She nodded and headed along the ravine. It led up to a small wooded plateau with vertical cliffs to the north, flanking the notch-like ravine, but with a long, bushy slope to the south-west, descending into a marshy vale that was proving very hard to defend. In addition there was the canal shore which mostly lay at the foot of a sheer, jagged precipice, and extended into a couple of small coves. All of this had to be defended by the battered remnants of the two companies that Ilgarion had left to guard the siege machines before leading the rest of his army across to the Isle of Besh-Darok two days ago.

There were few trees on the rocky plateau itself. Many varieties of hardy bushes had found niches among the mossy outcrops and the tufts of hill grass. The camp was a hastily erected cluster of meagre tents and Jarryc's was a canvas lean-to slung up against an upthrusting finger of rock near the brink of the drop overlooking the canal. Two Earthmother initiates were tending to several wounded on the grass nearby as Ayoni approached while twenty or so muddy and battered-looking soldiers were gathered around a cooking fire. A closer look told her that they were mostly from the Iron Guard, so these had to be the survivors Jarryc's message had mentioned.

As she hurried towards Jarryc's tent she glanced across the strait. The Isle of Besh-Darok was now only an expanse of pale, deathly grey, utterly covered by the consuming blight which had expanded outwards from the old imperial palace. The awful fear she had felt yesterday on beholding the advancing wall of greyness was still fresh in her mind, as was the terrible sight of people fighting and killing to get places on boats. Then of course some of the overloaded boats foundered partway across from the pilgrim tent city, hurling women and children into the cold waters. And even as the grey tide was sweeping towards the isle's western limits, the forces of Ilgarion and Huzur Marag had continued to clash, battling with deranged hatred as a mutual doom bore down upon them both.

All this Ayoni, Jarryc, Chellour and Baron Klayse had witnessed from the seer's boat as they rowed back across the channel. On making landfall, the Mogaun seers had gone their own way, intending to return to the forests of the north; Ayoni and Jarryc, Chellour and Klayse elected to move south-west to discover a stealthy way back to Sejeend, only to find themselves in the middle of a panicked rout of imperial soldiers. One of the two companies had been under Jarryc's command just days earlier and he had been unable to leave them leaderless in such desperate circumstances . . .

Now as she climbed old mossy steps to the rise and the small camp, Baron Klayse emerged from Jarryc's lean-to, his face grim.

'My lady,' he said. 'Your husband — and three others — await you within. I cannot tarry — the defences in the vale will not direct themselves!'

As he hurried away, clearly exasperated, Ayoni's spirits sank.

Three others? she thought. *Ilgarion and the Archmage Tangaroth — they survived . . .*

But she was wrong. As she entered, Jarryc rose to greet her as did Shumond, Lord Commander of the Iron Guard, and a startled-looking young man she recognized as one of the court mages. A fourth person garbed in capacious, dark blue hooded robes, remained seated and motionless. Something about him stirred the fringe of her perception, vague sensations of pain and anger . . .

'Countess, it pains me to greet you in these unfit conditions,' Shumond said before Jarryc could speak. 'Yet I am the bearer of a tragic news which must be heard and understood, no matter the anguish that it may cause to the listener. My lady — know that our dear and most puissant emperor, Ilgarion son of Magramon, is no more. He fell on the field of battle, defending the glory of the Khatrimantine Empire and its heritage to the very last . . .'

Ayoni kept her face sombre and downcast to mask her inner feelings of cold satisfaction, yet when she glanced at Jarryc his unhappy look seemed genuine. Something else was amiss, she realized . . .

'Yet such is the deadly peril what we face here and elsewhere,'

Shumond went on, 'the empire cannot afford to remain leaderless, its throne empty, its crown unworn. Therefore, myself and the senior officers of the Iron Guard and those nobles yet surviving have proposed that, in the absence of any issue, the crown be passed to another whose service and duty are unquestioned and whose ancestry provides the necessary royal association . . .'

At this point, the seated figure began to turn towards Ayoni who felt a dark foreboding. Then a trembling hand rose to push back the cowl, revealing a changed Archmage Tangaroth. His skin was pale, almost waxy, and one eye was bloodshot, but what caught the attention were the grubby, red-spotted bandages which had been wrapped around the lower half of his face.

'The Archmage suffered a terrible injury,' Shumond said. 'And is without the use of his voice, yet Gessik here is able to act as an intermediary . . .'

At this the young mage jerked suddenly and began to speak in a flat voice.

'I am prepared to overlook your past misdemeanours, Countess,' he said. 'Along with those of your Watcher colleague, your husband and even the Baron Klayse. All I require is your word that you will continue in what you have been doing – opposing and destroying the empire's enemies.'

It was an unbalancing moment, hearing speech coming from one man's mouth while meeting the furious glare of another who was the actual source of those words.

'You know that the crown should go to Magramon's brother's branch of the family,' she said, 'rather than his uncle's, which I believe is the trail of your own ancestry, Archmage.'

Tangaroth's hard gaze did not waver.

'What are you more interested in right now, Countess, arguing over dynastic details or trying to survive?'

Ayoni glanced momentarily at Jarryc who let slip the faintest glimmer of a smile.

'Very well, Archmage,' she said. 'I give you my word that I will oppose the enemies of the empire – all of them.'

'I am gratified by your words, if not your manner, but it will suffice.'

Shumond suddenly smiled widely. 'Unity is preserved — now we can plan the downfall of the enemy Mogaun.'

Then, within her thoughts, Ayoni heard the Archmage's own voice:

(*And always remember — my eyes are upon you.*)

How comforting, she thought as she bowed and left.

Part Three

Chapter Nineteen

Begin now thy revels,
Of sleepless dread,
And furious night.

Jedhessa Gant, *The Lords Desolate*, Act I, Sc. i, ll. 5–7

Locked within the recesses of his own mind once more, Corlek Ondene was the prostrate and unwilling witness to every sight and word and thought and act of the Shadowking spirit. And to his own sensibilities, for that journey through the monstrous, rushing intestine of the sea god Grath paled next to this crossing over to the Nightrealm. The open portal of the Shattergate contained only indivisible blackness and one step was all it took to plunge into it. Invasive and pervasive, the pressure of it ignored his garments and engulfed every part of his skin then seemed to seep inwards to probe at vein and bone, nerve and muscle.

And he was walking through it, pace slowing as he became aware of stone underfoot. The air was cold, smelling faintly of musty decay, and along with the hard scrape of his own dragging footsteps were the sounds of others coming from behind. Fearing unseen attackers, he turned – and vision surged upon him and he saw that he was standing in a narrow, arched passage made of stone cobbles. All seemed drenched in shadows, yet a peculiar radiance touched everything like ashen silver. And there, behind him, stood a dozen or more spectral figures, motionless and watching closely. Ondene felt fear turn into curiosity when he saw the great differences among them – there was an old woman with a shawl draped over her head and shoulders, a waggoner in a long, heavy tabard and a wide-brimmed hat, a scrawny man stripped to the waist, a hulking, bearded Mogaun warrior clad in fur and chain mail, and several others whose stares held an unblinking edge of insanity.

'Who . . . are you?' he said hoarsely.

No mouth opened in response yet a flow of whispering sighs reached him, a mingling of slurred voices talking among themselves . . . *He sees us . . . so this is the other . . . where is our master . . . yes, the vessel . . . so weak . . . our master will soon rise . . . our rewards . . .*

Ondene turned and fled the ghosts and their tenuous mutterings, spurred by a raw fear which filled him utterly. In panic he turned left at the next junction, found himself in a section of passage open to the sky, a canopy of black and dark-violet clouds which roiled and swirled in continuous turbulence but seemed to make no progress in any one direction.

As his fear abated, he emerged in a pillared chamber with three tall openings in the far wall. It was a large but shabby place with bare stone walls, dark grey mould on the columns, and a floor of five-sided tiles, many of which were cracked or loose. Two of the openings faced the brick wall of another building, so warily he crossed to the third beyond which there seemed to be a platform or landing. As he approached he saw that there were steps leading down between a black rock face and the adjacent building, then his viewpoint opened out and, struggling to comprehend, he halted on the threshold.

The stairs were a long rack descending into a peculiar leaden darkness and the shadows of a small square with a wrecked fountain surrounded by the low halls and houses of a small town. A few roofs further beyond was a large fortified wall which cut across, with smoke rising from its guard towers; on the other side was a district of narrow-peaked woodframe houses and next to that was a cluster of crude stone-and-earth tribal lodges, and next to that the log palisade of a stockade, then the porticos and cloisters of opulent townhouses, a ruined fort, a long, half-demolished viaduct, a high-walled temple on whose roof he could see sentries patrolling . . .

And on it went, sloping gently upwards from his vantage, a dizzying profusion of roofs and towers and arches, cabins and mansions and taverns, turrets and keeps and redans, all crammed together in a single, unbroken cityscape, or rather a patchworked vista of innumerable villages, towns and cities. The upper districts were lost in the darkness of distance, compounded by the deathly half-light which had no source yet which was all-pervasive, muting colours and casting a grainy silver patina over every surface.

Ondene tried to remember what he had witnessed and over-heard during Calabos' encounter with the Sleeping God, at least before the arrival of that spirit-wraith, and recalled that this was the world of the other path of Time, one in which the Lord of Twilight had triumphed. This Nightrealm was a living nightmare presided over by the Lord of Twilight, now called the Great Shadow. There was no death here, or at least no end to a ghastly experi-ence, no escape . . .

And now I'm trapped here, too, he thought grimly. *Is there anyone that I can trust in a place like this . . . ?*

A cold sensation made him turn and he saw the ghostly figures from before converging upon him. Their whispering touched the edge of his thoughts and he recoiled, retreating to the head of the long stairway as they drifted toward him.

Master . . . master . . . arise . . . awake . . . begin the war . . .

Choking on his own fear, Ondene plunged away down the steps, down into fractured darkness. But as he ran the fear began to change, its inward spiral turning into an upward surge of anger at the ghosts, at the Shadowking, at Calabos and the Sleeping God, and at this funereal realm. As the foot of the steps came nearer, indistinct figures emerged from the deeper shadows to discover the source of the clattering boots, first a few then a dozen or more, and yet more. Ondene could see the gathering crowd and sense the brooding menace in their manner. But the anger in him drowned all sense of caution as his gait slowed to a deliberate walk while hate began to grow out of his anger like a coiling vine that slowly filled up his thoughts.

'A stranger comes,' said someone in the crowd.

'Aye, from out of the fell tunnels,' said another.

'Is he a danger?'

'Only one way to find out!'

And with a roar the crowd surged forward. Ondene, mind dissolving in hate, charged down the last remaining steps and was engulfed. Heedless, the mob piled in on top of him, wielding fists, knives or clubs, and in the deranged confusion a scattering of fights broke among the ambushers themselves. Blood splashed on the cobbles, black in the ashen light. Ghastly wounds were given and received and terrible injuries abounded on all sides, yet none slumped into death or gasped their last. Several crawled away from the carnage holding severed limbs or trying to keep spilled innards in place. Screams, shrieks and shouts slashed the air and of Ondene there was no sign beneath the heaving press.

Then suddenly bodies were flying back, thrown out from the centre where a figure stood, fists clenched and burning with an emerald glitter twin to the radiance that shone from his eyes. He snarled at the sprawled and maimed ambushers, and hot green power leaked from his mouth.

'Overseer!' some cried. ''Ware overseer . . . !'

Watching them flee from the square, the Shadowking felt a certain exultation in the intense purity of Sourcefire as it coursed through his body. The traverse between that other world and the Nightrealm had swept him down into the undervaults of Ondene's mind but his stoking of the fires of primal anger and hate had opened the gates to the Wellsource and himself. So now Ondene was again confined to inner durance and he was once more enthroned with the Wellsource at his fingertips and a land to conquer.

He smiled, a hidden expression now that the edge of his Sourcefire had abated somewhat.

'Enthroned,' he said for the pleasure of hearing his own voice.

A thin, cracked laughter rang out from a gloomy mound of rubble to one side of the long stairs. Frowning, he walked towards the sound and saw how the mound was the collapsed debris from the front half of the tall brick building, and halfway up its jagged slope sat a wiry old man clad in rags. He stopped laughing as the Shadowking drew near and regarded him with beady eyes.

'What amuses you?' he said.

The old man stared for a moment, then burst out laughing again.

'And . . . and still they come!' he managed. 'Let me guess – you're going to persuade all the crews and chapters and militias to put aside their precious feuds and hatreds, to unite behind your banner and launch a war to free all of the Nightrealm from the Great Shadow's tyranny, yes?'

The Shadowking gazed at him thoughtfully, deciding to explore the limits of this paltry denizen's knowledge.

'No,' he said. 'I have come to take what is rightfully mine.'

That made the old man pause and give him a close look.

'Hmm, you don't look much like a naïve hero or a shadow artifice, which are the usual agents of misfortune who come along from time to time to make us forget the word "futile".' He coughed and spat. 'So you don't want to set us free, rather you just want to usurp the Great Shadow himself – well, that's not entirely novel but it's still rare enough to be refreshing. Very well, I'm your man, willing to swear fealty and offer whatever wise counsel I can dredge out of this aged head . . .'

The Shadowking watched him pick his way down the rubble mound.

'I never asked for your fealty,' he said. 'What makes you think that I need your counsel?'

'Because of all the questions you want answered, lord, and because I know who the local chiefs are and what some of their weaknesses are.'

The Shadowking smiled. 'Good, then I accept you into my service, but before you swear the oath of loyalty tell me your name.'

'Dar,' the old man said. 'That is all. And you, lord?'

A name, the Shadowking thought. *It needs be a name of strength and ruthless purpose – yes, I know which one . . .*

'You may call me Lord Byrnak,' he said, feeling the rightness of it even as he spoke.

'Byrnak,' Dar said. 'I'm sure I've heard that name before, long time since . . . hah, matters not. So, my lord Byrnak – I swear by all that I hold sacred to serve to the best of my abilities and with the utmost regard for discretion. Now – what is my first task?'

'When that mob fled my wrath, some shouted that I was an "overseer",' Byrnak said. 'Explain this to me.'

'Ah, the Overseers,' Dar said, nodding sagely. 'Put simply, the Overseers serve the Duskgeneral, who serves the Great Shadow. The Overseers have a number of tower strongholds all across the Nightrealm from which they range forth, some on the wing, some on foot, to warn, to punish, to slay, and just occasionally to reward.'

The Shadowking Byrnak gazed up at the walls of the square and the buildings beyond, eyes searching the receding proliferation of streets and roofs and domes and turrets.

'And the Duskgeneral,' he said. 'What manner of bastion has he?'

'A gigantic fortress called the Citadel of Twilight which sits against the sheer cliffs near the zenith of the Nightrealm. The topmost chambers of the citadel lead out onto the clifftop and the dream-courts of the Great Shadow, a column-ringed maze of shifting walls and buildings open to the sky.'

Byrnak smiled. 'Has he a throne?'

'A huge, jewelled throne in the shape of an upthrust sword which presides over the dream-courts from an imposing, stepped dais. And behind it is supposed to be the White Prison, a towering wall of ice in which the Great Shadow keeps certain favourite prisoners.'

'The Great Shadow clearly has much to defend,' Byrnak said. 'Who has threatened him?'

Dar snorted. 'The whole of the Nightrealm is littered with the ruined fortifications and wrecked war machines constructed by those who have sought to oppose him. But he has the fearful Overseers, the Duskgeneral's Murknights, and the echelons of the Black Host to call upon, a fearful army indeed.'

'Then we shall gather a still greater army,' Byrnak said. 'Who is the nearest and likeliest chief to dispose of?'

'That would be . . . Yanama, I would think,' Dar said, narrowing his eyes. 'Yes, he leads a small crew of rogues out of one of the Eyrie's underhalls. Not so important that his ousting would attract attention, but not so small as to be pointless.'

'Is it far?'

'If we hurry, we can reach the Eyrie before nightfall,' said the old man.

Byrnak grimaced. 'Day and night? Here?'

'Indeed, yes, a freezing fog-smothered night through which hungry powers and sly beasts hunt, my lord, for the likes of you and me! Come, let us be on our way . . .'

Through chilling, gloomy roads and winding alleys Dar led him, passing on more scraps of lore, names, places, locations of recent battles, the favoured tactics of the Overseers when they trawled for captives. Byrnak learned that there was no true death here, that however brutal and thorough the despatch, a victim's body would always regrow somewhere across the Nightrealm in certain gardens. He learned that the only food consisted of roots and tubers that grew in dark cellars, alleviated by a bitter berry beer made by brewers out on the periphery of the Nightrealm, near the immense cliffs that hemmed this grim land in on all sides. He learned that most weapons were of a kind of forgeable glass, that the ore was mined at several places and each one was the seat of a powerful chapter or group of militias.

As they stole through the shadows, Byrnak saw many people in groups or ones or twos, loitering, fighting, running, standing in doorways or leaning from windows, and nowhere were any children to be seen. And during his exchanges with Dar he got no sense that the old man thought or knew about the origins of the Nightrealm, in fact no sense of history at all. He thought on this, realizing that if there was no death then all the men and women he saw here were over three centuries old: could they all have forgotten the Shadowking war and the Lord of Twilight's triumph on this path of Time? Or was this the result of some deliberate glamour cast by the Great Shadow to make their memories short?

The Eyrie was a tall, ugly tower surround by a cluster of equally ugly buildings, some of which were in a state of partial or complete ruin. Several gangs and warbands had lairs in nooks and crannies on the ground and basement levels, leaving the rest to a powerful militia called the Roaring Gauntlets, led by one Cebroul. Yanama's crew was known as the Hangers and their underhall was beneath one of the half-demolished buildings, reached via a creaking, timber-shored tunnel which led crookedly through the ancient rubble. A pair of guards at the underhall entrance searched them both before admitting them. Emerging in one corner of a tall chamber, Byrnak quickly counted those present — nine, including the guards — and gauged their readiness and possible threat as fairly low.

'Visitors, huh?' said a balding man from a large, jutting ledge at the top of a rickety, wall-set staircase. The ledge bore a low pallet and a stool and had a pair of fastened shutters in the rough stone wall. 'You here for business or pleasure?'

Judging this to be Yanama, Byrnak gestured Dar to remain below, then started up the stairs.

'I'm your new recruit,' he said.

Yanama sneered. 'I take on blooded warriors, not novices. I will, however, take your jerkin, your boots and any weapons ye have.'

'I only have my fists,' Byrnak said as he neared the top. 'But they're yours.'

At the ledge he lunged at Yanama, who had drawn a curved black dagger to slash at Byrnak's throat. But Byrnak grabbed the oncoming wrist, turned in midstep and threw Yanama over his shoulder to crash onto the floorboards. The ledge shook underfoot. Byrnak then pounced on the dazed warband chief, hauled him up and dragged him over to the shutters which he opened with a single, savage kick.

'Don't come back,' he growled at Yanama before pitching him headfirst out the window. Turning back, he faced two of Yanama's henchmen who came howling up the stairs — one ended up sprawled in agony on the underhall floor while the other followed his chief out into the dense fog. The remaining seven looked at each other with expressions ranging from stunned amazement to naked fear.

'You have a new chief,' Byrnak said to them. 'Stay or leave.'

The seven fighters paused for only a moment before bending the knee and swearing an oath of loyalty as Byrnak descended the steps.

'Good,' he said, pointing at the now-unconscious man on the floor. 'And get rid of this.'

Dar was at his side, grinning and chuckling.

'Most efficient, my lord. Most, ah, direct. Now, what is your will?'

'Who is the most powerful chief in the Eyrie?' Byrnak said. 'Apart from Cebroul of the Roaring Gauntlets.'

'Kural of the Stone Wolves,' Dar said. 'A dangerous man.'

'Who are his deputies?'

Dar frowned. 'I'm not sure, but I can find out quite easily.'

'Do so, and find out which one hates Kural the most.'

The next day, Byrnak had the seven remaining Hangers training with knife and staff while Dar was away ferreting out the truth. He sooned returned with the news that Kural had three captains, one of whom he had viciously and sarcastically lambasted before the rest of the chapter just a couple of days ago. This captain, known as Domas, Byrnak contrived to encounter later that day in one of the upper halls, calmly introduced himself, praised Domas' tactics in a territorial clash a few weeks past (which Dar had learned of during his investigations). He then made several enigmatic comments about Domas' loyalty not going unnoticed, and let his mouth curl with contempt as he mentioned Kural's 'judgement'. Then he made his excuses and departed, leaving a puzzled-looking Domas in his wake.

The following morning, Byrnak went seeking an audience with Kural, accompanied by the best two of his seven fighters. Intrigued by this stranger who had so swiftly deposed Yanama, Kural agreed to the meeting and that was his undoing. Less than ten minutes after it began, Kural and two of his deputies lay hacked and insensible on the chamber floor while Domas sat off to one side, disarmed and bound by Byrnak's men. Byrnak then disclosed his powers with a small demonstration of Sourcefire, holding a clay bottle in a fire-wreathed hand and reducing it to a charred and smoking ruin. Domas stared, fear and uncertainty writ clearly in his features.

'First the Stone Wolves,' Byrnak said, sitting opposite him and speaking in a low voice, as if he were confiding in an equal. 'Then the Roaring Gauntlets and the Eyrie, then the district, then a domain, then . . .' He smiled. 'The Nightrealm needs a new purpose, a new strength, a new ruler. Are you with me?'

A revelatory light came into Domas' eyes and he nodded.

With Domas' and Dar's help, Byrnak circulated the story that

Kural had been plotting with another militia in a neighbouring district to remove Cebroul and disperse the Roaring Gauntlets. Three days after Kural's fall from power (and the subsequent exile of his body parts to a faraway district), Byrnak was peremptorily summoned to an audience with Cebroul in the Skyhall, the topmost floor of the Eyrie. Byrnak smiled when it came, issued orders to Domas and Dar, then left to ascend the tower's levels.

It was the most luxurious chamber Byrnak had yet seen in the Nightrealm, certainly when compared to the rundown shabbiness prevalent everywhere else. Banners hung all around the oval walls, racks of spears were stacked to left and right, and vine-oil lamps cast a silvery glow over the black pillars and the grey tiles. Cebroul was seated on a tall throne of some red-veined stone, flanked by scores of subordinates and guards and glowering as Byrnak entered by himself. The leader of the Roaring Gauntlets barely waited for Byrnak to take half a dozen steps into the hall before launching into a venomous tirade, claiming that Kural's loyalty had been beyond question, that his military skills would be hard to replace, and that Byrnak was a pox-ridden vermin who deserved to be dismembered . . .

Byrnak kept silent as the rant wound on, standing a short way back from the middle of the hall, right between two large pillars. At last Cebroul ran out of insults and snarled: 'So what do you have to say for yourself, eh?'

Byrnak frowned, gave a small shake of the head. 'Can you hear it?'

Mutters of outrage at this behaviour went round the assembled underlings.

'Hear what?' said Cebroul, anger reddening his face. 'What?'

Byrnak struck a listening attitude for a moment, then smiled. 'Something unavoidable.'

A low rumble came up from below and the Skyhall trembled. Then without further warning most of the floor fell in, just suddenly broke apart in a roaring cascade of masonry, tiles and screaming members of Cebroul's court, including Cebroul himself, all plunging through billowing dust. Byrnak seemed to be safe where he was, having previously made sure of the location of the supporting wall in the floor below, yet he backed away to the hall entrance as one of the far pillars toppled and crashed through the outer wall.

Byrnak had known that he would be summoned to the Skyhall and had sent a squad of trusted men with masonry backgrounds to prepare this devastating surprise. Their work was skilled and deadly – all except two of Cebroul's court suffered the half-death, and the collapse wrecked less than a third of the two floors below without endangering the rest of the building. With all the senior commanders of the Roaring Gauntlets gone, Byrnak moved to establish his authority in the Eyrie and when next morning one of the nearby militias carried out a raid on an outlying Gauntlet guardpost it was the perfect excuse for a swift retaliation. When his men returned laden with trophies and weapons, it set the seal on his claim to the mastery of the Eyrie.

The morning after the counter-raid, Byrnak was in the Skyhall with Dar, taking stock of the damage while a few labourers were attempting to shore up the weakened outer wall. Suddenly there were shouts of warning and the sound of discarded tools. Byrnak looked round to see a large, winged figure clambering in through the ragged gap in the Eyrie wall as the labourers darted away in panic.

'Oveerseers,' said Dar. 'What's their interest . . . ?'

The Overseer was nearly ten feet tall and had a man-like body, but the skin seemed rough and the face looked distorted, the jaw overlarge and the flinty eyes recessed beneath a bony brow. The pinions of its leathery wings jutted well above the shoulders, indicating a prodigious span.

'You're the one I seek,' the Overseer said in a deep, rasping voice as it strode towards Byrnak.

Byrnak regarded the newcomer, sensing a raw but semi-disciplined power in him. He knew that he could master this Overseer but realized that the consequences of such an act might forestall his plans. Better to mask his own powers and to see and judge.

Coming to halt a few feet away, the Overseer towered over Byrnak and stared down at him with undisguised despite.

'So Cebroul's been cut down to size, has he? Matters not – he was an insect, just like you and no doubt you'll go the same way. In the meantime I've come to make sure you understand about the levy.'

'What levy?' said Byrnak.

'The levy of the Black Host,' the Overseer growled. 'Cebroul's was ninety able bodies a month, but from you I want a nice round hundred in six days' time, understand? I can see that you've got some of the power in you but just be sure that you don't get above yourself – you might end up with bits of you spread over a wide area, eh?'

Impassive, Byrnak nodded and the Overseer grunted.

'Worms, that's what you people are. Worms.'

He walked back to the break in the wall, climbed out then looked over his shoulder: 'Don't forget – one hundred. Even if you have to include some of your own.'

Then dark wings spread, beat the air once, twice, and he was gone.

Byrnak was surprised at how calm he was, in spite of the searing hate that had boiled up during the encounter. He stared at the ragged opening in the wall then went over to it, beckoning Dar to follow. Standing before it, both gazed out at the sweeping vastness of the Nightrealm, a colossal city of cities, endless shadowy districts and domains, a glittering darkness strewn with the silvery pinpoints of lamps.

'Where did that Overseer come from?' Byrnak said.

'Orlag Tower,' Dar said, pointing.

Byrnak looked and saw a tapering spire with a bulbous apex rising from a confusion of roofs about twenty miles away. It was roughly twice the height of the Eyrie and looked strong and defiant.

'I wonder what it would take to bring it down,' Byrnak said.

Dar began to laugh. 'I know of something that might be useful,' he said. 'Very useful!'

Conscious of the gathering crowd watching from the riverbank, Tashil tried to concentrate on paddling the small skiff across the

Valewater towards the grey-shrouded south bank. Beside her was Sounek, likewise wielding a paddle, while in the snub prow sat Dardan who, for once, was wearing his habitual hooded cape and appeared restless in the bright light of late morning. In his lap was a bulky leather pannier containing a rack of stoppered vials, each one full of a different liquid or powder which had been hurriedly garnered from north Sejeend's few apothecaries in the last couple of hours. At least one of them, it was hoped, would turn out to be of use against the grey blight.

As she paddled, Tashil tried to focus on the task in hand but her thoughts kept drifting back to the valedictory encounter with Calabos and his Daemonkind allies just a few hours ago. *A dark and perilous realm*, was how he had described his destination, and Tashil had wondered how monstrous a place it could be compared to the dark perils the Watchers had faced these last few days. But then it was a place which had produced the sorcerer Jumil who had then conjured a proliferation of evil acts and atrocities culminating in the desecration of the grey blight. Tashil's imagination pictured a shadowy land peopled with montrosities and in a constant turmoil of violence and pain, and she gave a small shudder.

The skiff was past the midpoint and approaching the opposite bank. Tashil glanced over her shoulder, checking on the rope which trailed from the sternpost down into the water where a series of bladders buoyed it all the way back to the north bank. There a squad of longshoremen stood ready to haul the skiff back from the other side if signalled to do so by its crew.

When they approached the far bank closely, Tashil and Sounek stopped paddling and a small iron anchor was tipped over the side with a hefty splash. This close, Tashil was able to see more of that vile, deathly blanket – it came up to the bank and hung over in pale, ragged curtains, or extended down a nearby, sloping shingle almost to the water's edge, recoiling visibly when wavelets surged up the slope. As she was studying the blight, Dardan unbuckled the pannier and flipped back its cover, then produced a pair of heavy gauntlets from a side pouch.

'So, which one first?' said Sounek.

Dardan sniffed as he considered the rack of vials. Then he gave a thoughtful smile.

'Well, there is one attack I've been eager to try since this began,' he said, then raised a fiery hand and hurled a single firedagger bolt at the nearby, blight-swathed shingle.

The burning shard of power plunged into the greyness and almost immediately the surrounding area erupted in a writhing forest of tentacles and stems, strange bulbous growths which burst open in displays of squirming flowers, bizarre jointed limbs several yards long, some of which lashed out towards the skiff and its occupants. Sounek waved frantically at the north bank and the longshoremen hauled the skiff back from the commotion. It took more gesturing to get them to stop, and since the wild outburst soon subsided Tashil and Sounek had to haul in the anchor and paddle back to where they had been. Much to Tashil's irritation, Dardan was visibly amused at the entire episode and was still chuckling as he pulled on one of the heavy gauntlets.

'So now we know that it likes Lesser Power sorcery,' said Sounek. 'Thrives on it, even.'

'Let's see how it copes with this,' Dardan said, picking out one of the vials and hurling it over onto the blight-covered beach. As they watched, the blight quickly ate through the glass vial, letting the contents – an amber fluid – flood out only to be summarily absorbed.

'And that was?' said Tashil.

'Corroding Elixir,' Dardan said, frowning.

Sounek smiled. 'Next, if you please.'

Thus one by one Dardan worked his way through the rack of vials and each time the result was the same – no effect. At the sixteenth, Dardan declared himself done with the useless process and doffed the gauntlet. Tashil sighed, picked it up and put it on, then selected the next vial, which held a fine white powder, and threw it onto the beach. It spun through the air and there was a tiny breaking sound when it landed, sending the contents flying out onto the surface of the blight . . . which dissolved on contact with the powder, forming large gaps through which plain brown earth showed.

'Well done,' said a voice from nearby. 'A fascinating discovery but unfortunately, too little, too late.'

The speaker was standing a few yards downstream on a raised stretch of the bank, He was clad from head to foot in night-black armour whose surfaces caught no light but instead carried a leaden glitter which shifted across the limbs and torso in a slow, continuous swirl. As Tashil watched, the slotted visor seemed to melt and shrink to reveal the pale, waxen features of a man framed by the close-fitting helm.

'I am High Captain Vashad of the Black Host,' he said. 'Soon to be governor of this province.'

'You sound very sure of yourself,' Sounek said.

'I have every reason to be,' the High Captain said, his manner vaguely dreamlike. 'The force of Fate is with us, not you.'

'How very reasonable,' Dardan mocked. 'What a devastating argument – perhaps we should just put down our weapons and await the inevitable.'

'Yes, you should,' Vashad said, undeflected by Dardan's sarcasm. 'But you won't – you'll gather together your feeble armies and deploy whatever inept sorcery this world provides, and you'll fight and resist us every step of the way, and every step along that road will be paved with your bones. There shall be only defeat, pain and death for you before the end comes and all of this world is joined with the Nightrealm in the long-denied union.'

Tashil laughed. 'How blind! You think you can reach everywhere, and you think that you know or can know everything, a logical impossibility.'

Vashad smiled faintly. 'We know all that is necessary to know, yet even that which we do not know still lies within the scope of the known and thus there is nothing which is truly unknown.'

Tashil exchanged incredulous looks with Sounek and Dardan, then said, 'How invulnerable do you imagine your master's realm to be?'

'We know of those who have passed through the Shattergate,' Vashad said. 'But the Great Shadow is the master of life and death there so any and all machinations and insurrections will prove fruitless and futile. So, my answer is – completely invulnerable.'

Tashil nodded. 'And how invincible is your army? Oh, you do have an army, don't you?'

The High Captain's smile widened perceptibly and he turned slightly, throwing out one gauntleted hand in a theatrical gesture. On cue, the grey blanket of the blight began to bulge in many places to either side and some way back from where the encounter was taking place. Then the bulges split along their bases and peeled back like mouths, disgorging black-armoured troops in their hundreds, then thousands, marching lock-step into ranks facing across the Valewater. And every one of them was an archer bearing a grotesquely adorned bow nearly as long as he was tall.

'Yes, I do have an army,' Vashad said. 'This, however, is only the spearhead echelon but I am sure that it will suffice.' The metal of his helm began to flow across the contours of his face, and a moment later the slotted visor had reformed. 'I shall permit you to return to the other side before our attack begins. May you die well.'

As he walked away, Dardan looked over his shoulder and began waving at the longshoremen. As Sounek hauled up the anchor and the rope tautened, pulled them back, Tashil gazed despairingly at the serried black ranks that moved as one, drawing long, strangely tipped arrows and making them ready. Feeling a sense of foreboding she focussed her thoughts into farspeech . . .

Inryk?

(Yes, Tashil . . .)

Have you been watching?

(With magesight, yes. It looks bad.)

You have to get anyone out in the open along the dockfront indoors or under cover before the arrows fly . . .

(We're already doing that – what about you?)

She glanced at the north bank, gauging the runing distance from the low jetty up the wharf and back to the nearest warehouse.

I think we can make it, she thought. *But it could be close.*

(It would be a help if we knew what those arrows will do.)

I expect something between agonizing and horrific.

(Oh good, I do love surprises!)

Dardan, overhearing, rolled his eyes while the skiff rocked and wallowed as the rope was hauled in.

Pain started to well up from Tangaroth's jaw shortly after the war council began but he bore it with iron determination, forcing himself to remain alert as that upstart, Count Jarryc, gave an outline of their defences. Characteristically, Jarryc's summary was bleak, as if he sought to challenge any optimism by painting as forbidding a picture as possible. Shumond responded with a far more balanced view of their successes as well as the challenges that they faced, penned into this small upland with their backs to the Great Canal.

At least he was spared the presence of Jarryc's harridan wife and that backstreet conjuror, Nyls Chellour, although the bombastic Baron Klayse was in attendance. Combined with the effort of feeding his words through the mouth of his proxy, Gessik, it constituted a considerable strain on his stamina. Soon after arriving with Shumond and the remnants of the Iron Guard, he had contemplated having Jarryc and the others executed for treason. But a swift appraisal showed that had he done so the morale and resolve of the 150-odd troops would have collapsed. In the wake of the grey engulfment of Besh-Darok, it had proved a wise decision. Having survived the first day and night of fighting, the defenders of this small upland enclave found the Mogaun attacks becoming less frequent with fewer warriors involved. Scouts and lookouts reported signs of fighting among the Mogaun, a most pleasing development. But this was tempered by the news that there were less than two days' worth of stores left, which presented them with a stark choice: obtain more supplies from nearby Belkiol, by either stealth or raid, or try to stage a breakout followed by a headlong retreat south to Sejeend.

As emperor-elect, Tangaroth found neither prospect appealing, the former for its high degree of risk, the latter for the great indignity it would inflict. Through Gessik, he said to Jarryc and Klayse: 'Gentlemen, I understand the gravity of our position and would ask you to allow me some moments to ruminate on these matters by stepping outside. My thanks ... Shumond, wait a moment.'

Looking grim, Jarryc and Klayse left the tent and once the tent flap swung back into place, Tangaroth beckoned Shumond closer.

'Is it true about the stores?' he murmured through Gessik.

The Lord Commander of the Iron Guard nodded.

'Yes, your majesty, and that's with the men on quarter-rations.'

'What course of action would *you* choose?'

Shumond considered it a moment. 'The breakout,' he said, 'with a side raid to try and lay hands on some mounts.'

Tangaroth nodded and sat back in the rickety chair, feeling another surge of pain in his face.

'You may be right,' he said. 'But I need seclusion to think . . .'

'As you wish, majesty,' Shumond said, heading for the tent entrance.

You too, Gessik, he thought to his attendant. Gessik's eyes widened in surprise, but he made no objection and followed the Lord Commander outside.

Once he was alone, Tangaroth let out a shuddering gasp and raised a trembling hand to his head. With the other he fumbled within his enfolding robes and brought out a cluster of chain-berry leaves which Gessik had picked for him that morning. Carefully he pulled aside the bandage and one by one slipped them into his ruined mouth. There was pain for a moment or two, then the sap of the leaves began to dull the torment.

He remembered how the battle with the Mogaun cavalry had wavered back and forth, even as that ghastly grey tide was advancing towards them all. In the end it had been a riderless horse, driven mad by arrows in its flanks, which had reared up and struck Tangaroth full in the face with a lashing hoof. When he fell from his mount, Ilgarion saw and came riding over to help and was himself unseated by a Mogaun spearman. Wounded, he was still able to despatch the spearman before going after his wandering horse, only to walk straight into a long limb of the consuming greyness which had stretched ahead of the leading edge.

One eye-witness said that the emperor had not even had time to draw his sword before being engulfed by the grey blight. After that, the battle was lost and the survivors faced a desperate rush to the canal in the hope of finding a boat or any floating debris.

Tangaroth was lucky enough to be carried by members of the Iron Guard back to one of the longboats that had been used to ferry the troops over the night before.

The chainberry sap was spreading a vaguely warm numbness through his face and down into his neck. He felt almost able to cope.

Yet I am not an emperor, he thought. No crown or coronation could make me into a monarch, but I must shoulder this burden and safeguard the empire – I must.

Shumond was right – breaking out of this enclave then retreating to Sejeend was the only real option, now that it was clear that no help would be coming from the capital. He had repeatedly tried to contact his mages there by farspeech but without success, which caused him no end of dire speculation.

He sat back in his chair, thoughts wavering between the worries of their predicament and the lulling soporific of the chainberry. He also desperately needed the services of a healer, which was another reason for a swift return to Sejeend. The prospect of losing the ability to speak for good filled him with horror . . .

Then, at the edge of his undersenses, he felt a tremor of power nearby and a change in the air. Someone or something had appeared in the tent behind him, yet for all that he had no weapon about him he felt oddly calm. His instincts urged him to reach out to Gessik, or even the Countess, for help, but the presence made no move and seemed to possess no aura of ill intent.

Who are you? he said in his thoughts.

'One who would see you crowned emperor,' said a calm, male voice.

A figure in dark, opaque armour stepped into view. The newcomer also wore a long cloak of some shimmering deep red material with a dark blue lining. The armour, however, had a smoky, gleaming radiance which surpassed the gloom within the tent, and was clearly invested with great power.

You are from the grey shroud which has swallowed the isle of Besh-Darok, Tangaroth thought. *Why have you come here to say such things?*

'To offer you a pact, majesty, and to heal your wounds if you so wish.'

Tangaroth stared up at the smooth black visor which masked the man's face, set in a swept, fluted helm which rose to a strange coronet of short, bifurcated tines.

Heal this . . . wound? Why?

'Call it a gesture of good faith, a token signifying ancient but common bonds.'

Before Tangaroth could reply, a cold, sharp tingling raced through the lower half of his face and there was an odd metallic taste as he felt the shattered pieces of his jaw shift yet with not a hint of pain. Several ripples of heat passed through his mouth and a faint resonating sound accompanied each one. Then the tingling coldness receded from the muscles and the flesh, leaving a dull ache in his teeth but, mercifully, not a sign of the bone-grinding torment from before. With shaking hands he pulled away the dressings and touched his lips and face while probing the inside of his mouth with his tongue. And as the exultant relief made tears sting his eyes, a small, hard part of him was thinking – *Now I am beholden, now I have an obligation . . .*

He breathed in deeply, trying to steady himself.

'I thank you, ser,' he said hoarsely, savouring the sound of his voice. 'You have removed a great burden from me, for which you have my deepest thanks. But you mentioned some kind of treaty, as well as ancient and common bonds, which I am eager to explore further with you. However, you can quite openly regard my face whereas I have yet to see yours.'

Almost before he reached the end of the sentence, the helm's visor altered, melting, flowing aside to reveal the man beneath. It was a youthful face, yet very pale, with near-white hair and frost-grey eyes which were like twin glimpses of some desolate emptiness. And it was face that Tangaroth found disturbingly familiar.

'Be welcome, ser,' Tangaroth said. 'Yet I must repeat my first query – who are you?'

'I am known as the Duskgeneral, militarch of the Overseers and suzerain of the Black Host of the Great Shadow.' The pale lips twitched in amusement. 'But once I bore another name and, briefly, another title. I too was once an emperor.'

Tangaroth could feel his heart thudding in his chest as the

reasons for the man's familiarity emerged from his memories, the realization that a younger version of his face could be seen everywhere in Sejeend and across the empire . . .

'Are you . . . truly Tauric, son of Kerrigan?'

'I have the honour to bear that name, but I am not the Tauric who sacrificed his life for the sake of his people.' A bleak look came into his eyes. 'The final battle of the Shadowking war took place in the very depths of the Void and was so savage and destructive that the course of Time itself was ruptured, split in two. Along one stream the Shadowkings and the Lord of Twilight were defeated and history unfolded as you have known it. But along the other they triumphed and all the world was enslaved and plunged into a terrible domain called the Nightrealm, a pit of deathless, never-ending servitude.'

The man calling himself Tauric shook his head. 'For long ages we have played out the roles of futile conspiracy and revolt for his brutal pleasure; I have become his Duskgeneral and commander of his Black Host, and buried all that I was out of sight, out of my conscience. But now that his hunger and pride has led him into this assault upon your world, I and others are determined that it will prove to be his undoing.'

Tangaroth listened closely, his thoughts in upheaval as he strove to perceive the truth or otherwise of this tale. Part of his mind wanted hard proof or some form of corroboration, while another facet was certain on a visceral level that Tauric was all that he claimed to be. Unable to resolve this, he reasoned that it was the proposed pact which was of more immediate importance.

'You mentioned a treaty, ah, Lord Tauric,' he said. 'What would it entail?'

'An alliance, majesty,' Tauric said, leaning forward. 'I have led a small, hand-picked force through to this world, supposedly to establish a beachhead in advance of the main army. My intention, however, is to take my men off this island and join with you in preparing to resist the approaching invasion. But my master's agents are rife amongst the Mogaun and it is they who stand in my way. Will you help us to overcome these mutual enemies?'

The sense of rightness was almost overwhelming. To know

and understand that they both faced the same enemy – that was brotherhood.

'What help can we offer?' Tangaroth said.

Tauric's smile sharpened. 'Your spirit of generosity humbles me, majesty. Very well, my plan is that, under cover of night, a ship bearing my men will sail along the canal and attack Belkiol from its waterfront and northern boundary. If your army can launch a raid in force on the southern boundary about half an hour before as a diversion, our assault will catch them unawares and wipe them out.'

'The Mogaun in and around that town outnumber us by nearly four to one,' Tangaroth pointed out. 'Such a ploy as yours would require excellent timing.'

'You have a well-developed sense of strategy, majesty,' Tauric said. 'And I concur completely with your appraisal, but what I propose is this . . .'

As the black-armoured figure and the cloaked Tangaroth leaned together, a pair of little eyes peered at them from a clump of weedy grass at the foot of the rock wall at the rear of the tent. The eyes belonged to a small bushfox which also possessed a pair of sensitive, twitchy ears. The bushfox had been stalking tiny rodents earlier when something inexplicable led it through the undergrowth to the back of the tent, then to edge its snout under the waxed canvas and then to wait and watch and listen.

And less than fifty yards away, on the other side of the jutting pillar of rock, Ayoni and Chellour were crouching behind bushes, hearing what the bushfox was hearing and trying to make sense of it. But before long the little creature was distracted by insects buzzing outside the tent and when it crept off in pursuit the fragile bond was lost.

'Who was that?' Chellour muttered. 'And that story about another world . . ?'

'Tangaroth seems to believe him,' Ayoni said. 'Especially after his mouth was healed.'

They looked worriedly at each other.

'Shumond will support whatever Tangaroth decides,' Chellour said. 'What will your husband say?'

Ayoni gnawed her lip. 'It depends on how Tangaroth explains it – I doubt that he'll mention the appearance of someone claiming to be the Emperor Tauric!'

'We have to tell Jarryc about this immediately,' Chellour said. 'That infiltrator seems to be playing some kind of convoluted game – I mean, why would this Duskgeneral want us to attack the Mogaun? Why not just attack either us or them first?'

'We need to know more about the grey blight, as well,' Ayoni said. 'I'm sure Tashil and the others could tell us more, but I'm still having no luck with farspeech. Perhaps we should keep trying every half hour or so . . . What is it?'

Chellour's brow was furrowed with concentration. 'Our little spy has given up chasing twigflies and I've got him back to the tent . . . ah, Tangaroth is alone again . . . and that slightly disturbing attendant of his, Gessik, has reentered . . .'

'Then Tangaroth will be calling the others back in,' Ayoni said with a half-smile. 'So we'll have to wait to see what Tangaroth tells them – I'm sure that Jarryc's account will be an entertaining one!'

So slow, the return of his conscious mind, so agonizingly slow. Through the limpid darkness of no-self, only the impressions of feelings seeped, followed by bubbles and motes of thought. Connections began to form, here, there, above, below, before, behind, around and across – then a toppling rush of linkages and he suddenly knew he was sitting in a dark, dank place, sitting on cold, damp stone, sitting with one arm cradled in the other, a hand of broken, seared fingers . . .

There had been pain, and that was the only memory that came back to him at first. But thought joined with thought with flitting remembrance with emotion with smell with texture with physical action with sounds with voices shouting his name . . .

It seemed to hang before him, echoing in his head, yet something made him hesitate, something in him which longed for another name, a hungry, savage name. But with a surprising ease he stifled that inner longing and instead turned his attention to all the new sounds he was hearing, cries, reverberating hammer blows, footsteps, moans, the clatter of chains, a guttural, demanding voice . . . uttering questions in heavily accented Yularian, he knew with a shift in his mind, like some dislodged foundation of knowledge suddenly dropping back into place.

And although the stinking, glimmering gloom of these pillared dungeons never changed, he became conscious of changes outside, how the silver radiance from the small, high windows grew opaque and how a moist chill poured down into these vaulted chambers. There was day and night out there, he was sure of it.

Then, during one of those chilly nights, a pleasingly destructive havoc came to the vile prison. Down one of the columned corridors a roar went up and he could just make out figures capering and gathering in the silver lamplight. Very soon, cudgel sentries were rushing off to quell the riot, including the pair who guarded his own fenced-off area of the great chamber. Then over the yammering clamour he heard a heavy thud from directly above, from the shadow-masked heights of the dungeon. Fragments of stone fell clicking on the floor, followed by a trickling hiss of dust. Followed by another impact and a cracking rumble and the shattering noise of broken masonry slamming into the flagstone floor. Amid the panicking cries and the tormented shrieks and the billowing powdery dust, he was cowering from the extravagant turmoil when strong hands gripped his shoulder and turned him.

'Calabos – you are safe now.'

Calabos.

That was the name, his name, the key for the lock, the seed for the soil, the crack in the dam, the candle in the abyss, the spark for the tinder.

'Qothan,' was all he was able to say through his choking emotions as he recognized the other two Daemonkind, Viras and Yostil, reaching down to him. Then his deliverers lifted him with beating wings, up to the ragged hole in the ceiling and out into a foggy night.

For a moment he caught sight of an empty cobbled road hemmed in by stone walls but his ascent continued, speeding on through streaming mists. Occasionally the murk parted to show the roofs of countless buildings crammed together, their deserted streets resembling canyons of shadow broken by the infrequent silver glints of lamps. And every glimpse revealed the same cityscape, the same collision of differing styles of architecture as well as differing functions. Calabos shivered as he recalled the words of the Sleeping God – '. . . *the Nightrealm's tilted territories . . . districts make war upon districts with unrestrained savagery . . .*'

Moments later, a great, broad tower emerged from the ashen mists. Calabos' bearers banked to the right, losing a little height then slowing as a wide gap in the side of the tower came into view. Lamps burned within and figures both sitting and standing were visible. Qothan and his brothers alighted gracefully just inside the hole, carefully depositing Calabos on the tiled floor. Calabos managed to stagger a couple of paces before his legs went from under him and he fell in a sprawl, his senses spinning, his damaged hand full of stabbing pain.

'Here, now,' said a woman's voice as one of the Daemonkind pulled him upright. 'You'll need to get yer strength back first and get that hand seen to – *then* go for a walk!'

Gasping, and feeling a sting of embarassment, he glanced up to see Qothan crouching beside him.

'We were lucky enough to encounter Kerna and the Horn-ghosts, her warband, after we crossed over . . . and lost you. Without her help it would have taken much longer to track you down.'

'By which time you would have succumbed to Urku's tender mercies,' said the other voice. 'But it was most pleasing to work with people who look like Overseers but aren't.'

'I'm deeply indebted to you,' Calabos said as he turned to look at his benefactor . . . and stopped, staring in astonishment. The hair was lighter and longer, and there was a scar on her chin and a graze along one side of her jaw, but it was Keren. Every line of her face, the steady appraisal of the eyes, the air of experience, all of it leaped from the oldest, deepest memories, those bequeathed by Byrnak.

'Keren?' he murmured

She frowned and gave a little smile that made his heart lurch. 'No – Kerna,' she said. 'I'm the chief of this band of idealistic rogues, and this . . .' she indicated the chamber with an outstretched hand, 'is our sumptuous barracks, full of homely comforts and a stack of sharpened weapons. I'll have our adept, Guldarem, look at your hand when he gets back from foraging. In the meantime, Calabos, be welcome with us.'

As she turned to speak with one of the thirty or so men relaxing about the chamber, Qothan, Viras and Yostil helped Calabos over to an empty alcove in the side wall. After several cloth-wrapped bundles were stacked inside, against the wall, Calabos sat down heavily on a stone bench and sighed.

'How long, Qothan?' he said.

'It has been nearly seven days since we passed through the gate,' the Daemonkind outrider said, then tugged open one of the bundles. 'But we still have your sword.'

The sight of its crosshilt and scabbard jutting from with its wrappings was a gratifying relief. All was not lost – but, seven days!

'The Sleeping God said that Time runs faster here,' he said. 'But we've no way of knowing how fast compared with our world. We'll have to assume that events there are happening much slower than here, and lay plans for finding a way to this Great Shadow's court.'

'That may prove difficult,' Qothan said and went on to describe the Nightrealm to him, first in terms of life and the half-death, how people lived and fought, and how there appeared to be no memories stretching back more than a few years, with a kind of folk memory of long-past great battles, including one or two collective uprisings against the Great Shadow himself. Then he laid out the strategic picture, the warband and the chapters, and the militias who answered to the Overseers who maintained the Great Shadow's dominion from their towers. They in turn answered to the Duskgeneral whose cliffside fortress, the Citadel of Twilight, provided the only way of reaching the dream-courts of the Great Shadow. In addition to the Overseers, flocks of Nighthunters guarded the airborne approaches there, and elite echelons of the Black Host manned the cliff fortifications.

'And I have to tell you Calabos, that I have suspicions about these Overseers,' Qothan said, anger smouldering in his eyes. 'It may be that they are the Daemonkind of that other world, enslaved and corrupted.'

Calabos nodded. 'Yes, of course. Then that may mean that Orgraaleshenoth is alive, here.'

Qothan's eyes widened as the realization sank in.

'The great prince,' he said. 'He was the first to rebel.'

'But even if he were still here, there would be no guarantee that his independent spirit has survived this terrible place.' Then Calabos glanced at Kerna, who was laughing with some of the Hornghosts, and felt his hope lift a little.

'So we have to get from here to the Citadel of Twilight,' he said. 'Then enter it unseen and find the way to the Great Shadow's courts. It's going to require stealth, subterfuge, and a river of luck . . .' He looked over at Kerna again. 'And some local help.'

'From speaking with her,' Qothan said, 'I am sure she would be keen to aid us, but she is engaged on a task of great importance to her – she intends to rescue her sister Nilka from the dungeons of a militia chieftain called Grachek . . .'

'Her sister?' Calabos said apprehensively.

Qothan frowned. 'Apparently so.'

'So if we offer our help in her cause, she may help us in turn.'

'I'm afraid that bargain has already been made, Calabos,' Qothan said. 'Our help in her rescue attempt is the return favour for their help in freeing you.'

'Ah, I see,' said Calabos, sitting back. 'Still, I'll raise the matter with her later – we at least need some kind of map that will get us to this Citadel . . .'

And perhaps I can discover more about her sister, he thought, feeling both fascinated and fearful at the possibility that it might be Nerek, the mirrorchild of Keren which Byrnak had created.

An opportunity presented itself an hour later when the foraging party returned and Kerna introduced him to the Hornghosts' adept, a lanky, balding man called Guldarem. He gave Calabos' damaged hand a quick examination then nodded.

'Pretty straightforward,' he told Kerna. 'Typical of Urku's boys, but I'm surprised he still has all his fingers – they must have been busy when they brought him in!'

As he started work, cutting away dirty bandages and cleaning out wounds, Kerna gave Calabos a quizzical look.

'I never did get a good explanation from your winged friends about where you've come from,' she said. 'Care to try?'

Calabos already knew what Qothan had told her, and decided to keep their story as straight and uncomplicated as possible. 'There are other lands beyond the Nightrealm,' he said, wincing as Guldarem touched a fractured finger bone. 'Our land is quite different from yours and is under attack by the Great Shadow's forces. But we will not surrender to his greed which is why we need to get inside the Citadel of Twilight.'

Kerna's eyes widened for a moment before she burst out laughing.

'I know a good way inside,' she said. 'Turn up at the citadel's gates and proclaim loudly that the Duskgeneral is the bastard offspring of a burial boy and a vine worm! I'm sure the Murknights'll be more than happy to invite you across the threshold!'

There was a collective roar of laughter from the nearby warband rogues, and Calabos nodded and grinned along with it.

'But seriously,' he said once the mirth had subsided, 'if you wanted to get inside, how would you go about it?'

Smile fading, she gave him a hard look. 'I wouldn't – it would be an invitation to perpetual torment in the Duskgeneral's iron cells. I have heard of a legend supposedly telling of a great rebellion against the Great Shadow in which legions of the Black Host sided with the rebels and got as far as the outer dream-courts. I don't know the details . . .' She shrugged. 'I've had the half-death a few times – makes it hard to remember everything.'

'Old man Culri might know,' said Guldarem, glancing up from Calabos' hand from which the pain was slowly lifting. 'He always claims that he holds on to his memories through the half-death.'

'That sounds promising,' Calabos said. 'I'd like to meet him.'

Kerna grimaced sardonically. 'Later, then, once the night is over.'

As she turned away to speak with one of her men, Guldarem straightened and pronounced the fingers healed, their bones rejoined.

'But you really shouldn't put too much strain on the hand for a few days,' he said. 'And wear a gauntlet – the skin will be a little frail for a while.'

Calabos nodded and thanked him, noticing the beads of sweat on his forehead. The hand felt cool and numb, but the fingers worked and all the cuts were closed scabs.

'May I ask you something?' Guldarem said.

'Please do,' said Calabos.

'I cannot help but wonder if you have been an adept of the Well before this,' he said nervously. 'Whenever I drew upon the flux I noticed that it was eddying towards you, very slightly. Forgive me if my query intrudes . . .'

'No, it does not,' Calabos said. 'The answer is yes, although I wonder if it means the same in my land as it does here. Tell me, have you every heard of something called the Lesser Power, or the Godriver?'

Guldarem shook his head. 'But Culri might recognize them.'

With that, he excused himself to go and work on some of the others men's wounds. Calabos regarded him for a moment then returned to the alcove where the Daemonkind were resting. Qothan looked up.

'How are your wounds, friend Calabos?'

He held up his hand in answer, working the fingers.

'Cured, yet still in need of recuperation,' he said, sitting beside the hulking Daemonkind outrider.

'There may not be time for such,' Qothan said. 'The woman Kerna wants to launch the rescue raid by the end of the next day, which means that we will have to be in position for it.' He gave Calabos a considering gaze. 'Are you going to play a part, and will you wish to carry your blade?'

'Yes, and yes,' he said. 'But let me ask you this – have you had occasion to employ sorcery since our arrival?'

Qothan exchanged looks with Viras and Yostil.

'Yes, and it was an unnerving experience.'

'Why?'

'The powers of the Israganthir derived from the Wellsource but through another part of the Void,' Qothan said. 'Here, the flavour of it is tinged by other strains of power, and thus it behaves differently.'

Calabos nodded. 'That's what the Sleeping God said, that when the Lord of Twilight triumphed here, he seized the other powers and combined them with his own . . . but I've felt nothing through my undersenses, no feeling of power woven into the air and the surroundings as it is back home. Perhaps I should attempt to form a thought-canto but I'm unsure of the risk.' He snorted in self-reproach. 'Truly, the timidity of an old man . . .'

'Calabos,' said Qothan. 'I had not wished to mention it before now, but you no longer look like an old man. Since passing through, your hair and your beard have become utterly black and I see few lines in your face.'

Reflexively, Calabos reached up to finger his beard, then squinted down at a tuft held out and saw black not grey curls, And a closer look at his hands and arms revealed fuller, more muscular flesh.

'Was it the journey here that has caused this?' Qothan said.

'Perhaps,' Calabos said. 'Certainly, it greatly affected my mind. You should know, however, that my elderly appearance was an adopted disguise, whereas this is how I really look.'

'A mask,' said Viras. 'To hide your long-lived nature.'

'Just so, although I also moved from place to place to keep from arousing suspicion . . .'

Just then, there were sounds of a commotion near the arched doorway at the rear of the chamber. Calabos glanced over to see a couple of Kerna's Hornghosts struggling with a bald, gangling man in shabby garments whose protests quickly grew louder.

'Let me be, you . . . villains – *cutthroats*!'

Calabos and the three Daemonkind drifted over to observe, along with most of Kerna's warband, while she glanced once at the disturbance then contined her discussion with two of her serjeants. As Calabos drew near, Guldarem joined him from the side, indicating the beggarly captive.

'No need to go looking for old Culri,' the adept said. 'He's come to you!'

'. . . yer filthy hands off! I seek the sword-bearer, the one who has crossed the unseen bridge!'

Calabos exchanged a look with Qothan, then looked back. The two brigands restraining the old man tried to bind his hands but he squalled and screeched and fought them. Certain that the old beggar had been referring to him, Calabos was about to speak up when Kerna finally stepped forward.

'What is all this racket? I can hardly hear myself think!'

'We spotted this old bag o' bones skulking around in the lower halls,' said one of Culri's captors. 'When he tried climbing up the outer ledges, we grabbed him and brought him up here.'

The old man ceased his struggles and glared at the speaker.

'Once there was a time when you were kinder to me, Losker,' he said. 'But that was four or five half-deaths ago for you, back when you marched with Gonderlak . . .'

The man called Losker paled at this and Culri went on, passing his angry gaze across the gathered warriors. 'There are others here I recognize, yes, almost half of you I knew well, but now you don't know me at all . . .'

'There's one thing I do know,' said Kerna, standing over him. 'That I'm getting a headache listening to your drivelling!'

Culri regarded her with disapproval. 'I knew you, too . . .'

'Do you know me, old man?' said Calabos, pushing to the front.

The moment he laid eyes on Calabos, joy flickered in his face, then awe and a little fear. At a gesture from Kerna, the guards released him and he hesitantly went up to Calabos and studied him.

'What do you hope to find?' Calabos said, amused at this.

'So long, so long . . . only the absence of darkness,' Culri said. 'I remember your face, Calabos, remember it despite the ocean of years that have washed through this realm of darkness . . .'

Kerna came over and addressed Calabos. 'All right, he can stay for now, but once you're finished questioning him he's to leave. I don't want him listening to what don't concern him.'

'As you wish,' Calabos said and guided the old man over to the alcove as the other warriors lost interest and dispersed around the chamber. Culri glanced at the three Daemonkind for an amused moment, then faced Calabos before he could sit down.

'You'll not succeed,' he said. 'You'll fail and end up in that ice prison of his, if you deny your nature!'

Calabos was taken aback. 'We have skills and powers at our

disposal and a weapon of surpassing might, which may mean little in the face of the Great Shadow's hordes. But somehow we have to find a way into his courts to confront him there.'

'What an elaborate way to commit suicide,' Culri said with unconcealed derision. 'Unless you accept the foundations of your nature.'

Calabos was silent for a moment, coldly certain of the old man's meaning.

'The "nature", as you put it, is gone for ever,' he said. 'Torn out by the very blade which I have brought to this place with the intention of testing its powers on him!'

Culri shrugged. 'The time will come and you will know what has to be done. In the meantime, just how do you imagine you'll even get as far as his courts?'

Calabos smiled. 'It is my understanding that this had been achieved at least once before.'

'Just the once, the culmination of Omizar's campaign,' the old man said. 'And he had the one thing that could unlock the Duskgeneral's citadel – the armour of a Murknight.' Then he laughed. 'Of course, he also had a huge army at his back . . .' Glancing around him at Kerna's warband, he laughed again.

Calabos gritted his teeth and suppressed his irritation. 'So how would I lay hands on a suit of Murknight armour?'

'By killing a Murknight.'

'Of course.'

Culri looked over his shoulder at Kerna who was glowering at him from the middle of the big room.

'I fear that my time here is almost done,' he said. 'Look for Murknights after dark, mostly – they enforce the Duskgeneral's orders to the high chiefs, and there is rivalry between them and the Overseers who see themselves as the hand of the Great Shadow . . .'

'Where would I find one?' Calabos said.

'Not on the streets, you may be sure. They're the messengers of power so they'll only leave the Citadel on missions of import . . .'

Two Hornghosts sauntered over to stand behind him, a silent warning. Culri shrugged and, pretending not to notice them, started to stroll towards the chamber entrance. But he paused to give Calabos a sidelong look.

'Only the half-death can make you forget your nature,' he said. 'Do not squander the opportunity.'

Then, with a jaunty whistle, he passed through the shadowy doors and was gone, leaving Calabos caught between frustration and bleakness.

The fog of night cleared at last, revealing the eye-defying dark and close-packed roofscape of the Nightrealm, a black and glittering panorama of buildings crammed relentlessly against each other and sloping up towards a gloom-shrouded convergence. There was no source of true light, only the strange, all-pervasive ashen radiance so it was difficult to make out far-away details or to gauge distances. But Calabos thought he could just discern a wide array of sheer cliffs with a huge fortification at their midpoint, reaching to their full height. It was, he reckoned, perhaps fifty or sixty miles away.

Here and there across the crowded, colossal city, tapering towers rose above the chaos of roofs and streets, each a leaden column with a bulbous bastion at its apex. One of Kerna's serjeants told him that they were the tower fastnesses of the Overseers, and when Calabos asked where Kerna's sister was being held, the man pointed to a cluster of squat, conical forts about fifteen miles upslope.

'The Red Scabbard,' he said. 'The lair of Grachek's Daggerdogs.'

Calabos nodded, his mind turning over ideas for the forthcoming raid. A short while later he went to Kerna with a plan to which she listened carefully. When he finished she paced back and forth, mulling it over and occasionally glancing over at Qothan and the other Daemonkind. At last she nodded.

'I like it,' she said. 'We'll do it your way.'

The rest of that morning and afternoon the Hornghosts spent hurrying in twos and threes through less well-used streets on their way to the vicinity of the Red Scabbard. Due to their stature and the bulky visibility of their wings, the Daemonkind were forced to travel across the rooftops while watching for any observers, above or below. Calabos, accompanied by two of Kerna's most skilled men, followed her own route through the ebony districts and was the last to arrive. By the first onset of evening, everyone was in position and the raid began.

Posing as Overseers, Qothan, Viras and Yostil forced their way
into Grachek's Red Scabbard fortress under the pretext of an
inspection demanded by the Great Shadow himself. With this asser-
tion they demanded and got access to the prison levels, leading
various officials and warders through the cell-flanked passages while
Kerna and the Hornghosts followed, eliminating guards and barri-
cading doors into other areas of the Scabbard. Calabos was with
Kerna, guarding the approaches when news came back that her
sister Nilka had been found alive. When she finally appeared with
Qothan and the others, looking battered and bruised, Calabos was
privately amazed to see that she was indeed Kerna's twin. Yet Nilka
was possessed of a vibrant charisma that made Kerna seem mild
and easygoing by comparison.

But misfortune struck as they retraced their steps out of the
prison corridors. The balconied entrance hall by which they had
entered was the scene of fighting as Hornghosts battled
Daggerdogs in shadowy, pillared cloisters. A burly, one-eyed man
in skins and wood armour emerged onto the overlooking balcony
and bawled, 'Lay down your weapons! You're outnumbered, you
can't win! Surrender and I'll promise you a quick half-death, no
torture . . .'

It was Grachek. Then, behind him, another figure came into
view, at which many of the Hornghosts muttered fearfully. It was
a man in a full suit of armour which shimmered smokily and
whose visor was sculpted like a face. The dark figure casually
crossed its arms, as if relaxed and expecting some entertainment.

'A Murknight,' Kerna muttered to her sister who spat an oath
and ordered her men to close ranks.

Calabos stared up at the newcomer, at the armour, then in
farspeech said: *Qothan, get me up there!*

Immediately, the Murknight unfolded his arms and the visor
face spoke: 'Who are you?'

But Qothan and Viras already had Calabos in their grip and were
lifting him up onto the balcony. Grachek tried attacking with an
axe but a sweeping wing talon pitched him over the balcony. The
Murknight drew his own heavy blade to meet Calabos' weapon,
the sword of powers, and at the first clash the Murknight's blade

shattered. Yet even as the Murknight flung the useless sword aside his free hand flared with emerald power and jagged bolts sprang forth. As Calabos and the Daemonkind countered this attack, their enemy whirled and dashed away along an upper corridor.

Calabos, Qothan and Viras gave chase, eventually cornering him in a high chamber decked with banners and grim trophies. Prepared for the Murknight's attacks, Qothan and Viras were swift to lay hands on him and tear him limb from limb. But when the first arm was wrenched from the shoulder not blood but a heavy black vapour poured forth. At the same time, all resistance ceased and the black-encased form fell apart in the Daemonkind's grip, armoured sections clattering to the floor amid boiling gouts of the same black, leaden mist.

By the time Calabos and the Daemonkind rejoined the Hornghosts, with the Murknight armour lashed to Qothan's back, Daggerdog reinforcements were arriving. Led by Kerna and Nilka, the Hornghosts withdrew from the Red Scabbard along planned escape routes through tortuous back-alley mazes choked with icy night fog. The pre-arranged meeting place was the top floor of an abandoned chapterhouse, by a ruined Skyhorse temple. But when Calabos and the Daemonkind reached it, someone was waiting for them – the old man, Culri.

'So you got the armour,' he said. 'Did the Murknight give you a good fight?'

It was a long room of rotten floorboards, cracked rafters and large gaps in the roof tiles through which the chill moistness of the night vapours trickled.

'The thing dissolved,' Calabos said. 'Melted away into black smoke. What are they?'

'It is said that they are all sorcerous images of one man, one of the Great Shadow's enemies from the earliest age of the Nightrealm.' The old man tightened a ragged brown cloak about his shoulders and met Calabos' gaze. 'But listen – there is news from across the realm, news that I'm sure you will find intriguing.'

Calabos glanced at Qothan who had doffed the burden of armour and was retying the pieces into a more comfortable load. Qothan gave a wintry smile and a faint shrug.

'So what's your news?' Calabos said. 'Don't tell me that street crime has risen again.'

Culri laughed darkly.

'One of the Overseer strongholds, Orlag Tower, has fallen to the new chieftain of the Roaring Gauntlets, an easterly militia army. This chieftain rose from being the headman of a petty warband just a few days ago, and already he's challenging the Nightrealm's rulers. Do you want to know his name?'

All the old man's words seemed filled with foreboding, but Calabos merely nodded. 'Tell me.'

'He calls himself Byrnak,' Culri said. 'Byrnak the Protector.'

Calabos was stunned, caught up in a gathering wave of realization, and his body felt as hollow as a bell in which fate and doom began to toll.

Chapter Twenty

Faces of night dance with faces of day,
Ghosts of ice dance with ghosts of fire,
Swords of hate dance with swords of blood,
While the weavers of fate dance alone.

Mogaun seer chant

Smoke from the burning waterfront buildings drifted through the streets of northern Sejeend, a grey haze that was growing murky as the afternoon wore to its close. From a third-floor window overlooking Yarram Square, Tashil sniffed the charred air and gazed south. More smoke was rising from unseen locations close to the fortified garrison of Hubranda Lock where High Steward Roldur, Dardan, Inryk and a handful of nobles and about 500 men were struggling to hold against the growing ranks of the Black Host. With evening approaching, conditions for a successful assault on the garrison would be greatly enhanced.

A woman was screaming with grief somewhere down in the the square, screaming her son's name over and over again, and feelings of grim sorrow passed through Tashil's thoughts. Even though a hasty evacuation had begun before the attack of the archers, hundreds, perhaps thousands, had perished in the ensuing rain of death. Now the north of the city was largely deserted, although some houses and estates on the fringes had been swamped by the sick and the elderly, and children separated from their parents. The main roads north and west to the Rukangs were filled with continuous streams of refugees, about whom brigands and kidnappers circled like flies drawn to a dying animal.

All in less than a day, Tashil thought. From the appearance of Vashad and his Black Host this morning to the encirclement of Hubranda Lock – just a matter of hours.

The arrows fired across the Valewater by the Black Host's archers had turned out to possess a range of deadly qualities. Some had burst on impact in fiery gouts, spreading flame across roofs; some had razor-edged splines which sprang out just after entering a victim's body. Others, however, seemed to be half-alive and burrowed into the body, killing from within, while still others broke apart into clouds of insects with lethal stings and bites.

After that deluge of horror, the mass of the Black Host crossed the Valewater on barges captured at the Silver Landings and other wharfs along the eastern bay. Disorganized and lacking clear orders, some squads of the city guard had charged the first wave of invaders and were cut to pieces. The same happened when Baron Cortain led thirty Roharkan heavy horse against them – just two riders had managed to escape the enemy's hooked spears and pole-axes. The remaining groups of guards or imperial troops either fled north and west, or sought refuge within the staunch walls of Hubranda Lock.

While Dardan and Inryk went to lend aid to the High Steward's defences, Tashil, Sounek and Dybel had gone in search of the high priest of the Earthmother temple north of Sejeend, talking with them a grisly cargo in a wagon.

'Right, we're just about done here,' came Sounek's voice from behind her.

Turning back from the window, she saw Dybel tying a cloth hood over one end of a four-foot hollow cane tube which he then fitted into a canvas sack alongside another nine or ten. There were another three sacks full of the same sitting next to the door.

Tashil nodded. 'Good. Have the scouts come up with any other suggestions for a likely course?'

Sounek laughed. 'Every way is as good or as bad as any other,' he said. 'You can approach the gates of Hubranda Lock from north or south, along narrow streets, or from the west along that big road with the statues – it matters not for those Black Host troops are everywhere. They've also posted more archers on the roofs of buildings closest to the garrison so any approach is going to come under attack from them as well as any on the streets.'

'That's why we need to send a party and one of the sacks up onto the roofs overlooking the northern course.' Tashil said.

'A very exposed position,' said Dybel. 'Even after sunset.'

'I know,' said Tashil, 'which is why I'll be the one to take charge of it.'

Sounek and Dybel objected strenuously and in unison, pointing out a multiplicity of reasons why either of them was better qualified for the role, vying with each other for it. But less than an hour later it was Tashil who was leading six reliable guardsmen with shields on their backs, through the rear courts of a deserted residential terrace which adjoined the lairages and goods yards behind the trading houses that faced Hubranda Lock. The failing light offered cover from observing eyes but concealed underfoot hazards like the rotting refuse of overflowing middens and the vermin it attracted. More than once she bit back a curse when their passage through the stinking darkness disturbed packs of rats and sent them swarming around their feet.

After breaking through an old wooden gate, they found that the ostler's quarters by the stable had a doorway into the mercantile building. From a tiled scullery a servant staircase led up to the first floor – Tashil knew that there were six floors and a loft and knew from scout reports that Black Host archers were firing into Hubranda Lock from balconies on the top floor. But she also knew that there were black-armoured sentries on every level, a tricky obstacle to silent infiltration.

It took a combination of stealth, detours along window ledges and the thought-canto Smother for them to finally reach a sturdy ladder which led up to the loft. But with magesight Tashil quickly saw that the loft's flooring was either rotted with damp and woodworm or missing altogether, and decided that they would have to climb up onto the peaked roof itself and traverse the length of the building that way. To her surprise it proved a straightforward route for them all, with plenty of tiler pegs to provide solid footing, then a climb up to the peak and down the other side to bring them to the corner directly above the archers on their balconies.

There were other archers in the building opposite, just visible in the dusk, but she knew that she had to deal with the nearer ones first and hope that her guardsmen's shields would give her enough time.

Tashil turned to the man carrying the sack of tubes, a lantern-jawed Kejani called Habrul.

'Let's have two to begin with,' she whispered.

Habrul nodded, quietly pulled two from the sack and passed them to her. Tashil laid them softly on the tiles and slid them down to rest on the guttering, one poking over the front, one over the side. A flight of arrows leaped up from the unseen archers below, causing her to freeze and hold her breath for a moment. Then she removed the hoods on the upper ends and wound the tear cord of the front-facing one around her fingers. She paused, remembering how that morning the vial of bone-dust had eaten into the grey blight and later how Dardan's second vial had stopped a Black Host swordsman in his tracks, its contents chewing through the inky armour in seconds then through the man beneath. It had been an ugly sight, but a revelatory one. After that they had raced to a burial grove and filled a wagon with plundered bones, then headed north to the Earthmother temple at Harring. There, she had persuaded the high priest to let them use the big flour mills to grind down the bones, and then to bless the resultant powder.

Consecrated bone dust, she thought as she prepared herself. *It seems absurd yet it works . . .*

'Be ready with the shields,' she muttered and sharply tugged the tear cord. Then she gripped the upper half of the tube and swung it to and fro along the edge of the guttering and the bone-dust poured out to fall in pale clouds.

Sounds of surprise were followed by curses and the first gasps of fear, but by then more dust clouds were falling on the balconies round the corner as well.

Dardan, she said with farspeech. *Time to move – now!*

(*We're going, we're going . . .*)

Then from the corner of her eye she saw an arrow hurtling towards her and for a second thought that death had found her . . . until a shield swept down and the arrow hammered into it, splinters flying as a gleaming black spike punched through it, missing the guardsman's arm by a finger's width. Tashil snatched another dust tube out of the sack, tore off the hood and called up the thought-canto Ram in her mind. Then she raised the tube to level it at the archers on the building opposite, yanked on the tear cord and cast Ram down the tube. A bolus of bonedust shot from the other end, leaving a trail in the gloom as it arced across the street and burst against the stonework, enveloping most of the building's frontage in choking clouds. The shrieks of torment rising from the nearby balconies soon began to be echoed from over there.

Suddenly one of her shieldmen cried out as he was dragged backwards and tossed aside. Driven by fear and instinct she threw herself sideway, up the slope of the roof, and turned with her hands still gripping the dust tube. It slammed into the upraised sword arm of a black-armoured invader and bonedust residue was jarred loose, covering the man's helm and shoulders. He managed one downward cut which she parried with the tube, which broke apart, then he groaned and staggered backwards, dropped his night-black blade and began to claw at his helm's faceplate. Howling with pain he went down on his knees and rolled down to the eaves and gripped the guttering with one hand. Tashil caught a glimpse of gore and the paleness of exposed bone before he fell and was gone.

There seemed to be a long suspended moment when all she did was half-sit, half-lie on the side of the roof, listening to the sounds of fighting and cries near and distant, as if the battle had somehow dropped away.

Then a large arrow thudded into the roof tiles a few feet away and promptly split into half a dozen coiling snake things. Eyeless, they began to squirm towards her until Habrul seized one of the bonedust tubes, tore at the cord and upended the contents on them. As they writhed and hissed, blackening amid the layer of powder, Habrul grinned.

'Even their false creatures are slain by our ancestors' bones . . .'

Then another arrow flew out of the night and struck the roof at his feet, bursting into flame. In a moment he was a gasping,

screaming mass of fire, so blinded by pain that he lost his footing
and fell burning to the street below.

Shaken, Tashil swore and ordered the rest of her shieldsmen over
to the other side of the roof. Even as they scrambled up, she felt
a tickle of farspeech – Dardan.

(*Can you see what is happening?*)

We've had to seek cover from those cursed archers, she said. *What do
you mean?*

(*We've been fighting our way through, and the bonedust has worked
wonders. But all of a sudden they're pulling back, towards the wharfs
between here and the sea gates, it seems. We're almost at Hubranda Lock's
main gate and no one's here to stop us.*)

I don't know, Dardan, she said, pulling herself back up to the
peak of the roof. *Let me take a look . . .*

Cautiously, she peered over the coping stone, using magesight
to study the buildings across the darkened avenue of statues. But
the roofs and windows seemed empty, lightless and abandoned,
and she was sweeping her gaze along the row of roofs when something large flew past overhead,

Mother's name! she thought. *Are they sending winged troops against
us now?*

Her guardsmen had drawn their swords and she was fumbling
for one of the bonedust tubes, when a voice came down from
the darkness.

'Tashil Akri – be not alarmed, for we are friends.'

Sitting up straight she saw two winged figures descending from
above, carrying a third between them. One of her men still had
a hooded lamp and she told him to open it a little as wings beat
the air and the newcomer was set down with feet astraddle the
roof's peak. By the meagre yellow glow Tashil recognized him as
Calabos' cousin, Coireg, attired in grey breeks and an unadorned
tabard that left his arms bare, the plain garb of a temple novitiate.
But there was a difference to him now, an iron calm in his manner
and the light of enigmatic purpose in his eyes.

Tashil got to her feet. 'Greetings, Coireg – am I right in thinking
that the Daemonkind have entered the fray?'

Coireg nodded. 'Pericogal, captain of the *Stormclaw*, was

reluctant to involve his crew in this conflict but once I reminded him of the divine writ of my task he became more amenable.'

'And what task is this?' she said, at once feeling a ripple of fore-boding.

'Nothing less than the defeat of the pitiless enemy that assails us.' He smiled wryly. 'Or at least, I am charged with an under-taking necessary to that end. I was with the *Stormclaw* at Nydratha when Ondene succumbed to the Shadowking again and fled through the seagod Grath, followed by Calabos. But once they were gone, the Sleeping God spoke again and laid upon me a task whose enormity I am still unable to grasp, yet which I must carry out. And part of that includes taking you with me!'

She stared at him, unsure whether to frown or laugh. 'Take me where?'

'To the heart of the war,' he said. 'We are flying north to near Besh-Darok at the behest of the Sleeping God who said to tell you that those closest to you will soon need your help.'

'Ayoni and Chellour?' she said. 'What kind of danger are they in?'

'I'm not certain,' Coireg said ruefully. 'The Sleeping God only mentioned "dread fetters". This seems to be an abiding aspect of the pronouncements of gods – some are starkly apparent, others annoyingly opaque. But I'm afraid you'll have to decide as we are leaving now.'

As he spoke, another pair of Daemonkind swooped out of the night to alight on the roof.

'We are ready, friend Coireg,' said one. 'Are we needed?'

'A moment, Besarl – the lady Tashil is considering her duty.'

Tashil bit back a harsh retort while trying to gauge her value to the defenders here against the uncertainties of this god-appointed task. Farspeech with Ayoni and Chellour would have helped her decide but there had been neither word nor response from either the entire day.

'Very well,' she said. 'I'll go with you, but I'm taking *these* with me.' She raised the shoulder sack, now holding just three bonedust tubes.

Coireg glanced at Besarl who nodded.

'We can bear this load,' the Daemonkind said.

Minutes later, Tashil was rising from the roof, both hands holding on tightly to the heavily muscled arms that were lifting her. Gusts of wing-struck air swirled about her and as the roof and her guardsmen dropped away, her stomach quivered with the hollowness of vertigo. Closing her eyes, she reached for the Lesser Power then sought Dardan through farspeech.

Dardan, I'm with some new friends and allies . . .

(*Yes, the High Steward is having talks with their leader, fellow called Agasklin.*)

And I'm with Coireg and some of the Daemonkind — we're flying north to Besh-Darok to help Ayoni and Chellour.

(*Hah! First Calabos and now you! Have to say that I am less trusting of those winged monsters than you!*)

I'm safe and will remain so, she replied. *Do you think that you can hold Hubranda Lock?*

(*For a time — our new allies have helped throw them back across the Valewater, but they seem to have a limitless source of reinforcements . . . who knows what that Vashad character will try next?*)

The Daemonkind were higher now, and she could see the whole of Sejeend spread out beneath her, the scattering of lamps across the north with dull red glows from fires along the route of the fighting and flashes of sorcerous battle near the riverbank. Then there were the bright torches and beacons on the ramparts of Hubranda Lock, illuminating scores of guards and the standard of the High Steward wavering in a faint night breeze. By contrast, the south bank was an expanse of darkness, with only the vague hint of shadows shifting within shadows, a dark featureless stage for the Black Host.

Be careful, Dardan. I pray that we'll meet again.

(*Aye, just watch your back, Tash, and . . . walk in the light.*)

As the farspeech bond was severed, the Daemonkind began heading northwards. Tashil drew her rough woollen shirt up against the rushing cold and wondered what Calabos was doing in the Nightrealm and if he had encountered Corlek Ondene yet.

Be safe, Calabos, she thought. *And come back to us.*

The fall of Orlag Tower was a glorious sight.

After the warning encounter with the Overseers, the old man

Dar had taken Byrnak downslope to an area of great destruction, an expanse of gutted and demolished buildings. Under the fallen columns and arches of a temple, in the vaults beneath, he had shown Byrnak a long barrel-roofed chamber strewn with rotting sacks, heaps of bricks, crates of dusty arrowheads – and a hulking, wheeled shape like some massively built wagon. Its framework was of immense timbers that could only have been plundered from a substantial building, and its wheels were of stone and timber and rimmed with some tough red substance. But atop it was a device that made Byrnak's eyes widen – a single, wooden column more than a yard across, lying lengthways and turning on an axle driven by double handcranks at the rear. The front end was socketed into a large, conical piece of stone whose surface bristled with deep-set, carefully slanted arrays of glittering black blade shards.

'A great many years ago,' Dar had said. 'A valiant but cunning fool named Gonderlak raised the Nightrealm in revolt against our eternal lord and master. He had his artisans build this, the Mawl, then decided that he wanted another still larger one and it was that which he used to break down the gates of the Duskgeneral's citadel. But his siege failed and in the vast carnage of half-deaths, knowledge of this original was forgotten.' He grinned. 'Except by a few . . . although in all honesty, I learned of this from an old man I used to know.'

Thus Byrnak brought in the workers and labourers of his ally militias as well as his own, had a ramp built and the Mawl hauled up to street level, all covered with hides and decrepit canvases. Then by night, a risky journey through the haunted fog to a well-guarded barn not far from Orlag Tower.

The hours building up to the assault were a masterpiece of misdirection which Byrnak personally managed. The Roaring Gauntlets, and their allies the Bloodrats and the Hook Order, announced that another senior militia, the League of Fists, had gravely insulted their women and their collective honour and would pay a heavy price. They then launched a series of raids on the League's territory, exercises in savagery, maiming rather than killing outright and wrecking buildings or their contents. The

League of Fists was a known ally of the Overseers of Orlag Tower and was so infuriated that they called on the Tower for help.

Which was what Byrnak had been hoping for. As most of Orlag's dozen and a half Overseers swooped down towards the League's embattled strongholds, Byrnak moved his hundred-strong gangs into position near the tower. Then he sent in the Mawl.

Pushed and pulled by scores of helmed warriors, the war machine rumbled towards its objective from upslope, gaining a deadly momentum. The point of the spinning stone ram struck the base of the tower, pierced the stonework and chewed its way through. The two men madly cranking at the rear were thrown off by the initial impact but others quickly took their place. Then, under the lash of bellowed orders, the men on the ropes turned about and dragged the Mawl back upslope before turning about to propel it down towards the tower once more, aiming the stone ram at a different spot.

The war machine teams managed to knock four gaping holes in the tower's base before Overseers began appearing and attacking. But by then it was too late – large cracks ran between the holes and spread upwards. Then shards of stone flew as large blocks began to fragment, an internal support cracked loudly and the tower's weight shifted, grinding the shattered blocks into dust. Byrnak was watching gleefully from the flat roof of a tall tavern as the tower tilted and its looming mass began to topple. There was a rushing roar and the huge spindle broke in the middle and split into long vertical shards. A shuddering thunder filled the air as Orlag Tower fell, its vast pieces hammering any other buildings into a long swathe of rubble beneath clouds of dust . . .

Byrnak reached for power, just enough to enhance his vision which showed that the Mawl had escaped being crushed by the tower's death. He laughed at this, breaking off when a large winged form crossed his field of vision and swooped towards the tavern roof. Byrnak's guards readied spears and slings but he halted them with a raised hand as the Overseer fetched up with perfect grace to alight on the roof's low wall. It was the one who had warned Byrnak.

'You!' he said. 'I had a feeling that you were going to be trouble.'

'Well, I hope you're not disappointed,' Byrnak snarled.

The Overseer grimaced unpleasantly. 'When we rebuild we shall bury your bones in the foundations, and when you come back from the half-death we'll find other uses for you.'

At his gesture another five Overseers clambered up over the low roof. The guards gasped and backed away towards the steps, but Byrnak just laughed. Without another word the Overseers launched themselves at him.

He left it until the last moment, then released the pent-up energy of the Wellsource in one spiralling wave of radiant force. Slashed and ruptured, his attackers were hurled backwards and off the roof altogether, apart from one, the spokesman, whom he held in the pitiless grip of his power, suspended in midair.

'There is a new power in the Nightrealm,' he cried. 'And the old shall give way to the new, a new purpose, a new belief – do you hear me?'

Then without waiting for a reply he tossed the battered Overseer off the tavern roof. Breathing heavily, he stood for a moment savouring this first true moment of delving into the Wellsource. Which was different here, he noticed, in its taste, its texture, its imperative, and its primal undertones. The savagery of that other Wellsource was here tempered with something else, a deeper sense of nuance, and a greater flexibility. Perhaps it could offer new ways of coercion . . .

Someone began to applaud behind him, a faintly metallic sound. Byrnak turned to see that all his guards had fled, and that a single opaque form stood there watching him. It was a man, clad from head to foot in dark, shimmering armour with the front of the helm open, revealing a pale, youthful face.

'Greetings,' the stranger said. 'That was a marvellous demonstration of untutored brawn – I like that, it shows great promise and could lead to a rewarding future, depending on the choices you make.'

Byrnak sneered. 'There's no time here and no true death, so how can there be any future?'

'Perhaps it would be more accurate, then, to distinguish between life, such as it is, and the no-life of my master's White Prison, which of course is without any present or future.' The armoured man smiled faintly. 'I've heard that you're calling yourself Byrnak — is that true?'

'Yes — so who are you?'

'I have the honour to be known as the Duskgeneral, commander of the hosts of the Great Shadow.' He sketched a mocking bow. 'An interesting name, Byrnak — almost no one here remembers it, but I do. I remember . . .'

Byrnak regarded him closely, realizing that this was only a far-flung image and that the real Duskgeneral was elsewhere.

'I'm coming for you,' he said. 'I mean to have it all, and I'll destroy you if you stand in my way.'

'How refreshingly direct,' the Duskgeneral said. 'And very reminiscent of how he was in the beginning. In fact . . .' He stared at Byrnak for a long moment, then a slow smile crept over his features. 'Is this a ploy of his, to send an unknowing fragment of himself off into the hinterland in the hope that it will return in strength? Well, we've played that game before but never while prosecuting a war for another world!' He laughed. 'I accept the challenge and and shall prove my worth! Till we meet again, Byrnak the Protector!'

Still laughing, the Duskgeneral turned to walk away, his form melting away. A pace or two later all of him had wispily dissolved into the shadows.

Byrnak glowered at the spot where he had vanished.

'This is not a game,' he muttered. 'And you will beg for death before it is done.'

The night was full of confusion and the clash of arms. Ayoni moved carefully through the darkness, using magesight to find a safe path through the undergrowth but not daring to use farspeech for fear of discovery. Tangaroth and his pawn, Gessik, were out there, just waiting for any sign of her or Chellour.

Anxiety at not knowing the fate of Jarryc and the others assailed her, almost threatening to overwhelm her emotions. But she held on to cold, hard calmness as it were a rock amid a stormy sea. Nothing would be served by a surrender to sorrow and uncertainty — she would press on and discover the truth and the truth would not break her.

They had crept out of their enclave via the northern ravine, travelling in groups of ten or a dozen. Tangaroth's orders were clear – they were to make a stealthy approach to the hilly western quarter of Belkiol, where the Mogaun still had a foothold in the town, and attack their positions. He claimed to have concluded a pact with the leaders of the Black Host which, having secured the main part of Belkiol, was pursuing the Mogaun savages and Carver fanatics into the northern hills. All this he announced just after nightfall in person, with his miraculously healed and voluble mouth.

Ayoni and Jarryc and the others had been stunned, but had no time to react or argue as Tangaroth ordered the deployment to begin straight away. And barely half an hour after emerging from the ravine, Jarryc's group, including Ayoni and Chellour, had been ambushed by Shumond and the Iron Guard. As lamps went out and everyone scattered, Ayoni had become separated in the midst of a gentle vale full of bushes. And now that she had reached the crest of the rise on the other side, she could pause to get her bearings. Magesight was more useful in daylight, but after dark could only make her surroundings a little clearer, or sometimes pierce weak illusions. It was possible to enhance her sight with a thought-canto but she could not take the chance that Tangaroth was alert to any use of the Lesser Power in the vicinity.

Feeling tired, grimy and scratched, she leaned against a mossy boulder and stared out into the darkness. To the east she could hear shouts and the occasional clang of weapons but that was the direction of the Great Canal and the presence of the Black Host. That left her with the choice of heading for the original goal, the western quarter of Belkiol, or returning to the enclave, or risking a use of farspeech . . .

It was tempting, but Tangaroth was already a powerful mage and with this Duskgeneral as his ally there was no knowing what other lore he now had at his disposal. It seemed that retracing her path to the enclave might be her best chance of rejoining Jarryc and the others. She turned south and was about a dozen paces further on when she heard wings flap overhead, large wings . . .

'Countess,' said a familiar voice from above, 'Wait . . .'

Looking up, she gaped in astonishment as a pair of winged creatures descended, bearing none other than Tashil Akri clad in traveller's robes and carrying a long pack on her back. Once Tashil
was safely on the ground, the two women embraced happily, but
before Ayoni could speak another person arrived in the same
manner, a bare-armed Coireg who smiled and nodded.

'Greetings to you both,' Ayoni said while looking closely at the
four winged figures, taking in their burly and vaguely reptilian
countenances. 'Forgive me, but if I didn't know any better I would
say that your friends are – Daemonkind?'

Tashil nodded. 'Besarl and his companions have borne us all the
way from Sejeend this night, and yes, that was the name they once
had. Before all this, however, they adopted more usual appearances
as the crew of the *Stormclaw*.'

Ayoni smiled, surprised yet calmly accepting it as part of the
stream of events that she was caught up in. 'So how fare matters
in Sejeend?' she said.

'So much has happened,' Tashil said sadly, 'that it would take a
perilous amount of time to relate it all. Suffice to say that the
blight has consumed half the city and invaders called the Black
Host are trying to seize the rest.'

'And you are both here,' Ayoni said. 'Why?'

Tashil glanced at Coireg who maintained an air of calm amusement.

'The pronouncements of gods?' Tashil said to him, then looked
back at Ayoni. 'A certain higher agency let it be known that those
close to me here would soon be in danger, a warning I took to
mean yourself and Chellour. But it turned out otherwise . . .'

'I wouldn't say that our situation is without difficulties,' Ayoni
said.

Tashil shook her head. 'Jarryc and Chellour are safe, holed up
with two score of soldiers in a tumble-down hunting lodge about
a mile north of here. No, it seems that the divine foreboding
referred to my family . . .'

Ayoni could see the fearful worry in her eyes, despite her
apparent composure. 'You're sure?'

Tashil nodded but it was Coireg who spoke.

'It is true, Countess — I have seen it through the bond placed upon me by the Sleeping God. The Great Shadow's Black Host has seized most of the town north of here, along with several hundred prisoners who have been confined to the ceremonial chamber of the Twilight Temple. The floor of the temple has been scribed with intricate patterns and the prisoners have been divided into eleven groups, with ten arranged in a circle and the last placed in the centre around which a number of gold statuettes has been arrayed. Familiar?'

Ayoni felt a chill of horror. 'Mother's name . . .'

'Most of my family had come to make the pilgrimage to the Carver's Ascent in the city of Besh-Darok,' Tashil said in a level voice. 'Several of them, my father included, were taken prisoner when the Black Host swept into Belkiol — they are among those being held at the temple.'

'That ritual must not take place,' Ayoni said, as memories of the ceremony she had witnessed came flooding back. 'Is that why you're both here?'

'It's why *I'm* here,' Tashil said, glancing darkly at Coireg. 'He has other matters to attend to.'

'I have been appointed to a crucial task,' Coireg said. 'Over on Besh-Darok Isle.'

'Divinely appointed, I assume,' Ayoni said. 'What does it involve?'

'I am . . . constrained not to reveal that to anyone.' He gave a wry laugh. 'Such that I cannot even frame the words on my tongue, Countess, but both of you must accept that the work I have been charged with is vital, and so perilous that I may not survive to see it through. Yet I must try.'

Ayoni was sobered to hear the gravity in his voice and gave a nod of assent, even as she itched to know.

'Time is our first enemy,' Tashil said.

'Exactly so,' Coireg said, looking over at the four Daemonkind who stirred and one by one spread their wings and flapped aloft. Two of them descended towards Coireg and with neat accuracy plucked him up into the air. 'Farewell, Tashil, farewell, Ayoni — we shall not meet again. Farewell, and walk in the light . . .'

As they watched the small group of figures recede into the

upper gloom of the night sky, Ayoni said, 'He sounds as if he believes it.'

'He does,' Tashil said, 'with a certainty that's almost unnerving.'

'Excuse my curiosity,' Ayoni said. 'But what is in the bundle you're carrying?'

Tashil smiled. 'A weapon that harms the Black Host soldiers. I'll explain as we walk.' She swept her gaze across the sky, then pointed up the shallow dale Ayoni had recently crossed. 'Your husband and the others are that way.'

As they hurried through the bushy undergrowth, skirting dense walls of foliage or jumping small streams, Tashil sketched out the terrible events which had struck Sejeend. But her account of the last deadly day, from the discovery of the bonedust's effects to the attacks of the Black Host and the arrival of the *Stormclaw*, left Ayoni amazed and horrified.

'How can the empire withstand such a hammerblow?' she said.

'I don't think that it *can* survive,' Tashil said. 'With the capital in ruins and the emperor dead, the regional governors will take what they can seize – assuming that the Great Shadow's invasion fails.'

A short time later they encountered one of Jarryc's lookouts who led them into a wood and a large, dilapidated cabin where Jarryc and Chellour and their men had found hidden shelter. After the happy and relieved reunions, Tashil outlined the situation at the temple at Belkiol and the prisoners' impending sacrifice. Faces were grim as Ayoni told how she had witnessed the same ritual in the city of Besh–Darok, which led to the vileness of the Blight. There was no dissent when Jarryc gave the order to break camp, only an eager determination.

As Jarryc's forty or so soldiers began making their way north through the woods, one of the far scouts arrived with news of Baron Klayse who had likewise gone to ground with nearly fifty men less than a mile to the west. Jarryc and the scout agreed on a birdcall signal before the scout left to find the Baron once more and guide him to the southern boundary of Belkiol. An hour further on into the depths of the night the two parties finally met, in a sparse wood near a cluster of charcoal burner huts and on the other side of a low ridge from the town of Belkiol. While Jarryc and Ayoni swiftly apprised Klayse of the foul sacrifice being prepared at the temple, Tashil and Chellour had emptied one of the bonedust tubes and distributed the powder among those with small leather pouches along with instructions for its use.

Over the low ridge the wood thinned out to be replaced by a patchwork of tilled fields whose meagre crops had already been trampled into the mud by other feet. Ayoni and Tashil were at the front, leading the column of men through the darkness, choosing paths through the fields, past empty pens where chickens and pigs had been kept. Ahead, the town of Belkiol was a dark, spread-out mass of low roofs with a scattering of lamps and torches, and one flickering orange glow where a building was on fire, sending a funnel of smoke and sparks into the sky. Tashil gestured to the eastern side of town, where the Temple of Twilight was located.

Stealthily they headed along the southern boundary in that direction. But as Ayoni and Jarryc, with Tashil and Klayse, led the column up a path between the wrecked gardens of two houses, figures emerged from doors and shadows and torches flared. In the glow, Ayoni saw that they faced six black-armoured swordsmen of the Black Host while behind them, looking nervous and uncomfortable, were the Iron Guardsmen who had come with the Archmage as well as another thirty or so ordinary imperial soldiers.

One of the Black Host swordsmen raised an arm and pointed at them.

'Traitors, every one of you, traitors who would oppose the just commands of your emperor. Bow down now, or face the punishment of the blade.'

None moved or spoke, although swords were calmly loosened in their scabbards. The armoured figure surveyed them and nodded.

'So be it,' he said, drawing his own sword, a long, crooked shard of blackness.

'Wait, captain,' came a voice from the shadows. 'Let us not be too hasty with these wilful strays – I shall speak to them myself.'

'By your command, your majesty.'

Tangaroth stepped unhurriedly from the shadows, still garbed in the long, dark hooded robe, but when his face came into the torchlight Ayoni had to stifle her surprise. Only a few hours ago he had spoken to a gathering of officers with a healed mouth and face which had shown no sign of the earlier horrific injuries. Now his features were marred by a swathe of glittering blackness which spread across his face in a ragged blotch from the right cheek across the mouth and chin and ended beneath the left jaw. It resembled the gleaming armour worn by the Black Host yet when he spoke it stretched and moved like flesh. There was a smile upon the lips but it seemed slightly skewed while the eyes were clearly deranged.

'Why do you persist in this rank folly, Count Jarryc, Countess Ayoni?' Tangaroth said. 'The rewards of the empire await you, yet you choose to flout my express will . . .'

'The rewards of what empire?' Tashil said. 'Ilgarion is dead and the capital is half-destroyed, half in chaos.'

'Ah, the impertinent Mogaun child,' he said, looking at her. 'Know that the Iron Guard has offered me the crown, which I have reluctantly accepted for the good of the empire, an empire that is greater than one monarch or one city.'

'But not so great that you would refuse aid from those who have come to conquer,' Jarryc said. 'Your majesty.'

Tangaroth gave him a hate-filled stare and moved closer to stand before him.

'You . . . know . . . *nothing*, rebellious upstart! These men and their valiant general are our friends and allies, and they have promised to help destroy our enemies . . .'

'But I know something which you do not, *majesty*,' Tashil said.

His head swivelled her way. 'And what would that be? Some noxious Mogaun recipe, or the colour of your father's socks . . .'

Tashil's smile was almost feral and Ayoni could sense the sharp heat of her enmity.

'No – I know what harms our enemies.'

In a single motion she flung out one clenched hand towards Tangaroth's face, her fingers springing open to release white bone-dust powder. Even as the pale cloud enveloped his head, the Black Host captain was drawing back his sword to cut her down. But Jarryc shoulder-charged him, hurling him to the ground.

There was a chorus of shouts as both sides surged towards one another, with the Black Host soldiers leading. But more handfuls of bonedust were thrown and the black-armoured swordsmen stumbled and went down. A choking, gasping shriek cut through the clamour and eyes turned to see Tangaroth writhing on the ground.

Ayoni had watched in horror as the bonedust powder attacked his face and the black flesh turned mottled grey and began to slough off. But the powder was not stopping there.

'The rot goes deep,' said Tashil, regarding the dying, would-be emperor with dispassion.

By now the brief spasm of fighting had come to a halt as the gurgling screams of the six Host soldiers became a chorus of torment. One of the fighters who had backed Tangaroth was staring in terror at one of the disintegrating bodies for a moment before turning away to be loudly sick.

'You men of the army and the Iron Guard,' Jarryc said. 'You see how your loyalty and trust have been betrayed. Are you going to keep fighting for this offal . . .' He indicated the now-still corpse of Tangaroth, 'or will you put up your swords and join us in a grave task, to free captives being held in the temple and thereby prevent an abominable sacrifice?'

There was scarcely any hesitation – the opposing soldiers sheathed their blades and clasped hands and exchanged grins with those they had so recently faced at swordspoint. But then a scout came running with news of Black Host swordsmen, a score or more, approaching from the town. Ayoni turned to Tashil but she was already extracting a bonedust tube from the long canvas sack.

'I think I know how to deal with these vermin,' she said.

True to her word, she sent a cloud of dust billowing into the gap between the nearest two buildings just as the enemy swordsmen came running through it. Jarryc then led his men past the convulsing black forms and up into the streets of Belkiol. Ayoni and Tashil were at his side, sharing his astonishment at discovering that there were no other Host soldiers to be seen. A few lamps guttered here and there with the brightest glow emanating from the doors of the Temple of Twilight, a slope-sided building with tall windows masked inside and out by heavy red banners. Inside, resistance was slight, a handful of Black Host soldiers who charged the large force of liberators only to be downed by the bonedust once again.

Down on the temple floor, amid complex pattern markings, trussed-up groups of Mogaun captives were crying out to be released. Ayoni and Chellour were the first to start cutting bonds, closely followed by Tashil and the others. Moments later they heard Tashil cry out and looked up to see her weeping as she embraced a group of tribeswomen, one by one, then turned to face an elderly man who came through the crowd with severed ropes still trailing from his neck and wrists. Tashil put her hand to her mouth for a second before embracing him tightly. Ayoni felt emotion sting her own eyes as she saw this, a kind of fierce joy that her friend was reunited with her family.

Then one of the soldiers guarding the outside came dashing in to tell Jarryc that a handful of Mogaun were outside, bearing a truce flag and asking to speak with him. Ayoni shook her head, feeling as she were a leaf caught in a rushing river of events. She said as much to Chellour, who chuckled.

'Well,' he said. 'What will the next one be?'

'I'd say . . . probably nothing good . . .'

Her voice trailed off as she saw Baron Klayse hurrying through the crowd towards them, his face serious.

'Countess,' he began. 'I cannot interrupt your husband – he's talking with the Belkiol Mogaun. But I had to tell you . . .'

'Tell me what, Baron?'

'Up on the temple roof there is an odd enclosure,' he said. 'Beneath it are several contraptions on tripod frames, things that act like those neareye devices only they also make the darkness lighter . . .'

Ayoni was grim. 'What did you see?'

'A flotilla of small ships heading this way along the Great Canal,' he said.

'Could they be friendly?' said Chellour.

Klayse shook his head. 'The devices bring distant things nearer, and I could see that every deck was crowded with more Black Host soldiers.' He looked at them both. 'At most we have less than an hour before they start coming ashore. And I doubt that Tashil has enough powder for them all!'

From the attic window of a strange lodging house just within spearcast of the Citadel of Twilight, Calabos could see Byrnak's army making its steady, unstoppable progress up the last mile or two to their mutual goal. The fog of night had just lifted, revealing a wide swathe of bright pinpoints in the perpetual dusk, all the lanterns of that army's many thousands of warriors fighting against the Black Host, pushing them back street by street. Overseers soared and wheeled above, indistinct winged shapes which occasionally swooped down to harry fighters on the ground only to be driven back by bristling clusters of long spears. And whenever they employed sorcerous means of attack, they drew a similar, savage response from Byrnak and the dozen or so adepts he had somehow brought into his service.

It was just four days since the fall of Orlag Tower, during which Byrnak had either persuaded or coerced entire knots of chapters and militia chieftains to join his campaign to defeat the Great Shadow. In that time, Calabos had conferred with Qothan and Culri, then with Kerna and Nilka, trying to figure out a way to penetrate the inner and higher floors of the citadel – assuming that the Murknight armour would unlock the gates.

At last a plan formed: they would wait until Byrnak's army was about an hour from the citadel before approaching the citadel's gates, led by Calabos in the armour and the Daemonkind posing as Overseers and with some thirty of Kerna and Nilka's Hornghosts dressed as Black Host soldiery. Kerna and Culri and a few others would be trussed up with convincing-looking bonds and presented as newly captured rebel leaders who were to be rushed to senior commanders for questioning.

This had met with general approval, except from Culri who insisted that they should also devise a fall-back plan in case the first one failed, for whatever reason. This they duly did by adapting one of the rejected ideas in which the Overseers would carry Calabos in the Murknight armour up to one of the citadel's higher balcony ledges, followed by the others.

Thus it was that Calabos, wearing most of the black eldritch armour (which proved surprisingly light) was standing at that window, gauging the speed of Byrnak's upslope advance. But as he watched the mile-distant clash under the radiant, unending shadows of the Nightrealm, his thoughts drifted into wondering what was happening back in the other world – some seven or eight days had gone by here but there was no way of knowing how much time had passed for Tashil and Dardan and Ayoni and the others. Had they failed to stem the Great Shadow's invasion, or were they still holding on in the hope that deliverance would come?

This is what is meant by the burden of responsibility, he thought. *An unbearable weight and an uncertain fate. How will I have to change so that I can bear it?*

There were footsteps coming up the stairs behind him and he turned as Kerna came into view.

'Is it time?' he asked.

She nodded so he left the window and followed her down to the ground floor where the rest were preparing themselves. Nilka handed him the black helm and when he put it on he found that the faceplate was quite translucent from within. Culri gave him the gauntlets and Qothan held out the sword of powers, sheathed in an intricately embossed leather scabbard stained black and studded with dark green stones. It was splendidly barbaric.

A short while later he was leading his procession towards the citadel's gates from the easterly direction. Squads of Host fighters, swordsmen and archers, were hurrying downhill or taking up positions on roofs and balconies overlooking the main approaches. Many noticed the prisoners and their escort but none sought to impede them.

Then the tall ebony gates were looming before them, smooth black doors flanked by massive statues of snarling Nighthunters. Calabos glanced at the motionless horrors as he led the infiltrating party straight up to the gates . . . which stayed firmly shut for a long, long moment. Thinking desperately, he raised one iron fist to hammer on the dull black surface but before he could do so there were thuds and the heavy scrape of gears and bars in motion . . . and the gates swung slowly open.

Black Host officers were waiting in the big oval antechamber but bowed on seeing a Murknight in the company of three Overseers. Calabos barked the line about rebel prisoners destined for interrogation and the officers waved them through. Spurred on by relief and the edgy fear of being in the midst of the enemy, Calabos led the party at a sharp pace up a set of lead-grey steps to a high-ceilinged corridor which ran in a long curve around a huge central hall where the main staircases wound upwards on fluted red columns. However, Calabos had gleaned an alternative route from Culri's long-lived recollections and turned right along the corridor, heading instead for lesser stairways which led up past the outer balconies, restrooms and other galleries. According to Culri, there were several of these secondary networks of stairs and passages, most of which rose to the highest of the Citadel's thirty-three levels. It was just a matter of sustaining the plausibility of their deception for as long as possible.

It got them as far as the seventh floor when they encountered a Murknight on a square gloomy balcony overlooking a training room. The Murknight stopped Calabos as he led the others along the balcony, but when Calabos shook off his hand and tried to continue the Murknight gave an angry shout and drew a broad-bladed battle-axe. Instinctively, Calabos snatched out the sword of powers to parry the incoming blow and cleft the axe's haft clean through. The Murknight already had a long dagger out and was closing with it so Calabos, rather than pull back for another full cut, seized the upper part of his swordblade, just below the hilt, and dealt a brutal hack to the Murknight's side.

There was a burst of dazzling silver-green light, illuminating the balcony and the room below for a moment, and the Murknight let out a strange, high buzzing cry before collapsing to the floor in a welter of armour sections and dense black fumes. Host soldiers were already mounting steps on the other side of the balcony, some fitting arrows to bows, so Calabos led everyone in a dash to an archway leading out to the next set of stairs.

After that it was a series of confrontations, bluffings and pursuits through the glittering black passages and chambers of the Citadel. At length they came to a hall full of low benches where Calabos called a halt, took off his helm, and told them all that he would have to go on alone.

'How foolish can one man be?' said Culri. 'No, this is not a task for you alone.'

'The captains of this place now know who they are looking for,' Calabos pointed out. 'So the moment any enemy sees a Murknight in the company of three Overseers they'll be unlimbering their swords not rolling out the carpet!'

'He's right,' said Kerna. 'He'll stand a much better chance by himself but that leaves us with the problem of how to get out.'

'Find your way to one of the balconies,' Calabos said. 'Qothan and his brothers might be able to ferry you down to safety . . .' He glanced at Qothan who gave a slow, serious nod.

'But friend Calabos, you take all the risk of this task upon yourself – should you not have even just one of us three go with you?'

In the silvery half-light Calabos could see the worry in the Daemonkind's half-man, half-reptilian features, and his own trepidation almost made him change his mind. But he hardened his resolve.

'I understand your concerns, Qothan, but even the presence of just one of you would be enough to draw unwanted attention and suspicion.'

Qothan frowned but did not dissent, while Culri glared.

'This is an idiocy,' he said. 'You'll die in this place, and then what will it all have been for, eh?'

'Go in peace, Culri,' Calabos said as he put the helm back on. 'If we do fail, keep yourself alive, old man, and watch out for another, better hero.'

So saying he raised one hand in farewell to Kerna and Nilka, to Culri, to Qothan and Viras and Yostil, then strode away between two banks of benches towards a square open door in the far wall. It took an effort of will to keep walking.

But his judgement proved correct and he was able to avoid the various search patrols sweeping through the corridors, and once or twice managed to bluff his way past squads of Host guards. And as he climbed floor after floor, they became infrequent and even the sounds of battle grew quieter. Once he risked a glance from a small balcony on the twenty-second floor and looked down to see Byrnak's army gathered at the foot of the Citadel, and furious fighting taking place on some of the lowest balconies.

By the time he reached the twenty-ninth floor, there were no Black Host soldiers to be seen although a few formally attired men and women wearing masks passed him in the darkly opalescent corridors from time to time, or were noticed in rooms and halls that he walked by. The light changed too, becoming a little brighter and softer, almost pearly. On the thirtieth floor he doffed his helm but carried it in his right hand as he went in search of the next set of stairs.

The corridors and rooms here were busier, and everyone wore a mask of some kind, whether plain or elaborate, some like caricatures of faces, others resembling animals while a few attempted to depict an idea or quality like War or Death. Few if any regarded Calabos directly as he walked along, for which he was thankful, guessing that they saw him as far beneath notice.

Then his search took him into an oval room, along a high balcony where a handful of masked spectators were gazing down at something. When he went to the balustrade for a look, what he saw rooted him to the spot.

Two men were fighting with spear and net, a tall, grey-haired man in battered leather harness and a younger burlier man wearing furs and crude mail, his black hair tied back in tribal manner. The tall man was Ikarno Mazaret, and his opponent was the Mogaun chieftain, Yasgur. Yet their contest seemed more like mock fighting with both uttering stagey snarls and grunts as if they were play-acting.

'Quite a display, don't you think?' said a woman's voice from behind him. 'I don't particularly care for these puppet games but my husband promised them to the clades of the court, hence this.'

Without turning, he said, 'Your husband? Who would that be?'

She laughed. 'Why, the Duskgeneral, of course. Now which court clade are you from, may I ask?'

He turned to see a blonde-haired woman in a blue, high-collared gown and a winged half-mask decorated with shiny green feathers. For a moment he smiled as she regarded him, then her eyes widened, her smile faded and her mouth trembled.

'Highest, forgive me . . .' she stammered. 'We had no warning from the harbingers . . . and I would have recognized you – it has been a long time since you last used this guise. I might be the only one here who remembers it . . .'

Realization struck — *She thinks I'm him, the Great Shadow, come down from my throne to slum it with the mortals. This could be useful . . .*

'Your loyalty is most welcome but I do not wish attention drawn to myself so — calm composure will suffice.'

She nodded and forced a smile back into her lips.

'Good,' he said. 'Yes, these diversions are quite interesting — where does your husband obtain such subjects?'

'Oh, they are only rivenshades provided by the White Prison, highest.'

'Correct,' he said quickly. 'Can you show me other similar jousts?'

She nodded and led him through a series of chambers in which pairs of people both familiar and strange fought each other with a variety of weapons. As before, the fighting was more like a flourishing display than real combat, but as soon as first blood was drawn they went into a murderous frenzy. He saw an Alael and an Atroc attack each other with long cleavers — the sight made his blood run cold.

After that he asked her to show him the most direct path to 'his courts'. She gave him an odd look then took him down a mottled blue corridor where sombre-coloured tapestries showed scenes in motion, past a room where blood-red statues stood in iron-voiced chorus, through a purple-jewelled chamber from whose ceiling scores upon scores of limbs and heads hung and writhed, along a black-and-silver tiled gallery where mouths great and small spoke or snarled or muttered from the walls. Then as they climbed a spiral staircase, she paused a few steps ahead of Calabos and turned to look down at him with a sly smile.

'There is much about you that puzzles me,' she said. 'And much to think upon, and . . . I think that you are not the Great Shadow after all.' She laid a soft, accusatory fingertip on his armoured chest. 'I think that you are the other one, Byrnak — yes, you're the Twilight Lord from the other place and you've come to the Nightrealm to wrest away his power even as he invades your world! The symmetry is so daring.'

He smiled. 'Very perceptive of you, but aren't you afraid that I might have to kill you to maintain my secret?'

She sniffed. 'Your secret is safe, mighty Byrnak. Only I would recognize your face because I'm the oldest of the Duskgeneral's wives — the Highest last wore that appearance more than two thousand years ago, since when he has tended to blend and mingle features for his own amusement.'

'Two thousand years?' he said suddenly.

'Why, yes. It seems that Time is faster here than in your world and has become faster since the Triumph, which was about three thousand years ago . . . or is it four? As for you killing me — well, so far I'm still alive.'

With another smile she continued on up the stairs and he followed, his mind full of thoughts about Time. If the three centuries since the Shadowking war translated into three millennia or more here, then it was possible that no more than a day had passed since he and the Daemonkind had stepped through the Shattergate. If Tashil and the others were still holding out . . .

'Do you get to hear anything of the invasion of the other world?' he said. 'Does it go well?'

She shrugged. 'Black Host echelons are still being sent through the gates, and my husband divides his time between conducting the invasion and directing the defence of the citadel.' She laughed. 'How delicious! He's down on the battlements and you're already near the apex . . .'

From the top of the stairs they emerged into a wide, oval chamber that was dimmer and colder than the floors below. Small niche lamps cast a hard silver glow on the pentagonal tiles underfoot and the bas-relief sculptures of war that covered the walls. A ramp of shallow steps curved round the wall to a tall, open archway and as they climbed the air grew distinctly icy.

The archway led through darkling shadows and up a ramp to a wide platform open to the black, glittering canopy of the Nightrealm's sky. Ahead was an arresting view along the easterly cliffs with all their fortifications and towers while to the right was the entirety of the Nightrealm itself, a vertiginous, astonishing, reason-challenging carpet of buildings, a frozen avalanche of cities, its roofs and towers and lamp glints sloping away, merging into a distant, murky glimmer.

To the left of the arch a wide, plain stairway led up a dozen steps or so to an open gate in the cliff-edge battlements, passing between two slender and seemingly unmanned guard towers.

The Duskgeneral's masked wife was sitting on a low retaining wall that curved along to the foot of the cliff steps, and watching him closely.

'What will you do if you succeed?' she said. 'Will you free everyone from the White Prison, and replace them with us?' She shivered. 'It might be interesting to see them emerge, to see her.' She glanced over her shoulder at the cliffs. 'Sometimes, when I come up here, I can hear her calling to me – sometimes I can hear her weeping . . .' She stood and walked over to stare down at the Nightrealm. 'I've been alive too long, too many sights, too many memories. Perhaps you should kill me after all – the half-death might be a blessing, if that is what is in store for such as I . . .'

'I don't know what will happen if I succeed,' Calabos said. 'All this will change . . .'

'You could change that face of yours,' she said. 'Or mine – would you do that for me?'

He stared at her, with a cloud of half-suspicions coalescing in his thoughts.

'Well, since you've seen my face,' he said, 'Won't you show me yours, that I may come to the correct decision?'

'As you wish, ser.'

And when the feathered mask was removed, he saw that it was indeed Suviel Hantika.

He smiled sadly and fitted the Murknight helm back on his head, then adjusted the harnessing of the scabbard so that the sword of powers was in the right position for drawing over the shoulder.

'Have a care, lady,' he said. 'I am neither of those that you imagined me to be, but if Byrnak does come this way he would not hesitate to slay you.'

Without another word, he strode away from her and began to mount the stairs that led to the dream-courts of the Great Shadow.

When he left Tashil and Ayoni on that bushy slope, Coireg had been on the point of rebelling against his terrible duty. But he had already given the directions of their journey to Besarl and the others earlier so while fear and doubt racked him, the Daemonkind loyally lifted him into the night sky and commenced the flight towards Besh-Darok.

They flew across the dark straits of the Great Canal, the wide waterway created by the defeat of the Shadowkings when the dread towers Gorla and Keshada and their vast, encircling fortifications had collapsed into the tormented depths. A few moments later only the faint, radiant greyness of the Blight was beneath them, a smooth blanket whose dips and bumps were the only indication of natural landmarks, now smothered. The Daemonkind banked north and before long a wide stretch of the canal came into view in the darkness, a place where either bank bulged outward for this was where Keshada had stood three centuries ago.

The Daemonkind slowed and Besarl spoke above the flap and rush of beating wings.

'Is this close enough, friend Coireg?'

'Yes, but should we perhaps be lower . . . ?'

Besarl laughed. 'Have no worries – we shall not relax our grip and soon you shall be pastwalking with us in the pit of Time.'

Coireg nodded, trying to feel assured and calm even though his stomach was churning and his heart was racing. He knew that Captain Ondene had experienced this leap through time, as had Calabos, and it was the latter's account which was going through his mind, at least the unsettling parts thereof. He tried to tell himself to look forward to the unknown, to expect some kind of exhilaration . . . then Besarl said: 'Now, friend Coireg – close tight your eyes!'

Even as he did, his sense began to shift and gave the impression that he was suddenly moving in a circle very quickly. And although his eyes were shut, grey threads leaked into his vision from either side, turning silver as they interwove, then white as they began to coil into the centre. Then the spiralling hub of it surged towards him and he cried out as his sense of balance swung to and fro. His ears were full of his own voice and panicky breathing, hissing and roaring . . . but after an interminable time these sounds grew quieter and more rhythmic, even as the inpouring white traceries lost their meshlike texture, merging into an irregular whiteness rushing by beneath him . . .

A snowy landscape, its purity broken by trees, farmhouses, fences, and there was the rhythmic beating of Daemonkind wings bearing him through the sky. Ahead the towering mass of Keshada loomed and below he could see where a great number of riders had recently passed, churning the snow and mud right up to the tower's wide open gates.

'Shall we enter?' Besarl said.

Shivering, Coireg pointed up. 'The ramparts . . . will be quicker.'

They alighted on a deserted parapet where only grey banners moved listlessly in the fitful icy breeze. Coireg warmed himself by beating his hands against arms and legs, and thought of the journey that lay ahead, through Keshada to the chambers where the Lord of Twilight's realm had started to invade the world. From there they would fly across the Realm of Dusk to the vicinity of Hewn Mountain where he would discover if the Sleeping God's buried imperative would take them all into the death throes of the old after all, would carry them safely into the black dream of a ruined world . . .

Ikarno Mazaret would be there, fighting for dear life along with the rest, Bardow and Yasgur, Suviel and Gilly, Tauric and the witch-horses. But he would see none of them and would be unable to save any of them.

'I once had a brother,' he told Besarl as the Daemonkind handed him a torn, discarded tabard. 'I wish he could have known that I defeated my inner darkness and found the strength to stand against the outer. But even now he'll not know.'

'All that arises from the Void returns to the Void,' Besarl said. 'If you have done this, he will know.'

Coireg thought on this for a long, illuminated moment, then bowed deeply. 'Thank you, Besarl – I am changed by your words.'

'This is as it should be, friend Coireg,' the Daemonkind said. 'Shall we commence?'

'We shall.'

As Besarl led the way into the halls of Keshada, Coireg thought – *So this is the end which becomes the beginning, but will the beginning take us to a worthy end?*

Chapter Twenty-one

From the mountains I came,
With a song and a smile,
But with torch and sword,
I descend into the abyss.

Gundal, *The Doom Of Gleoras*, Ch. 2, v.

Hand over hand, with fingers punching holes and ledges in the sheer rock face, Byrnak climbed towards the fortified dream-courts of the Great Shadow. Below, the siege raged, with the most intense fighting taking place around two immense holes which the Mawl had bored in the outer wall before the defenders destroyed it with well-aimed sections of masonry. There was also a savage clash on one of the lower ramparts from which scaling ladders and nets hung.

It was a satisfyingly brutal sight. His demolition of Orlag Tower had earned him a reputation for ruthless, irresistible purpose which he turned to good account in his dealings with other district chieftains and leaders. Almost as important were the adepts who were drawn to his own overt mastery of the Wellsource, and persuaded by promises of tuition to pledge their loyalty.

The higher he climbed, the harder it was to distinguish among the press of warriors at the foot of the Citadel. The glimmering gloom blurred details and reduced those struggling thousands to a heaving, dark grey mass. Glancing down for a moment, he laughed and continued his ascent.

When he was halfway up he changed direction and traversed the cliff face towards the citadel and leaped onto a wide, ostentatiously carved balcony. From there he rose through the remaining floors of the citadel, killing all those he met. Crowds of foppish, masked people screamed and ran from the bifurcated black shard of a sword with which he slew and maimed.

This is the full pleasure of dominion, Byrnak thought. *And when I throw down the unworthy lord of this realm, I shall bring a new order to its every road and life. I shall need every hand and every back when I begin the true conquest of all the other worlds that lie beyond.*

As he strode bloody-handed through the halls, he turned part of his perceptions inward, curious to know if the original spirit of this host body was conscious of all that was transpiring. Past inspiralling veils Byrnak's inner eye flew till he came upon a narrow place where the opaque core of the man Ondene still resided, a misty knot of images and memories wrapped tightly around a dull spark, the embers of his hope, no doubt.

At last he reached a cold chamber and a curved ramp that led to the very roof of the citadel itself. Out in the icy darkness, with the silver-grey cliffside battlements stretching out to either side, Byrnak stood right at the edge of the rooftop platform, staring out over the Nightrealm, and roared and laughed in triumph and defiance. Then he turned to face the fortified cliffs and the great stairway that rose to an open gate, and with an easy agility ran across to climb the steps three at a time.

Slender towers topped by lookout chambers flanked the gate but both were as vacant as the flagstone street beyond. Yet for all the absence of guards or anyone, the sense of being watched by innumerable observers was all-pervading. Poised on the gate threshold, Byrnak glared at the dark windows of a tall, elaborate, flat-roofed building opposite, certain that he had glimpsed figures at them. Then he stepped across the threshold – and the building faded from sight as another, smaller one with steep, peaked roofs slowly appeared in its place. Moments later, it too dissolved into a pillared temple with a bell tower jutting into the road.

Such transformations were taking place all around him as he walked warily along the street that led straight on from the gate. A city of silent, impermanent buildings, walls and gables that melted into one another, doors that stretched into yard entrances, archways that shrank to windows. And roads which changed direction, became dead-ends, or even grew new junctions and side streets.

Byrnak glowered as the road he was following was suddenly cut off by the flowing appearance of a row of terraced cottages, just as a large villa on his right parted to reveal a new turning. He knew that he was being steered through this flickering, hazy maze, and knew that he could seize control of it if he wanted, and freeze everything in place.

'Play your games,' he bellowed to the changing waves of masonry. 'It will only delay your doom, not alter it!'

As he strode down the opened way, other details came to his notice, like the huge, dark columns that rose from the midst of these mutable courts and stretched up to vanish in the upper darkness. Also, as nearby buildings and those beyond twisted through their changes, he would occasionally catch a glimpse of something else as changeless as the towering columns, a massive, sloping dais almost half a mile away, up whose face a rack of steps rose to a wide platform where there was a throne in the shape of a huge, upraised sword. Behind the throne was a pale grey, faintly mottled wall stretching some distance above and to either side, while upon the throne itself . . .

Was there a shadow-swathed figure seated there? Did burning eyes full of ancient hate gaze steadily across that intervening distance? Byrnak could make out no details but did feel the pressure of that implacable presence, to which he uttered a burst of harsh laughter and walked on.

Roads closed and roads opened, alleys turned back on themselves, stairways became bridges. Then the street he was following narrowed to a brick passage ending in an antechamber with an archway which led out to a pillared cloister encircling the packed earth of an arena. Tiers of seats banked back on all sides, and they were crowded with onlookers, only it was a crowd as wayward and spectral as the buildings of the Great Shadow's dream-courts. And just as silent.

But Byrnak was unconcerned with such spectators, knowing that his arrival here presaged a duel with either the Great Shadow himself or his champion. Would it be the Duskgeneral, he wondered, or some other monstrous servant?

'I am ready,' he bawled to the wavering watchers. 'Come forth to your defeat!'

For a moment, nothing, only the jostling crowds, soundlessly laughing and talking, changing seats, pointing down at the arena floor, all a fluctuating throng. Then a figure emerged from the shadowed cloisters on the other side, a man garbed in the armour of a Murknight and carrying a longsword on his back. Yet he knew immediately that this was not the Duskgeneral – he knew what aura-taste to expect from that one. No, this was another . . . who nevertheless provoked an undercurrent of familiarity in him.

'Who are you?' he sneered. 'What feeble opponent has the Great Nothing sent out in his cowardly stead?'

The Murknight made no reply, instead reached for the hilt jutting over his shoulder and drawing out a long, straight blade which glittered silver and green. As Byrnak looked at it, something in him quailed.

'I have come here to put an end to gods and would-be gods,' the Murknight said. 'Not to grovel before them.'

Byrnak's anger at the thread of quivering fear within surged into rage at these words. 'You'll do more than grovel when I'm done with you!' he snarled, then drew his own sword and charged.

Calabos had followed a similar route through the maze city, more than once pausing to glance backwards when he felt that he was being followed. But when he saw no one he continued on his way past the variable exteriors of buildings and down the roads which seemed to beckon to him. He was crossing a stone bridge, whose balustrade decoration changed three times on his way across, when running footsteps made him turn quickly, hand reaching for his sword.

But it was the old man Culri who came to a staggering halt before him, bending to lean on his knees, gasping for breath.

'Curse these . . . deranged . . . streets . . .'

'Curse you for being a stubborn old man,' Calabos said. 'This is the very heart of peril! Go back, now!'

Regaining his breath, Culri mopped sweat from his face with a grubby sleeve. 'I've come a long way for this and now I'll see it through to the end.'

Calabos shook his head. 'You're a fool, old man.' Then he turned to resume walking.

'Ah, yes, I've been a fool and worse before this, Calabos,' Culri said with a chuckle. 'But in such a venture, are you any less of a fool than I?'

'Perhaps, since I know more about the danger than you.'

Their conversation continued in this bantering style for a time, interspersed with observations and speculations on the inconstant city through which they travelled. Before long, they were heading along a narrow street only to have the buildings on either side curve inwards to form the arched roof of a dim tunnel which sloped down and ended in the darkened cloister of an arena.

From the shadows Calabos watched the fur-and-mail-clad figure of Corlek Ondene emerge from another archway, his face almost aglow with the force of the spirit which possessed him. As he roared his challenge at the ghostly throngs who crowded the arena seats, Culri glanced at Calabos, then the Ondene-Shadowking, and back.

'Is this it?' he said under his breath. 'Is this where all beginnings end?'

'Stay out of sight,' Calabos told him and strode out from the shadows.

'No, wait . . .'

The Shadowking calling himself Byrnak looked round at Calabos and sneered. 'Who are you? What feeble opponent has the Great Nothing sent out in his cowardly stead?'

Calabos felt the power radiating from Byrnak and knew he was much stronger than before. He could also feel the heat of the Wellsource stirring at the edges of his own senses, hungrily waiting. *Too soon for that*, he thought as he reached up for the hilt of the sword of powers, drew it across his shoulder and held it two-handed before him.

'I have come to put an end to gods and would-be gods,' he said. 'Not to grovel before them.'

A trembling rage seized Byrnak and his distorted features reddened.

'You'll do more than grovel when I'm done with you!'

Then he wrenched out his blade, a five-foot jagged black shard, raised it behind and across his shoulders and charged.

Calabos watched the black blade coming, gauging Byrnak's onrushing force and the likely arc of the attack. When it came, the pitch-black sword made a faint keening sound as it sliced the air, cutting straight through the spot where Calabos' neck had been. Calabos had dived forward at the crucial moment, half-turning and trying to hook Byrnak's feet with one of his legs. But Byrnak spotted this ploy and leaped over the entrapping limb, stumbling a step or two even as Calabos rolled to his feet.

They faced each other for a long moment, and Calabos could sense Byrnak's hate rolling off him, a palpable corrosive. Then the Shadowking stepped forward with a thrust that Calabos ducked, then a second and a third. Then he made a fourth which turned into a savage cross cut which Calabos met with a heavy parry that turned into a trial of strength.

As the two blades ground against each other, Calabos heard the sword of powers give forth a faint discordant note of frustration as it failed to bite into the other.

Byrnak grinned across the locked swords.

'I took this little cutter off one of those Overseers,' he said, 'then cut him to pieces with it – I wonder how well yours cleaves offal!'

'This is not a butcher's weapon,' Calabos said, turning suddenly towards where Byrnak was holding the hilt of his sword, letting his own blade go down. As Byrnak staggered forward, Calabos lifted one foot and rammed it into his side, throwing him off-balance. Byrnak roared in fury but managed to roll through the fall and regain his feet. He gave Calabos a murderous, hooded stare.

'Enough jousting,' he growled and flung out his free hand. Blazing knots of power leaped from it and streaked towards Calabos. Even as they were in flight, he charged. Calabos reached instinctively for the Lesser Power and found himself mentally grappling with the turbulent force of the Nightrealm's version of the Wellsource, to which the Great Shadow had wedded both the Lesser Power and the Earthmother's Gift. He struggled to form

the thought-canto Cadence, not because he could not envisage its
elements but because the circle was too easily disrupted by the
power on which he was drawing. Then it was too late and the
bolts of Sourcefire reached him . . . and the sword of powers swept
and caught them all on the flat of its blade which shone and rang
with a new, rich tone.

Byrnak saw this happen as he lunged forward, bringing his
sword down in a vertical blow. And Calabos saw doubt in his eyes
in those last fractions of a second, and brought up his glowing
sword to block the downward stroke. And this time when the
black blade met the silver-green, it broke with a loud iron crack
which reverberated around the arena. Calabos wasted no time and
struck home, thrusting the sword of powers into Byrnak's side,
almost to the hilt.

A look of utter disbelief was stark upon the Shadowking's face.
Calabos, gasping for breath, imagined for a moment that he could
feel that impalement, an echo of a memory left to him by the
original Byrnak . . .

Then the Shadowking before him, clothed in the flesh of Corlek
Ondene, sank to his knees, one trailing hand still limply holding
the shattered stump of his sword.

'What is . . . happening . . . ?' The Shadowking gazed up at
Calabos. 'How can you be . . . standing there . . . ?'

Calabos swiftly pulled the sword out, and the blade bore not a
smear or spot of blood. Byrnak looked frozen with horror, quivering eyes darting here and there as unsettling whispering sounds
leaked from his slack lips. Then the first spirit-wraith began to
emerge from his upper chest, a darkly opaque and writhing mass
oozing from beneath layers of fur and chain mail. Byrnak's eyes
rolled back, showing the whites, and a second tore itself away from
him, and a third and a fourth . . .

Suddenly Culri was at Calabos' side, tugging on his arm.

'Calabos, use the sword on me . . .'

'What? Have you lost your mind?'

'Quickly, curse you!' the old man cried. 'You don't have to use
a killing stroke – just piercing the skin should be enough . . .'

Angry, Calabos shook him off. 'Leave me be . . .'

But then Culri shrieked in fear, staring past Calabos who turned to see a dark flock of spirit-wraiths converging on him. He backed away in panic, almost choking on nightmarish fear, hacking madly at them with the sword of powers, but even severed they still came on . . .

Then he was engulfed in a swirl of grey forms which one by one dived into his flesh. He ceased to feel his body as a normal carriage of skin and bone but as some hollow shell which shook with the incursion of every intruder, which rang with a growing rapacious chorus, but in which his own cries of terror were increasingly drowned out. Eventually the last spirit-wraith sank into his unwilling flesh, leaving him sprawled on the floor of the arena, leaning on one elbow while his other hand still gripped his sword. It was deathly quiet now and even the soundless, restless crowds were gone, although Corlek Ondene lay groaning on his back some distance away and Culri was staring wide-eyed and fearful from the cloisters.

Within Calabos chaos ruled, a raging tumult of maddening voices. His attempts to envision this grotesque invasion depicted it as monsters battling amid a sea-storm, or fanged predators fighting across a shifting desert, or fire-creatures skirmishing in a cavern of black ice. But now an ashen army of macabre phantoms fought and clashed there, some seeking domination while others tried to grow stronger by devouring those who were weaker . . .

Through the powerless misery of his prostrate posture, he became aware of Culri crawling towards him on hands and knees, while of Ondene there was no sign. Soon the old man was close enough to warily poke his shoulder.

'Use the sword, Calabos,' he said, tears in his eyes.

'Could not . . . even if . . . I wanted,' he managed.

'You have to, somehow!' Culri glanced over his shoulder. '*He* is bringing us to him!'

Then Calabos noticed that beyond the arena, the flickering buildings of the Great Shadow's dream-courts were flowing past on either side as the arena moved steadily towards the immense sword throne dais. And he could imagine a great dark figure upon the throne, beckoning with a crooked finger . . . but was that his imaginings, or did he truly see that?

'You have to take the sword and pierce me with it, Calabos,' Culri said. 'I once had a brother, you know, a mighty warrior who would have been surprised to know that I could remain loyal to my duty, especially for three and a half thousand years, my duty to the Sleeping God . . .'

'How can you . . . know about the . . . Sleeping . . . ?' Then he paused as a suspicion of astounding enormity began to form in his mind.

'I had to find the end to find the beginning,' the old man said. 'Then wait for the end to come round again so that I could bring you the Sleeping God's gift. Find the strength, Calabos, use the sword.'

'Coireg . . .' Calabos muttered, gripped by anguish.

'The very same . . .'

'I cannot . . .' Then something black clawed its way to the front of his mind and spoke: '*I will grant your wish, worm!*'

The spirit-wraith drew back his sword and plunged it into Coireg's chest, then twisted the blade. Calabos howled with fury and sorrow and wrenched back control of his body, but only in time to see his old friend die on the arena floor beside him, and all he could do with his strengthless form was inch his hand onto Coireg's outflung arm.

Then a strange thing happened – something pale and opaque appeared in Coireg's open, dead eyes, then passed out of them, a small, slowly twisting scrap of gossamer which for a moment or two just glided towards Calabos, drifting serenely through the air . . . then leaped suddenly at his eyes. Before he could react it was there, a flash of white that spiralled down into the recesses of his mind. And there, in the wreck of his mind, amid the roaring confusion of savage spirits, he found himself with a bright spine of light, picturing it held in his hand like a dazzling sword . . .

The sword of the mind, whispered a fading voice he knew could only be Coireg's, his final words.

He knew what he had to do and, from his view of the arena's progress through the mutable city, he knew that he had little enough time to do it in.

Tame all these frenzied spirits, break the urge of their voracious desire, bind them to his will, *then* hope that somehow they could help him stand against the Great Shadow.

And somehow I doubt that he'll do me the favour of confining himself to swordplay.

When the Shadowking Byrnak disintegrated into a swarm of spirit-wraiths tearing themselves from his body, Corlek Ondene wanted to utter a scream of exultation. Yet even as the last of them departed, fleeing the radiant presence left by Calabos' sword, Ondene was left struggling to regain control of his faculties, trying to cope with senses that had been battered and distorted by the savage usurper Byrnak.

The glimmering dusk of the Nightrealm seemed like a dense welter of shadows. He lay on the hard dirt floor of the arena and groaned, vaguely aware of voices a short way off. Then a trembling mote of light appeared above him, growing as he watched into a pale grey oval which looked for all the world like a pair of hands raised to a face. The apparition then swiftly elongated into a featureless misty figure who lowered its hands to reveal the face of a young man.

'Corlek,' he said. 'You have to move, you have to get out of the arena – look, there's a few archways over there . . .' A flickery outstretched hand pointed.

'Wh . . . why . . . ?' he managed, the word feeling like stones in his throat.

'We have a task, you and I, just as Coireg and Calabos have, so come now – up! Or do you wish to face the Great Shadow in your current state?'

Ondene almost laughed at that, but forced himself onto his knees then lurched upright and staggered over to the perfect black of the cloisters, following the pale spectre through one of the arches. Beyond it, he was led along roads flanked by deforming, distorting buildings, dark and surreal frontages that exuded menace and madness. More than once he called out to the pale figure as it wove and floated on ahead, asking its name, wanting to know where it was taking him, demanding to know, cursing it for not answering yet still stumbling on after it, fearing the alternative.

At last, after a score of louring streets, a trail of sepulchral canyons all woven into an endlessly changing maze, Ondene emerged from a high-walled passageway to find his spectral guide waiting in a curiously static chamber decorated with relief geometric patterns, except that every line was in the form of a chain.

'You have done well to regain body control so soon after an expulsion,' the apparition said.

'So – are you ready to tell me just who you are?' Ondene said through gritted teeth.

'You know who I am,' came the reply. 'On the towertop at Nydratha, amid the perpetual storm, the Sleeping God looked deep into you and examined your every thought, and laid bare the possible threads of your fate. And I did so, too.'

Ondene struggled to understand. 'When I was trapped in the Shadowking's shadow chains, I felt that there was some kind of spark in there with me, one small flame in the dark – was that you?'

'It was merely the bond that joined me to you, one weak enough for the Shadowking to pass over yet strong enough to survive all his casual brutalities. Thus I am here.'

'And who are you?'

The ghostly youth smiled faintly and shrugged. 'You may call me Tauric, though the name is to me as the seed is to the tree.'

Ondene stared, scarcely believing it. 'And I brought you all the way from Nydratha?'

'You brought the bond,' Tauric said. 'Is this sufficient for you because we have little enough time left for what has to be done – the battle between Calabos and the Great Shadow is about to begin.'

'And what is our task?'

'We are to free a few prisoners,' the spectral Tauric said as he led the way out of the chain-adorned chamber. Ondene followed down a short, plain passage beyond whose end he caught sight of a pale wall mottled with shadows. Then he emerged from the passageway and beheld the White Prison.

A wall of foggy, frosted grey stretched up and up and up, becoming lost in the ice-black heights of the Nightrealm. It loomed to the right, almost to where the rear wall of the courts met the cliff-edge fortifications; to the left it extended to the stepped incline of the massive throne dais and beyond. But everywhere upon its deathly, opaque surface was proof of its countless captives, be it jutting, frozen limbs and heads, or faces gazing wide-eyed and softly blurred beneath the surface, or the uncertain dark shapes of those buried deeper.

Ondene approached the wall, his thoughts gripped by a kind of fascinated dread as he contemplated the people trapped within it. Here was a bearded man in his middle years, frozen in the act of clutching a book to his chest; next to him, a young man dressed like a farm worker but holding a broken sword in his hand; there, a matronly woman shielding a boy child with one arm and holding out the other; further along, a warrior in battered armour, his fists held clenched at his side,

'Here are all the vanquished,' the ghostly Tauric said. 'The courageous and the foolhardy, all determined to overthrow the Great Shadow, and all doomed to fail. Places like the Nightrealm are founded on the wild exercise of power and gods are the manifest dreams of power. Thus in this place, only a dream can defeat a dream.'

Ondene gave a wry laugh. 'You?'

'So I hope,' Tauric said. 'But speaking as a dream, I cannot do this alone.'

Ondene reached out to touch the wall of the White Prison, and snatched his hand away from the raw bite of bitter cold.

'How can we free them from this?'

Tauric drifted closer. 'By waking them from the dream.' And so saying, he raised one hand and lightly tapped Ondene on the shoulder.

A wave of stinging coldness flashed through him and he staggered forward with surprise, put out a hand reflexively . . . and gasped when it passed through the opaque surface unimpeded.

'Step into it,' Tauric said. 'I will lead you through this ice-bound dungeon, but be ready for strife – the enemy awaits us at the prison's heart.'

The pale Tauric then calmly glided into the grey wall and after a moment's hesitation, Ondene walked after him, closing his eyes just before his face met the opaque surface . . .

. . . and opened them to find himself drifting amid numberless, frozen prisoners, looking up and down and seeing them in their hundreds, receding into foggy murk. Tauric was above him, a gauzy figure beckoning, so he looked in that direction and began floating up. Together they wove in and among the captives and as they did so Tauric touched this one or that with the stroke of translucent fingers across a forehead or a tap on the shoulder. Blank eyes filled with emotion, heads turned and limbs jerked into life, and when Ondene glanced back he saw a string of them following . . .

Quite soon a long channel of brightness appeared out of the gloom and several moments later Ondene emerged into a shining, glassy corridor lit by tiny lamps whose silvery radiance reflected from every surface. Ondene could see that the passage's far end opened out into some kind of chamber drenched in an emerald glow, and when he pointed that way Tauric nodded.

'You will need strength and purpose for what is to come,' he said. 'And much else besides.'

Then suddenly he was flying away towards the end, and when Ondene gave chase he discovered that the ice of the White Prison was hard underfoot. When he reached the chamber he saw that it was a large, glittering concavity lined with frozen faces, and with a wide round hole at the centre encircled by a low wall. A flashing green refulgence poured up from it, spreading bright highlights all around the chamber and casting an emerald hue upon Tauric who was standing by the open hole, staring across it at a figure clad in dark, highly ornamented armour which encased him from head to toe.

'Welcome to the chaining room of the White Prison, shortly to become your new home.' The figure made a sketch of a bow. 'I am the Duskgeneral, guardian of the Nightrealm, commander of the Black Host.' His visored helm turned towards Tauric. 'I knew someone dangerous was approaching but never imagined that it would be you. It must disappointing for you to discover how weak your allies are.'

The ghostly Tauric shook his head. 'Oh no, not disappointed, but I am surprised at how insecure *you* seem to be. Your vast armies, your towers of Overseers, your Citadel and even that armour you're wearing – it all suggests that both you and your master feel very precarious indeed. Surely you have the courage to at least show us your face.'

For a long, tense moment there was no response, then as Ondene watched the Duskgeneral made a small gesture and the faceguard of his helm melted away to reveal the pallid features of a young man who in every respect resembled Tauric. An ugly hate filled the eyes, even though the lips smiled sardonically.

'Ah, smug sanctimony, a long absent but not entirely forgotten miasma,' he said. 'You sound like one of those Rootpriests – I'm sure you remember how well they fared after the destruction of their sorcerous powers. You should ready yourself for a similar fate.'

'You should be more concerned about your own fate,' Ondene said. 'When Calabos defeats your master . . .'

The Duskgeneral–Tauric directed a contemptuous glance at him. 'What is this that you've brought to this place? What capering pet?'

'This, my dear Duskgeneral, is the Prince of Change,' said the pale Tauric. 'He is your doom.' He turned to the glittering curved wall and made a beckoning gesture. At once, a translucent female figure emerged from it, bowed briefly to him then glided smoothly over to Ondene, arms outstretched. Ondene stared fearfully at her approach, flinching when she reached him, and as she slipped into his form he heard a voice say, '*Greetings, Corlek – my name is Ffion . . .*'

'Enough of this infantile masquerade,' the Duskgeneral snarled. 'Let's have an end to it.'

He drew forth a curved, black sword whose ridges and grooves captured the green glow of the Wellsource. Then he came round the well towards Ondene who backed away, looking imploringly at the ghostly Tauric.

'How can I . . . ?' was all he got out before the Duskgeneral was upon him, swinging his vicious warblade down towards his neck. Crying out, he instinctively raised his arm to ward against the blow, catching the edge on his upper arm . . .

The blade shattered, hot green traceries of power flaring from the pieces as they flew. Ondene felt the shock of the impact but no wound or pain, only the force of it which threw him and the Duskgeneral backwards. At the same time, he heard a fading cry from within: the woman Ffion, he was certain. In the next instant, a second apparition, male this time, detached himself from the wall and swooped down towards him. And Ondene heard:

'*Greetings, Corlek — my name is Shaleng.*'

The spectral Tauric spoke to him as he swayed upright.

'You are the Prince of Change, Corlek — you are the weapon that will master him . . .'

'My hands will do what my sword could not,' growled the Duskgeneral-Tauric who charged, mailed fists flailing.

Ondene locked his own hands together, ducked the swinging arms and slammed a mighty blow into the centre of that armoured chest. The Duskgeneral was knocked off his feet with such force that he turned over to land on one side. The clashing impulse only made Ondene stagger but still he heard a faint, expiring shout in his mind . . . and again, a misty figure flitted down from the chamber wall, whose frozen faces now seemed to look on with a desperate intensity.

'*Greetings, Corlek — my name is Avalti.*'

And in his mind the ghostly Tauric said, 'Fight him — your every blow will erode his godhead.'

Thus with each successive clash, Ondene became more confident while the Duskgeneral grew steadily weaker. And a procession of fleeting presences came to Ondene, sacrificing themselves so that he could continue the battle.

So at last the armour was cracked and ruined, and the face was bruised and bloody, yet still the Duskgeneral fought to rise. As Ondene watched, he seemed to gain a little strength as the Wellsource's radiance pulsed brighter in the icy chamber. Then the ghostly Tauric was by Ondene's side.

'The conflict between Calabos and the Great Shadow hangs on a knife edge,' he said. 'Yet we must trust that it will end in victory, and prepare for that eventuality.'

'Are we going to try and destroy the Wellsource, as before at the end of the Shadowking war?' Ondene said.

The pale Tauric shook his head. 'There is no Void here which could absorb or heal the ravaging consequences of such an act. No – the only course open to us is to seal the Wellsource off from this world for ever.'

Then he drifted forward, enveloping Ondene with his mistlike form for a second, then his presence was there in Ondene's thoughts like a river of song.

'So, let us prepare.'

Ondene understood his intent and purpose, seized the feebly struggling Duskgeneral and hauled him across to the low wall around the Wellsource. Just inside, a series of narrow steps spiralled down into the dazzling depths and without hesitation he climbed over, dragging the Duskgeneral with him.

Calabos' campaign to quell the spirit-wraiths with the sword of the mind had turned into a running battle throughout the vaulted heights and crumbling crypts of his thoughts. They soon understood the nature of this new threat and began to act in concert against him, then started to join together, unifying into larger ones . . .

All the while the dark arena progressed towards the huge throne dais, and odd silhouettes and glimmering shafts of silver chased each other across the dirt floor. As Calabos snatched the occasional glance at their destination, it seemed that there was a tall dark figure, cloaked in writhing shadows, standing up on that dais, beckoning . . .

Within, Calabos took the fight to the largest of the spirit-wraiths which, in his mind, took the form of a squirming, many-tentacled horror not unlike the sea god Grath. With the sword of the mind he hacked off tendrils and long, coiling cables and wove a web of white symbols about it. The spirit-wraith tried to escape by dividing itself but could not achieve such an act of self-dismemberment. Then the symbol-net flashed and the spirit-wraith was his, its voracious desire broken, its will bound to his own. And when he turned it loose on its lesser brethren, they soon succumbed to the potent stealth of the sword of the mind.

When he opened his eyes upon the arena, its smooth passage

was slowing to a halt and the leading edge of its structure was transforming into a tall ceremonial arch as the foot of the throne dais stairs came nearer, ever nearer. Still grasping the sword of powers, and with the cowed spirit-wraiths poised and obedient in his mind, he got to his feet and saw a dark, cloaked figure coming down the stairs.

I know all about you, Calabos, said a mountainous voice. **I know all about the sword of powers and the flensing of the original Byrnak — but your singular weapon cannot harm me since I cannot be expelled from myself. I am whole and indivisible — I am the master of all ritual, I create beginnings and endings.**

The Great Shadow deliberately descended the last few steps then stalked through the ceremonial archway and into the arena. The deepest shadows seemed to condense about him like the ragged tails of a huge cloak, with only half-glimpsed details of heavy barbaric armour, and the merest suggestions of a face, the dull, emerald glitter of an eye, the grained ivory of teeth bared in a snarl. The rest was swamped in darkness.

Calabos casually hefted the sword of powers and balanced it over his shoulder, almost striking a pose of theatrical audacity. *I don't know if bombast and swagger is of any use at this crux,* he thought. *But they certainly feel right and besides, I am after all my own audience!*

'Know this, o mighty pestilence,' he said. 'I have come to cast down your throne and break your crown, and I have not come alone.'

As he said this, the tame spirit-wraiths in his mind were preparing several thought-cantos and even discussing among themselves possible tactics.

There is a thin line between defiance and insolence, the Great Shadow said, his voice rolling like thunder around the arena. **But I am not unforgiving — bow down before me, pledge your undying loyalty and I shall withhold my burning need for retribution. You would prove valuable to my growing dominion — I could give you a new name, the Dawngeneral, perhaps ...**

Calabos uttered a disdainful laugh. 'The captain offers passage aboard his sinking ship,' he said. 'How generous, how oblivious to your encroaching doom.'

You should awake to the reality of what surrounds you, Calabos – you may have defeated that crippled image of myself, but do not imagine that his broken fragments offer a way of doing me the slightest harm. You are at the heart of my realm, embraced by peril – all that remains is for me to decide the manner of your passing.

The dark shifting shape of the Great Shadow had come to a halt near the centre of the arena so, smiling, Calabos began to pace leisurely around him.

'What made you do it, I wonder?' he said. 'You have an entire world here in which to stage your every whim and fancy and a population open to every machination of compulsion and persuasion. Yet through the veil of time and happenstance you have tunnelled to lay hands upon my world – why? What reason could prompt such an aggressive outbreak?'

The Great Shadow's laughter was deep and wide and full of menace.

What reason do I need besides the guiding star of my divine inspiration and the rule of might?

Calabos' smile widened a notch. 'Ah yes – what you can reach you can grasp; what you can grasp you can take.'

Exactly – all else is either subordinate or a distraction, much like you.

The tall figure then raised an arm into the air, and ragged shadows rippled up it like hungry smoke, coalescing into the shape of a heavy, double-headed battle-axe, its black surfaces elaborately etched, its haft weighted with a large, silvery jewel. As Calabos watched, the upper tines of the axe blades began to glow with a hard, white radiance and the Great Shadow spoke.

I am the source of beginnings in this place, and also the father of endings – here is yours!

He swept the axe down to level it at Calabos. In that instant, Calabos felt fear and an intense alarm from senses stretched wide by the protective activities of the spirit-wraiths within. Afterwards, he was not sure if it was his own instincts or theirs which saved him, but there was a reflex urge to leap backwards and a swift casting of the thought-canto Ram to carry him further than his legs could manage. There was a darkening of the prevalent gloom and a sound like a thousand mouths sighing in the moment before . . .

Before something immense came crashing down on the spot where Calabos had been standing. It was a building, a tower of some kind that struck the ground at an angle, spire first. Calabos landed near the pillared cloister just an instant before it did and even as he rolled he felt the gigantic impact and heard the shattering din. The tower broke and the crushing, collapsing weight sent cracked masonry flying in all directions. On hands and knees and still holding the sword of powers, Calabos scrambled behind one of the cloister columns as chunks of stone banged and thudded to left and right. A large spinning piece struck the third column along from his position, smashing it into splintered debris.

At last the roar of destruction faded to nothing, a silence disturbed by the click and rattle of small fragments seeking rest.

And footsteps.

Calabos rose from his crouch, turned and moved out from the cloister shadows. The fallen tower lay across the arena in a long mound of rubble around which a fine haze of dust was settling. Of the Great Shadow there was no sign but there were others there instead, five others whose names he knew all too well.

'Ah, our brother,' Thraelor said with a languidly cruel smile.

'Our lost brother,' said Kodel, regarding Calabos thoughtfully.

'Our treacherous brother,' growled Ystregul, the Black Priest.

'Our reluctant brother,' Grazaan said grimly.

'Our enemy brother,' said Byrnak. 'Come to break thrones and crowns, to pit himself against us and ultimately to fail. Concede the futility of your task, brother, and join us.'

Calabos stared back at the face that was so like his own, then surveyed the rest. All five Shadowkings were arrayed in a curve before him, all attired in fabulously intricate suits of armour seemingly fashioned from a gleaming opaque substance, each with a different colour, gold, crimson, jade, amber, and blue. And each bore a long-hafted, double-headed battle-axe.

He laughed and shook his head, while conferring inwardly with his spirit-wraiths.

'So you would rather indulge in this play-acting,' Calabos said. 'This dance of masks amongst the shadows. Forgive me, but I have no desire to take part in your little ritual. Put off your masks and face me, or are you truly the Great Nothing?'

The Shadowkings in turn all shook their heads and in unison said, 'The insolence of an insect,' then suddenly leaped forward. Calabos lurched backwards, thinking they were coming for him but instead they converged on a spot several yards in front of him. Their forms darkened and grew amorphous, merging as they rushed together into a single, tall figure cloaked in writhing shadows.

You will be consumed, the Great Shadow thundered. **The devouring of your flesh will become a new ritual for the Nightrealm**.

Again, Calabos felt the panicky, piercing warning and threw himself sideways, just as something burst up out of the arena floor. At first he thought it was a rough pillar as thick as a man, then saw it bend and curve down towards him, black jaws gaping in an eyeless head. Like a grotesque serpent of stone, it undulated in his direction, forcing him to run. The Great Shadow's laughter boomed around the arena as a second, a third and a fourth erupted from the rubble-strewn floor and began seeking him out. The murky half-light of the cloisters could not conceal him from their pursuit and as he dodged and dashed from their snapping heads, he knew that the moment of extremity was upon him.

To the bound spirit-wraiths within he said — *The time is now. Are you prepared?*

(*Yes, Calabos, but we will need something more to be sure of victory.*) *What?*

(*The sword of the mind's pattern rests in your inner thoughts — release it to us and we will destroy this god for you.*)

He hesitated for only a moment or two, during which he sidestepped a lunging stone serpent and dealt it a blow with the sword of powers, which merely clanged and rebounded.

It is yours, he said. *Go!*

As he released them, his senses blurred and he seemed to see himself from several angles at once, crouched behind a tilted section of tower wall. Then the spirit-wraiths glided away from him, their forms vaguely manlike, dark knots of hands holding blazing white blades while all their faces were his own.

In his mind's eye he followed them as they flew up to where the Great Shadow hovered above the rubble mound and converged upon him there. As battle commenced, Calabos found himself darting madly from the stone serpents who redoubled their savage attacks. They were also more closely co-ordinated, keeping him trapped in the section of the cloisters across which the tower had fallen. Only the rubble and wreckage that was piled on the rampart above the cloister and down onto the arena offered any kind of refuge. In his mind's eye, he could see how the spirit-wraiths had surrounded the Great Shadow, and were attacking him with swift hacking lunges. But his own situation was becoming precarious as the stone serpents began ramming their heads into the sheltering rubble, steadily knocking it away.

The impacts not only peppered him with sharp fragments, they also threatened to collapse the slope of shattered masonry at his back. One of the stone serpents was now visible, its toothless, jaws thudding shut just a few feet away. Calabos watched the encroaching sorcerous beasts with bleak grimness, trying to gauge his chances of ducking past either of them then running for some other more likely bolthole . . .

Then the fleeting images in his mind went black. An awful sense of dread gripped him before a deafening bellowing came from the stone serpents which thrashed about for a moment before falling to the ground with a massive shattering sound. As the reverberating echoes faded away, Calabos warily emerged from his refuge and looked around at the arena. The serpents lay in broken pieces upon the floor, while a turmoil in the heights above the dream-courts cast shifting patches of radiance across the now-unchanging nearby buildings.

(*Calabos* . . .)

He glanced about this half of the arena and up at the long mound of rubble. Seeing nothing, he trusted to his undersenses and hurried through the cloister to the other side of the arena and saw a tall dark figure waiting there. It made no move as he approached, and as he came nearer he could see that its shadowy bulk was flickering, almost rippling. Closer still, he saw the features of the Great Shadow but his form was now a patchwork of his own funereal substance and the smoky shapes of Calabos' spirit-wraiths moving in a slow swirl around him.

(*Calabos — the Great Shadow cannot be destroyed. The very essence of his being runs through the Wellsource and is bound tightly to the under-pinnings of the Nightrealm.*)

Hearing the spirit-wraiths tell him this with his own face while unhurriedly weaving around the Great Shadow's darkling form was greatly unsettling, and his heart sank.

'Is there nothing that we can do?' he said.

(*Something has already been done — Corlek Ondene . . . and another, await us at the heart of the White Prison, by the Wellsource itself. The Duskgeneral has been subdued but as with the Great Shadow it cannot last. However, Ondene's companion insists that there is a solution.*)

'Which is?'

(*Exile. The Great Shadow must be taken to the Wellsource, but we are unable to move him as all our powers are devoted to subjugating him.*)

Calabos stared at the eerily calm images of his own face drifting around the frozen darkness of the Great Shadow.

'So what are you asking of me?'

(*We do not ask — we can only offer the solution. It is for you to decide. In this case, the only way to move the Great Shadow is for you to carry him to the Wellsource yourself. It will be a taxing burden, in many ways.*)

Calabos swallowed hard.

'To become a host for him, you mean.'

(*You will be bearing us too — whatever ruse of deceit he tries to employ, we shall be there to keep him shackled and you safe.*)

'And how would I do this?'

(*Walk forward into this form of his. Your sight will dim for a moment then return. And we must not tarry in this.*)

Calabos breathed in deeply, then laughed. He gazed up at the shifting high gloom and the huge pillars that rose up to vanish there. Then he glanced at the throne dais and the pale, looming wall of the White Prison. But when he stepped determinedly into that dark embrace it was with eyes tight shut.

The shaft leading down to the fount of the Wellsource was like the neck of a bottle, its bright, emerald narrowness widening to a dim, grey cavern. From the very centre of the hard, flat floor the burning flux of the Wellsource rose in a quivering column of power too bright for ordinary eyes. Ondene was standing a few feet away, watching over the sullen, glowering figure of the Duskgeneral–Tauric while the other, spectral Tauric was investigating the Wellsource, studying it closely.

'You cannot win,' the Duskgeneral was muttering. 'My master's essence and power is spread throughout the Nightrealm. It matters not if you bring him here and disperse that which you hold captive, for he will rise again.'

'So you say,' Ondene said. 'But since you have nothing to say that I wish to hear, you are only wasting your breath.'

'Unfortunately, he is telling the truth,' said the other Tauric.

Dismayed, Ondene turned to regard him, shielding his sight from the Wellsource's dazzle, but before he could speak a newcomer descended from the entry shaft and clambered down the rough blocks which bridged the drop to the floor. It was Calabos, attired in the shimmering armour of a Murknight, and carrying a longsword in a harness over his back. Ondene felt a surge of relief and joy but his smile froze on his lips when he saw the drawn and haggard look on the man's face, the trembling in his features and the scarcely veiled mortal dread in his eyes.

Calabos took a few faltering steps towards the Wellsource, then blinked and turned away from it.

'Unburden me of him,' he said through clenched teeth. 'Now! I command you!'

As Ondene watched, his armoured form grew blurred as an ashen haze gathered around him like a larger ghostly figure. This enclosing form began to darken and obscure Calabos, and Ondene noticed that strange shapes were also moving in the dense opacity, undulant shapes whose faces were that of Calabos.

Even as a shocked Ondene took this in, Calabos himself emerged from the menacing form, almost seeming to force his way out. Trembling and gasping, his face pale, he managed to stagger a couple of steps before collapsing to the ground. But Ondene was already at his side.

'I nearly ... very nearly didn't get here,' Calabos said. 'His poisonous thoughts were like a river of vermin washing through my mind – every step was a struggle against savage desires and gross illusions, despite my spirit-wraiths' help.' He grimaced. 'And I came close to surrender, to embracing it ...'

'My master will embrace you all,' snarled the Duskgeneral. 'See! His divine essence surges against your inferior sentinels ... throw off these shackles, Great Shadow, and crush our enemies!'

Shadows writhed about the tall figure and as Ondene and Calabos watched, hints of a snarling face became visible. It took a step in the direction of the Wellsource, and a second, then the spirit-wraiths together uttered a droning song, each with Calabos' face. The Great Shadow came to a halt but his hate was a palpable thing in the dim cavern, an invisible, choking miasma.

(*Soon all of our efforts will be exhausted*) said one of the spirit-wraiths (*You must decide what to do and soon.*)

Calabos shook his head. 'Since his essence is bound to the Nightrealm, he cannot be obliterated, so presumably destroying him would also destroy this place and everyone in it.' He looked at Ondene. 'So what is left to us? And who is this companion of yours?'

Then the spectral Tauric drifted into the group and smiled.

'Greetings, Calabos, poet and mage – we've come a long way, you and I.'

Calabos stared a moment, then chuckled. 'So the Sleeping God bequeathed a second gift, hm?'

Tauric nodded sadly. 'But more sacrifice than gift, Calabos,' he said. 'In this place, fates entwine and doom looks both ways ...'

His words were drowned as an insensate bellow of rage shook the cavern. All eyes glanced over at the shadow-wreathed form and Ondene felt a stab of panic to see that one of the spirit-wraiths' faces had turned into a darker, more brutal visage.

(*Time is short*) sang the others as they converged on the usurper.

Calabos gripped Ondene's arm as he tried to rise to his feet. Ondene helped, supporting some of the man's weight with a hand about his waist.

'So what must be done?' the poet-mage said.

'Surrender,' growled the Duskgeneral from where he lay prone upon the cavern floor. 'Bare your throats, accept the knife . . .'

'Exile,' said Tauric. 'The Great Shadow cannot be eradicated, therefore he and the Wellsource must be ousted, expelled. The augmented powers of this Wellsource are open to me and together with the spirit-wraiths' abilities we may be able to turn this cavern into a prison.'

'Will that suffice?' Ondene said.

'No, it will not,' Tauric said. 'Once sealed, the prison must be gradually detached from the Nightrealm before its bonds with the vestigial Void are severed, then it must be thrust still further down, into the Void beneath the Void.' He smiled sadly. 'But neither I nor the spirit-wraiths are capable of wielding and guiding the Wellsource without a living host – only the visceral essence of living flesh will permit me to override the Great Shadow's connection to it and create the deepest connection. The Duskgeneral is wholly his creature and is thus irrevocably corrupt . . .'

'So it has to be one of us, yes?' Calabos said. 'Then I'll do it.'

Ondene stared at him, at the pallor of his skin, at the exhaustion writ so clearly in his lined features. And was suddenly aware that the spectral Tauric was staring too.

Then he and Tauric exchanged a look, and understanding came to Ondene in a wave of clarity and purpose.

'I'm sorry, Calabos,' he said, 'but it has to be me.'

The older man drew away from him, forcing himself to stand unaided with a visible effort of will.

'No, Corlek – you do not have the knowledge and skill with these powers, not to mention very many years of experience . . .'

'But the truth is that you're at the end of your strength,' Ondene said. 'You've given so much to get this far, and given almost everything to carry an unbearable burden to this place. You must let me finish the task – after all, the Sleeping God appointed me the Prince of Change.'

There was another guttural roar of fury which was only muted, not silenced.

'There is no more time, Corlek,' said Tauric. 'Are you prepared?'

'Yes, but Calabos must be removed to a place of safety.'

'It shall be done.'

'Curse you, no . . . !'

Ignoring Calabos' anger, Ondene stood still as Tauric rushed towards him. A moment of misty envelopment . . . and then that illuminating presence was permeating his thoughts and sense once more. Almost unconsciously he drew on the torrential flux of the Wellsource, lifted Calabos as if he were as light as a child and then rose up through the shaft to the chaining chamber of the White Prison. There were dozens of people there, former prisoners who shielded their eyes from Ondene-Tauric's radiance as he emerged and carefully laid Calabos on the chamber floor.

'Well,' said the poet-mage, levering himself up on one shaky arm. 'I can see that you've made up your mind . . .' He closed his eyes for a moment then opened them again. 'There – I've told the spirit-wraiths to obey you as if you were me.'

'Thank you, Calabos,' Ondene-Tauric said. 'Give my farewells to all the Watchers and the Daemonkind.'

'I shall. Now go – do what must be done.'

Ondene-Tauric turned to one of the onlookers. 'This chamber will soon be very dangerous for you all – you must leave quickly, and take my friend with you. Can you do this?'

They nodded wordlessly and some hurried to lift and carry Calabos. As they made for the way out, Ondene-Tauric descended the bright shaft and returned to the cavern. There, the Duskgeneral was crawling towards his master, the Great Shadow, whose form was a turbulent storm of amorphous distortion amid which the spirit-wraiths fought to maintain control.

He wasted no time and swooped down to stand in the full, dazzling rush of the Wellsource. He was about to wrench free the step blocks to block the entry shaft with, when an object came clattering down from above. It was Calabos' sword of powers, still in its scabbard. Ondene-Tauric smiled and moved it to one side

before continuing with the task. Soon the shaft was full of broken
blocks being woven shut with webs of verdant Sourcefire. Suddenly
the diminishing aperture was closed completely and Wellsource
power flooded around the cavern.

After that, Ondene found himself left increasingly to one side
as the godlike being within him began to employ the Wellsource
in astonishing and unfathomable ways. He had heard and learned
something of the Void during his extraordinary adventuring, and
it seemed to him that this cavern was actually the shrunken remnant
of this world's Void, wrecked and curtailed when the Lord of
Twilight triumphed — here. And as the Tauric deity worked, the
emerald radiance of the Wellsource spread throughout the cavern
and across the uneven walls in slow, rippling waves, losing its
dazzling glare as it did so, calming and dimming. At the same time
a strange, fine haze began to rise and gather like drifting layers of
smoke, swirling and thickening. An occasional flash of ruddy light
pierced the haze, revealing glimpses of a much wider underground
cavescape than Ondene had already seen, as if the cavern had
somehow become many miles across.

The Tauric deity ignored this and continued to labour at its
tasks, sealing the boundaries of the Great Shadow's prison and
preparing to detach the cavern from the Nightrealm.

In the cavern itself, distance had ceased to have meaning and
the glowing mist gave a dreamlike quality to the twilight-softened
vistas of hills, vales, moors and rolling downs which now stretched
impossibly all around. Of the Great Shadow and his servant, the
Duskgeneral, there were no signs, the raging howls having all but
subsided. A tense hush held sway for a while until a single, dark
writhing shape came gliding out of the mists, one of Calabos'
spirit-wraiths.

(*The Great Shadow comes*) it said. (*War comes.*)

Then Ondene gasped as the fount of the Wellsource blurred
and flowed, becoming a white-walled fortress upon whose
ramparts he stood while the battlements teemed with thousands
of brightly armoured fighters, all wearing Calabos' face. He was
himself attired in silver-green mail and a flowing, pure blue
cloak.

The end is in sight, said the Tauric deity in his mind. *But our Enemy has regained some of his strength and is coming against us with an endless hunger in his spirit and a trembling fear in his heart. You must hold him back until the task is done – you must!*

Then barbarous horns blared in the murk-veiled distance and the bellowing of a myriad savage throats shook the air. A moment later a long line of indistinct, opaque shapes appeared in the enclosing mists, then took on solidity and detail as they emerged – and this was only the leading edge of a vast horde of glittering black creatures, galloping along on two, four or even six legs. Without pause they charged across open ground towards the Wellsource fortress, urged on by tall armoured knights mounted on grotesque lizard-like beasts with a multiplicity of eyes and mouths. Battle was joined.

In the demented clangour of unrestrained brutality, events seemed to blur into one another. From hand-to-hand combat on the battlements, Ondene went to fighting from horseback within the fortress courtyard, then outside the walls, except that his mount turned into a great armoured beast resembling an ox or a bear. Then it changed again into a massive, golden drakken while the Wellsource fortress became a huge ship surging through stormy waters, an immense dromond with a dozen masts and bristling with war machines. From amidships the glowing stem of the Wellsource poured up to spread across the still-present cavern roof and downward, lighting up the depths.

The fight went on against waterborne attackers as well as those diving from above. Ondene was just leading an assault on a flotilla of boats crammed with armoured predators, when an ominous rumble sounded and a great shudder shook the cavern.

The prison leaves the Nightrealm, and descent has begun, said the Tauric deity. *Down, further down into the Void beneath the Void we are plunging, drawing taut the Wellsource's ties to the Nightrealm, drawing forth the Enemy's poison until finally the bonds will part . . .*

A bestial howl of fury ripped through the air and the waters erupted with monsters, coiling, writhing horrors that flung themselves against the flanks of the Wellsource dromond . . .

Which changed again, becoming a high-walled citadel even as

the heaving, thrashing sea froze into a desert of wind-sculpted dunes and outcrops of worn rock. Around the foot of the walls, enemy legions swarmed, raising scaling ladders that were living creatures. But the quivering continued in the cavern, which Ondene felt underfoot as he steered his golden mount down to the citadel ramparts and dismounted. He glanced up at the high, glowing roof then out at the hazy distance, hoping that Calabos had found a safe place after throwing his sword down the Well shaft, hoping that all this was helping the defenders back in Sejeend and Besh-Darok . . .

We descend — the Void beneath the Void beckons and the knot of fates tightens!

Then the desert gaped and the Great Shadow rode up from darkness on a serpent-headed horse, at the head of an endless army which poured across the desert like a dark tide. Ondene felt the stonework quake beneath his feet, then cried out in surprise and fear when the approaching horde rose in the air on blurred wings like a vast stormfront and bore down on the citadel . . .

But the cavern shook from ceiling to floor, from wall to wall and darkness fell for a moment like a great eye closing . . .

Everything . . .

. . . paused . . .

And when the darkness lifted, the cavern was how it had been at the beginning only now the flow of the Wellsource was a diminishing spout of radiance while the entire cavern trembled and vibrated. Before the fitful, fading emerald light, a roaring dark figure fought with a pale, ghostly one. Ondene, feeling dizzy, forced himself upright and staggered towards them a pace or two, not sure what to do. Then his foot knocked against something on the floor which clattered and looking down he saw a sword lying bare and gleaming on the uneven, shaking rock. *Calabos's sword of powers*, he thought as he quickly snatched it up and moved towards the struggling gods.

All is done, said Tauric in his thoughts. *The last bonds have been severed and the Wellsource is but a candle guttering out its last. We will fall through the Void beneath the Void for eternity and our essences will gradually slow and dissolve into the slumbering sea from which Fate draws its catch. Are you prepared, Corlek?*

'I am,' he said. 'Just let me strike one last blow!'

And the Great Shadow, once Lord of Twilight, once the five Shadowkings, threw a glare of limitless hate over his shoulder at the oncoming Ondene.

'I will devour you both!'

'I care not,' Ondene cried as he drew near. 'For after us, you will feast only on nothingness!'

And with a straight-arm thrust he drove the sword of powers into the Great Shadow's upper chest. The Enemy, still grappling with Tauric, gave a harsh, despising laughter but that soon turned into a shriek of surprise and agony as the swordpoint speared into the dense, ragged vapour of his form. Releasing the god Tauric, the Great Shadow recoiled from Ondene and the sword of powers, the wound in his chest leaking black smoke, and then lunged towards the flickering, failing fount of the Wellsource. And as he reached for it, the waning glow died. Corlek Ondene heard him utter a single, senses-shattering howl of fear and loss . . . then the indivisible darkness of finality fell and he knew no more of the light.

Epilogue

There are no endings,
Only a river of beginnings,
Rushing onwards for ever.

Mogaun proverb

As the cavern of the Wellsource began its descent into the Void beneath the Void, the first visible effect elsewhere was on the soldiers of the Black Host. In Oumetra and Adnagaur, or rather the grey, blighted plains where those cities had stood, the Host's patrols out into the lands beyond became less frequent and kept closer to the Blight's deathly borders. In Alvergost, where the Host was under concerted attack by a determined Carver army from Anghatan, the black-armoured troops pulled back to within the Blight itself. At the Great Canal, by the Blight-smothered Isle of Besh-Darok, the companies of the Black Host broke off from pursuing Mogaun warriors and retreated to the town of Belkiol where they clashed with the imperial remnants under Jarryc's command, now allied with the local Mogaun.

At the half-effaced city of Sejeend, the battle that raged all along the banks of the Valewater faltered and the Black Host fell back to the cliffs while their archers staved off attacks by the Daemonkind. And in the gloomy precincts of the Nightrealm, Byrnak's siege army broke through the gates of the Citadel of Twilight, even as the ground underfoot trembled ominously and the Overseers launched ferocious, near-suicidal attacks from above.

Then at last, the cords of power that joined the Wellsource to the Nightrealm were stretched too far in the pitiless gulfs of the Void beneath the Void, and gave way. As the cavern of the Wellsource became a true prison and fell unhindered into oblivion, a string of consequences were taking place. The Blight darkened and began to shrink, splitting and cracking as it withdrew from the lands and the cities that it had consumed and shrouded. But more dramatic were the reactions of the soldiers of the Black Host – some stopped in mid-motion and fell lifeless to the ground, while others screamed and collapsed in convulsions. Still others broke apart into sections of armour as the very substance of their beings turned to oozing, black vapour. Roughly a third of their number were unaffected yet abandoned their positions and fled back to the Shattergates, seeking to return to the Nightrealm.

A handful, however, threw down their weapons and cast off their enclosing helms, revealing men and women whose memories were of life in the Nightrealm prior to their recruitment into the Black Host. None of them showed any desire to return there.

In the Nightrealm itself, entire legions of the Black Host rebelled against their commanders while the Murknights to a man perished where they stood. And with the Overseers either fallen in flames from their towers or hiding in inaccessible refuges, the chieftains of the chapters and militias were fighting for what advantage they could. Tremors and quakes shook the Nightrealm from end to end, yet Qothan and the other two Daemonkind kept their vigil at the top of the Citadel of Twilight, hoping that Calabos would still appear. The Great Shadow's dream-courts had become a bizarre maze of buildings and streets frozen in mid-change, an insane vista of twisted, distorted walls and roofs. They had already ascertained the whereabouts of the Shattergate portals, four being distributed among the ten cliff-side bastions, with the fifth located on the Citadel's thirtieth level.

Then at last Calabos emerged, carried on an improvised stretcher, as a huge crowd of people also came forth, thousands of weary-looking men and women. But when Qothan suggested that he and the Daemonkind start immediately for the nearest gate this was rejected – Calabos was determined to see that all his fellow escapees reached some kind of sanctuary, for they were most of the former captives of the White Prison and thus deserved peace and protection.

And it was achieved. As Viras and Yostil guided parties of them down through the citadel, Qothan sought out Kerna and Nilka who agreed to help the former prisoners find a safe refuge away from the fighting. Almost three days later the last of them left the Citadel, and Calabos had begun to make a good recovery. Three days on from the imprisonment and exile of the Great Shadow – as well as Corlek Ondene and the god Tauric – the terrible quaking had waned to just the occasional tremor, and the quality of the light was changing, brightening. Even the air was starting to smell fresher.

Three days on, only the Shattergate in the Citadel remained open so Calabos agreed that it was time to go, wondering if several days here was still only a matter of hours back in the world that was his home. From the platform on the Citadel's roof he gave the Nightrealm's vast cityscape one last look and raised a hand in farewell before following the Daemonkind down into the Citadel of Twilight to find their way back.

When the Daemonkind Besarl and his three companions landed in Belkiol's town square less than a day after the destruction of the Blight and the Black Host at Besh-Darok, Tashil Akri had asked after Calabos' friend, Coireg, but they were not forthcoming.

'What little we know,' Besarl had said, 'we have sworn not to reveal, lady. Not even to our brothers and sisters aboard the *Stormclaw* shall we relate our experiences – our vow is a sacred one.'

Which Tashil had to accept and although the curiosity gnawed at her, she had other matters on her mind, namely the reunion with her family. Seeing her aunts and her father among the captives in the temple, their necks and limbs bound with rope, had been a soul-wrenching moment before all her fears had turned to relief amid bursts of sobbing. In the hours afterwards, when the Black Host returned to Belkiol and terrible fighting ensued on the northern outskirts of the town, she had all but made up her mind to stay with her family should she and they survive.

But just one day after the rout and dissolution of the invaders, her father declared that the Akri family would be leaving for northern

Khatris without delay. But when he asked Tashil to go too, she had looked about her at the wrecked town and the houses and halls full of refugees and the wounded and knew that she had to remain. The knowledge of Atemor's death had also come to stand between them and Tashil had found it easier than she thought to say farewell.

Once her family had departed Belkiol, Tashil turned her attention to helping where she could with the healers or with the temporary shelters, or with translation for Jarryc as he strove to forge a working relationship with the Mogaun chiefs and elders.

But two days later, she had word from Dardan and Sounek in Sejeend, asking if she could return quickly to attend a council called by several nobles to determine the succession. Ilgarion and Tangaroth had died without issue, so the stage was set for a potentially ruinous power struggle which the Watchers and High Steward Roldur hoped to stall with their own candidate for the crown, Count Jarryc. Thus it was that on the morning of the third day after the end of the invasion, Tashil was being carried through the icy sky towards Sejeend by Besarl and his Daemonkind brothers.

It was mid-afternoon under a clear blue sky when the winged group finally alighted on the fortified ramparts of Hubranda Lock. Dardan and Sounek were waiting for her, the former trying to look stern while the latter wore an unabashed grin.

'At this rate,' Dardan said, 'you'll be rushing off to join the Daemonkind on their ship.' Then a smile broke through the gruff exterior. 'Don't reckon they'd be able to handle you, m'self!'

Tashil laughed. 'Ser, I have many important tasks to complete here before I depart for other lands, like guiding you into the embrace of a good tailor!'

'He'll join the Carvers before he gives up that forest cloak of his,' Sounek said. 'Good to see you back, lady – your presence and the substance of your personal account should add weight to Count Jarryc's stature in these nobles' eyes.'

She nodded. 'Of course, if Calabos were here, we would be on firmer ground.' She smiled at them both, concealing her blackest fears. 'So, has anything been heard from him?'

Dardan and Sounek exchanged a look and a sly smile that made hope leap in her.

'There has been word,' Sounek said. 'About an hour ago two Daemonkind emerged from the ruins of the palace, from the Shattergate there which is still apparently open – unlike all the others. They said that Qothan and Calabos were following on, but so far the sentries watching the place have reported nothing.'

Tashil thought this over, remembering with perfect clarity Calabos' vow to return.

'I am sure that he will be here,' she said.

'He's a tough old fox,' Dardan said. 'I know he will.'

'When is this council of nobles due to commence?' Tashil said.

'This evening,' said Sounek.

'Good – then there's time enough to cross the Valewater and see what remains, yes?'

To which there could only be agreement. And as they left, Tashil noticed Besarl and the other Daemonkind altering their forms, shrinking back to the appearance of tall, stern people.

From the main gates of Hubranda Lock they walked downhill towards the riverbank. Every street bore the scars of conflict, fire-blackened doors and windows, floods of water from burst tanks and pipes, families tugging belongings from the rubble of their homes. However, there were also many soldiers present, helping to clear away piles of wreckage or patrolling watchfully while labourers and arti-sans worked to shore up walls or repair roofs. There was misery aplenty to see, which made Tashil feel almost helpless with sorrow, but there was also the selfless compassion of ordinary people striving to help each other while refusing to break under the burden of grief.

Yes, she thought. *I belong here, where there is work to be done.*

A few moments later they passed into the dockside district and Tashil got her first proper view of the east bank since the disap-pearance of the Blight. From the air she had had a glimpse of a dark, featureless swathe of ground stretching from beyond the cliffs and the north curve of the bay all down the bank, south along Gronanvel. But this close it resembled acres upon acres of tilled earth, blank except for a few jutting remnants of heavily constructed walls. Tashil felt that her sombre mood was shared by Dardan and Sounek as they all hurried across the sole restored bridge, feeling the new timbers shift and rattle underfoot.

On the other side, a few huts had been erected and a dozen guards in city livery were keeping an eye on a gang of labourers who were digging into the riverbank in search of wharf foundations. Sounek had a word with the guard officer who nodded and let them pass unhindered.

A muddy path led up a steady incline towards the main level on which this part of the old town had been built, and thence off in the direction of the great notch in the cliffs through which the river Kala had poured. Tashil could only stare about her in silence, remembering street after street of ancient buildings while her eyes gazed upon nothing. Then a shadow passed over the ground before them and the great winged form of a Daemonkind swooped down to land before them. Tashil's sudden alarm turned to elation when she saw that it was Qothan.

'Friend Qothan,' she said. 'It gladdens my heart to see that you are in good health. May we assume that Calabos is also hale and hearty?'

As he folded his wings, Qothan regarded her with a vague amusement. 'Honoured Calabos is well, friend Tashil. He suffered greatly during his struggle with the Great Shadow and gave more of himself than he will admit, such that he lacks the strength to greet you with farspeech. Thus I offered to fly ahead to announce his arrival and explain this silence on his part.'

Tashil glanced at Dardan and Sounek and saw her own worries reflected in their expressions.

'What of Corlek Ondene?' she said.

Qothan shook his head. 'We know only a few details, those at least that Calabos mentioned – he was there at the heart of the Great Shadow's dream-courts and saw what had transpired before Corlek Ondene and the Sleeping God imprisoned themselves with the Enemy and his servant, the Duskgeneral, before sending that prison off into the infinite depths of the Void beneath the Void.' The Daemonkind was sombre. 'They gave everything.'

For a moment or two all were silent.

'So Calabos knows what happened,' said Sounek.

'I take it that he is descending the Kala gully,' Dardan said to Qothan.

'I offered to fly him down from the cliffs,' Qothan said. 'But he would have none of it.'

'That sounds like him,' Dardan said. 'We'd best move along smartly, then, before the old fool breaks a leg.'

As they hastened up the muddy track, Qothan explained how strange the return had been, how slow compared with the outward journey and how gruelling it had been for both of them. They were climbing to the elevated ground where Hojamar Keep had stood, and listening to Qothan's descriptions of the Nightrealm, when she heard Dardan curse. Looking up quickly she just saw a half-naked figure disappear into the opening of the Kala dale.

'Who—' she began to say before Dardan cut her off.

'Bureng!' he said. 'That pirate vermin, I recognized him with magesight – come on!'

As they dashed forward, Qothan leaped into the air and hurled himself towards the notch in the cliffs. Anger and fear lent Tashil an almost limitless vigour, and also filled her mind with a river of images. She remembered how the deranged Bureng had led an army of the undead up from the wharfs, and recalled that ghastly battle on the night-bound, rain-lashed workshop roof. Everyone had assumed that he had died either in the fighting or when the Blight later overwhelmed the eastern half of Sejeend, but now her mind was creating the worst of speculations.

When the three Watchers reached the narrow, brown waters of the Kala they found themselves to be involuntary spectators of a harrowing, tensely balanced situation. On the opposite bank of the rushing river, the pirate Bureng, wearing only a loincloth, had Calabos on his knees with a long dagger held to his throat. The pirate was grinning nastily at Qothan who stood several yards away on the same side, his hooded eyes filled with a level fury, his clenched, taloned hands gleaming with silvery, deadly radiance.

'Ah, Dardan, Sounek and Tash,' Calabos said hoarsely. 'Forgive me for not rising to greet you . . .'

'Cease your prattling, host,' said Bureng. 'None of these insects can come between my pretty blade and your neck. But if they bow down to me, I may make them into useful pets, even the winged one . . .'

Bureng's words and his manner were intense and focused but Tashil could see that physically he was near the end – his grimy body was covered with scars and one arm seemed to have been broken and reset at a slight angle.

'I will never be your pet,' growled Qothan. 'We do not serve the likes of you – we destroy them.'

'Ah, but he is your friend, is he not?' Bureng said, yanking on a handful of the robes Calabos wore. 'Are you ready to see his blood redden the river, or will you rejoice when he sinks into the nethermind to be consumed?' Saying this, he bent to crane his face into Calabos' then snapped back up to regard Qothan once more.

'What can this avail you?' Sounek said smoothly. 'Kill him and nothing will stay our retribution, but release him and surrender to us and we'll see that you are . . . cared for.'

Bureng laughed at this. 'Cared for! Yes, in an iron casket, maybe? You're pitiful fools, all of you. No, when I come into my greatness I will care for you, better than poor Rikken cared for me in the end, gave me enough strength to endure and to wait – hah, no!'

Qothan took a step forward and stopped when the dagger pressed into Calabos' neck and drew forth a hairline bead of blood.

'Time for the final stroke, I think,' Bureng said. 'Time for a new king of shadow to arise.'

Then, swiftly and calmly, he took the dagger from Calabos' neck, brought it up and slashed open his own throat.

Dardan uttered an oath and Tashil cried out in surprised horror. As Bureng fell to his knees, blood drenching his body, Calabos moved away a few feet and shook his head when Qothan tried to drag him further back. Bureng was grinning when his eyes showed the whites and he toppled backwards, legs splaying. There was a long, drawn-out moment of dread, then Tashil saw the very thing she feared beginning to rise from the body.

'Calabos, please get away!' she cried. 'Qothan – take him, fly with him . . .'

'No!' Calabos said. 'It must end here, here and now, and only I know what has to be done.'

Yes, but have you strength? she thought, seeing the exhaustion in his face, the darkness around his eyes and the muscle twitching in his cheek.

Yet he drew a deep breath and got to his feet as the spirit-wraith wrenched itself free from Bureng's corpse and began drifting towards him. Smoky tendrils writhed around a dark, vaporous core and began to reach out towards his face as it came nearer. When the first of them touched the skin just above the eye, Tashil saw his head jerk very slightly but still he did not duck away. Rather, he waited until several of the vile tendrils were in contact before bringing up his hand and holding it in front of the spirit-wraith. For a space Tashil thought that it would continue along its path to engulf his hand and then his face, but instead it stopped. Calabos' gaze was unwavering, implacable, and after a moment or two there was a bright, passing flicker at the heart of the spirit-wraith . . . and its tendrils retracted. Calabos then slowly began to push it backwards, further back until he was standing over the body of the pirate. Then he guided it downwards, down into the pirate's chest.

'Die the death,' he said and straightened.

The corpse stirred, the chest inhaled and the arms twitched, as did the feet, then with an ungainly effort it sat up. Disarranged eyes blinked and a ghastly glee twisted the mouth, but only for a moment. A slack hand wavered up to finger the gaping wound in the neck and a look of tormented horror passed over the features for a second before it quivered and slumped onto its back. Its last breath was a quiet, grisly sound.

Calabos smiled and leaned back against the bare rock of the gully side, then slid down into a sitting position. Meanwhile, Tashil and the others splashed their way waist-deep across the Kala and Qothan came over to crouch beside him.

'I am here,' Calabos said with the carefulness of the utterly weary, 'by virtue of the sacrifice of dear and noble friends. It is so heartening to know that I still have some left!'

As they helped him to stand and walk gingerly out into the sunshine, he surveyed the devastation and the bare earth.

'So – how is Ilgarion, and dear Tangaroth?'

'Dead,' said Dardan.

Calabos arched an eyebrow. 'Any arguments over the succession yet?'

Sounek grinned. 'There's a big one scheduled for this afternoon. But we have plans, involving the Count and Countess of Harcas . . .'

Calabos gave an approving nod. 'Hmm, perhaps if I have a brief nap . . .'

Tashil laughed and hugged him. 'Lasting a couple of days, perhaps!'

Calabos glanced at her and smiled. 'You may be right, come to think of it.'

As they walked down towards the Valewater, Tashil said, 'So is that the end of the Shadowkings and the Lord of Twilight?'

Calabos, poet and mage, did not answer for a moment, then said: 'Yes, they are gone, finished, ended. But I can't help remembering something that my friend Coireg once told me. He said – "Evil acts do not require the hand of an evil god".'

'And what about good acts?' said Qothan. 'What about their origin?'

Calabos smiled and shrugged.

'Does it matter?'

POCKET
BOOKS

Michael Cobley
Book One Of The Shadowkings Trilogy
SHADOWKINGS

It has been sixteen years since the dazzling Khatrimantine Empire fell
to the vast hordes of the Mogaun. Sixteen years since the invaders'
evil deity, the Lord of Twilight, was shattered into five hosts, five lost
souls destined to become the Shadowkings. Sixteen long years since
the forces of the Earthmother and the Fathertree were defeated, and
the Rootpower magic itself was destroyed . . .

But for Suviel, one of the few surviving mages, it was not a final
defeat. Nor was it so for Ikarno Mazaret, Lord Commander of the
Knights of the Fathertree. They and their companions face a deadly
struggle against terrifying odds in their fight for freedom.

Byrnak, one of the many warlords who squabble amid the Empire's
ruins, discovers that he is one of the five Shadowkings and thus compelled to bring the Lord of Twilight into fleshly being. Across the
battlefields and dreamscapes of the land, he is driven ever closer to
this goal.

These lives and uncountable others will be changed forever when the
Empire's last valliant defenders take arms against ancient sorceries
and new terrors.

ISBN 074341599X
PRICE £6.99

POCKET BOOKS

Michael Cobley
Book Two Of The Shadowkings Trilogy
SHADOWGOD

A harsh winter is settling in across the land and the Shadowkings' deepest, darkest plans are hatching . . . the worst is yet to come.

Ikarno Mazaret, now Lord Regent, still grieves over the death of his beloved, the mage Suviel. Ranging forth from the city of Besh-Darok, he takes ever more perilous risks. Tauric has been crowned Emperor yet feels increasingly powerless to influence events. Despair begins to taint his every decision. Keren Asherol remains haunted by her shattering encounter with one of the Daemonkind, while her twin, the mirrorchild Nerek, is dogged by sinister omens.

And far to the north the Shadowking Byrnak broods on his towertop. Mistrustful of his fellow-Shadowkings and harried by a ghostly fragment of the Lord of Twilight, he knows he must utterly crush the Imperial remnants and their allies, despite the powers of the goddess Earthmother.

ISBN 0743416007
PRICE £6.99

**POCKET
BOOKS**

This book and other **Simon & Schuster** and **Pocket Books** titles are available from your local bookshop or can be ordered direct from the publisher.

Please send cheque or postal order for the value of the book, **free postage and packing within the UK,** to SIMON & SCHUSTER CASH SALES PO Box 29, Douglas Isle of Man, IM99 1BQ
Tel: 01624 677237, Fax: 01624 670923
E-mail: bookshop@enterprise.net
www.bookpost.co.uk
Please allow 14 days for delivery. Prices and availability
subject to change without notice